R. L. STINE

HORROR HIGH

DEADLY LOVE

SCHOLASTIC

Scholastic Children's Books
An imprint of Scholastic Ltd
Euston House, 24 Eversholt Street
London, NW1 1DB, UK
Registered office: Westfield Road, Southam, Warwickshire, CV47 0RA
SCHOLASTIC and associated logos are trademarks and
or registered trademarks of Scholastic Inc.
Series created by Working Partners

Grave Intentions
First published in the US as *The Boyfriend* by Scholastic Inc, 1990
First published in the UK by Scholastic Children's Books, 1992
Text copyright © R. L. Stine, 1990

Fatal Kiss
First published in the US as *The Girlfriend* by Scholastic Inc, 1991
First published in the UK by Scholastic Children's Books, 1992
Text copyright © R. L. Stine, 1991

Deadly Rumours
First published in the US as *The Dead Girlfriend* by Scholastic Inc, 1993
First published in the UK by Scholastic Children's Books, 1994
Text copyright © R. L. Stine, 1993

This edition published in the UK by Scholastic Ltd, 2009

ISBN 978 1407 11661 7

British Library Cataloguing-in-Publication Data
A CIP catalogue record for this book is available from the British Library

The right of R. L. Stine to be identified as the author
of this work has been asserted by him.

Printed in the UK by CPI Bookmarque, Croydon, CR0 4TD
Papers used by Scholastic Children's Books are made from wood grown
in sustainable forests.

1 3 5 7 9 10 8 6 4 2

This is a work of fiction. Names, characters, places, incidents and dialogues are products of the author's imagination or are used fictitiously. Any resemblance to actual people, living or dead, events or locales is entirely coincidental.

www.scholastic.co.uk/zone

R. L. STINE

HORROR HIGH

GRAVE INTENTIONS

One

Am I going to do it? Olivia asked herself.

She looked down the brightly-lit mall at the blur of faces, shoppers balancing packages, pulling young children, peering into colourful display windows, teenagers walking in twos and threes, beginning their Friday night prowl.

Of course I am, Olivia decided, a smile spreading slowly across her face. Once I get something in my mind, I always go through with it.

"Daddy's little go-getter." That's what Edward Collier, Olivia's father, always called her. His highest compliment: "Daddy's little go-getter. She'll never take no for an answer."

There were lots of compliments from Dad, Olivia thought bitterly, walking quickly away from the meeting place by the bookshop, crossing the wide aisleway, then stopping. I was Daddy's girl, "a *real* Collier".

1

Of course, thought Olivia, her smile now completely gone, that didn't stop him from leaving. That didn't stop him from running off with that cheap-looking redhead, off to Tucson or some crazy place. Her mother refused to tell her where.

She hadn't heard from her father since, not even on her sixteenth birthday.

Mum had done all right, though, thought Olivia. Tiny, meek little Mum. Well, she wasn't so meek when divorce time came around. She must have taken Daddy for every penny he had, which was considerable. The two of them had lived really well ever since. Mum and Olivia. They enjoyed being rich and not having Daddy around.

At least Olivia did.

Daddy's little go-getter didn't miss Daddy at all.

So why was she standing on the edge of this mall now, watching the Friday night crowd pour in, thinking about him?

Break-ups.

That was why.

Family break-ups. Boyfriend break-ups.

Break-ups weren't so sad. In fact, they could lead to better things.

She thought of Ben. His wavy blond hair. The dimple in his left cheek when he smiled that funny, lopsided smile. She wondered what Ben was doing tonight while she was supposed to be meeting Josh.

What was that song on the loudspeaker? Some ancient Elvis song from the fifties. "Don't Be Cruel."

Olivia nearly laughed out loud. Don't be cruel?

Why not?

It was a cruel world.

She was about to do something really cruel. And, she had to admit, she was enjoying it already.

She turned and caught her reflection in a shop window. Not bad, she thought.

She knew she was beautiful. Why should she force herself to have false modesty and pretend she didn't know, like some simpering young thing in one of those embarrassing Elvis films Josh had forced her to watch on TV?

She had the Collier good looks. That's what her father always told her – usually as a dig at her mother. She had the high cheekbones, the perfect, straight nose, the clear blue eyes that always seemed to be opened wide, the proud, high forehead, and the sunlight-blonde hair, so smooth and straight that it looked beautiful even cut so stylishly short.

The Collier good looks.

Maybe that's why she and her mother could never be that close, as close as other girls and their mothers. Or was that something from a stupid fifties film, too?

3

Her mousy little mother. She always looked so small and funny inside the glamorous fur coat she wore everywhere with the collar pulled up almost over her head. It always made Olivia laugh – to herself, of course.

She couldn't blame her father for wanting a little more.

Yes she could.

Break-ups.

Well, of course break-ups were on her mind tonight.

Two wiry twelve-year-old boys on skateboards came whirring down the aisle. One of them nearly barrelled into her. Olivia jumped out of the way just in time. "Hey, you –" She stopped herself.

The mall security guards would catch them sooner or later.

And she didn't want to call attention to herself. She was hiding, after all. Hiding from Josh.

Hiding from her boyfriend.

She thought of how Josh smelled. Sort of fresh. Almost flowery. Soapy.

It almost made her sad.

Almost.

Was that him across the mall at their usual meeting place?

No. It was some other guy in jeans and a red hoody.

She leaned against the concrete column, the back of her head resting against a sign announcing some kind of mall band concert.

What kind of idiots would go out of their way to listen to a band playing in a mall? It was no wonder people turned their noses up at the suburbs. Everything here in Middlewood was so . . . tacky. Olivia knew she would move to New York as soon as she graduated. Enrol in a few modelling programmes. And with her fabulous looks and drive, well . . . who knew how far she could go?

Which was one reason why Josh had to go.

There he was now. Hurrying to the bookshop entrance where they always met. Late again.

He'll be late his whole life, she thought, surprised by her bitterness. He'll never catch up.

He stopped in front of the open entranceway, looking from side to side. He seemed to relax. From across the crowded aisle, she could see that he looked relieved.

He thinks I'm late, too. What a laugh.

Look at him, she thought disapprovingly, pressing herself flat against the column so he couldn't see her. That's how he dresses for a date. Those faded jeans, torn at the knee. That stupid T-shirt. Probably not even a clean one.

He did have that wonderful, soapy smell, though. And when they were all alone late at night in the front seat of her car, he . . . Well, why get into that?

She was standing him up, after all.

And watching him while she did it.

She shifted her jacket to her other hand. Across the wide aisle, Josh started to pace back and forth in front of the bookshop. He looked at his watch. He jammed his hands into his jeans pockets and continued to pace.

He's short, she thought. Why hadn't she ever noticed how short he was? And his jeans are so baggy.

Look how nervous he's getting. He knows I'm never late.

And he knows I've been losing interest in him. I haven't been too subtle about that, have I!

You're cruel, Olivia, she told herself. Actually, it's one of your most admirable qualities.

How else to survive in a cruel world?

Josh would have to find it out sooner or later.

Why not sooner? This was good for him.

He stopped pacing. He ran his hand back nervously through his thick, black hair.

She had loved to pull on Josh's hair, tug at the back, tease him, pulling until it hurt. Now it just looked greasy to her.

Get a haircut, she thought.

No. Don't go overboard, Olivia. You love his hair. Don't deny it. You love the way it tickles your cheek when he puts his head on your shoulder and pulls you close.

I'm not giving in, she thought, shifting her weight against the column. She straightened her blue jumper, the one her father had bought because it matched her eyes so perfectly. It was getting a bit tight now. Why did she insist on wearing it?

I'm not running over to him. I'm just going to stand here and watch him squirm. I'm enjoying this too much.

He looked angry now. He stopped pacing and stood with his hands in his pockets, looking down the aisle towards the cinema at the end.

"Breaking Up Is Hard To Do," Olivia thought. What was that? An old song title? Well, she knew it wasn't going to be easy with Josh. He was so dramatic, so moody, so theatrical.

Josh wanted to be an actor. And he had the dark good looks for it. He looked a lot like the actor Matt Dillon. Sounded like him, too.

The previous spring, he had invited Olivia to come and see him in the lead role in *Julius Caesar* at his school across town. Olivia obligingly came, worrying if her BMW would be safe parked on the street across from the three-storey brick school. The neighbourhood certainly didn't look very appealing. She had locked the car and hurried into the building, surprised by how tacky and run-down everything looked.

Josh had been good. He had a clear, expressive voice, and he looked very handsome on stage. But everyone else was terrible, the scenery was practically non-existent, and the lights kept flickering.

Afterwards, Josh was so excited. He was positively high! Olivia told him how good he was. But all the while she was feeling sorry for him. If only his aunt could afford to send him to a decent school, like Glenview, where Olivia went. Then maybe he'd have a chance to get somewhere with his acting ambitions.

But his old aunt had no money at all. And she hadn't wanted to become Josh's guardian in the first place. She didn't care if he went to school or not. She lived in her own grey world.

A world I don't ever want to be pulled into, Olivia thought, watching Josh across the mall. Two guys she had never seen before had stopped to talk to him. She could hear them laughing about something, but Josh didn't join in, and he kept looking past them, looking for her.

This anxiety will help Josh's acting career, Olivia thought. Heartbreak. An actor needs some heartbreak in his life to draw on during his performances, right?

"Heartbreak Hotel". Wasn't that an Elvis song, too?

Why do I have Elvis on the brain? she wondered. I guess Josh looks a little like the young Elvis, the Elvis in all those films. Was that why Josh liked watching those old films so much?

Time to go home, she decided suddenly.

The two guys had headed on to the cinema. Josh was

alone again, pacing back and forth in front of the bookshop entrance.

This is so mean, she thought, turning her back on him and heading to the doors that led to the car-park.

So why do I feel like laughing?

Two

"So you just stood there and watched him?"

Amy's voice rose several octaves as she asked the question. Olivia pulled the phone away from her ear before the high-pitched voice did any damage. She could just picture Amy, lying on her stomach on her bed, a shocked look on her angelic little face.

"Yeah. It was kind of . . . interesting," Olivia said. She knew that would get a reaction from her friend – and it did.

"Interesting? Olivia – that's so cold!" Amy cried.

Amy was always so sweet, so nice to everyone. So angelic. Olivia loved shocking her, making her voice rise.

Across town, Amy, lying on her stomach on the bed, in the oversized man's shirt she used for a nightshirt, looked at the phone as if to ask, "Am I really hearing right?" Her brown hair, falling in tight curls down her neck and shoulders, was still wet from the shower. She shivered.

10

But she knew that it was Olivia who was making her feel cold.

How can this person be my friend? The question flashed through her mind. And then: Why has Olivia changed so much?

They had been friends since grade school. When Amy's family moved out of Middlewood to the less fashionable area known as Westside, the friendship had continued, mostly over the phone.

Olivia had always been a little snobbish, Amy realized. But she was so smart and funny, and so pretty, and such a good friend, someone you could always talk to, confide in, tell just about everything.

So when had she turned so cold, so mean?

Had she been that way all along, and Amy simply hadn't noticed?

No, Amy thought, as Olivia's voice continued to murmur in her ear. No. Olivia has changed. Since the divorce, I guess . . .

"You'll have to meet Ben," Olivia was saying. "I think you'll really like him. He's very good-looking, and—"

"He goes to Glenview?" Amy asked.

"Yeah. He's a senior this year. He's already been accepted at Yale. Everyone in his family goes to Yale."

"Nice," Amy said. She didn't really know what to say.

"I – I'm just so surprised. I mean, totally. I thought you and Josh were really serious."

"We were," Olivia said. "Too serious. It wasn't good for either of us."

"What do you mean, Olivia?"

"I mean Josh has no money and never will have," Olivia replied, talking very quickly, the way she always did when she got excited. "Sure, I care about him. But a person has to be practical, too."

"Practical?" Amy truly was shocked, more by Olivia's voice than anything else. She sounded so hard, so removed, as if she were talking about a stranger.

"I'm thinking of both of us," Olivia said, not meaning to sound as defensive as she did. "I mean, how do you think Josh feels being driven around in my BMW all the time?"

"I don't think it bothers him," Amy said drily. Then she added, "You know, Josh wouldn't mind taking the bus once in a while."

Olivia laughed. "Get real. I'm really going to take the bus with a BMW sitting in the garage!"

This isn't the first time she's bragged about her car, Amy thought, brushing back her wet hair uncomfortably. "What kind of car does Ben drive?" she asked, unable to keep the sarcasm from her voice.

"He has one of those cute Mercedes soft-tops," Olivia

said. "A red one with a white top."

Which did she check out first – Ben or his car? Amy wondered. Then she scolded herself for starting to sound as cold as Olivia. This is just an act Olivia is putting on, Amy thought. She doesn't want to let on to me how bad she feels about breaking up with Josh. She probably doesn't even want to admit it to herself. So she's putting on this cruel act, pretending to be tough.

"Are you sure you know what you're doing?" Amy asked her old friend. "Josh is crazy about you."

"He's just plain crazy," Olivia said. "D'you know what he's been doing lately? He gets the bus over here in the middle of the night and climbs in my bedroom window. Just to talk."

"Very romantic," Amy said, trying not to sound jealous.

"Are you kidding?! If my mother ever found out, she'd – she'd ground me for a month!"

And that posh BMW would just sit in the garage, Amy thought.

"Josh is too melodramatic," Olivia continued. "He's too theatrical for me. He's—" There was a series of clicks on the line. "Hold on, Amy – I've got another call coming in."

The phone went silent at Amy's end. Frowning, she sat up. She threw the phone down on the bed and went to get a towel to dry her hair.

"Hello?" Olivia asked brightly. She had a good idea

13

who was calling. "Oh, hi, Josh." Keep it casual, she told herself.

"Hey – I'm still at the mall," he said. He sounded very upset. She could just picture the look on his face, his dark eyebrows low over his eyes. He was probably biting the skin off his lower lip the way he always did.

"What? *Where* are you?" That's good. That sounds really innocent.

"I thought we had a date, Olivia. You were supposed to meet me – remember?"

"Huh?" She laughed. She knew the laugh would really infuriate him. "Oh, good lord! I completely forgot!"

Silence on his end.

More silence.

A click. And then the dial tone returned. She listened to the steady hum for a few seconds, then remembered that Amy was waiting on the other line. "Hello, Amy? Hi. I'm back. That was guess who."

"What did he say?" Amy asked, sitting back on the bed, the towel wrapped around her hair.

"Not much. I told him I just forgot." Olivia giggled.

"I can't believe you're being so mean. Why are you playing these games with him, Olivia? Why don't you just tell him you don't want to see him any more?"

"Come on, Amy," Olivia chided. "It's much more fun to

make him squirm for a while."

"You – you're not serious, are you?"

"No. I'm not. *Really.*" Olivia couldn't decide if she was serious or not. She surprised herself at how aloof she felt about what she was doing, about how little feeling she had for Josh.

She had thought she was in love with him, after all. But now she didn't feel much of anything at all. And deep down inside, she had to admit she did enjoy watching him squirm.

"I'd tell him straight out," she told Amy, "but you know how theatrical he is. He'd pull a big scene. Probably do the third act of *Macbeth* in my living room, have us all in tears." She laughed.

That's so cold, Amy couldn't help thinking again. I thought she cared about him. She really had me fooled. Had all of us fooled.

"I just think it'll be easier if I let him down slowly. You know, a few subtle hints. Then maybe let him see me out with Ben. That way he'll start to catch on."

"Olivia – really. You can't do that to Josh."

"Just watch me," Olivia said, admiring her dark red nail polish as she talked.

"Maybe we should change the subject," Amy said. "We've always been honest with each other, Olivia. But this time I—"

"You're right. Maybe we should change the subject."

15

Olivia laughed, trying to keep it light, but it sounded phoney even to her.

Silence for a few moments.

Finally Amy said, "Did you buy that winter coat you were looking at? The one with the fur hood?"

"Oh, there were two I really liked," Olivia told her. "I couldn't decide which one I liked best. So I bought them both."

There was silence at the other end. Olivia thought she heard a short gasp. She loved shocking Amy. But it wasn't much of a challenge. Amy was so simple and nice, and she shocked so easily.

"I'm so spoiled. It's disgusting, isn't it?" Olivia said.

"Yes," Amy answered quickly. "It is!"

"Hey, I think I hear my mother roaming around again – for a change. She never can sleep. I'd better get off."

"OK. See you," Amy said.

"I'll call you tomorrow." Olivia hung up the phone. She took a deep breath and stretched. She was feeling pretty good.

She listened to her mother's muffled footsteps retreat down the carpeted hallway. Poor Mum. She's always so nervous, so restless these days.

On an impulse, Olivia picked up the phone again. She looked through her directory for Ben's number.

Should I call him?

Why not?

It rang four times before someone picked it up. Silence. "Hello, Ben?"

Someone yawned loudly on the other end.

"Ben, is that you?"

"Yeah. Who is it?"

"It's me. Olivia. Did I wake you?"

Another yawn. "No. I mean, yes. I guess you did. What time is it? Hi."

They talked awkwardly for a few minutes. It didn't take Ben long to wake up.

"I'm surprised you're not out on a Friday night," Olivia said coyly.

"No. I stayed home in case you called," he cracked.

He has a good sense of humour, she thought. I like that. She decided to go ahead and ask him out. "Are you busy on Saturday night?"

He seemed a little surprised by her directness. "No. I don't think so. I mean, no."

"D'you want to go and see a film or something?"

"I'll pick *something*," he joked. And then he added, "Hey, aren't you going out with that guy from across town?"

"Well, no," she said quickly. "Not exactly."

"Great!" he said, suddenly very enthusiastic. She could picture his blond, wavy hair, his round cheeks, which made him look like such a little boy. He was probably blushing. He seemed to blush all the time, getting all rosy for no reason at all. "See you on Saturday," he said.

"See you on Saturday."

She was still replaying the conversation half an hour later, lying under the covers, watching the shadows of the trees outside her window shift and dip across the wall.

She couldn't have been asleep for more than an hour when she was woken by a loud clambering at the window.

She pulled herself up with a startled gasp.

Framed by pale yellow moonlight, Josh was climbing into the room.

The moonlight made his skin look green. And he had the strangest look on his face.

Olivia's breath caught in her throat.

"Josh – what do you want?" she cried.

Three

He stood by the window, eerily framed in the pale moonlight, catching his breath, staring at her across the dark room.

She pulled the satin sheet up to her chin protectively. "Josh, what are you doing here?" This is the end, she thought angrily. These middle-of-the-night visits have *got* to stop.

"It's a beautiful night," he said, still staring at her as he wiped his hands. Climbing the tree to her second-storey window was not an easy feat.

"So?"

"So come on." He flashed her his famous smile. Even in the near-darkness it was a fabulous, winning grin. "Get your car. We'll go for a ride."

"Huh? Are you crazy?"

"Yeah." He laughed. He took a few steps towards her.

"Josh, how did you get here?"

19

"Flew."

"Have you been drinking?"

"Yeah. I had a coupla beers while I waited for you at the mall. Come on – get dressed." She had left her jeans on the chair beside the bed. He picked them up and tossed them to her.

She ignored them. "You took the bus here? Doesn't your aunt know that you sneak out at night?"

"I don't know what she knows," he said. "We don't talk much."

"Well, I really don't think—"

"Stop wasting time," he said, pacing impatiently.

She suddenly saw him pacing at the mall again, looking so unhappy.

"Get dressed. Let's go for a ride. You know. Do something exciting, something no one else we know is doing. Dare to live, know what I mean?"

"Is that from a play?"

"Owen's with me," he said, ignoring her sarcasm. "He's waiting outside."

Olivia didn't really like Josh's friend Owen. With his short, spiky hair, the diamond stud in his ear, and the heavy metal music rattling on his iPod all the time, he was such an adolescent. What was he trying to prove – that he was cool or something?

She looked at Josh, his face half in shadow, half out.

What was I trying to prove by going with Josh? she wondered. That I was cool? That I wasn't who I am? Sure, he's handsome. Sure, he's exciting to be with in a crazy sort of way. But he really isn't my type at all . . .

Josh was my teenage rebellion phase, she decided with sudden certainty. That's it. He was a phase I went through. Every teenager has to go through a rebellion phase, right?

"Come on, Olivia. Let's get moving! We're wasting time. What are you thinking about?"

"Nothing," she said.

"Well, all right. Get dressed. Owen's waiting. We'll drive to the Promontory. It'll be beautiful." He saw that she wasn't making a move to get up. "Just for a few minutes. Just so we can say we did it." She never could resist him when he pleaded like that, like a lost little boy.

"Well . . ."

"And I promise I won't come here in the middle of the night any more. OK?"

"You promise?"

"Well . . . I won't come very often." He laughed, expecting her to laugh too, then stopped abruptly, surprised by her hard expression. "What's wrong?"

"Nothing. Everything," she said, realizing that she was going to give in one last time, that she was going to go along

21

on this wild escapade out to the cliffs in the middle of the night.

"I waited at the mall two hours for you," he said. "Come on. You owe me."

Now she laughed. "I owe you? Well, I guess I have no choice then." She turned and lowered her feet to the thick, wool carpet. "Do you mind turning around while I get dressed?"

"Hey, Ol – since when are you so modest?" He leered at her.

Ugh, she thought. He's so immature.

What did I ever see in him?

This is the last time I'm going anywhere with him, she thought, pulling on the jeans, then searching her drawer in the darkness for a jumper.

"It's so warm for October," he said.

"Spare me the weather reports," she said drily.

She didn't realize he had stepped up behind her. He put his arms around her and, turning her around, kissed her, tentatively at first, then harder.

He *does* have his good qualities, Olivia thought, returning the kiss. Then she shoved him gently away. "Owen's waiting, remember?"

"He likes to wait," Josh said, reaching for her again.

He smelled so sweet, so soapy sweet. She kissed him again.

No. This was crazy.

"Come on. I'll get the car." She pulled away from him and headed to the hallway. She grabbed her jacket, and they sneaked down the front stairs and out the front door.

Owen was waiting in the driveway, his iPod plugged in, as usual. The moonlight seemed to emphasize his bad skin. He was wearing a lightweight zip-up jacket with the collar turned up. He grinned at Olivia.

She gave him a short wave and headed to the garage, pulling on her jacket. Climbing behind the wheel of the BMW, she took a deep breath. The leather smelled so good. She put the car into neutral and Josh and Owen pushed it backwards down the drive. If she started it in the garage, Olivia knew, it was certain to wake her mother. This wasn't the first late-night drive the three of them had taken.

But it's the last, she thought, as Josh climbed in beside her, grinning excitedly, and Owen folded his long legs into the back seat. She started the car and headed towards the high cliffs at the edge of town that everyone called the Promontory.

The houses on both sides of the street were dark. There were no other cars on the road. "Turn on the radio," Owen said, leaning over the back of the seat. "It's Metal Maniacs Hour."

"No way, man," Josh said, lowering his window, letting in a blast of cold air. "We're listening to the quiet. Just listen to that. Beautiful, huh?"

He looked over at Olivia, who kept her eyes straight ahead on the curving white line in the middle of the road. She was more tired than she had thought, and driving was taking all of her concentration.

The houses gave way to woods, then open fields as they headed out of town. The Promontory was a popular make-out spot for Middlewood teenagers. But of course it would be deserted this time of night.

A large moving lorry honked its horn as it headed past, startling Olivia. She gripped the wheel tighter as she turned on to Cliff Road, more of a gravel path than a road. The moon had disappeared behind clouds. Trees whispered and shook in the darkness.

"I feel *good*!" Josh shouted exuberantly out of the open window as the car sped over the gravel.

"Can't you close that window? It's freezing," Olivia complained.

He turned to look at her, surprised that she wasn't getting into the spirit of things. "Hey, lighten up," he said. "This is great! This is awesome!"

She didn't reply. She skidded to a stop as the gravel road abruptly ended at a low fence made of logs. A few metres beyond the fence, the high granite cliffs jutted out, overlooking the town.

Josh leaped out of the car, shouting up at the sky.

"Hey – you forgot to close your door!" Olivia called angrily after him. But he didn't hear her. He was already half running, half skipping to the cliff edge.

Owen climbed out of the back, tinny drum rhythms escaping from his headphones. Olivia held the car key in her hand, thinking about locking the car, then decided it was silly. No one else would be foolish enough to be up here at three o'clock in the morning.

She walked around to the other side of the car, the ground soft and wet beneath her trainers, and closed Josh's door. Then, dropping the car keys in her jacket pocket, she started walking slowly towards Josh on the cliff edge.

"Hey, it's a lot colder up here," she complained, zipping up her jacket as the cold wind gusted about her.

"It's great!" Josh called, a dark shadow against a darker sky. "Come here! Take a look!"

She shivered. Was it the cold? Or the cliff edge? She had always had a problem with heights.

Josh took her hand and pulled her close to him. "Look – the whole town." He pointed.

"It's all dark," she said without enthusiasm. "All sane people are asleep."

His arm tightened around her waist. "Hey, you're a lot of laughs tonight," he said softly, bringing his face close to hers.

"It's too cold. I thought it was warmer out," she said.

"I'll warm you up." He squeezed her waist again.

She looked for Owen. He was off by himself a few metres away, sitting on a large rock, staring down into the dark valley that held the town, his foot tapping to the music that pounded in his ears.

Why am I here with them? Olivia asked herself, as a strong blast of wind pushed her towards the jagged cliff-edge. Why aren't I home asleep, safe in my bed, like every normal person in town?

She thought of her mother padding around the corridors at all hours, unable to sleep. What if her mother happened to look into Olivia's bedroom and see that she was gone? I'd be history, Olivia thought with a shudder. I'd be dead meat. She wouldn't let me out of her sight for the next decade!

And then I couldn't go out with Ben on Saturday night . . .

"Hey, Josh – what are you doing?" Olivia's voice caught in her throat. She looked up to see him standing ostrich-like on one leg at the very edge of the cliff.

"Just trying to get your attention," he said, laughing. "You seem to be somewhere else tonight."

"Josh – stop it! You're frightening me!"

"All right!" he cried. "I think I finally *do* have your attention! Now, for my next trick . . ." He started hopping up and down on one foot, his other foot stretched up in the air behind him.

"No, please! Stop! You'll fall!"

And as Olivia said the word, Josh slipped and fell over the edge.

Four

The sky seemed to blacken. The ground started to spin.

"Josh?"

She blinked her eyes, then opened them wide, thinking that when she opened them, he'd be back where he had been, standing on one foot, hopping up and down on the cliff-edge.

But there was only darkness.

"Josh?"

Her heart felt as if it had stopped beating. She wasn't sure she could breathe.

She took a step to the edge. But she was too dizzy.

"Josh?"

He poked his head up from below the surface, a wide, delighted grin on his face. "Gotcha!"

She just stared at him open-mouthed. She couldn't speak.

He laughed. "Aren't you going to help me up?"

"You – you –"

"It was a joke." He reached his arms over the rock surface and started to pull himself up. "There's a little ledge here. Fooled you, huh?" He looked up at her expectantly.

"You creep," she muttered angrily, her heart beginning to beat again.

"See? You really do care!" he said, laughing.

"That wasn't funny, Josh."

"It wasn't really supposed to be funny," he said, pulling himself all the way up, standing up with a groan, and dusting off his jeans. "I guess it was like . . . performance art."

She made a disgusted face and turned away.

"Hey – what's wrong?" he asked, coming towards her. "You always used to enjoy my little performances."

"Well, I didn't enjoy this one!"

"Hey – what's going on?" Owen called from across the darkness. He had lit a cigarette, and all she could see was the glow of it.

"Huh? You missed it?" Josh called, disappointed.

"Missed what?"

"Never mind," Olivia said quickly. She no longer felt upset or frightened. Her anger had forced away those feelings. What a stupid, mean trick to pull!

"Hey, watch! I'll show you!" Josh yelled.

Owen stood up to get a better view.

A gust of wind battered all three of them. "Stop it, Josh!" Olivia cried. She turned and started going towards the car. "I'm leaving. Are you two coming with me?"

"One second," Josh said, holding up a finger. "I just have to do my little performance for Owen. Now watch carefully . . ."

"No – don't!" Olivia screamed. "I mean it, Josh! It wasn't funny the first time. It was horrible! I'll never speak to you again if—"

"You'll like it better the second time," Josh said, looking to see if Owen was watching.

"Josh – I'm warning you!" Olivia took another few steps towards the car. Her trainers were soaked through from the wet ground. She felt cold and uncomfortable. "Are you coming?"

She turned round to see Josh back on the cliff-edge, balancing again on one foot. "Ta-daa!" he cried, a gleeful smile on his face.

The smile suddenly faded as Josh's eyes opened wide in horror.

Olivia saw his expression change. Then she looked down and saw why.

A large chunk of stone was crumbling beneath Josh. The cliff-edge was breaking away.

"No! No!"

He threw his arms up as he began to drop and frantically grabbed for the edge. But it crumbled in his hands.

"No – Josh!"

His head disappeared, and then his flailing hands.

She heard his body hit hard against the side.

"No – Josh!"

She heard him scream all the way down.

Then from down below she heard a cracking sound, the sound of eggs breaking.

This wasn't a joke.

This wasn't a performance.

This was real.

This was a death.

Olivia didn't even realize she was running until she reached the car.

She could hear Owen calling to her, his voice high-pitched and frightened, but she couldn't make out the words over the siren of her panic. The siren was drowning out everything. It seemed to echo between her ears, so loud, so unbearably loud.

She couldn't think.

She couldn't hear.

Was Owen calling to her? Was she running away? Was she climbing into the car, fumbling in her jacket pocket for the car key?

"Olivia – come back!"

She couldn't hear anything. The siren had taken over her brain.

"We've got to help him! Olivia! Come back!"

What was he saying?

Come back?

But how could she?

If she stayed, her mother would find out she had sneaked out. Her mother would find out everything. Everyone in town would know what she had done.

How could she stay?

Her mother would take away her car. Take away her credit cards. Take away . . . everything.

For Josh?

Stay and have her life ruined for Josh?

She'd stay – if it weren't already too late.

But she heard him fall. She heard the horrifying sound when he hit the bottom.

She'd probably be hearing it for the rest of her life.

No. No way. No way, Josh.

Poor, dead Josh.

"Olivia – come back! We've got to help him! We've got to save him!"

Help him?

Is that what Owen was yelling?

The siren was just so loud, so overwhelmingly loud. Maybe if I drive really fast, the siren will go away.

The car was already in reverse. She was already backing away from the low fence.

No way. No way, Josh.

I can't ruin my life for you. I was going to break up with you, anyway. Don't you see? You're just not right for me. You're just not my kind. You understand, don't you?

Don't you?

The tyres squealed as she floored the accelerator pedal, and the car began to race over the gravel road, slipping from side to side, noisily spitting a tidal wave of gravel behind it.

Lose my car? Lose my . . . reputation?

Ben's face flashed into her mind. He looked so good to her. So safe.

Sorry, Josh.

I'll get help.

Don't worry. I'm not abandoning you. I'll get help.

That's what she'd do. As soon as she got home, she'd dial 999. She'd tell them to hurry to the Promontory.

She'd save Josh after all.

She wasn't running away. She was running for help.

She started to feel better. The siren faded to a low, insistent wail.

I'm getting help. Owen will understand.

I'm getting help.

The tyres squealed as she turned on to the Town Road. She realized she was going too fast.

But I have to go fast. I'm getting help for Josh.

As soon as I get home.

As soon as I can.

She didn't see the lorry until it was too late.

She saw the lights first. She wondered why she was suddenly bathed in light.

She thought it might not be real. It might be part of her panic, like the siren.

But the lights grew brighter.

They were lorry headlights. The lorry swerved to avoid her, but the road was too narrow.

By the time Olivia realized she was about to be hit head-on, it was too late to react.

The lights grew brighter, brighter, seemed to surround her.

Everything was glowing.

And then the siren was drowned out by the sound of breaking glass and bending steel.

And the lights gave way to darkness.

Five

The blackness lightened to a murky grey. Shadows in a dark fog. Clouds. Heavy, grey clouds. Then nothing at all.

She opened her eyes.

The room was a blur. A dark, warm blur. It was very still. Unearthly still.

The quiet is deafening, she thought.

And then she realized she was awake. And the room, coming quickly into focus, was her bedroom. She happily recognized the light through the open window, the shadows from the trees on the familiar flowered wallpaper. The two framed Picasso prints over the bookshelf next to the desk.

Home. She was home.

She raised her head, testing it. She raised her left arm, then her right. She stretched.

I don't hurt. I'm OK.

She sat up quickly.

I feel fine.

I must be dreaming. She yawned. No. The lorry was a dream. The headlights, those blinding, yellow headlights weren't real. The accident wasn't real. It never happened.

I'm fine.

She pushed down the bedspread and the satin sheet and started to climb out of bed. But a sudden fluttering at the window made her stop.

Just the curtains?

No. She heard a scrabbling against the side of the house, a soft thud.

That's odd, she thought, pulling the sheet back up. Why is the window wide open in October?

There were other things that puzzled her. The quiet was one of them. Except for the soft thuds outside, it was so eerily quiet.

Where was her mother? Why wasn't she waiting at her bedside for her to wake up?

Because there was no accident, she told herself. Because it was all a dream.

A dark form filled the window. It moved quickly, struggling, pulling itself into the room, one leg, one arm, then another leg. It stepped into the square of moonlight.

"Josh!" she cried.

"Ssshhh." He raised his finger to his lips, his eyes glowing like dark jewels.

"Josh – you're OK!" We're both OK, she thought.

His smile seemed to warm the room. "It's a beautiful night," he whispered. "Come on, get dressed. Let's go for a walk."

"A walk?"

She wondered what time it was, what day. How had she got back to bed?

She had to remind herself that she had been in bed all along. In bed dreaming a terrible dream.

"OK." She got up quickly, feeling as light as air, and floated across the room to pull a designer tracksuit from her drawer.

"Hurry," Josh whispered, sounding very excited and happy.

She was dressed in an instant, headed for the door, then hesitated. She walked over to Josh, grabbed his arm, squeezed it hard.

He was real.

He was really there.

He laughed. "What's the matter with you?"

"Nothing," she said. Why go into it?

She remembered that she had decided to break up with him, not to see him any more. I'll have to tell him, she thought. It won't be easy, but I'll have to tell him. Maybe I'll tell him during our walk.

They were outside now, and starting to jog. It felt so good to be moving, to feel the cool wind on her face.

She jogged a little faster, leaving Josh behind.

"Hey, wait for me!"

He'll always be a little behind me, she thought. He'll never really be able to catch up.

It was still so silent. The silence was almost *thick*.

It must have been very late. No cars moved. The houses were dark. The wind blew but the trees didn't move. The fallen brown leaves, scattered all over the ground, stayed in place as if nailed down.

Strange.

Olivia jogged a little faster.

"Hey!" Josh called from a few metres behind.

She didn't turn around. It felt so good to run, to move, to be OK.

"Hey!"

She looked back without slowing her pace. She was running really fast now, and not in the least bit out of breath.

"Hey!"

Josh, she realized, looked angry. What was his problem?

She turned again. A street light cast a cone of white light down on him. His eyes were narrowed, his mouth pulled back in an angry frown.

He looks frightening, Olivia thought.

And her next thought frightened her even more: He's not running with me. He's chasing me.

"Hey!"

She knew she was right. She picked up speed. She glanced quickly back. Josh picked up speed, too.

He was gaining on her.

Why was he doing this? Why did he look so frightening, so angry? She wanted to stop. But she was afraid.

Where were they?

The houses were gone. The woods gave way to flat fields. She could see low, black hills against the purple night sky.

How far have we run? It doesn't seem as if we've been running that long.

"Hey – you . . ."

His voice sounded so angry, so filled with hatred.

He's going to catch me, she thought, feeling her legs begin to ache, feeling her chest begin to heave for breath. He's going to catch me, and then . . .

And then?

A cold shudder ran down her body.

She forced herself to run harder. Every step hurt now, every thrust of her legs sent a flash of pain up her back. But she knew she had to keep running.

"Olivia – stop!"

She ignored his angry call, gulped in a mouthful of air, and ran, her trainers sinking into the wet ground.

Ground?

Where were they?

The ground seemed to dip, then rise again. The soft ground gave way to granite.

The Promontory.

They had run to the Promontory. He had chased her to the Promontory. Had this been his destination all along?

She was only a few metres from the cliff-edge. She stopped, gasping for breath, her entire body throbbing, pulsing with pain. She spun around.

"Josh – stop!"

He came running right at her, his expression fixed in hatred.

"Josh – why are you doing this?"

He seemed to pick up speed rather than slow down. He was only a couple of metres away now. His dark eyes burned into hers. His mouth opened wide, and he tossed his head back in a silent scream.

"Josh – stop! *Please!*"

He ran past her, ran right over the cliff-edge. His legs scissored in mid-air. His hands flailed wildly above his head. He spun, turned to face her, an accusing look on his face. Then he started to drop.

It was Olivia's turn to scream. She closed her eyes tight and tossed back her head, and screamed and screamed.

No sound came out.

When she opened her eyes, she was in a very bright, white room.

Her mother's face loomed over her.

Olivia could see the criss-cross of lines at the corners of her mother's eyes, the small pores of her made-up cheeks, the crumbs of orange lipstick on her lips. She could see her mother's face so clearly. There was a damp path down the makeup on her cheeks where tears must have recently trickled.

Her mother's smile was broad. Too broad.

"She's coming out of it now," a woman's voice said from somewhere behind her mother.

"It's starting to wear off," another woman said.

Her mother's smile grew even wider. She leaned down over Olivia until they almost touched noses.

"What?" Olivia asked.

"She'll be fully awake soon," one of the unseen women said.

"She did very well," the other added in a hushed tone.

Her mother's face didn't move. It hovered above Olivia like a pink balloon.

I'm still dreaming, Olivia thought.

"You're going to be fine," her mother said, her smile still fixed. The face retreated a little. Tears formed near the tangled criss-cross of age lines.

Yes, I'm going to be fine because I'm still dreaming.

She tried to sit up.

Everything hurt.

I'm paralysed, she thought, and the sweet calmness of the dream sensation gave way to panic.

"Hey . . ."

"You're going to be fine," her mother said softly. The tears ran down the already defined tracks on her cheeks.

I don't believe you, Olivia thought.

She struggled to sit up. When that didn't prove possible, she struggled to move her arms. That wasn't possible, either.

"Help – Mum –"

"She's fully awake now," a voice said.

"That's a good sign," the other voice added.

Who *are* those women? Olivia wondered angrily.

"Don't try to move," her mother said.

"I can't," Olivia told her, her voice tiny, like a baby's voice.

I'm a baby again, she thought. I've just been born.

Crazy thought.

I've been drugged or something

A crazy thought that was probably true.

She looked past her mother with her frozen, tear-stained

smile to the white tiled walls, the bright fluorescent lights, the white-uniformed nurses standing side by side in the doorway.

I'm in a hospital.

And I'm not dreaming now.

It all seemed too much to take in. It was using all her strength, all her concentration to *see*.

"You're going to be fine," her mother repeated, like a song chorus.

You always were a bad liar, Olivia thought.

She hated the smell of her mother's make-up. So orangey. So ugly.

She drifted back to sleep with the smell clinging to her nostrils.

"She needs to sleep," a nearby voice said.

"You really were lucky," her mother said, a few days later. She sat stiffly in a folding chair beside the hospital bed, her fur coat on her lap. "Your beautiful face wasn't touched."

"Just about everything else was," Olivia groaned.

"Olivia, really. Don't complain. A lorry like that. You could have been – you could have been . . ." She bit her trembling lower lip. "A few broken bones. Really, dear. You should be so grateful. "

"Yeah. Grateful," Olivia repeated.

Whatever painkillers they were feeding into her arm made her feel as if she were not completely in the room. She felt as if she had swapped places with her shadow. Her shadow lay braced and bandaged on this hard hospital bed. Her real body – and her mind – were off somewhere else.

She was continually drifting off to sleep, sometimes in the middle of conversations. She wasn't allowed visitors yet, only her mother. The visits tired her out. She wished her mother would stop staring at her so intensely. She wished they would stop pumping stuff into her, so that she could think straight.

"In another few weeks, you'll be strong enough to begin therapy for your leg," Mrs Collier said matter-of-factly.

"Yeah. Well, I'm so grateful for that, too," Olivia said sarcastically.

"Just stop it, Olivia. Let's take this one day at a time."

"Don't you mean one *cliché* at a time?" Olivia cracked, knowing she was giving her mother a hard time and not caring.

"This has been a terrible shock for all of us," Mrs Collier said, deciding to ignore her daughter's sarcasm. "When I got that call from the police at three in the morning that you – that you were in an accident and . . ."

Olivia realized she hadn't explained a thing to her mother.

"What were you doing out, Olivia? Why did you sneak out of the house?"

She just didn't have the strength to get into it now. Drifting halfway between the real world and the shadowy world induced by the painkillers, she hadn't even thought about that horrible night.

Hadn't even thought about Josh.

She drifted off to sleep, wondering how she would ever explain.

"Owen?"

Olivia tried to sit up, then remembered that she couldn't. She looked for her mother, but she wasn't there. It was Owen sitting awkwardly in the folding chair now.

His face was flushed. His eyes darted nervously from her face to the floor. His hands were clasped tightly in his lap.

"Owen?"

"Hi, Olivia. Are you awake? I mean—"

"No. I'm talking in my sleep. Owen, are you OK?"

"Yeah. Fine." His face turned a little brighter red. "Your mum says you're going to be fine."

"She says it four hundred times a day," Olivia said bitterly, rolling her eyes. They were the only part of her she could move without any pain. "So it's got to be a lie."

Owen just stared at her. "You're pretty beat-up, huh?"

She laughed a dry laugh. It made her broken ribs hurt. "Good question, Owen. Got any others?"

He pulled at the diamond stud in his ear.

They sat in silence for a while. He stared at her. She had the feeling that he was waiting for something.

Finally he broke the silence. "Aren't you going to ask me about Josh?" He asked it angrily, accusingly.

What's wrong with me? Olivia wondered. Why *didn't* I ask about Josh? Is it just these awful drugs? Am I losing my mind? Am I trying to shut out all memories of that night?

"Well, Josh died," Owen said, shouting now. He jumped to his feet, his face filled with disgust. "Josh died, Olivia. He didn't make it. He died that night. And you didn't even bother to ask me about him."

Six

Amy came to visit a few days later. Or was it the same day? Olivia couldn't keep track of time, didn't even try.

"Sssh. I brought you something," Amy said, whispering, acting very secretive as she dug in the big, floppy embroidered bag she always carried.

"I like your hair," Olivia said.

"My hair? I haven't even brushed it." She continued to rummage in the bag. "Here it is." She looked behind her to the door to make sure no one was coming in.

Olivia laughed at the secrecy. "Amy – what on earth . . . ?"

Amy handed her a Snickers bar. "Quick – hide it."

"A Snickers bar? Amy – I'm touched!"

"Just hide it," Amy insisted, "before they take it away from you. I reckoned this is probably the one time you won't be watching your weight."

"What a thoughtful present," Olivia said, slipping the chocolate bar under the sheet.

The girls talked, animatedly at first, then awkwardly in fits and starts. They both realized that they had less to talk about now that they didn't go to the same school or have the same friends.

They talked about Olivia's broken bones, and about how her mother was taking it all. And they talked about Amy's classes and a boy she had met at the mall.

Then, as if she had been leading up to it all along, Amy said, "Owen told me about . . . Josh."

"Yeah," Olivia said, reaching over to adjust the tube that was still stuck to her wrist.

"It – it must be so hard for you," Amy said, staring intently into Olivia's eyes, searching for something there.

"Yeah. Well . . ." Olivia didn't know what Amy expected her to say. And why was she staring at her like that?

The silence grew really awkward. "I wish I felt more," Olivia said, mainly to fill the silence.

"What do you mean?" Amy looked very surprised.

"I mean, it's so awful. When Owen told me that Josh was dead, my first reaction was, Now I don't have to break up with him."

Amy's mouth dropped open. "Really? That's really the first thing you thought?"

Uh-oh. I've gone too far, Olivia thought. I've been too honest. I should have known better. I should have known that would shock Amy.

It shocks me, too, in a way.

"You really didn't feel *anything*?" Amy asked, shifting uncomfortably on the small folding chair, her hands playing with the straps of her bag.

"I guess it just hasn't sunk in," Olivia said, beginning to feel tired again, wishing Amy would just leave.

"Oh."

"I mean, I'm just numb, I guess. You know. From the painkillers and stuff. I'll feel it later. I'm sure."

Amy just stared at her, much the way Owen had.

'Well, I know it sounds a little cold . . .' Olivia started to say, and then decided she had nothing to be defensive about.

My feelings are my own business, she told herself. I don't have to explain how I feel to Amy, or Owen, or anyone else. I'm the one who saw Josh die, after all. I'm the one who saw him fall off the cliff. I'm the one who saw the look on his face when he knew he was falling.

That's horrible enough for one lifetime.

You ran away, a voice inside her said. You didn't help him. You ran away.

I hurried to get help, was Olivia's reply to herself. I would've got help for him if that lorry hadn't . . .

Who cares? Josh is dead, and I'm lying here wrecked.

Who cares?

Stop staring at me like I'm some disgusting kind of cold fish.

As if reading Olivia's thoughts, Amy jumped to her feet. "I've got to get going. I didn't realize how late it was."

She didn't even look at her watch, thought Olivia. She has no idea how late it is. "Thanks for coming," she said.

"Get better soon," Amy said. "Make sure you rest."

"What else can I do?"

Amy laughed, a nervous giggle. "I'll come back sometime. I mean, when I can. Bye." She hurried out of the room without looking back.

"What was it – something I said?" Olivia asked aloud.

She settled her head back on the pillow.

"So what? So what? So *what*? Sorry, Josh. But so what?"

"You're not going to study tonight, are you, Olivia?"

"No, Mum. I was just carrying these books up to my room. I have a date tonight."

"Oh, I'm glad." Her mother collapsed wearily into the oversized living room armchair and raised her feet on to the footstool. "You've been working so hard, I've been a little worried about you."

"Well, I missed six weeks of school, you know."

50

"I'm very pleased by how well you're doing, Olivia," Mrs Collier said, raising her feet to examine her ankles, which were swollen. "The therapist says your leg is coming along so nicely, you can probably stop by Christmas time."

"Maybe then people will stop treating me like an invalid," Olivia said, and started out of the living room, forcing herself to walk without a limp, even though her leg really throbbed with pain.

"I haven't seen Amy around in quite a while," Mrs Collier said, not noticing that Olivia was trying to leave. "Did she come and visit you in hospital?"

"Yeah. Once," Olivia said, allowing more bitterness to escape than she had intended. She quickly added, "I guess she's just really busy. It's hard, you know, to keep up with kids from other schools."

She started to leave the room again, but again her mother refused to let the conversation end. "And what about Josh?" she asked. "Did you say you were meeting him tonight? I haven't seen him once the whole time you..."

Olivia uttered a silent gasp. Her mother kept talking, but her voice seemed to fade as if someone had turned down the volume control.

I never told her, Olivia realized.

She never asked anything about Josh, and I never told her.

She doesn't know a thing. She doesn't know that Josh is dead. Doesn't know why I was out in the middle of the night. Doesn't know anything.

And doesn't really *want* to know.

Any other mother would have demanded an explanation, Olivia told herself. Any other mother would have wanted to know every detail.

Maybe I'm lucky.

Lucky that she doesn't care enough to ask.

I don't care, either.

So, we're both lucky.

"I'm not seeing Josh any more," she said, finding it easy to keep her voice flat and emotionless.

"Really?"

Mrs Collier was trying to play it cool. But Olivia knew how much that news would thrill her. Her mother never could stand Josh, mainly for the same reasons that had Olivia planning to break up with him.

"I have a date with Ben tonight," Olivia said.

"Benjamin Forrest?"

Olivia nodded.

"Sarah Forrest's son? How nice." A pleased smile formed on Mrs Collier's face.

"I'm glad you approve," Olivia snapped. It bothered her to see her mother so happy.

"I didn't mean – Well . . . it's just that Benjamin is much more appropriate."

"Appropriate?" Olivia laughed, a scornful laugh. "What a word!"

Why am I giving my mother such a hard time? she wondered. I *agree* with her that Ben is more appropriate.

It's just not her place to say it.

I should tell her that Josh fell off a cliff and died. Just to see her squirm. Just to see her come up with an *appropriate* response.

But instead, she shifted the books she'd been carrying to her other arm, and walked quickly up to her room to get ready for her date with Ben.

"I love that jumper, Ben," Olivia said. "Is it cashmere?"

"I guess. I'll let you touch it if you wash your hands first." He gave her that adorable lopsided grin, the one that made the dimple appear in his left cheek.

She laughed and rubbed the sleeve of the pale blue jumper. "Yep. It's cashmere."

"My grandmother gave it to me," Ben said, blushing a little as Olivia kept her hand on his arm.

He had insisted on taking her to the winter dance at Garland High, the school he had attended before switching to Glenview. "It'll be a laugh," he said.

Olivia didn't know any of the kids there, and the whole idea of going to the dance seemed like a real downer to her, but she didn't want Ben to think she was a bad sport, so she agreed with a smile.

"Maybe I should dress down a bit," she had said when he told her his plans for the evening after arriving at her house. She was wearing a silk vest and a short suede skirt over black tights.

"I think you look OK," he said, a little uncomfortably.

She liked his shyness. He was so incredibly good-looking, she thought, a little shyness made him more human.

"Shall we take my car?" she asked. She was so accustomed to driving Josh around, the question came automatically.

"No way," he said. "Look." He led her to her front door and pointed to the drive. Basking in the light from the porch was a brand-new silver Jaguar.

Olivia's mouth dropped open. "It's yours?"

"My grandmother gave it to me." Ben was grinning now. He ran a hand quickly through his wavy, blond hair.

"*Nice* grandmother!" Olivia exclaimed.

"Well, she's very old and very rich," Ben said seriously. "And very lonely. And I'm her only grandson."

"Lucky you," Olivia said, resting her hand on his arm again. "I guess we'll be going in style to the Garland High hop!"

When they got to the Garland High gym, everyone seemed so glad to see Ben. A steady stream of kids kept coming up to greet him and ask him how he was doing at Glenview, and if he missed his friends at Garland.

Ben seemed right at home with these kids. I thought this was supposed to be a laugh, Olivia thought, a little resentfully, seeing how excited and pleased Ben was to be back here. "Good lord – look what that girl's wearing," she said, pointing to a girl in a brown, fringed skirt and white boots. "How tacky."

"I think it's kind of sexy," Ben said, almost defensively.

"They could have spent some money on decorating the place a little better," Olivia griped. "I mean balloons and crêpe paper streamers? Please!"

But to her surprise, Ben didn't join in her laughter. "It doesn't look so bad. You know, they can't afford to have their dances at a hotel ballroom, the way we do at Glenview. Everyone seems to be having a good time, anyway, don't you think?"

Olivia quickly agreed. "Yeah, it's great," she said, trying not to sound as unenthusiastic as she felt. "Oh, no! Look at that girl's hair! Unbelievable!"

Ben looked at her, an odd smile on his face. "Olivia, you're such a snob." He said it jokingly, but there was definitely a tone of disapproval in it.

I'd better be careful, Olivia thought. Ben doesn't seem to appreciate my sense of humour.

She danced with him to the blaring music over the terrible loudspeakers and tried to join in shouted conversations with his friends, who seemed pretty nice. It was about eleven o'clock when she asked to leave for the first time. And by eleven-thirty, he had said goodbye to everyone, and they were walking across the street to the car.

"I told you it would be a laugh," he said, his arm casually around her shoulders. His coat smelled like the gym.

Mine probably does, too, Olivia thought unhappily. "Yeah. I like your friends," she said, working hard to sound genuine and enthusiastic.

She sat very close to him as he drove her home. A heavy frost had settled over the lawns. As they drove past, the ground looked silvery white, as if it had snowed. She nestled her head against Ben's shoulder, looking up to see if he seemed pleased by it.

"D'you want to go to a film or something next weekend?" he asked, his eyes straight ahead on the road.

"Yeah. I do," she said softly, secretly feeling as if she had scored a victory. Ben was hooked, definitely hooked.

She inhaled deeply. "I just love the smell of a new car," she said happily.

He kissed her goodnight at her door. He started to end the

kiss, but she grabbed his head with both hands and pulled him towards her, pressing her lips against his in a long, lingering kiss. Finally he headed back to his car, a goofy grin on his handsome face.

She stood and watched him get into the car. He pressed down on the accelerator, making the engine roar, the blast of exhaust white against the darkness of the night. Then he backed silently away.

Score one for Olivia, she thought, as she turned the lock and entered the house. He's just right for me. A little lacking in the sense-of-humour area, maybe. But he can be shaped up.

She hurried up to her room and was getting undressed when her phone rang. She glanced at the clock. It was a few minutes after midnight.

Who could it be?

She picked it up after the second ring, her arm tangled in the sleeve of her shirt. "Hello?"

She heard crackling at the other end. It was either a bad connection or someone was calling long distance.

"Hello?" she repeated, a little louder.

"Hi, Olivia." A boy's voice, sounding very far away. "It's me."

"What?"

"Olivia – it's me. Josh. How you doin'?"

Seven

Olivia didn't reply.

She had dropped the phone.

The voice. It *was* Josh's voice, she thought.

But that's impossible. Of course, that's impossible.

Someone was playing a cruel trick on her. But who could it be?

Who could sound so much like Josh? Who would want to scare Olivia, to make her feel bad?

Owen?

Was it Owen? She hadn't seen him since that day in hospital. Since the day Owen had come to tell her that Josh was dead.

Owen was so angry with her, Olivia remembered, so shocked that she hadn't asked about Josh immediately. So outraged when Olivia didn't cry at the horrible news.

Outraged. That was the only word to describe it.

Owen was the only one who knew that she had run away from the Promontory that night, that she hadn't stayed to try and rescue Josh.

But I didn't run away, she insisted to herself.

I drove away as quickly as I could to get help.

She wished she had had a chance to explain that to Owen.

That creep. She never had liked him. He was so ugly with that pockmarked face, and that awful spiky hair.

He was just stupid enough to make that phone call and pretend to be Josh.

But she knew it couldn't be Owen. Owen had such a high-pitched, scratchy voice. There was no way he could sound so much like Josh.

So exactly like Josh.

She shivered, and realized she was still undressed. She hurried over to her chest of drawers, stepping over her clothes, which she had tossed on the floor, and pulled out her warmest pyjamas.

What is going on? Who would play such a stupid, mean joke?

The question repeated in her mind. She just couldn't answer it.

It took hours to fall asleep. And then she slept fitfully, waking up every few hours, thinking the phone was ringing.

Sunday was spent doing homework and watching endless, boring old films full of stupid romance on TV.

She thought maybe Ben would call, but he didn't. So she called him after dinner, and they had a nice, short chat.

He's never asked me about Josh, she realized. Of course, he never knew Josh. But he did know that I'd been going with someone for a long time.

And he's never really asked about my accident, either.

That's strange.

Maybe he just doesn't like to bring up unpleasant subjects, she thought. A lot of people are like that.

The next day was a blustery, cold day that showed winter was getting serious. Low, grey clouds hovered overhead as she set off for home in the late afternoon after her French lesson. Even though it was still afternoon, it was as dark as night, an eerie, heavy darkness that made it feel as if it might start to snow at any minute.

I wish I had the car, she thought, even though her French tutor lived only a couple of streets from her house. She pulled the fur hood of her coat up, and picked up her pace. The cold made her foot throb, but she forced herself not to limp. Any change in the weather made her foot and ribs and shoulders ache. It was just something she was going to have to live with, she realized.

As she approached Trafalgar Avenue, the street lights

60

flickered and came on. The sudden light startled her. It made everything suddenly look different. New shadows shifted and played across the pavement.

It took Olivia a few seconds to realize what had happened. She stared up at the street lamp above her head, and for a split second, the yellow light reminded her of the lorry headlights, the headlights that had seemed to grow and grow, widen and widen until they were all around her.

With a silent gasp, she looked away quickly, turning her gaze across Trafalgar Avenue, one of the busiest roads in Middlewood.

Leaning against a bus-stop post across the street, illuminated by a circle of yellow light from a street lamp behind him, she saw a young man staring at her.

"Josh?"

He didn't move.

She froze.

She recognized the red hoody. He had worn it a million times.

"Josh?"

The traffic light was against her. A steady stream of cars poured down Trafalgar Avenue, people on their way home from work.

Except for the hoody, Josh seemed all yellow and black, bathed in light from the street lamp.

He stared at her, unmoving. And she stared back.

It can't be.

It's impossible.

Josh, you're dead.

She knew her eyes were playing tricks on her. It had to be another boy, another boy with black hair, bold, black eyes, and a red hoody. Another boy who leaned just like Josh.

Who looked just like Josh.

She heard his voice again, the voice on the phone on Saturday night. "Hi, it's me. How you doin'?"

The voice from so far away.

The light changed.

He didn't move. He leaned against the narrow yellow post, staring straight ahead at her. She shivered. Not from the cold.

She had to know the truth.

"Josh?"

She started across the street. But a city bus ran the red light, roaring through the crossroads.

Olivia leaped back to the curb, startled.

When the bus had passed, she looked across the street.

Josh had gone.

Eight

O livia rolled over with a weary groan and tugged hard at the covers. The bottom of the sheet pulled out from under the mattress. She sat up. Now I'll have to remake the bed, she thought. She couldn't stand to have her feet sticking out from under the covers.

She stood up in the darkness and glanced at the clock on her desk. Twelve-fifteen.

Why can't I get to sleep?

It was chilly in the room, even in her pyjamas. Maybe I should close the window, she thought. She pulled the sheet down and tucked it in. Out on the street a car drove by, its radio blaring.

I'll never get to sleep, Olivia thought, climbing back into bed. I'm not even tired. Maybe I should get up and work on my book report.

The scrabbling sounds outside the window made her sit

up with a start. She heard scraping noises. Trainers against the tree trunk.

No.

It wasn't possible.

She had to be imagining it. The way she had imagined seeing Josh standing on that street corner.

She uttered a soft cry as a hand grabbed the window ledge from outside. A head popped up, hidden in shadow.

No.

Olivia gripped the edge of the bedspread, pulling it up to her chin as if to shield herself.

She leaned over and, her hand trembling, struggled to turn on the bedside lamp. She nearly knocked it over, finally managing to click it on just as Josh pulled himself into the room.

He grinned at her, that warm, familiar grin, and walked stiffly away from the window into the yellow light. He was wearing black, straight-legged jeans and a worn, leather jacket.

"Hi, Olivia." His voice was a whisper, almost ghostly.

"Josh?"

"Yeah. It's me."

Don't scream, don't scream, don't scream . . .

She realized that she'd been holding her breath.

"But . . ."

"How are you?" Still a whisper.

He looked pale in the yellow light, and thin. He took a few steps towards her, limping slightly, holding his left leg stiffly.

"But – Josh – you're dead!"

Olivia didn't recognize her own voice. Her throat felt so tight, it was hard to breathe. She suddenly felt cold all over.

Don't scream, don't scream, don't scream.

"Huh?" His mouth dropped open. His face filled with surprise. He shook his long, wavy hair as if shaking off her words.

Olivia gripped the bedspread, staring into his bewildered face. He looks different, she thought. So thin, almost wasted away.

"What did you say?"

She coughed. Her throat felt tight and dry. "Dead," she said, the word sounding odd, not sounding like a real word. "Owen said you were dead, Josh."

"Huh? Really?"

He looked stunned. He pulled out the desk chair, turned it around, and sat down on it backwards, leaning his chin against the chair back. "He said I was dead?"

"Yeah. He told me. He said you didn't make it. That you—"

"But why would Owen say that?" He gripped the back of the chair and made it rock to and fro.

He's alive, she thought, starting to calm down, starting to

get over the shock of seeing him climb into her room again. He's alive. He's really sitting there.

To her surprise, she realized she had mixed feelings about seeing him, sitting there, rocking the desk chair up and down. She had got used to the idea of him being dead.

Am I glad to see him? she asked herself.

Not really.

Mainly, she realized, seeing him made her feel less guilty.

"Yeah," she said, "why *did* Owen tell me that?" Her shock was beginning to turn to anger. "Was that some sort of stupid joke he was trying to pull?"

"Poor guy," Josh said softly, staring down at the plush carpet, not picking up on Olivia's anger. "He must've been in shock. He was so upset about – about what happened that night."

"He was so upset, he *thought* you were dead?" Olivia pulled herself up and leaned against the headboard. Why did she feel so cold? The room seemed to grow even colder after Josh entered.

"I guess," Josh said. A sad expression crossed his face, an expression she had never seen before.

It's not just sad, she thought. It's mournful.

"Well, where have you been for the past two months?" she asked. The question came out more angry than concerned.

Her tone seemed to surprise him. "I was banged up really

badly," he said, looking into her eyes. She noticed that he was holding his left leg stiff, straight out in front of him. "I had a lot of broken bones, some internal bleeding and stuff. They took me to a hospital across town. I've been there the whole time."

"I'm sorry," she said.

You're supposed to be dead, she thought.

I felt so bad. I felt so guilty. Why did I have to go through all that for nothing?

Why did Owen do that? Out of spite? Out of anger? Did he do it for revenge, because I left him there that night?

"I wanted to call you," Josh said. "But my hands were bandaged. I looked like a mummy. My aunt tried to call, but there was never an answer at your house. Maybe she was trying the wrong number. She isn't too bright these days."

He shifted uncomfortably on the small chair. "It was so terrible, so unbearable," he said in a low, flat voice. "All the time in hospital. All those weeks. Know what I did? I pretended I was in a play, that I was just playing a role, that it wasn't really happening to me. Pretty pathetic, eh?"

"You look good," she said, ignoring his question, looking him up and down.

You look like a skeleton, she thought.

"So you really thought I was dead?" He scratched his

head. A grin crossed his face for some reason. "That explains it, I guess."

"Explains what?"

"Why I never heard from you. Why you never visited. Why you hung up on me the other night."

"I was in hospital, too," Olivia said, sounding defensive.

"You were?" He stood up. Olivia noticed that it wasn't easy for him. He had always been so agile, so athletic. But now his legs seemed stiff. He seemed to move with real pain. "What happened to you?"

"When you fell, I – I ran for help."

It's the truth, Olivia thought. Why do I feel as if I'm lying?

"Yeah?"

"Yeah. I started driving to town to get the police, or an ambulance or something. But I – I was so upset, I had an accident. I was unconscious for a day. But I guess I was lucky."

"We both were," Josh said with real emotion. "I've missed you a lot."

He hurried to her, leaned down, put his arms around her shoulders, and kissed her. Olivia kissed him back, suddenly feeling emotional, too.

He's real, all right, she thought. He's not a ghost.

The kiss lasted a long time. She grabbed the back of his head and held him to her.

What am I doing? she thought.

Ben's face flashed into her mind.

Pressing her lips against Josh's, holding his head, gripping his long hair, she felt terribly confused.

I *do* feel something for him, she thought.

Don't I?

Or am I just relieved that he's OK?

This isn't right. This isn't what I want.

So why am I doing it?

Again, Ben's face flashed into her mind.

She pulled back suddenly and dropped her hands to her side. He stayed there, leaning down over her, his dark eyes burning into hers.

"I really thought you were dead," she said.

"I'm not. I'll prove it," he said, and kissed her again.

Something's wrong, she thought. Something's different.

This kiss was much shorter. She heard noises, footsteps on the landing.

"My mum – she's up."

"OK. I'd better go. I'll pick you up on Friday night," he whispered. "I'll prove to you I'm not dead."

"Friday night?"

"Yeah." He kissed her again.

"But, Josh . . ."

She had to tell him about Ben. She didn't really want to go out with Josh.

But she did.

She was so confused.

He disappeared through the window. She listened to him slide down the tree.

Something is different about him, Olivia thought. His kiss. It felt different. Just not the same.

Trying to figure out what it was that was different, she fell into a troubled sleep.

Nine

"Well, I'm sorry, Ben. I'm disappointed, too." Olivia blew on her nail polish, cradling the phone on her shoulder.

Ben whined on the other end.

She didn't mind the whining. She was pleased that her breaking their date had got him so upset.

"Well, what about tomorrow night? I'm sure the same film will be on tomorrow night."

Ben had to go somewhere with his parents tomorrow night.

"Well, maybe next week," Olivia said, glancing at the clock. She was supposed to meet Josh at the mall in five minutes.

Oh, well. Let Josh wait a while, she thought. It wouldn't be the first time. She thought of that night back in October when she had hidden behind a post and watched him wait. What a laugh!

Why won't these nails dry?

Now Ben was asking if he could stop by later. No way.

"No, that's not a good idea, Ben. My mum is really sick. It's flu. That's why I promised I'd stay at home."

He wanted to talk more, but she hung up, careful not to smudge her nails. What a good liar I am, she thought. Even I believed that story. Josh thinks he's such a good actor. But I can act circles around him!

Josh.

Was she really going out with Josh?

More to the point: *Why* was she going out with Josh?

She really didn't feel anything for him any more. She didn't like admitting it – even to herself – but she had felt that tiny little bit of disappointment on learning that he was alive.

She tried to force that thought from her mind. It was an unspeakable thought, after all. But somehow it kept drifting to the surface.

So why *was* she standing Ben up so she could go to the cinema with Josh tonight?

Frankly, she admitted, she didn't know.

She was sure that after spending the evening with Josh, she'd be able to start sorting things out in her mind.

Ben was so sweet, so boyish, so charming. So right.

It had to be guilt. That was the only reason she was pulling on her best Ralph Lauren jumper over her designer jeans, giving her hair one more quick brush, and hurrying downstairs to get the car.

"Night, Mum," she called. "Don't wait up!"

What a laugh. Her mother had never cared enough to wait up, not once.

"You and Ben have a good time!" her mother called from the study.

"Right!" Olivia called back.

What she doesn't know won't hurt her. She doesn't even know that I thought Josh was dead. She doesn't have to know that I'm seeing him again.

She grabbed her big, expensive, fur-lined coat. She always felt so safe and protected in it. She stepped into the garage from the house entrance. The light went on automatically. She slid behind the steering wheel of her mother's new BMW. The leather seat felt cold against her hand. The car started with a gentle hum, and she backed down the drive and headed for the mall.

Josh was pacing back and forth in front of the bookshop. *This is where I came in,* Olivia thought drily.

He looked so pale.

That was the first thing she noticed about him.

The high fluorescent lights made everyone else look yellow. But Josh's skin, Olivia immediately noticed, was white, nearly as white as flour.

He was wearing the same black jeans and leather jacket. His black hair was brushed straight back and tied in a short ponytail. He was limping slightly as he paced, favouring his left leg.

She had the sudden urge to turn around and drive to Ben's house. She hadn't been looking forward to this date. In fact, she'd been dreading it, in a way. Dreading what they might talk about. Dreading what they couldn't talk about.

"Hi, Olivia!"

Too late. Josh had spotted her. A crooked smile crossed his face.

That's not his smile, she thought. His smile was always so straight, so open. That's not his smile at all. It's a stranger's smile.

Oh, just knock it off, she scolded herself. Stop looking for differences.

Of *course* Josh is different. He fell off a cliff, remember? He broke nearly every bone in his body. He was in hospital for two months.

That could make you seem a little bit different.

"Hi, Josh. Sorry I'm late." She took his hand. It was ice cold.

"Cold hands," she said, startled. His hands were always so warm. He was always so warm. He'd walk around in his shirtsleeves in the coldest winter weather and never seemed to notice that everyone else was freezing.

"Oh. Sorry." He pulled his hand away with an apologetic smile. He seemed really nervous. "The film's started already," he said, leading the way across the mall to the cinema, limping as he walked.

The film was some kind of action comedy with a lot of shooting and police chases. Olivia couldn't concentrate on it. It seemed so strange to be sitting next to Josh, sitting so close to him in the dark again.

A few minutes into the film, he slid his arm around her shoulder. She leaned against him, her eyes on the screen.

What was that smell?

She sniffed once, twice, then stopped because Josh was beginning to notice.

It was slightly musty, sour like old fruit.

Or meat that had gone bad.

She turned her head away, but the stale smell followed her.

Josh had always smelled so sweet.

What was causing that sickening stench?

Ten

"Josh is alive," Olivia said, unable to suppress a grin.

Amy's mouth dropped open. She turned positively pale. "No!" she cried when she could finally speak.

"Yes. He's alive. I went out with him last night."

Amy put her hands over her ears and shook her head, her tight, brown curls seeming to vibrate around her. "I don't think I'm hearing right, Olivia. Josh—?"

"He's alive," Olivia repeated, enjoying her friend's shocked reaction.

It was Sunday afternoon. Mrs Collier had gone out shopping again. Amy had dropped by unannounced, the first time Olivia had seen her since the hospital visit.

"But – but – Owen told me—"

"Me, too," Olivia interrupted. "What's Owen's problem, anyway?"

"I don't know. I haven't seen him," Amy replied, still

stunned. She flung herself back on to the crushed velvet sofa, rested her head against the back, and stared up at the elaborate crystal light fixture suspended from the ceiling. "Whew. Olivia. Really. Just let me catch my breath. What a shock."

"Tell me about it," Olivia said drily, tucking her legs beneath her on the big, overstuffed armchair. "He climbed in my bedroom window last week. Can you imagine?"

"At night?"

"At night. I was terrified. I thought I was seeing a ghost."

"But Josh is OK? Really?" The colour still hadn't returned to her face.

"Yeah. Pretty much. He limps a little. I guess he was injured pretty badly by the fall. He's been in a hospital across town for the past two months. But he seems perfectly OK now."

Except for the cold hands and the weird smell, Olivia added to herself. But what was the point of mentioning that to Amy?

"Wow," Amy said. She closed her eyes tightly. "Wow."

"I should call Owen and tell him that was a really rotten joke he pulled," Olivia said, more to herself than to Amy. "It's really the sickest thing I've ever heard. And I believed him."

"Of course. Me, too," Amy said, opening her eyes. "Why

would he tell a stupid lie like that? It's so cruel. Owen's a pretty strange guy, but I never thought he was cruel."

"I never liked him," Olivia confessed. "I only put up with him because of Josh."

"And you really went out with Josh?"

"Yeah. Last night. I had to break a date with Ben to do it."

"Ben?"

"Yeah. You remember Ben. Blond hair. Really tall. Has a great smile. And a Jaguar." Olivia laughed.

Amy was thinking too hard to laugh. "Josh is really alive? How come he never called you?"

Olivia shrugged. "He was badly hurt. He asked his aunt to try, but you know how flipped-out she is. She probably doesn't remember how to use a phone. Besides, I was in hospital for over a month, too. Josh didn't know that."

"And you're going out with Ben now?"

Olivia nodded.

"Well, are you going to tell him about Josh?"

"No. What for? I think I can string them both along for a while."

"Won't Ben get suspicious when—"

"Ben is so crazy about me, he'll put up with anything I do," Olivia said. She realized it sounded a bit boastful, but it was the truth.

Amy made a disapproving face.

"Don't look at me like that," Olivia said, only half teasing.

"You're awful," Amy muttered. She was only half teasing, too.

The two girls stared at each other without any real warmth. Olivia realized that she couldn't be as close to Amy as she had been. They had obviously grown apart.

It's not my fault, Olivia told herself. Amy's just changed. What right does she have to sit on my sofa like that and judge me?

"Well, how do you feel about it?" Amy asked, still struggling to understand. "Do you still like Josh?"

Olivia yawned. The conversation was becoming tiresome to her. She had enjoyed shocking Amy with the news and watching the stunned expression on her face. But now she wished Amy would go home.

"I don't really know if I like Josh or not," she said flatly. It was kind of fun trying to shock Amy with her coldness.

"Huh?"

"I don't think I like him any more. I mean, as a boyfriend. I guess I just . . . feel guilty."

"Guilty? What do you mean? Because you thought he was dead, and he wasn't?" Amy pulled herself up straight and leaned forward, her hands on the knees of her faded jeans.

Olivia realized that Amy didn't really know the details of that night. She didn't know that Olivia hadn't stayed to help rescue Josh. That Olivia had driven off without seeing if Josh was dead or alive.

"I mean, I feel guilty because I'm the one who drove him to the Promontory that night. He wouldn't have fallen if he hadn't been showing off for me."

"Oh. I see." Amy seemed disappointed by Olivia's answer.

What does she want from me? Olivia asked herself.

She decided to change the subject. "Let's talk about *you* for a while, Amy. What's new in your life?"

Amy sighed and flopped back against the sofa. "Nothing compared to you," she said. "I'm sorry, Olivia, but I just can't believe that Josh is alive. It's like – like a miracle! And you're being so calm about it."

So cold, she means, Olivia thought. "So are you going out with anyone?" she asked, running her hands back through her short blonde hair.

Amy shook her head. "No. My life is as boring as ever. I had my hair highlighted last week. See?" She lowered her head so Olivia could see the blonde streaks among the dark curls. Olivia hadn't noticed the change. "That's about the most interesting thing that's happened to me."

Olivia laughed, but quickly cut it off, realizing it wasn't an appropriate response. Amy was really feeling sorry for herself. Olivia just wasn't in the mood to cluck sympathetically and say, "There, there."

She was grateful when the ringing telephone interrupted their conversation.

"Hello. Josh? Hi." She gave Amy a meaningful look.

"Let me talk to him," Amy said. She leaped off the sofa and grabbed the phone from Olivia's hand. "Josh? Is it really you? It's me, Amy."

Amy's dark eyes were wide with excitement. She was breathing heavily.

"I – I can't hear you very well," she said, frowning. "You sound so faint. Like you're very far away."

Josh said something. Amy obviously had to struggle to hear him. Olivia wished she'd give back the phone.

"Josh – I'm so happy!" Amy gushed. "I'm just so glad you're OK. Owen told us – well . . . never mind. I'm just so glad! I can't wait to see you sometime. Here. I'll give you back to Olivia."

She handed the phone to Olivia. "He sounds weird," she said. "Very far away."

"It's just a bad connection," Olivia said, raising the receiver to her ear. "Hi, Josh. What? You'll have to speak up. There's a lot of static or something."

He continued to talk quietly. It was as if he couldn't raise his voice. He asked her out for Friday night. "Yeah. I guess," she said, thinking of Ben. They chatted a few minutes more, but she really couldn't hear him. It wasn't just the background static. It was also the fact that his voice sounded weak and thin. Tired.

When she hung up, Amy was pulling on her jacket. "I guess I'd better be going."

"I'm so glad you dropped in," Olivia said, putting on a sincere smile, then adding, "stranger."

Amy stopped at the door, and turned back with a concerned look on her face. "You know, Josh's been through so much. You should be straight with him, don't you think? You really should tell him about Ben."

Olivia shrugged. "It's too interesting this way," she said, holding the door open for her friend. "I think I'll just play it out and see what happens."

Eleven

Olivia swung easily and the ball sailed over the net.

"Perfect," Rod, her instructor, said, flashing all 320 zillion perfect, sparkling white teeth. "Placement. Placement."

What does *that* mean? Olivia asked herself, shaking her head.

I'm going to have to say bye-bye to you, Rod, if you keep up that "placement" nonsense. She had the sneaking suspicion that she could probably beat him in a real game.

"Pick a spot, then place it there," he said, wiping his tanned forehead with a white handkerchief.

I haven't worked up a sweat. What's *his* problem? Olivia thought. "Hey, can I work on my backhand a while?" she called. She was paying for it. Why couldn't she work on what she *wanted* to work on?

"OK, sure." He stuffed the handkerchief back into the

pocket of his tennis shorts. "I'll hit a few to your left. Let's see your backhand. Try to smooth it out today, OK?"

Smooth it out?

What did *that* mean?

Was she losing her mind, or was Rod just an inane idiot?

This was definitely the last day for Mr Smile Face. He hadn't given her a single pointer she could use. And with the rate he charged per hour, she expected a little more than "smooth it out."

He tapped the ball to the left. She jogged easily and smacked it back, using her backhand. She loved the *ping* the ball made on contact with the racquet. It was her favourite part of tennis. That little *ping*. So satisfying, somehow. She could hear dozens of *pings* all around her, as people played on the vast indoor courts of the private tennis club.

Look at that fatso over there, wearing a parachute for tennis shorts, she thought, sniggering at the woman chasing a ball across the next court. If I looked like that, I wouldn't play tennis. I'd shoot myself instead.

Another high bouncer from Rod. She reached back and returned it easily.

"Smooth. Very smooth. Nice follow-through," he called.

"Thanks a bunch."

"Time out. I've got to collect some more balls," he said, running across the court to get the ball basket.

Olivia sighed and lowered her racquet. She looked down the row of courts. A guy down at the end court looked a little like Ben. Not quite as good-looking.

She thought about Ben. He had come over on Sunday night and they had gone for a long drive in his Jag. It was a clear, cold night. He had wanted to park up at the Promontory. She had hesitated at first and started to make an excuse. That was a place she never wanted to visit again.

But then she decided, what the heck

It was just a place, after all. Just a rock cliff.

Just a make-out spot.

Just a place to get close to Ben.

She could probably push what had happened there out of her mind. It had been months ago, anyway.

What the heck.

And to her surprise, being back on that high cliff overlooking the town, being back on the very spot where the rock had crumbled and Josh had fallen, wasn't disturbing to her at all.

Josh had lived, after all.

Josh was OK.

Everyone was OK. So why should she feel funny about being back there?

It was so warm and cozy in the Jaguar with Ben. The windows all fogged over, and they were in their own world, their own little cocoon. Not on the Promontory. Not in the boring, little town of Middlewood. But locked away in their own tiny space capsule, just the two of them, so close, so close.

When that carful of teenagers drove up behind them with their lights on and the radio blaring, laughing and honking the horn, Olivia just wanted to kill them.

What right did they have to bring her back down to earth?

Sighing, she looked back to the tennis club waiting area. Ben was supposed to pick her up after her tennis lesson. Maybe he was early.

When she saw Josh back there behind the mesh wall, she uttered a low cry of surprise.

Josh?

What on earth is *he* doing here?

He was pacing back and forth behind the wire-mesh wall that separated the courts from the spectator area. Why was he walking so stiffly? His limp seemed to have got much more pronounced. Both legs appeared stiff now.

She raised her racquet over her head, trying to get his attention. Then she quickly lowered it.

His skin.

What on earth was wrong with his skin?

He looked positively green.

Maybe it's just the lights, Olivia thought. But there were

other people watching the matches from behind the mesh wall, and their skin looked perfectly normal.

With that stiff-legged walk and the greenish skin, he looks just like Frankenstein's monster, Olivia thought.

"Hey, Olivia . . ."

She realized Rod was calling to her. But she couldn't take her eyes off Josh. Was he sick or something?

"Hey, Olivia . . ." How long had Rod been calling? "Don't lose your concentration. Come on!"

"I'm ready," she said, turning back to face the net. But she couldn't get the sight of Josh out of her mind, the green face, the pained, straight-legged walk.

"Remember your follow-through," Rod said, lobbing a ball over the net.

She had to run for this one. She was off-stride and the ball hit the edge of the racquet and bounced into the next court. "Sorry."

Rod sent one into the back court. This time she got there in time and, using her backhand, sent it sailing over his head.

"Out!" he cried.

Oh, who cares? she thought.

She turned back. Josh had gone.

Maybe it wasn't Josh, she thought. Why would Josh be here, anyway? He doesn't know I have a tennis lesson this afternoon. And why would he be all the way over on this side of town on a school day?

"Time's up," Rod said, smiling, twirling his racquet in his hand. He walked around the net and joined her on her side of the court. "Good workout?"

"Yeah. Fine," Olivia said without enthusiasm. She turned around again, searched the waiting area. No Josh.

"I like your racquet," Rod said. "I was going to buy that one, but I couldn't afford it."

"Yeah. It's good," Olivia said, looking down at the racquet. "See you next time." She started towards the locker room.

"OK. Good backhand," Rod called after her. "We'll work on it more next time."

She didn't reply, just kept jogging off the courts. Maybe he isn't such a bad instructor, she thought. I mean, a tennis instructor doesn't exactly have to be a genius.

She showered quickly and changed back into her school clothes, carefully folding her tennis shorts and T-shirt into the canvas bag she had brought. Ben was waiting at the door. "How'd you do?" he asked, giving her a warm smile and carrying the bag for her.

It was a cold, sunny day. She zipped up her jacket. "Fine. The instructor is a real idiot. But I got in some practice on my backhand." She followed him across the street to his car.

"I can't wait to get you on the court at the country club

this spring," Ben said, tossing her bag in the back, then sliding into the driver's seat. "I'll give your backhand a workout."

"Are you any good?" Olivia asked.

"No," he replied. "Not very. Just good enough to be school champion."

"Big deal," she said. She started to make a joke, but her breath caught in her throat.

Josh.

It really was Josh. He was standing close enough to be seen clearly now.

He was leaning against the brick wall in the half-empty car-park beside the tennis club, his hands shoved into his jeans pockets. Even in the sunlight, his skin looked green.

Almost reptilian, Olivia thought queasily.

Josh had been looking at the ground, but now he looked up and directed his stare at them.

Does he see us? Olivia wondered.

He must. He's looking right at me.

Ben reached into his pocket for the car keys, dropped them on the floor.

Olivia stared across the street at Josh.

Josh's eyes caught hers. They suddenly seemed to glow ruby-red, like the red eyes in a bad flash photo. Glowing red eyes like a dog's eyes at night.

Twelve

"So tell me again," Ben said, standing very close to her at the entrance to their school, making Olivia back up till she bumped into the cloakroom door. "Why can't you go out with me both Friday and Saturday night?"

She gave him a playful little shove to give herself breathing space. A couple of girls she knew giggled as they passed by in the fast-emptying corridor. "I have to get home," she said, trying to avoid the question. "Why are you pushing me into the cloakroom?"

He grinned and took a big step forward, forcing her further back. "Just answer the question."

"Really, Ben. You're being a pig."

"Oink. Oink."

Olivia hated it when he tried to be playful. It just wasn't the right style for him, she thought. She liked him much better when he was serious and quiet and played it straight.

"I've already explained to you," she said wearily, shoving him again, a little harder this time, then dashing out into the middle of the hall so he couldn't back her up again.

"Hello, Mr Munroe," they both said, as their French teacher passed by, probably on his way to the staffroom. The paunchy, middle-aged teacher nodded and smiled and kept walking.

"I have to work on Friday night," Olivia lied. "I missed so much school because of the accident, Mum insists that I spend one weekend night studying. That's the whole reason, Ben. So stop being insulted."

Was he buying that story?

Yes. He seemed to be.

"Well, fine," he said, kicking at the wall plaster down by the linoleum floor with the toe of his boot. "So why don't I come over on Friday night, and we'll study together?"

"No way," she said, her grin mirroring the devilish grin on his face. "If you came over, we wouldn't study, and you know it."

"We could study," he said. "Really."

"No. Really," she insisted. "No way. At least not this weekend, OK?"

"Well . . ."

She loved how disappointed he looked.

"I'm really serious," she said. "I want to graduate on time.

I don't want to have to do an extra term because of that stupid car accident. I *have* to catch up with the work. Understand?"

"Of course I do," he said, brightening a little. "Of course."

She looked both ways to make sure no one was in the corridor, then kissed him quickly on the cheek. "Thanks," she whispered.

I love the fact that he's so gullible, so trusting, Olivia thought, pulling on her jacket. I'm also glad that Josh lives way on the other side of town. It makes it so much easier to keep Ben and Josh from knowing about each other.

She realized she'd have to break up with Josh soon. She didn't really care about him at all. But he was useful. It was kind of fun to keep Ben guessing, to make him uncomfortable. And the idea of having two boyfriends at once really appealed to Olivia. It was a lot like having two winter coats, she told herself. It was nice to be able to trade them off.

On Friday night she drove across town to meet Josh. He slid into the car, holding something carefully out of sight. Suddenly he reached for her, and something silver glinted in his hand. "Josh!" gasped Olivia, jumping. The car swerved.

"Surprise," said Josh, pinning a corsage to the shoulder of her coat. "Oh," said Olivia. "How nice."

They went to a small dance club in his neighbourhood.

"Why is it called Barks?" Olivia asked, carefully locking the BMW.

"You'll see," Josh said, climbing stiffly out of the car.

Once inside, the reason for the club's name became obvious. There were giant dogs painted on all the walls. "This place is really tacky," Olivia said, shaking her head as she surveyed the awful dog paintings and then the small dance floor with its flashing strobe light.

"And what is that awful moose head doing on the wall?" she asked. "Moose don't bark!"

"I knew you'd like this place," Josh said, laughing.

His cheeks seemed to sag when he laughed, Olivia noticed.

He looks so different, she thought.

"The sound system is good," he said, leading her on to the dance floor. "And it doesn't get too crowded."

There were six or seven couples on the floor, dancing to a fast, rhythmic number. Olivia looked across the dance floor at a particularly ugly wall painting of a German shepherd rearing up on its hind legs with its head tilted back in a howl.

"Come on, let's dance," she said, shouting over the music. "It's better than staring at these paintings."

He took her hand. Again, his hand was ice cold. He smiled at her, his old, familiar smile. But it seemed somehow lifeless, as if it were a real struggle for him to smile.

He seems so different, she thought, as they started to dance, bumping into other couples until they found a space for themselves on the small rectangular floor. He was always so lively, so theatrical, so excited about everything all the time.

Now he was dancing half-heartedly with her, almost in slow motion, hardly moving his feet at all.

The rhythm slowed into a slow salsa beat.

He moved closer to her, holding her with his cold hands.

That smell again.

That musty odour.

The odour of decay.

"Josh – are you wearing cologne or something?"

"What?" He struggled to hear her over the deafening sound system.

"Are you wearing cologne?" she repeated, shouting right by his ear.

He made a face. "Of course not."

He laughed, an unpleasant laugh.

I've never heard that laugh before, Olivia thought, staring into his face.

He's like a stranger, she thought. He's just so different.

Then suddenly he stopped dancing and held his hand up to his mouth.

"Josh – what's the matter?"

He didn't reply. Maybe he didn't hear her over the blaring music.

He seemed to flicker on and off under the flashing strobe light. One second he was bright and colourful in the red shirt he wore over his faded jeans. The next second he was shrouded in darkness, a dark figure holding his mouth, walking stiffly off the dance floor.

"Josh?"

She followed him. "Hey – wait. What's the matter?"

He bumped into a girl in a white T-shirt and short skirt and just kept going. The girl turned around angrily, surprised by his rudeness.

Olivia wasn't sure whether Josh wanted her to follow him or not. It was as if he'd forgotten about her.

He stopped in front of a floor-to-ceiling mirror against the back wall and peered into it as he fiddled with something in his mouth.

Reluctantly she came up behind him. "Josh – what's the matter?"

"Oh nothing," he said, removing his fingers from his mouth. He turned to face her, looking embarrassed.

"Nothing?"

"Loose teeth. That's all."

She laughed, then realized it wasn't funny. "Aren't you a little old to still be losing your teeth?"

He stared at her coldly. "It's just loose," he said. "It'll be OK."

She suddenly realized that it must have been caused by his fall off the cliff. He'd never wanted to talk about the injuries he had got from the fall. And, of course, neither did she.

She assumed that he was pretty badly hurt, but that he was basically OK now. But the fact that he suddenly had a loose tooth made her wonder.

"Josh – your legs. You've been limping. Is it because—"

"They'll be fine," he said quickly, not letting her finish.

He suddenly looked very tired.

They stared at each other awkwardly. "My legs are all right," he said finally. "I guess I'm doing a lot better than I ever expected." He laughed for some reason, a bitter laugh.

"You've got to get some sun," she said, touching his shoulder. "You look positively green."

He shrugged. "Maybe I'll charter a private jet and fly to the Bahamas."

"Hey, Josh – that's not your kind of joke. That's *my* kind of joke."

"You and your mother have a winter holiday every year," he said thoughtfully, ignoring her remark. "Maybe you'd like to take me along this year." He reached up and played with his loose tooth, turning back to the mirror.

What a thought! Olivia nearly laughed out loud. She

could just picture her mother's reaction if Olivia asked to bring Josh along to St Croix.

What a thought!

She was sorry she had said anything about his looking so green. She was sorry she had brought up his appearance at all.

She was sorry she had gone out with him.

He used to be so exciting, she thought bitterly, watching him in the mirror as he fiddled with his tooth.

"Want to dance some more?" she asked, trying to get him away from the mirror and end their conversation at the same time. "That's why we came here, right?"

He turned around slowly. "Let's get a Coke or something first, OK?"

"Yeah. Sure. Why don't you do that? Ill wait over by that table for you."

He nodded agreement and, walking stiff-legged, practically dragging his left leg after him, he headed towards the bar on the other side of the dance floor.

He really does look green, she thought.

I think he was more badly injured in the fall than he's letting on to me.

I think his knees are really damaged.

And his face . . .

Suddenly he stopped at the edge of the dance floor.

What's his problem? Olivia wondered, staring across the room at him. Why did he stop there?

"Oh good lord – no!"

She didn't realize she had screamed out loud.

Her breath caught in her throat. She suddenly felt sick.

She was sure she had just seen Josh reach up and pull a big chunk of skin off his face.

Thirteen

"You look wonderful, Olivia. Stand up straight."

"Mum, I *am* standing up straight."

'Well, maybe it's the dress then."

"Mum – just stop it," Olivia cried. "You're just trying to make me feel self-conscious."

Mrs Collier's mouth dropped open. "Me? Why on *earth* would I do that?"

Because you know you look like a frumpy little mouse in that dreadful evening dress you're wearing, and you want me to feel as bad as you look, Olivia thought. But she decided not to reply at all.

She walked side by side with her mother up the concrete steps of the old armoury and into the brightly-lit Main Hall. "Ugh! Those hideous portraits!" The walls were filled with gigantic, dark paintings of nineteenth-century town founders and other dignitaries.

"Olivia – please. Don't be so negative."

"What a place for a party," Olivia said, slipping off her coat and handing it to the young man behind the cloakroom counter.

"You just have to be nice and charming for a few hours," her mother said, fussing with her enormous fur coat. She couldn't manage to undo the top button. Olivia finally did it for her. "That's all I'm asking. It isn't that hard, is it?"

Olivia looked glumly around the draughty old hall. "I'll do my best, Mum."

Every year the Ladies Club had their winter charity drive here in the armoury. This year, her mother had volunteered to be chairwoman of the event.

Why not? Olivia had thought. She has nothing better to do.

But then Mrs Collier roped Olivia into coming and helping serve at the punch table.

It was going to be an endless night, Olivia knew, even though it was supposed to end at eleven. She had done everything she could to get out of it, even faking a stomach bug. But her mother wasn't falling for any excuse.

An entire Saturday night wasted, Olivia moaned to herself, adjusting the straps of her green velvet dress and making her way over to the gigantic crystal punch bowl on the table by the wall.

I could be out with Ben. Or Josh.

She hadn't seen Josh for over a week, not since that unpleasant night at that dreadful dance club. He had called a couple of times during the week and had actually sounded very pleasant, a bit more like his old self.

She and Ben had gone to a Will Ferrell film the night before, a very funny comedy. Ben had laughed like a lunatic. She had never seen him let go like that. He had a ridiculous laugh, she decided. She actually liked him a lot better when he was serious. But she was glad to see him loosen up like that. They had a really nice night.

And now here she was in the armoury, of all places, staring up at the dour, bewhiskered face of some old codger. Why was he posing with his hand in his shirt like that? Olivia wondered. Did he have an itch?

The hall filled quickly, mostly with old and middle-aged people in furs and formal evening wear. Olivia sighed wistfully. Is this *me* in forty years? she asked herself.

No way.

She plastered a smile on her face and, thinking about Josh, wondering what he was doing tonight, she started to serve punch in the crystal cups stacked beside the punch bowl.

"Aren't you Clare's daughter?" asked a woman in a violet strapless gown.

"Yes, I am," Olivia said through her plastered-on smile. "Would you like some punch?"

The woman was wearing purple lipstick that matched her dress. Her face was heavily rouged. She had wavy, silver hair, very stylishly short. "Certainly, dear. Your mother tells me that you're dating Benjamin Forrest."

Olivia, startled, spilled a little punch over the side of the cup. "Yes, I am." What was her mother doing – broadcasting it to the whole town?

"Well, I've known his family for years," the woman said, reaching out a violet-gloved hand to shake Olivia's free hand. "I'm Sylvia Norris."

"How do you do, Mrs Norris." Olivia handed her the cup of punch.

"He's a fine young man, and you're a perfect couple."

"Thank you."

Luckily a white-haired gentleman in a satiny dinner-jacket tapped Mrs Norris on the shoulder. She turned to greet him and they strolled off together chattering enthusiastically.

She's actually very well preserved for her age, Olivia thought. I hope I can still wear purple lipstick when I'm a doddering old geezer.

And she's right about Ben and me. We *are* a perfect couple.

So why do I keep going out with Josh?

102

It's crazy.

It's just not like me.

She poured out two cups of punch and placed them in waiting hands.

It's obviously a character flaw, she told herself.

That's what it is. Josh is just a flaw in my character.

I'm going to say goodbye to him next weekend. Maybe I should just write him a letter.

No. He would never believe it in a letter. The next thing I'd know he'd be climbing into my bedroom in the middle of the night, saying let's go for a drive, or something crazy, pretending he never even received it.

No. I have to break up with him in person. Face to face.

She pictured Josh's face. He used to be so good-looking.

She pictured his green complexion.

Then she saw the chunk of skin drop off.

That didn't really happen – did it?

Of course, she had imagined it. But why was he so different? Why did he act and look so different?

It's all over between him and me, she thought, pouring more punch, smiling like a robot at two plump, well-dressed women who returned the robot-smile.

That's it. I'm breaking up with him next Saturday night.

I don't care if he did almost die that night on the Promontory. That was his own stupid idea. The whole thing was his fault. Going there in the first place. Showing off like a fool on the cliff-edge. Falling.

I don't feel guilty any more. I just don't.

I don't feel anything. And I can't keep seeing him week after week, pretending that I still care about him because of that one stupid night.

Having made the decision, she banished Josh from her mind. She concentrated on thinking about Ben for the rest of the evening. He was so good-looking. So nice. So right for her.

She decided she even liked his silly laugh.

At about eleven-fifteen, Olivia's mother, looking flushed and excited after the successful evening, told Olivia to take the car and go home. "I'm going out with the Waynes and the Sturbridges," she said, squeezing Olivia's arm. "They'll drop me home later. Thanks for helping out, dear."

"Thanks for forcing me," Olivia said, and laughed so her mother would know it was a joke.

A few minutes later, she had wrapped her coat around her and hurried down the armoury stairs to the car-park. She started to hand the parking ticket to the attendant, and then stopped in surprise.

"Owen!"

It took him a little while to recognize her, probably because he had never seen her so dressed up. "Olivia?"

"How are you? I mean, what are you doing here?" she sputtered. He looked exactly the same, same bad skin, same spiky hair.

"I'm ... uh ... parking cars," he said somewhat defensively. "The pay is really good. And I get overtime for Saturday nights."

"Hey, that's great," she said with false enthusiasm. They stared at each other. She still had the parking ticket in her hand.

"So how've you been? I haven't seen you in so long," she said, wishing she could get her car and get out of there without having to make small talk with Owen.

"Yeah. It's been a while," he said, slapping his hands together, probably to keep them warm. He frowned.

"Listen, I've been seeing Josh," Olivia said, fumbling for something to say. "I'm surprised he hasn't mentioned you. He—"

Owen's face filled with confusion. "You *what*?"

"I've been seeing Josh. Something's wrong with him, don't you think? He looks so—"

"Olivia – what are you talking about?" Owen shook his head, a strange grin on his face. "You're having me on, right?"

"Having you on?"

"Yeah. That's a really bad joke, you know." He kicked at the curb.

"Owen, I saw Josh last week and—"

"Have you totally flipped out? Josh is dead. He's dead, Olivia."

"Owen, stop. He isn't dead. Why do you keep telling me that? I saw him last week. I touched him. I danced with him. He's not dead. Why do you insist on—"

"I don't get what you're trying to pull. Are you crazy, or what?" Owen glared at her angrily, searching her eyes as if trying to discover whether or not she was serious. "I only know one thing, Olivia," he said in a low voice she had to struggle to hear. "Josh is dead."

"But—"

"I went to his funeral. I saw him in the coffin. He was dead. Stone-cold dead."

"Owen—"

"Maybe you *think* you see Josh," Owen continued heatedly. "Maybe you imagine it out of guilt or something. I mean, you *should* feel guilty, you know. You left him there to die."

"I did not! I . . ." Oh, what's the use of trying to explain? she thought.

"Maybe you need some kind of help or something. I'm no shrink. Like I said, I only know one thing. Josh is dead. He's dead, Olivia. I saw him die. And I saw him at his funeral. He's dead. Forever. And that's the truth."

106

Fourteen

Olivia drove home slowly, carefully, her mind spinning from her conversation with Owen. She gripped the wheel to stop from shaking. Even though she turned the heater up full blast, she couldn't get warm.

She was still trembling when she climbed out of the car and entered the house through the garage. She changed into warm, comfortable clothes, a heavy wool jumper and soft, grey joggers. Then she made herself a cup of tea. But she still couldn't get calm, couldn't stop hearing Owen's frightening words.

I believe Owen, she decided.

But how *could* she believe Owen?

What did that mean? If she believed Owen, that meant she'd been dating a *ghost*.

And Josh was no ghost. She was sure of that.

"It doesn't make sense!" she screamed aloud, immediately

regretting it because she didn't want to wake Helen, the housekeeper.

She carried her tea from the kitchen into the living room, and turned on all the lights. The tea warmed her a bit. The trembling stopped.

There has to be a logical explanation for this.

There's a logical explanation for everything, right?

She sat down on the big, overstuffed armchair, curled her feet under her, and placed the mug of tea in her lap.

Let's just think about this . . .

But there was no way to think about it logically.

Josh was dead. Owen had told her that back in October in the hospital. Then in December, just a few weeks ago, Josh reappeared. He had been hurt, he said. And he looked and acted as if he'd been hurt. But he was alive. He was definitely alive.

Except for the fact that Owen insisted he was dead. And Owen had been at the funeral.

So that meant . . .

That meant . . .

What?

When Mrs Collier returned home shortly after one, Olivia was still sitting in the armchair in the living room, still staring at the wallpaper, the now empty tea mug in her hand.

"Good heavens, Olivia. I thought you'd be asleep."

"Well, no, I —"

"What a night!" her mother gushed. "And what a fantastic success. Do you know how much money we raised for the charity fund?"

"No." Olivia didn't pretend to be interested.

"It was a lot. Do you know what Mrs Norris said to me? She said . . ."

Her mother rattled on. Olivia tuned her out. Her voice became a quiet hum in the background of Olivia's thoughts. She nodded occasionally and said "Uh-huh" to make her mother think she was listening. She could go on like this for half an hour without taking a breath, Olivia thought. Well, let her. This is the highlight of her year, after all. Poor thing.

Olivia thought about Josh, trying to arrange the puzzle pieces of this mystery together. But the pieces just wouldn't fit.

Josh, even though he seemed different, was definitely Josh.

She thought about how he had changed. The green tinge of his skin. The stiff, straight-legged walk, the musty, stale odour, the loose tooth, the skin that peeled off like . . . like a zombie.

Night of the Living Dead.

Yuck.

She scolded herself for getting carried away. Now think logically.

Zombies aren't logical.

"I don't think you've heard a word I said." Her mother stood up and headed to the front stairway.

"Of course I did. I heard every word," Olivia lied. "Listen, Mum, I've got to go out."

Mrs Collier looked at her diamond-encrusted watch. "At this hour? Are you crazy?"

I *hope* I'm not crazy, Olivia thought.

"Uh . . . I'm just so wound up. From the party and all. You know. All the excitement. I can't seem to relax. I'm just going to take a short drive, just to get some fresh air."

"A drive? No, Olivia. Don't go driving late at night," her mother pleaded, wetting her finger and wiping something off the watch crystal. "Last time you went for a drive late at night, you—"

"I'll be careful, Mum." Thanks for pretending you care. "And I'll be back soon. Promise."

Olivia hurried past her mother at the stairway, grabbed her jacket and headed to the garage. "Be careful!" her mother called after her. "I really don't approve of this!"

I don't approve, either, Olivia thought, backing the BMW down the drive. I'd much rather be tucked safely into my nice, warm bed.

But I've got to know the truth. I've got to know what's going on here.

As she turned on to Fairview, the street that would take her across town to Josh's house, a feeling of dread began to form in her stomach.

She suddenly had the feeling that knowing the truth might be even more frightening than *not* knowing.

Fifteen

Josh's neighbourhood was so much more squalid than she'd remembered. The houses were so shabby, so small. They huddled together like little tents, one right after the other with hardly any front garden at all.

No wonder Josh always wants to meet on my side of town, Olivia thought, pushing the automatic lock button on the car door.

She slowed down as she neared his street. Across the narrow road, two scrawny dogs, looking like skeletons in her bright headlights, tipped over a rubbish bin. The lid clattered against the pavement and rolled into the centre of the street. The mangy dogs began pulling at a large package wrapped in brown paper, each snarling at the other to let go.

Olivia swerved to miss the rubbish-bin lid. The bony dogs were in her rearview mirror now. Even with the windows shut tight, she could hear their snarls and growls as they struggled to pull open the disgusting package.

Why do these people keep their rubbish out on the street? Olivia wondered, holding her breath as if trying not to smell it. And don't they ever feed their dogs?

Was that Josh's house up there? The small brick house with the newspaper stuffed in a broken window?

Yes, that was it. She'd been here once before.

Olivia slowed to a stop, but kept the car's engine running. The house was dark except for a single, low-watt bulb glowing over the narrow front porch. An old tyre sat in the middle of the front garden which was all weeds, weeds that hadn't been cut in months, bending first this way, then that in the shifting night wind.

Do I really know someone who lives *here*? Olivia thought.

How could I be going out with someone who has a tyre in his front garden and newspaper stuffed in a window?

And what am I doing here now? The house is dark. He and his aunt are probably asleep.

This is crazy. Totally crazy.

She glanced down at the clock on the dashboard. One-thirty.

Josh usually stays up till all hours, she thought, staring up at the dark house. Maybe he isn't asleep. I drove all the way over here. I have to talk to him.

If I knock on the front door, his old aunt probably won't hear it anyway, and he'll come to the door.

Having made up her mind, she pulled the car to the curb. There was no driveway. She'd have to park on the street. She turned off the headlights. The sudden darkness surprised her.

Can't they even afford street lights? she asked herself.

Oh, well. When I break it off with Josh, I'll never have to come to this awful neighbourhood again – unless it's part of some door-to-door charity drive.

Reluctantly she opened the car door and stepped out into the darkness. The wind was cold and strong. It seemed to push her away from the car. She pushed back, still clinging to the door handle.

This is a mistake. A stupid mistake.

No. I have to know the truth about Josh. I have to know – what?

If he's dead or alive?

The street was silent except for the wind. A narrow concrete walk, overgrown with weeds, led up to Josh's front porch. Low shadows clustered against the front of the house like hunkering animals, caught in the dim yellow light of the bulb suspended over the door.

Olivia's footsteps sounded so loud as she walked quickly to the front door. Down the street another rubbish-bin lid clattered against the pavement, startling her. She gasped. The two dogs were barking in the distance, fighting over the rubbish.

The smell of rubbish floated around her, carried by the wind. She held her breath and stepped on to the front porch.

For some reason she thought of the sweet smell, the smell Josh used to have whenever he held her close.

He didn't smell like that any more. He smelled just like the rubbish in the air.

She looked for a doorbell, but there wasn't one. The screen door, she saw, was torn at the top, one corner hanging down.

She took a deep breath and knocked gently on the door.

Josh – be awake.

Be awake, Josh.

Answer the door. And . . . be alive.

Tell me that Owen's a liar. Tell me that Owen has lost his mind. That Owen's been locked away, that he escaped and came to the armoury just to scare me, just to make me as crazy as he is.

I always hated Owen.

With that stupid diamond stud in his ear and his hair standing straight up, moussed and sprayed so carefully. He's so disgusting and stupid.

I never understood why you liked him so much, Josh. I never understood what you two talked about, what you two were always laughing about.

Owen's such a stupid, typical idiot.

The wind gusted, pulling open the screen door.

Olivia, startled, uttered a low cry, and raised her hands to stop the door from swinging out and hitting her.

It was as if a ghost had pushed open the door.

Then she scolded herself for getting carried away.

Don't lose it totally, Olivia, she told herself. She knocked on the door, harder this time.

She listened. No sounds inside the house.

Maybe Josh isn't even home. It would be like him to be out till all hours.

Maybe I made this whole trip for nothing.

But what choice did I have? Owen got me so upset, I . . .

She knocked again, pounding the door with her fist.

Ouch. That hurt.

Still no sounds inside.

OK. I tried.

She felt disappointed – and relieved.

She started to back off the porch, still listening for signs of life inside – and bumped into someone.

Felt hot breath on the back of her neck.

Felt a hand on her shoulder.

Her scream seemed to be stifled by the wind. The sound caught in her throat.

She screamed again.

She couldn't help it.

And spun around to look into Josh's face.

"Josh?"

His dark eyes stared into hers, unblinking. His face revealed no emotion, no surprise at seeing her there, no excitement, no delight by her unexpected visit.

No emotion at all.

"Josh? Are you OK?"

He didn't reply.

"Sorry I screamed like that." She suddenly felt embarrassed. She had screamed like a little girl. That wasn't like her at all. "But you scared me. I wasn't expecting . . ."

He stepped into the dim light.

"Oh."

She couldn't hold in her cry of surprise.

He looked so terrible.

His skin was pea-soup green. His eyes, still not blinking, were red.

Olivia stared into his face, feeling the fear sweep through her, feeling the terror overwhelm her, freeze her there, hold her like the plaster casts she had worn in hospital.

His skin was peeling. His forehead was pocked and cratered, as if pieces of skin had fallen off.

His black hair, once so beautiful, so silky and beautiful, looked as if it had slipped to one side. The skin was missing from his scalp and a patch of grey showed through from underneath.

His *skull*?!

"Josh!" she cried, unable to stop staring even though she wanted to look away, to turn away – to run away. "Josh – are you all right?"

The smell. The horrible smell.

It wasn't in the air.

It was coming from Josh.

It wasn't the rubbish, she thought, feeling sick. It was decay.

"Josh – why aren't you saying anything?"

He stared, unblinking.

"Josh – *please*! You're really *frightening* me!"

Finally he smiled.

The grin formed slowly, almost in slow motion.

I'm in a dream, Olivia suddenly thought. A slow motion dream.

Wake up, wake up, wake up.

As the grin formed, Josh's mouth opened.

"No!" Olivia screamed as she realized that his front teeth were missing.

He stepped forward, pressing her back against the torn screen door. He raised his hand. He was holding a corsage, a faded, tattered corsage, stabbed by a long, silver pin. Something dark dripped down the petals. He smelled like rotting meat. He grinned at her, his toothless grin.

"How about a kiss, Olivia?" he asked, his voice nothing but wind.

Sixteen

"Olivia – what's wrong? Why aren't you getting dressed?"

"I – I can't." Olivia lifted her head from the pillow with a groan. "I think I'm ill."

Her mother, already dressed in a very stylish black suit, shook her head, resting one hand on the doorway. "I knew you shouldn't have gone out driving around town at all hours," she said quietly.

She doesn't know how right she is, Olivia thought drily.

"Now you've caught that terrible flu that everyone is getting."

"No, I don't think so, Mum. I think I'm just exhausted. One day in bed, and I'll be OK."

I'll *never* be OK, she thought glumly.

I'll never get that hideous, decaying face out of my mind.

"Well, if you don't have flu, I really think you should make an effort to come to church," her mother said, adjusting the scarf that hung down the front of her pleated silk shirt. "Everyone will be asking after you. I received such nice compliments about you at the fund-raiser last night."

Like I'm a prized pedigree dog, Olivia thought bitterly. My, what fine lines she has, Mrs Collier. Could you put her through her paces for us? Make her heel or sit up and beg?

"I really can't go to church. I'm just going to sleep all day. I'm sorry."

Her mother looked more disappointed than concerned. "You know I won't be back till late tonight? There's a lunch at the Wilkersons'. And then I have that cocktail party and dinner at the Smiths'."

Well, that's good news, Olivia thought. So go. Please – go, go, go.

"Is there anything I can get you, dear? You *do* look very washed out."

Thanks, Mum. Be sure to get that little dig in before you go.

"No, thanks. If there's anything I need, I'll call downstairs for Helen."

"Oh, no! I gave Helen the morning off. She went to visit her sister for a couple of hours. I guess I shouldn't have, but I didn't know . . ."

That's even better, Olivia thought, burying her head

deeper into the pillow. I'll have the whole house to myself. "Go, Mum. You'll be late for church. Please give my regrets to everyone." She rolled on to her side, her back to the door. Maybe her mother would take the hint and leave.

A few minutes later, she heard her mother going down the carpeted stairs. A few minutes after that, she heard a car door slam and her mother's car start up and then drive off.

Now what?

Lie here all day and think about how my life has turned into a horror show?

Go back to sleep?

I can't sleep *forever* – can I?

What should I do? Pretend that last night didn't happen? Pretend that Josh hasn't become some kind of ghastly creature?

Olivia rolled over again, unable to find a comfortable position. She suddenly realized that being all alone wasn't exactly the best idea in the world.

Because all alone there was nothing to take her mind off what had happened.

And she would lie there and see his distorted, leering face with its green, crumbling skin, its patches of protruding skull, its missing front teeth, again and again and again.

"No!"

She sat up and dropped her feet to the carpet.

She started to stand up, but her ankle still hurt from when she had fallen on it, running away from him. She stepped down on it gingerly, then applied more weight. It wasn't so bad, she decided.

Had she really run in terror from Josh? Someone she had once thought she cared about, someone she thought she knew better than she knew anyone else?

Yes. She had leaped off the porch, dodging away from his sickening embrace, and had run through the tall weeds of the front garden.

It didn't seem real now. It seemed like a scene from one of those disgusting horror films on TV late at night.

But the faint, throbbing pain in her ankle told her it was real.

And the grinning green face she saw again and again in her mind told her it was real.

Last night, when she had run from him and tripped over the tyre in the middle of his garden and fallen into the wet weeds, she looked back up to the porch. Josh, she saw to her relief, wasn't coming after her. In fact, he hadn't moved. He stood stiff-legged, his back to the screen door, staring after her, the hideous grin frozen on his decaying face.

That smell.

Oh, that smell.

Her ankle throbbing with pain, Olivia had hobbled the

rest of the way to the car. As soon as she got home, she tore off her clothes, tossed them in the laundry basket, then jumped into the shower.

She had the longest shower of her life, making the water hotter and hotter, trying to wash away that awful smell, trying to wash away the sight of Josh, trying to wash away her fear, her confusion.

But the shower wasn't the answer. Stepping out, she felt as chilled – and as scared – as she had standing on that dimly-lit porch, staring into his unblinking red eyes.

Now it was Sunday morning and the horror of the scene clung to Olivia like a cold, damp fog.

I should've gone to church with my mother.

No. I've got to talk to someone.

I have to tell someone.

But who?

Amy.

Yes. Amy. Of course. Amy.

When it came right down to it, Amy was her only friend. The only one who knew Josh. Who knew all that had happened. Or almost all.

Amy was the only one who would understand. The only one who would believe her.

If *anyone* would believe it.

Olivia wasn't sure she believed it herself.

She walked across the room, stretching, stepping gingerly on her bad ankle, and picked up the phone from her desk. She dialled Amy's number and carried the phone back to the bed, sitting on the edge, staring out of the window at what appeared to be a grey, threatening morning.

Someone picked up on the sixth ring. "Hello, Amy?"

"Hi," said a sleep-clogged voice, sounding confused.

"Amy, it's me. Olivia. Did I wake you?"

"No, I had to get up to answer the phone."

"Funny line," Olivia said.

"I stole it from some TV show, I think. What time is it, anyway, Olivia? It's still the middle of the night, isn't it?"

"No. It's nearly nine. Can you come over?"

"What?"

"I really need to talk to you, Amy." Olivia was a little embarrassed by the neediness in her voice. She didn't like sounding like a helpless little girl, which she knew was how she sounded.

But for the first time in her life she really did feel helpless. For the first time in her life she really felt that things were out of control, that she was in a situation she couldn't handle.

It was a strange feeling. She hated it. She wished she sounded more together. She didn't like being so honest, so vulnerable, even with such a close friend. *Especially* with such a close friend.

"So can you come?"

"When? Now?" Amy still sounded half asleep.

"Yeah. Can you?"

"Can't we just talk over the phone, Olivia? I'd like to come, but I'm supposed to go over to my cousin's for lunch, and—"

"I really need you, Amy." This was so embarrassing! Why was Amy giving her a hard time, making it so much more difficult for her? "Something very scary happened last night."

"OK. I'll be there. Give me an hour or so, OK?"

"Oh, good. Thanks."

"Olivia?"

"Yeah?"

"Are you all right?"

"I – I guess. Yeah. No. I don't know. I'm all mixed up." She could feel herself start to crumble. She had the feeling she might cry, something she hadn't done in years and years.

So don't start now, she told herself, using all her strength to hold herself together. Don't start now.

What is there to cry about, anyway?

Just because Josh has joined the Living Dead?

Just because your boyfriend smells like rotting meat and his face is falling off?

Well, he isn't your boyfriend. You don't even care about him. And that's the truth.

126

You don't care if he lives or . . .

. . . dies?

"See you soon," she said into the phone, then walked over to the desk to put it back.

The sound at the window made her nearly jump out of her skin.

That scrabbling sound.

Someone tapping at the window.

Josh!

No. No – please!

She grabbed the top of the desk for support. Her knees felt weak, about to collapse. The room began to spin.

She was afraid to turn around.

Why was Josh climbing into her window in daylight? What was he doing here?

"Go away! Please – go away!" she screamed.

Seventeen

The tapping again.

It wasn't Josh.

Too light to be Josh. Josh would be pounding on the glass, demanding that she open up.

She saw his green face in her mind, that gruesome smile, the dark pit that was his mouth, the glowing red eyes.

Still holding on to the desk, she turned to face the window. A pigeon stood on the outer windowsill. It pecked at the glass. *Tap tap tap.*

Olivia, get a grip, she warned herself. You can't lose it because a stupid pigeon taps on the window.

Another shower maybe?

The hot water might make her feel better, help to cleanse away the memories, the pictures, the horrors of the night before that stuck to her skin like stale sweat.

She had a long, hot shower and shampooed her hair.

Drying herself off, she felt refreshed. A little better.

She got dressed quickly, pulling on a pair of jeans and a long-sleeved yellow cotton T-shirt. Then she went downstairs and made herself a breakfast of orange juice, cereal, and buttered toast.

She was dropping the breakfast dishes into the dishwasher when Amy's little Toyota pulled into the drive. Olivia ran through the front hall to let her friend in.

"Coffee!" Amy roared as soon as Olivia pulled open the door. "Make us coffee! I need a jump-start this morning."

"You do look a little out of it," Olivia said, examining Amy's pale face. "Late night last night?"

"No. Nothing special," Amy sighed. She followed Olivia into the kitchen. "Are you feeling better? You sounded so awful on the phone."

"I guess," Olivia said, filling the coffee maker with water.

"You – you sounded so scared, Olivia. Not like yourself at all." Amy pulled off her jacket and tossed it over one of the tall kitchen stools. She climbed up on to the stool next to it and leaned on the white worktop, watching Olivia measure out the coffee.

"I – I really don't know where to begin," Olivia said, hating this feeling of vulnerability that was so new to her, but eager to share everything with Amy. "It's about Josh."

129

"Are you still going out with him?" Amy stifled a yawn with her hand.

Olivia pushed the button on the coffee machine. "Yeah, I guess. I—"

"Him and that other guy. Ben."

"Yeah. Well, I'm going to break up with Josh. For good," Olivia said uncomfortably, sensing Amy's disapproval.

This wasn't the way Olivia wanted this to go. She wanted sympathy from Amy – not disapproval. She wanted some understanding. An explanation, maybe.

An explanation?

Who was she trying to kid?

How could there be an explanation?

"Listen, Amy, something weird is happening to Josh."

"Huh?" That seemed to wake Amy up. She sat up straight on the backless kitchen stool.

"I mean, I think Josh is ill or something."

"Oh. You mean like flu?"

"No. Not like flu. Some other kind of disease. Something really serious, I think."

"Olivia – how do you know? Did he tell you he's ill?"

"No. He didn't tell me. But – wait. Let me pour the coffee. Then I'll tell you everything." She reached in the cupboard for the coffee mugs. "It was really nice of you to drive all the way over here so fast. Sorry I woke you."

"That's OK," Amy said. "You sounded so . . . troubled."

Olivia poured the coffee. They added milk and sugar and carried the mugs into the TV room. Then, sitting beside Amy on the leather sofa, Olivia told her the whole story, starting with the date at the dance club, climaxing with the scene of horror on Josh's front porch the night before.

Amy listened in silence, taking long sips of her coffee. Her face remained expressionless. Olivia couldn't tell what she was thinking.

"And that's it," Olivia said. "Up to now, anyway. I just don't know what to think, Amy."

"I don't, either. I really don't," Amy said, staring down at her coffee mug thoughtfully. "You're right, I guess. Josh must have some kind of weird disease. Something that's making his body fall apart."

"But what could it be?" Olivia asked. "I've never seen anyone get a disease like that – not even on *Grey's Anatomy*."

It was meant as a joke, but Amy didn't laugh. She seemed to be thinking very hard about something. "The puzzling part is Owen," she said finally. "Owen says that Josh is dead."

"Yeah. When I told him Josh wasn't dead, he looked at me like I had totally lost it," Olivia said. "Owen says he went to his funeral. He still can't talk about the whole thing. He had tears in his eyes last night, Amy."

"This is all so weird," Amy said. "But there's a logical

explanation for it. I know we'll figure it out if we keep at it." She held up her coffee mug. "Can I have another cup?"

"Sure. Help yourself," Olivia said. "I want to—"

The phone rang, interrupting her.

She reached over the arm of the sofa and picked up the phone off the side table. "Hello?"

"Hello, Olivia. Man, I'm glad you're there." The boy's voice was frightened, breathless.

"Who is this?" Olivia cried.

"It's Owen. Olivia – you've got to listen to me."

"What? What's the matter, Owen? You sound so weird."

"Please – don't talk. Just listen. There isn't much time."

"Owen, please – what on earth are you talking about?" A feeling of dread was forming in her chest. She gripped the phone tightly, so tightly her hand started to ache.

"Olivia, I saw him, too."

"Josh?"

"Yes. I saw him." Owen's voice was trembling. It was hard to understand him.

"Owen, try to calm down," Olivia said. "I *told* you I've been seeing Josh. He—"

"Olivia – *please!*" He was shouting now. "You don't understand. Josh is back. Back from the dead!"

"What?!"

"It's true, Olivia. I'm so sorry, but it's true."

"Owen – you're not making any sense. Where are you?"

"Never mind. Just listen to me. He was dead. Josh was really dead. I did go to his funeral. I saw his corpse. But he's come back from the grave, Olivia. He told me."

"He told you?"

"He told me. Oh, lord, he looks so horrible. He's falling apart. I mean, really. Pieces of him are just falling off. And he smells so bad. He's rotting. Just rotting."

Olivia smelled that ghastly stench once again. Two long showers and she couldn't get rid of it. She pictured Josh's grinning, toothless face.

"Owen, listen—"

"*You* listen. Just listen," Owen continued, sounding even more frantic. Olivia could hear traffic noise in the background, a horn honking. Owen was obviously outside somewhere.

"He's come back to punish you, Olivia," he said, his voice trembling. "He's come back from the grave because he wants to pay you back – pay you back for letting him die."

"But I—"

"He knows, Olivia. He knows you ran away and left him. And he's come back to get revenge."

"Owen, stop – I . . ." Olivia's words choked in her throat. She suddenly felt terribly sick.

"You've got to run!" Owen cried, shouting over a passing

bus. "You've got to get out of there. Josh is on his way to your house – now! He's going to kill you, Olivia. He told me. He came back to kill you. He'll be there any moment!"

"Owen—"

She could hear the traffic in the background, but Owen didn't answer.

"Owen?"

The line went dead.

"What was *that* all about?" Amy asked, returning from the kitchen with a fresh cup of coffee.

"Josh. He—"

Olivia stopped and listened.

Yes. She had heard correctly.

There was a loud pounding on the front door.

Eighteen

"Why do you look so frightened?" Amy asked, putting her coffee cup down. "It's only someone at the front door."

The knocking repeated, a little louder, a little longer. The doorbell chimed.

"Are you OK?" Amy asked. "I'll get the door."

"No – Amy . . ." Olivia tried to stop her, but the words caught in her throat. Her heart thudding, she followed Amy into the front hall. "No! Don't!"

But she was too late.

Amy had already opened the door.

Ben walked in, shivering from the cold under his oversized wool coat. "Hi, I'm Ben," he said, reaching out to shake Amy's hand.

Amy introduced herself. Ben looked beyond her to Olivia, who was leaning against the wall, breathing a sigh of relief.

"Thank goodness. It's only you," Olivia said breathlessly.

Ben laughed. "What's that supposed to mean? Is that a compliment?"

"We have to go," Olivia said, unable to keep the fear out of her voice.

"Where are you going?" Ben asked, unbuttoning the heavy coat. "I just got here."

"Olivia – what's wrong?" Amy asked. "You look so frightened. Was it that call?"

"Yes. I . . ." She looked at Ben. He didn't know anything about Josh. He only knew that she had broken up with someone after her accident so that she could go out with him.

How could she begin to tell him what was happening? Especially since she could barely believe it herself.

"You'll think I'm crazy," she said, her heart still pounding in her chest.

"I already think you're crazy," Ben joked, flashing her a warm, reassuring smile. "Hey – do I smell coffee?"

"Yes. I've just made a fresh pot," Amy said.

"I'd kill for a cup," Ben said, rubbing his hands together to warm them. "It's freezing out there."

"We don't have time for coffee," Olivia said impatiently. "Josh – he's on his way here."

Ben's handsome face filled with confusion. "Josh?"

"He's coming here?" Amy asked, startled.

"That was Owen on the phone. He – he saw Josh. He knows Josh is back. He—"

"Who's Josh?" Ben asked, draping his coat over the bannister. "What do you mean he's back?"

"It's too long a story," Olivia said, closing her eyes, wishing she could just disappear. "And you wouldn't believe it, anyway."

"Try me," Ben said, walking past her into the kitchen. He sniffed the warm aroma from the coffee maker. "Where are the mugs?"

"Ben – you're not taking me seriously!" Olivia screamed.

Amy and Ben both stared at her, alarmed.

"Olivia—" Amy started.

"He's coming to kill me!" Olivia screamed. "Owen said Josh is coming to kill me!" She knew she sounded hysterical, but she didn't care. Somehow she had to get it across to her two friends that this was an urgent situation, that all three of them were in danger.

"But, Olivia, why?" Amy asked, walking over and putting a hand gently on Olivia's shoulder. "Try to calm down. What did Owen say to make you so – so frightened?"

Olivia pulled angrily away from Amy. "Josh has come back from the grave!" she screamed, feeling her face grow hot. "He told Owen. He's come back from the grave – to kill me!"

Ben stepped back from the coffee maker. He looked over to Amy, as if to say, What's wrong with Olivia?

"I'm not crazy!" Olivia shrieked. "Josh was dead. Owen went to his funeral. But now he's back. Do you understand? He's back! He came back to kill me!"

"Maybe we should get a doctor," Ben said, talking to Amy. "Is Olivia's mother at home? Is anyone else in the house?"

"No. No one's home," Amy said. She turned to Olivia. "Listen, why don't we all go over to my house?"

"You don't believe me – do you?" Olivia cried, squeezing her hands into tight fists, so tight her nails dug into her skin.

"We believe you're very upset about something," Ben said softly, slowly. "Why don't we go and sit down? Maybe if we discussed it—"

"There's nothing to discuss," Olivia said angrily. "Josh is dead. He's on his way. He's going to kill me. He could kill us all."

"OK. Then let's get out of here," Amy said, looking at Ben. "Get your coat, Olivia. We'll go to my house. Josh will never find you there."

"I don't understand," Ben said. "Is Josh the guy you used to go out with?"

"Yes," Amy said, pushing Ben towards the front hall. "Olivia can explain it all in the car."

"Explain about a guy who's come back from the grave?"

"You don't believe me! Well, I don't care if you believe me

138

or not!" Olivia cried. "I'm getting out of here." She started towards the front hall, but Ben grabbed her arm and pulled her back.

"I believe you," he said. But he didn't sound very convincing. "But I think we should sit down for a moment, have a cup of coffee, and discuss—"

Before he could finish his sentence, the front door burst open, banging loudly against the wall, making all three of them jump and cry out.

"Ben – you didn't close the door?" Olivia cried.

"I – I thought I had," Ben said, looking frightened.

The storm door slammed.

They heard footsteps in the hall.

Josh, walking fast, his eyes wide, stepped stiff-legged into the kitchen.

"Josh – stop!" Owen came running in behind him, his cheeks bright red, breathing hard, his face filled with terror. "Stop! Can you hear me?"

All three of them gasped as Josh staggered under the bright kitchen lights. It was hard to believe that it was Josh. He looked like a creature from a horror film. A large patch of grey skull protruded through a square bald spot in his hair. All of his teeth were gone. Purple liquid dripped from his eyes. His skin was as green as grass and seemed to be peeling off his cheeks and forehead.

He glared at Olivia, his mouth opened wide in a toothless grin. He staggered forward. It seemed to take every ounce of his strength for him to move. One arm hung limp at his side.

"Josh – stop!" Owen screamed. He turned to Olivia. "I tried to stop him. Really – I tried. But he won't listen to me. I don't think he hears me!"

"Josh . . ." Olivia tried to cry out to him, but her words choked in her throat. She suddenly felt as if she couldn't breathe, couldn't move.

I'm paralysed with fear, she thought. So this is what it feels like.

He's going to kill me. I know he's going to kill me. And I'm just going to stand here and let him.

"Olivia, I'm back," Josh said suddenly. His voice could barely be heard. It was a rasping whisper, like wind blowing through the crack in a window.

"Olivia, I'm back. I came back from the grave."

"No! Josh – no!" Olivia managed to find her voice and scream.

"You shouldn't have left me to die, Olivia."

Josh raised his good arm high in front of him. In his hand he held a large, black-handled kitchen knife.

Nineteen

"Stop him! We've got to stop him!" Owen cried.

He leaped at Josh, reaching for his broad shoulders.

With startling quickness, Josh spun away from Owen. Owen slammed hard into the kitchen worktop, looking dazed.

Josh, his dripping eyes staring into Olivia's, staggered forward. "I'm back," he said in his raspy whisper. "Olivia, I'm back."

With one quick chop of his open hand, Ben knocked the big knife from Josh's hand.

"Hey!" Josh cried out in surprise.

He dived for the knife but Olivia got there first.

She didn't even think about it. She grabbed the knife by the black handle, leaped at Josh, and plunged the blade deep into Josh's chest.

Bright red blood spurted out from Josh's hoody.

His eyes opened wide, first with surprise, then with terror. He stared at the knife. Then his eyes slowly went up to Olivia.

"No. This isn't right," he said, grimacing in pain.

He slumped to the floor and lay in a puddle of his own bright blood.

"No!" Owen screamed, grabbing Olivia and pulling her back, pulling her hard, angrily.

Olivia stared down at Josh's unmoving body. She felt numb. No feeling at all. Then bewilderment as Owen jerked her away.

Amy stood back by the sink, her hands up to her face. Ben leaned against the kitchen worktop, looking very frightened and confused.

"What have you done?" Owen cried. "You've killed him, Olivia. You've killed him!"

"I – what?"

What was Owen saying

What did he mean?

How could she have killed someone who was already dead?

Owen dropped down to the floor and bent over the body. He put a hand on Josh's neck. Then he placed the back of his hand under Josh's nose.

"Dead," he said, after a long wait. "He's dead."

"Now, wait a minute," Olivia started. "What's going on here? What do you mean . . . ?"

"It was just a joke," Owen said softly, looking up at her, still on his knees on the bloodstained floor.

"What?" Ben came up behind Olivia and put his hands on her shoulders.

Olivia leaned back against him, grateful for his support, for his caring.

"Owen – what are you saying?" Amy asked. She had tears running down her cheeks. She was shaking all over. Her eyes kept going down to the still body on the floor.

"It was just a joke," Owen repeated. He rubbed his fingers over Josh's face and held them up to Olivia. His fingers were green. "Just stage make-up," he said.

Olivia swallowed hard. "You mean . . . ?"

"It was all stage make-up. The green colour, the blacked-out teeth, the stuff dripping from his eyes. Him staggering around like Frankenstein's monster. It was all a gag, Olivia."

"Owen – you said you went to his funeral," Olivia said, beginning to realize what really had happened, the horror of what she had just done starting to sink in.

"Just a joke," Owen repeated sadly. "Josh and I cooked it up. To pay you back. To teach you a little lesson. That's all."

"But—"

"But now you've killed him," Owen said, his expression hardening. "Now you've really killed him."

Twenty

"Call an ambulance," Ben said, still holding on tightly, comfortingly to Olivia's shoulders. "Maybe he—"

"He's dead," Owen said, sweeping a large hand back nervously through his spiky blond hair. "It's too late for an ambulance."

"I – I'm going to be sick," Amy said, looking ashen. She ran out of the kitchen, holding her hand over her mouth.

"How could you just kill him like that?" Owen asked Olivia, sounding more accusing than questioning.

"But, Owen . . ." Olivia didn't know what to say.

"You saw the way Josh came at her with the knife," Ben said, coming to her defence. "She had to react – didn't she? She had to protect herself."

"That's right. It was self-defence," Olivia agreed quickly. Self-defence. Of course.

Self-defence.

Ben, you're a genius.

"I had to protect myself," she repeated. "He came at me . . . and I just reacted." She was starting to breathe normally, starting to feel a little more like herself.

"What a horrible joke," Ben said, looking down at Josh's body. "You know, Owen, you're as much to blame as Olivia."

"I didn't stab him with a knife," Owen said.

"But if you hadn't cooked up this whole thing, if the two of you hadn't planned for Josh to – to—"

"Why, Owen?" Olivia interrupted. "Why pull such a stupid joke?"

"I knew it was stupid," Owen said, sighing. He dropped on to one of the kitchen stools, his shoulders drooping, all of the energy seeming to drain from his body. "I told Josh it was really dumb. But it was that day in the hospital, Olivia. That day I came to tell you that Josh was dead. That's as far as we were going to take the joke. But then—"

"But then what?" Olivia demanded, anger replacing her fear.

"Then when you didn't even cry, when you didn't even look that upset, Josh decided to take the joke as far as he could."

"And you and he did the whole thing just to frighten me?" Olivia asked.

"You deserved it – the way you treated Josh. You used

him." Owen's voice softened. "Josh loved acting. And he loved make-up. You should've seen him after he got out of hospital. He was so turned on by the whole idea. He spent days just getting the right smell to make it seem like he was decaying."

"Ugh." Olivia made a face, remembering that sour smell.

"It was all just a stupid joke that went too far," Owen said sadly, shaking his head. "You're right, Olivia. I'm as much at fault as you are."

"But what are we doing to *do*?" Olivia demanded. "We can't just stand around here talking about it."

"We've got to call the police," Ben said, squeezing Olivia's shoulder.

She stepped away from him and started to pace back and forth. "We can't," she said, thinking hard. "Do you really think the police would believe this story? They'll just think that I killed him."

"But we're all witnesses. We saw what happened," Ben said.

"They won't believe any of us. They'll think we made up the story after Josh was killed," Olivia said.

Amy came back into the kitchen, still looking pale and shaky. "Olivia's right," she said, sitting down on one of the tall stools. "The police will never believe the true story. We've got to get rid of the body. Drag it out to the woods or something."

"Yes!" Olivia cried. She felt like hugging Amy. What an excellent idea! "Amy's right. There's nothing we can do for Josh now. Why should our lives all be ruined because of a stupid joke?"

Olivia realized she was breathing normally again. Her heart had gone back to its regular beat. She was starting to feel a lot stronger, a lot more in control.

"Yes, we have to get rid of the body," she repeated.

Ben shook his head. "It's no good," he said. "They'll catch us. Josh's family will know where he was going. They'll—"

"He doesn't have a family," Olivia interrupted. "He only has an old aunt who never knows where he goes. There's no way the police can trace this to us. No way. Especially if we take the body somewhere far away."

"No. I'm sorry. We have to tell the police. They'll believe the truth if we all just—"

Olivia glared angrily at Ben. 'Why are you being such a wimp?" she cried. "You know, *your* life will be ruined by this, too. Are you really willing to give up your entire future because of Josh's stupid joke?"

Ben didn't answer. He walked over to the back door and stared out of the window at the long, sweeping garden.

"Yeah. I guess you're right," Owen said reluctantly, staring hard at Olivia. "There's nothing we can do for Josh now."

Amy turned her head away. Her shoulders were shaking.

"Don't cry, Amy," Olivia said. "We'll be OK – once we get rid of the body." She wanted to go over and comfort her friend. But she was afraid she might start crying, too.

She didn't want to cry. She wanted to keep herself in control.

She wanted to keep thinking clearly, to stay alert.

They were going to get out of this mess.

She wasn't going to let Josh ruin her life.

She never should have got involved with him in the first place.

Amy suddenly turned back. "Owen and I will take the body," she said resolutely. She dabbed at her wet cheeks with a tissue.

"I'm not helping," Ben said, still staring out into the garden. "I won't stop you from doing it. But I don't think it's right. I won't help."

"That's OK," Owen said quickly, standing up and walking over to Josh's body. "Amy and I can get Josh into her boot. We'll take him to the woods near his house."

"Ben and I will clean up," Olivia said, looking at Ben.

"Yeah, OK," he agreed, looking very unhappy.

Olivia heard the front door open and close.

Everyone froze.

"Who's that?"

"Your mum?"

148

"It's Helen," she told them. "The housekeeper. Mum gave her the morning off. But now she's back. Quick –" she pointed to the body – "out the back door. Hurry!"

Looking frightened, Owen bent down and grabbed Josh under the shoulders. He started to pull. The body slid across the floor. "I think I can drag him," he told Amy. "Just get the door, OK?"

Amy hurried to the kitchen door and held it open for Owen.

"I'll call you later," Olivia said, listening to Helen's footsteps in the hall. "Good luck. I know we're doing the right thing."

Just get it out of the house, she thought.

She breathed a sigh of relief as Owen and Amy disappeared through the door, and the door slammed behind them.

Ben stood, leaning against the kitchen worktop, looking very upset.

Helen's footsteps grew louder, then fainter.

She's going to her room to change, Olivia thought. Then she'll come into the kitchen.

She looked down at the puddle of dark blood on the floor.

"Well, they've gone," Ben said quietly. "I hope the neighbours won't see what they're dragging to the car."

"The neighbours can't see. Their houses are too far away," Olivia said, thinking hard. "Besides, there're all the trees."

She went to the drawer and pulled out a small steak knife. Then she advanced quickly on Ben.

Ben looked up, surprised.

He saw the knife in her hand and, as she strode towards him, a purposeful look on her face, his expression turned to fear.

"Olivia – stop!" Ben cried. "What are you going to do with that?"

Twenty-One

Olivia grabbed Ben's left hand, turned it over, and sliced a long line across the palm with the knife.

Bright red blood seeped to the surface along the line of the cut, then quickly dripped to the floor.

"Olivia . . . ?"

Ben pulled his hand out of her grip, staring at the flowing blood, then at her, horrified.

"Helen!" Olivia shouted, tossing the knife on to the worktop. "Helen!"

"Yes?" the housekeeper called from down the hall.

"Could you come here, please? My friend has cut himself. I'm afraid there's a lot of blood on the floor. Could you help clean it up?"

Helen came rushing in. She was a short, chubby woman, with a round face that frowned in surprise as she saw the large puddle of blood on the floor. She looked over to Ben, who was busily wrapping his bleeding hand in paper towels.

"You should go to a doctor. You've lost a lot of blood," Helen said, hurrying to the mop cupboard.

"He'll be OK," Olivia said.

Ben glared at her. He strode past her and into the front hall, heading to the door, holding the paper towels tightly around his cut hand.

Olivia followed him to the door. "I'm sorry, Ben," she said, whispering so that Helen wouldn't hear. "I had to do something. I didn't want to hurt you. But it was the first thing I—"

"You're cold, Olivia," he said, his hand on the door handle. "You're not really human. I had no idea how cold you were."

He was out the door before she could reply.

She watched him get into his car, back down the drive, and roar away. Then she closed the front door, locked it, and hurried up the stairs to her room.

She sat down on the edge of the still unmade bed.

"I'm going to be OK," she said aloud.

I'm going to be OK.

This is all going to work out fine.

I'm going to be OK.

She repeated the word *OK* over and over until it didn't seem like a real word any more.

Then she realized that she was trembling all over.

*

She saw Ben at school on Monday. His hand was bandaged. He walked right past, pretending he didn't see her.

She sighed, feeling sorry for herself.

Ben, I care about you, she thought.

We've got to get back together. We're so right for each other.

She thought of chasing after him, running up behind him, throwing her arms around his broad shoulders. I'll beg him to forgive me, she thought. I'll beg him. I'll apologize a thousand times, throw myself on his mercy.

She stood in the middle of the hall, watching the back of him until he turned a corner and disappeared.

She tried to concentrate on mid-term exams, but it was nearly impossible.

Her mind kept wandering back to all that had happened.

Josh's face, his toothless, grinning, green face haunted her thoughts.

She couldn't study. She couldn't think straight.

On Monday night she called Amy to find out what had happened with Josh's body. But Amy couldn't talk. Her parents were in the room.

On Tuesday she drifted through two exams, struggling to concentrate. Afterwards, she was sure she messed up on both of them.

Wednesday and Thursday went by in a blur of studying

and more exams. On Thursday night she picked up the phone to call Ben.

But she put it back down.

What if he refused to talk to her? What if he refused to come to the phone?

After school on Friday, she thought of skipping her tennis lesson. But at the last minute, she decided to go ahead with it. A little exercise might do her good.

Maybe it would take her mind off Josh, off the blood-smeared kitchen floor, his body lying so still on the floor. Maybe it would take her mind off losing Ben.

I'll work up a good, honest sweat, she thought.

I've got to get my blood flowing again.

Blood.

She had to stop thinking about blood.

"I'm going to be OK," she said, juggling her school bag and tennis racquet as she passed through the glass doors of the tennis club.

I'm going to be OK. It wasn't my fault. No one will ever know.

Gary was her new instructor. He looked more like a wrestler than a tennis player, with his long, curly black hair, his biceps bulging out of his T-shirt, his broad chest. "Let's warm up a little first," he said, dragging a basket of yellow tennis balls on to the court.

The club was crowded, mostly with kids having their after-school lessons. Voices echoed off the high rafters. Olivia had never noticed how noisy the club was before.

Gary hit some easy ones over the net. Olivia stood in place, hitting them back with her forehand, swinging casually, the racquet light in her hand.

After hitting five or six balls, something made her turn around. She looked back to the spectators' area behind the mesh screen.

That's where Josh had stood, she remembered.

That's where he had stood, looking so green, so weird.

She remembered seeing him in the car-park afterwards, his eyes glowing red. It was so frightening.

And all so phoney.

Just a fake.

She couldn't believe Josh had played such an elaborate prank. All that make-up. All that time and work.

And where had it got him?

Into a shallow grave in the woods.

Or maybe no grave at all. Maybe he had just been tossed into some thick bushes or high weeds.

She should've tried Amy again. Or called Owen. She should've found out what had happened with the body.

But somehow it was just as well not knowing.

The body was gone. Josh was gone.

So why was she looking for him now?

"Olivia? Olivia?"

She realized that Gary had been calling to her for some time.

"Are you looking for someone?" he asked.

"No," she said, still distracted.

"Shall we play a game?" He twirled his racquet in his hand.

"No," she said. "I – I've got to go."

She couldn't concentrate. She didn't want to be there.

I can't play on this court, she thought. I keep having the feeling that Josh is standing back there, watching me, staring at me with those frightening red eyes.

"Olivia . . . ?" Gary called after her.

But she turned and ran to the changing room without looking back.

I've got to get out of here. Out. Out. Out.

I've got to stop thinking about Josh.

What's wrong with me, anyway? I didn't even care that much about Josh. Why can't I get him out of my mind now?

She answered her own question: because you killed him.

She changed quickly, then she drove around aimlessly for nearly an hour before heading home.

Maybe if I talk to Amy and hear the end of the story, I'll be able to put it out of my mind, she thought.

The end of the story. Would there *be* an end to the story?

She had read the morning newspaper every day, grabbing it as soon as she came downstairs, much to her mother's surprise. But there had been no story about anyone finding Josh's body in the woods. She watched the local TV news at six each evening. They didn't have the story, either.

So, maybe the story had already ended.

She just had to talk to Amy. See how Amy was doing. Maybe Amy was doing better than Olivia. Maybe she wasn't thinking about Josh, thinking about the murder every minute of the day.

Maybe Amy can help me get it out of my mind.

But when Olivia got home, her mother was there. She had to talk to her mother, pretend to have a conversation. She talked about her mid-term exams, how hard they were. She talked about her tennis lesson, making up some funny stories about the new instructor who looked like a wrestler.

That made her mother laugh.

Olivia, you're such a good liar, she told herself.

If only you could lie to *yourself.*

She wanted to go upstairs and call Amy, but Mrs Collier stopped her from leaving the room. "Helen's just about to serve dinner," she said. "She's made your favourite – leg of lamb. I have to go out tonight, but I thought for once we'd have a quiet dinner, just the two of us."

So Olivia had to make up more stories to tell her mother, stories about school, stories about Ben and what a great guy he was.

"You've barely touched your lamb," Mrs Collier said after a while.

"I – I'm not all that hungry," Olivia said, which was certainly true.

"Are you feeling OK? You look kind of . . . tired." Olivia's mother was constantly accusing her of looking tired.

Olivia looked up from her practically untouched plate at her mother. For a brief moment, she felt as if she might tell her mother what was troubling her.

You see, I killed Josh, Mum. He was playing a joke on me, trying to make me think he had come back from the grave, and I stabbed him in the chest with a knife. Then Owen and Amy took his body and hid it in the woods. And that's why I'm having a little trouble digging into this lamb on my plate.

Wouldn't that go down well?

Olivia couldn't believe she had even *for a second* considered telling her mother what had happened.

I must be *really* losing it, she thought.

Helen served apple pie with cinnamon ice cream for dessert. Olivia managed to get a little of it down. Then she excused herself, and gave her mum a quick kiss on the forehead – which startled Mrs Collier, who wasn't used to much affection from her daughter. "Olivia . . . ?" she started.

But Olivia was already running up to her room to call Amy.

She sat down at her desk, breathing heavily from running up the stairs. As she reached to pick up the phone, it rang.

Startled, she grabbed it before the first ring had ended.

"Hello?"

"Hi, Olivia." A boy's voice cut through the static on the line.

"Ben? Is that you?"

Muffled laughter on the other end. "No Olivia. It's me. Josh. I'm back, Olivia. This time I really *did* come back."

Twenty-Two

"See you," Josh's voice said over the static.

"Josh?"

"See you."

Then the line went dead. Olivia uttered a little cry and sat staring at the phone.

She saw Josh's green face again, the skin peeling off. And she saw him lying on her kitchen floor in the puddle of blood.

Real blood.

Really dead.

It had all been real.

And now he was back.

It has to be a joke, she thought, feeling cold all over.

Someone is pretending to be Josh.

But it sounded so much like him. She even recognized the muffled laugh.

But Josh was dead. She'd killed him. Felt the knife go in. Seen the blood.

Oh, help me. Somebody – help me!

I can't think straight!

I've got to figure this out. I've got to know what is happening!

She dialled Amy's number. It rang four times. Finally Amy's mother picked it up.

"Amy can't come to the phone now. She's very busy."

"Oh, please. I've really got to talk to her." Olivia didn't recognize her own voice. It was so pinched with fear, so . . . desperate.

"I'll get her to call you back."

Not good enough, Olivia thought. Not fast enough.

I've got to get out of this house, away from here.

"See you," Josh had said. Dead Josh.

"See you."

Did that mean he was on his way over to her house?

Dead Josh was on his way to . . . to do *what*??

Olivia dropped the phone, jumped up, and ran down the stairs, taking them two at a time. "Mum? Mum?"

"She's just left," Helen called from the kitchen. "Some club meeting or something."

I've got to get out of here, Olivia thought, her heart thudding.

I'll go to Amy's. She grabbed her coat from the cupboard and searched the front table for her car keys.

"I'm going over to a friend's," she called to Helen.

Helen called something back, but Olivia was already through the door.

Amy will know what to do, she told herself as the houses whirred by on both sides. It was a clear, cold night. Everything seemed to be in sharp focus, as if she were looking through a very expensive, fine camera lens.

Amy will know what to do.

But that was silly, wasn't it?

Why should Amy know what to do about someone who has come back from the grave?

Dead Josh.

Dead Josh . . . who wouldn't stay dead.

A few minutes later, she pulled the car into Amy's driveway and turned off the headlights. The front of the house was dark. The porch light wasn't on.

Olivia stepped out of the car and waited for her eyes to adjust to the total blackness. After a while, the black outline of the house loomed in front of her, against a somewhat lighter sky. Shrubs and a low, bent tree came into dark focus.

Olivia turned and looked back at the street. There were no street lights.

She had a sudden chill.

Wrapping her unbuttoned coat around her, she started walking quickly up to the dark house. The ground felt hard and frozen beneath her trainers. Her breath sent clouds of fog in front of her.

As she neared the front porch, she could see lights on in the back of the house.

I'm almost there, she thought, nearly tripping over a smooth stone placed at the edge of the flagstone path that led to the front door.

Why does it have to be so dark?

She regained her balance and started to jog up to the front porch.

Amy will know what to do.

I just need to talk to her, that's all.

She raised her hand to knock on the front door, then stopped.

She smelled him first.

That sour smell. That stench of rotting meat. But different from the phoney rubbish smell. Worse. Raw. Raw and rotting at the same time.

Then she felt the bony tap on her shoulder.

"Ohh."

She spun around, unable to breathe.

"Josh!"

In the darkness, she could see that one of his eyes was gone. There was nothing there but an empty socket.

"Olivia," he said, his voice a harsh whisper. "Why did you kill me?"

Twenty-Three

It was so dark.

The smell was overpowering.

Olivia realized she'd been holding her breath. Now she let it out in a loud gasp.

"Why did you kill me, Olivia? Look – I'm still bleeding."

He held up his shirt. The wound was large and dark.

"Josh – I didn't mean –" She looked for an escape route, but he had backed her up against the front door.

She turned away. She couldn't bear to look at the empty eye socket, at his sagging, crumbling skin, at the gaping, dark wound in his chest.

Even in the blackness of the night he looked terrifying.

"Why did you kill me?" he repeated, his voice so weak she could barely hear him, the words floating out over his toothless gums.

"Help! Somebody help!" she screamed at the top of her

voice, and started to run, her trainers slipping on the hard, wet ground.

"Don't run! It was so hard to come back!" Josh cried.

He was right behind her.

"No! Go away! Go away!"

"I went away, Olivia. But I came back."

He grabbed her shoulder. Then his hand slid down and he tackled her around the waist.

They both tumbled to the cold ground. He landed on top of her and pressed her into the dirt.

"No!" she screamed.

She was about to scream again, but stopped.

"Hey!" she said, pushing him hard, trying to shove him off her. "I can touch you." She grabbed his arm. "You're solid."

He was breathing hard from the short chase.

She reached up and touched his face. She pulled off a chunk of plastic make-up.

"You creep! You're not dead! This is still part of your ghastly joke!"

A broad, toothless smile formed on his face. "You're right," he said in his normal voice. "I'm alive." Then he added, "But the joke is over."

"Get off me! It's cold down here. You're ruining my coat!"

"The joke is over, Olivia."

166

"Did you hear me? Get off! What do you think you're doing? Ugh. You stink!"

She struggled to climb out from under him, but he was too strong.

"The joke is over," he repeated.

Reaching into his jacket pocket, he pulled out a switchblade knife and flicked it open.

"Josh – put that down!" she screamed.

The porch light came on. He looked even more gruesome in the shadowy yellow light.

And he looked angry.

"The knife is real," Josh said, staring down at her, holding the knife in front of her face. "It's real like me."

"Josh—"

"It's not a fake this time. It's not a retractable stage knife."

"Josh – *please!*" Olivia cried. "What do you *want*?"

"I want to show you that this knife is real," he said, bringing it down quickly.

Twenty-Four

He plunged the knife blade into the ground beside her head.

He was only trying to scare her.

"See?" he said, breathing hard. "It's real. A real knife."

With a burst of strength she shoved him off and struggled to her feet. He regained his balance quickly and stood beside her.

"Why, Josh?" she asked, watching the knife in his hand. "Why are you doing this?"

He turned away, and looked up to the front porch. The light had come on, but the door was still closed. When he turned back to her, his face was filled with hatred.

"Why? Because you didn't care about me." He angrily pulled off the phoney eye socket.

"But, Josh—"

"I loved you, Olivia." His voice broke on the word *love*.

"You were the best thing that ever happened to me. I cared so much about you. And then . . ." He looked down at the knife.

"I cared about you, too," Olivia said. But it didn't sound convincing even to her.

"Then when I fell off that cliff, you didn't care whether I lived or died."

"Is that what Owen told you?" Olivia asked quickly. "Well, that's a lie, Josh. That isn't true. I—"

"It *is* true!" he screamed, his dark eyes burning into hers. "You can't lie to me any more, Olivia. You didn't care whether I lived or died that night. And when Owen came to see you in hospital—"

"I was totally drugged in hospital!" Olivia cried. "I was hurt, *too*, you know. When Owen came to see me—"

"He told you I was dead, and you didn't even react."

"I was drugged. I wasn't myself, Josh. I cried for days."

He laughed, a bitter laugh. "It's no good, Olivia. It's no good. When you stuck that knife in me last Sunday, and I died a second time, you still didn't care."

"I was so upset—"

"You just wanted my body out of the way. That's all you cared about. I was just some mess to clear away. So you and your rich boyfriend wouldn't have your lives disturbed."

"Owen is behind all of this – isn't he?" Olivia asked, looking over to her car.

It was so close, yet so far.

If she could just get into the car and lock the doors . . .

"This is all Owen's idea, isn't it, Josh?"

He shook his head. He flicked the knife blade in and out nervously, staring hard at her all the time, his breath coming out in small puffs.

"Owen helped me. That's all," he said softly. "Owen helped. But I don't need help now."

"What do you mean? What are you going to do?"

She looked to the house. Why didn't the door open? Why didn't someone come rushing out to save her?

Couldn't they hear all the yelling out here?

He took a step towards her. "I'm not going to die a *third* time," he said, his voice without expression, flat and calm now.

Insanely calm, she thought.

He's crazy. Josh is truly crazy.

"I'm not going to die again," he said. "It's your turn!"

She backed towards the drive.

He raised the knife and lunged at her.

"No!"

He stumbled over the smooth stone at the end of the path, the same stone Olivia had stumbled over before.

The knife bounced out of his hand and landed at Olivia's feet. She bent over quickly and picked it up.

"You're wrong, Josh," she said. "It's your turn *again*!"

Twenty-Five

"Olivia – stop!"

Amy came running out of the house at full speed, wearing only shorts and a T-shirt.

Olivia turned towards her, startled, forgetting the knife in her hand. "Amy – what are you . . . ?"

She expected Amy to stop. But Amy ran right at her, pushing her hard, grabbing the knife out of her hand.

"Get away from him!" Amy screamed angrily.

Surprised by her friend's reaction, Olivia took a step back.

"Were you really going to kill him?" Amy screamed. "Haven't you done enough to him?"

She walked over to Josh and put her arm around him. He bent his head low, and she kissed him on the cheek.

"Amy!" Olivia suddenly felt weak. The yellow porch light flickered. Shadows seemed to circle her on the dark ground.

This isn't real, she thought.

"Amy – you were in on this, too?" she asked, struggling to get the words out.

Still holding on to Josh, Amy smiled triumphantly. "It was all my idea," she said softly. "Right from the beginning."

"But why, Amy? I thought we were best friends. I thought . . ." Olivia just stared at them, waiting for the shadows to stop spinning, waiting for the darkness, the incredible heavy darkness to lift.

"Why?"

"You had everything," Amy said bitterly, "and what did I have? Nothing. You had the big house, the expensive car – you had Josh. He was the one thing I wanted in the world." She looked up at Josh. He hugged her tight.

"But Amy—"

"It just broke my heart, Olivia. It broke my heart that you had Josh, and you didn't even care about him. You used him. Like you use everybody. It was all a game to you. You told me that yourself. He was a pet, a belonging, just one of the hundreds of things that belong to you."

"You're not being fair," Olivia said, staring hard at the knife, which was still clenched tightly in Amy's hand.

"Oh, yes, I am," Amy said heatedly. "Time and again you told me how Josh meant nothing to you. You were so *awful* to him. Standing him up and then bragging about it to me. Going out with Ben behind his back."

Amy was getting more and more worked up.

Olivia kept staring at the knife, wondering how over the edge Amy was, wondering if she was upset enough to use it.

"It was so ironic," Amy continued, her voice high and tight, her eyes wide with anger. "Because all the time you were telling me how little Josh meant to you, that's all I wanted – just Josh."

Before she realized it, Olivia found herself laughing. "Hey, listen, Amy – you're welcome to him. Really. Be my guest."

She started walking quickly to the car.

"*Don't laugh at me, Olivia!*"

In a fury, Amy leaped at her, holding the knife high.

"No! Stop!" Olivia turned just in time, and stumbled backwards on to the ground.

Amy raised the knife high, but Josh grabbed her arm.

"Let me kill her! Let me kill her!" Amy screamed.

But Josh gently pulled the knife from her hand and tossed it on to the ground. "Come on," he said softly, holding her close to him. "Easy. Take it easy." She was still breathing hard, but his words seemed to calm her. "Let's go inside. Let's forget all about Olivia. Let's forget this whole crazy time."

She glared at Olivia, then turned her face away.

They walked arm in arm up to the house.

They never looked back.

Olivia picked herself up and watched them until the door closed behind them and the porch light went off.

Then she picked up the knife. The blade slid easily into the handle.

It was a phoney stage prop.

At home in her room, Olivia sat at the desk, holding the knife in her hand, rolling it around between her fingers.

It's as phoney as I am, she thought.

Amy was right. About everything.

And now here I am, all alone. I've lost everyone.

There's no one left.

I don't have a friend, a single friend. Maybe I never did.

Because I never really knew how to care about any of them.

Before she realized it, hot tears were running down her cheeks, and she was sobbing.

It felt so strange.

I haven't cried in years, she thought.

I haven't cried since . . .

She thought hard. When? When?

I haven't cried since the night Daddy left us.

For once, she didn't hold her true feelings back. She let herself cry, the tears flowing down her cheeks. She cried until she was all cried out.

To her surprise, she felt a little better.

She wiped her eyes, then tucked the knife away in a desk drawer.

Then she took a deep breath, picked up the phone, and dialled Ben.

He picked up on the third ring.

"Ben?"

"Hi . . . Olivia."

"Ben, I have to talk to you," she said. "I – I'm back from the grave."

He didn't understand what she meant.

She hoped he'd give her a chance to explain.

R. L. STINE

HORROR HIGH
FATAL KISS

One

"I'd like to propose a toast to Jack and Lauren," Mr DeMarco announced. He raised his fluted champagne glass above his head and held it there until the large, crowded room grew quiet.

Jack tried to hide behind Lauren, but she turned and pulled him beside her, her expression playfully scolding. "This is embarrassing," Jack whispered.

"Get used to it," Lauren told him, holding him in place with both hands so he couldn't escape. "My dad *loves* embarrassing people. It's his hobby."

"I know, I know," Jack replied, shaking his head, his eyes on the front of the large rec room where Lauren's dad was still holding his champagne glass in the air, waiting for all the guests to raise their glasses.

Jack and Lauren had been a couple since sixth grade, so Jack knew exactly what to expect from her parents. Both of them were warm, and outgoing, and generous. Too generous, Jack sometimes thought.

They smother you with kindness. That's how he sometimes described them.

Jack felt smothered by this lavish party, with the enormous, seemingly endless buffet table, the overstocked bar, the five-piece band out on the terrace, the young waiters parading around in their black dinner-jackets, carrying silver trays of salmon and caviar hors d'oeuvres.

After all, it was a little too early to celebrate.

Jack and Lauren had received preliminary acceptance at Princeton, but nothing official yet. And Jack might not be able to go anyway. He was still waiting to hear about his scholarship.

Jack and Lauren had urged the DeMarcos to wait a while before having the party. For one thing, it was only November. They still had the rest of their senior year at Glenview High to finish.

But, Mr DeMarco, in typical fashion, had insisted on throwing this huge, expensive party. "Don't worry about it," he had said, his youthful face beaming happily, one big arm around each of them, crushing them both in an affectionate hug. "We'll throw another party after the school year. Or maybe *two* parties – one for each of you!"

Jack and Lauren finally gave up trying to discourage him.

"What's the point?" Lauren asked, as they were sitting in the front seat of her father's BMW, parked up by Rainer Point, overlooking the town. "Dad will always be Dad."

"But it's so rubbish!" Jack exclaimed unhappily. "I mean, throwing a party for us for no reason."

"I wish you wouldn't say 'rubbish' all the time," Lauren said, squeezing his hand affectionately. "I mean, we're going to Princeton, you know – not just any old uni."

They both laughed.

"You're a snob," Jack said.

"And you love it," she replied and kissed him for a long time.

Jack did love it, he had to admit. He liked everything about Lauren. He liked how her wavy, blonde hair caught the sunlight, how soft it felt in his hands. He liked staring into her wide, hazel eyes. He liked the way people said she looked like a model, like a young Kate Moss.

He liked walking down the hall at school with her, holding hands. "You know we're a cliché," he'd tell her. "I mean, the football quarterback and the Homecoming Queen? Get real!"

"I don't feel like a cliché," she'd reply in her serious way. "I just feel like me."

He had to admit he didn't at all mind that they were a cliché. Being with Lauren always made him feel good. And he was proud of being the starting quarterback of the Tigers.

He'd been voted player of the year last year. That was pretty good.

Jack liked the fact that everyone thought of him and Lauren as a couple. And he liked the fact that other kids were jealous of them. And of him. He didn't think about it a lot, but when he did, he admitted to himself that having this long, steady relationship with one girl was maybe the most admirable thing about him.

Other kids, even his best friends, even Walker, his very best friend, seemed sort of aimless to him. Immature.

Jack liked being responsible. Maybe it was because his father had been so irresponsible. Running off without a word, leaving Mrs Singleton to bring up Jack and his younger brother Charlie.

How could he *do* that to us? Jack often asked himself.

He never came up with a satisfactory answer.

Lauren's parents seemed to have such a close, stable relationship. Maybe that was why Jack liked them so much.

He realized he liked being with the DeMarcos as much as with his own family. When he didn't feel smothered by their wealth, by their enthusiasm, by their generosity.

Now he found himself looking around the large, brightly-lit rec room, crowded with kids from school, relatives of both families, and a lot of people he'd never seen before, and *definitely* feeling smothered.

"We should never have agreed to this," he whispered, leaning against Lauren.

"We had no choice, remember?" she whispered back, as her father rambled on with one of his endless, meandering toasts.

"But it's so embarrassing," Jack moaned, staring across the room at his friend Walker, who was leaning against one of the sliding glass doors, staring back at Jack with his eyes crossed and his tongue hanging out of his mouth.

"Don't think of it as a going to Princeton party. Think of it as a going-away party for me," Lauren said, playfully stepping down hard on his foot until he winced in pain, her eyes straight ahead as if concentrating on her father's toast.

Jack was tempted to pour his Coke down the front of her dress, but managed to hold himself back.

He had almost forgot that Lauren and her parents were going away. Off to Paris for a week. Mr DeMarco had some sort of architectural business to take care of, so why not turn it into a spur-of-the-moment family holiday?

He glanced at his mother, in her flowing fuchsia-pink dress, which was just a little too tight on her plump body, her platinum hair piled high on her head, standing in front of Mr DeMarco, glass in hand, listening so intently.

For a brief moment, Jack felt real envy. He wanted to be in

the DeMarco family. He wanted to go on unplanned trips to Paris, too.

Oh, well, some day soon, I *will* be a member of the family, he thought, glancing affectionately at Lauren.

". . . I'm so proud of these kids . . ." Mr DeMarco was saying at the front of the room.

And then Mrs DeMarco looked away from her husband and gasped.

Mr DeMarco stopped abruptly in mid-sentence. All eyes turned to where his wife was staring – to the buffet table, where Lauren's little white cat had leaped up and was enthusiastically sampling a good helping of the salmon mousse.

"Oh, Fluffernutter!" Lauren cried, letting go of Jack's hand and rushing towards the buffet table.

One of the waiters got there first and lifted the still-chewing cat off the table, setting it gently down on the tiled floor.

"I think that was a sign that I've been talking for too long," Mr DeMarco said, grinning. He held up his glass one more time. "To Jack and Lauren," he announced, looking for Lauren. He couldn't see her because she was down on the floor scolding her cat.

There was a clinking of glasses, and conversations resumed around the room. Jack breathed a loud sigh of relief, took a long gulp of Coke from his glass, and headed over to thank Lauren's dad for the toast, even though he hadn't really heard much of it.

"Hey, man," Walker caught his arm. "Watch out for those caviar thingies. I tried one, but it tasted really fishy."

"I'll be careful," Jack said dryly.

Walker was tall and lanky, the tallest one in the room even though he was only seventeen, and still growing. He should've played basketball, Jack thought. He never could figure out why his friend wanted to be a footballer.

"What kind of a party is this without any pizza?" Walker complained, only half serious.

"It wasn't *my* idea, man," Jack said, sighing. "You want to go out for a pizza? I'll go with you."

"Yeah. Sure," Walker said sarcastically, glancing down at Lauren who was still on the floor playing with Fluffernutter, unaware that she was getting white cat hair all over her dress. "You ready for Friday night?"

Jack nodded. What with all the excitement over being accepted at Princeton and the party, he hadn't had much time to think about the game. "Lincoln isn't that good," he said.

"They're ace!" Walker exclaimed, pushing his heavy, black-framed glasses up on his narrow nose. "They beat Westerville thirty-five–nil, and we could only tie with Westerville."

"They got lucky, man," Jack said, grinning. "They're rubbish. Totally rubbish. We can take 'em."

He saw Mr DeMarco coming towards him, so he slapped Walker's hand in a low five and started to push his way through the crowd to meet him.

Mr DeMarco, chewing a fried chicken drumstick, beamed at Jack, raking back his thick, brown hair with one hand. He's so proud of his hair, Jack thought. He's always telling everyone how he's forty-five and still has every hair on his head.

"Hey, thanks for the toast," Jack said, trying to sound enthusiastic.

Mr DeMarco brushed chicken crumbs from his wide red tie. "I think I went on a bit too long, but I just couldn't help it." He flung an arm around Jack's shoulder, nearly knocking Jack over. "I'm just so proud of you two!"

"Thanks," Jack said uncomfortably.

"You know, I have a little bet on the game on Friday night," he said confidentially, his arm still around Jack's shoulders, guiding him towards the hallway that led to the rest of the house.

"You're betting on Lincoln?" Jack joked.

Mr DeMarco stopped for a moment, then laughed. "No way," he said. "You're going to take the Tigers to the state championship. I know it."

"Well . . . I don't know," Jack said, feeling his face grow hot. "We've got some tough games. And with Jergens hurt . . ."

"You just have to throw more," Mr DeMarco said. It was one of his steady themes. Jack was too generous, he was always saying. Jack should forget about sharing the glory. He should throw the ball more. The team should ride on Jack's arm.

"I don't think Coach Hawkins would agree," Jack always replied.

"Who *cares* about Hawkins?" was Mr DeMarco's answer. "He's a chemistry teacher. What does *he* know about football?"

Jack never won this argument. He seldom won any argument against Lauren's father. Mr DeMarco was too powerful and too insistent. He never gave up until he got his way.

"Listen, Jack, I meant everything I said in that toast," he said, turning serious, his face close to Jack's. "Keep making me proud, son. I know you will. I know you and Lauren both will. Keep making me proud. You know, when you graduate from Princeton, there'll be a place waiting for you in my firm."

Jack's mouth dropped open in surprise. "Really?"

It was a generous offer. Mr DeMarco's architectural design firm was the biggest in the state and was rapidly getting a national reputation.

Jack planned to do architecture at Princeton. His dream

was to build amazing skyscrapers, to change skylines. Now it looked as if his dream would almost certainly come true.

"Thank you, Mr DeMarco. That's just awesome," he exclaimed. "I really don't know what to say."

Mr DeMarco was looking past Jack, back into the room. The glass doors had been opened. Outside, the band had started to play, and people were drifting out on to the large, flagstone terrace to dance. "I can't believe what a beautiful evening it is," he said to Jack. "Imagine? Twenty degrees in November? It's like spring out there. Luck just seems to rain down on you and Lauren."

"I guess so," Jack said, still thinking about Mr DeMarco's amazing offer. He said goodbye to him and headed excitedly over to Lauren, who was talking animatedly, circled by friends from school.

It took Jack a while to separate her from the group. Then he led her out on to the terrace, which was lit by pale pink paper lanterns strung around the sides.

"If the trees weren't bare, I'd think it was summer," Lauren said, taking a deep breath of the fresh, cool air. "What were you and my dad talking about?"

Jack couldn't hold in the news a second longer. He told Lauren about her father's job offer.

"That's so exciting!" Lauren cried. She kissed him enthusiastically.

Walking with his arm around her shoulder, he led her across the crowded terrace. The swimming pool was drained and covered with its winter canvas tarpaulin. He led her past it, past the small pool house and into the large, sloping garden, away from the lights and the music. They stepped over the wet grass, walking around the carefully trimmed evergreens and shrubs.

"I shouldn't have complained," he said softly. "It's turned out to be a great party. Totally awesome. "

"I think Fluffernutter stole the show," Lauren said, snuggling against him.

"Fluffernutter stole the salmon," he corrected her. "I should've brought *my* pet. That would liven up the party."

"Your snake?" She made a disgusted face. "Yuck."

He pretended to be hurt, as he always did when she insulted his snake. "I think Ernie is cute," he teased.

Lauren started to say something – but only managed a choked gasp as a dark figure, arms raised to attack, leaped out at them from behind a tall bush.

TWO

Jack threw his arms up as the dark figure lunged at him, wrapping him in a tight bear hug.

"Charlie!" Jack yelped. "Are you *nuts*?!"

"You scared me to death!" Lauren cried, holding her hand up to her thudding heart.

Jack's seven-year-old brother let go of Jack, tossed his head back, and laughed. "Gotcha!"

"You got us, all right," Jack agreed, still feeling the effects of the shock. He reached forward and picked Charlie up off the ground.

"Hey – put me down!" Charlie protested, still laughing.

But Jack held his brother up over his head like a pair of weights and began to twirl him easily.

"Put me down! I'll puke on you!" Charlie screamed. "I had a big dinner, Jack! I'll puke on you!"

Jack quickly returned his brother to the ground.

"Don't be rude," Jack said, frowning.

"Well, you're stupid," Charlie repeated. He said the word a few more times. It was his favourite word. He said it all day long.

"Why don't you go inside and play in the sour cream dip?" Lauren suggested.

"You're stupid, too," Charlie told her. He turned and ran back towards the terrace. "I'm going to tell Mum you two were kissing and stuff!" he yelled before disappearing into the crowd.

"He's so cute," Jack said sarcastically.

"He *is* sort of cute," Lauren said, nestling her head against his shoulder. He smelled her hair. It smelled of coconut.

"He's a shrimp," Jack muttered. "He'll never make the team."

Mentioning the team made him think of the game against Lincoln the following Friday night. "I can't believe you're missing Homecoming," he said, not meaning to whine.

"I know. But what can I do?" She shrugged. "I'll be thinking of you."

"In Paris," he said, rolling his eyes.

"You can beat Lincoln without me, Jack."

"No. You're my good-luck charm," he said, only half kidding.

"That's what I am?" she cried, pretending to be offended. "I'm a good-luck charm? That's why you keep me around?"

"Hey – you're strong," Charlie admitted grudgingly.

"You're a featherweight," Jack said, straightening his tie and jacket.

It was true. Jack and Charlie didn't look at all like brothers. Charlie was short and slender. Jack was tall, broad-chested, with a thick football player's neck, muscular arms, and big hands. Charlie had curly black hair that he wanted kept very short because he didn't like it to be curly; small, dark eyes; and delicate features. Jack had straight, light brown hair that he kept short on top but down to his collar at the back, big blue eyes, and a large nose that looked as if it had been broken even though it hadn't. Charlie always looked serious. Jack seldom did.

"What were you doing behind that bush?" Lauren demanded, holding Charlie in place by pressing both hands against his shoulders.

"Hiding," he said.

"Hiding? Why?" Lauren asked, not letting him go, even though he was trying desperately to squirm away.

"To scare somebody. It's a party, right?"

Lauren laughed. Charlie scampered back out of her grasp.

"Charlie knows how to party," Jack exclaimed, putting his arm around Lauren's shoulder. She shivered. There was a chill in the air. "It's a party, so you scare someone."

"What *else* is there to do, stupid?" Charlie asked, sneering.

He nodded, teasing her. He liked it when her eyes lit up, and her face got all fiery. "That's all," he said. Then he quickly turned serious again. "You're missing the dance and everything."

"Oh, come on, Jack," she cried, giving him a hard, playful shove. "You don't care about the Homecoming dance, do you? You *really* wanted to stand up in front of all those gawking creeps – I mean, all of our classmates – and be crowned Homecoming King and Queen?"

He turned his glance towards the house. The band was taking a break, but people stayed on the terrace, standing in small groups, talking and laughing.

"I know it's all rubbish," he began.

"Yes. It's totally ridiculous," she interrupted.

"But it's kind of an honour," he continued seriously. "And it *is* our last Homecoming dance. I mean, we'll be graduating and everything. I mean. . ." His voice drifted off. He felt embarrassed. Everything he was saying sounded so nerdy.

She looked up at him, holding on to his arm, leaning against him, but didn't say anything.

"Well, you know how everyone expects us to be the perfect couple," he said. "I'll have to answer a million questions. 'Where's Lauren?' 'Why aren't you going to the dance?' 'Have you and Lauren had a fight?'" He shook his head. "It's going to be totally rubbish."

"Hey, I just had a funny idea," Lauren said, a sly grin forming on her face, her greeny-brown eyes catching the light from the half moon in the clear sky above them.

"Huh?"

"I think it would be really funny if you got a date for the dance."

He stared at her, his face filled with confusion. "What? What do you mean?"

She chuckled. "You know. Ask somebody else to the dance. It would be great. You'd show up with some other girl, and everyone would totally freak!"

He studied her face, trying to decide if she was serious or not. "You're kidding – right?"

"Of *course* I'm kidding," she replied. "But it *would* freak everyone out, wouldn't it?"

"You have a weird mind," he said. He wrapped his arms around her waist and kissed her.

The party ended a little after midnight. Jack's mother had taken Charlie home a few hours earlier. Now, suddenly feeling very tired, Jack said goodnight and thanked Mr and Mrs DeMarco.

Lauren, yawning loudly, walked him to the front door. "Don't look so sad," she said. "I'll only be gone a week. I'll send you a postcard from the Eiffel Tower. And I'll think of you all the time. I promise." She gave him a long, sweet kiss.

194

"See you in a week," he said despondently. He started out the door.

"Be good," she called after him. "Stay out of trouble."

Trouble? Jack thought, heading to his car. What a strange thing to say.

How could *I* ever get into trouble?

Three

Jack stormed into the locker room and heaved his helmet across the room. It hit a locker with a loud *clang* and bounced on to the floor.

"Come on, man," Walker urged, slapping Jack's shoulder pad. "We'll get 'em next half. It's not so bad."

"It's nine to nil," Jack growled, kicking his helmet hard as it rolled over to him on the cement floor.

"Hey, we'll catch 'em," Barker, a running back, yelled, sitting down on the bench across from Jack. "I almost broke one, you know. If I hadn't slipped. . ."

Jack looked towards the doorway as his team-mates entered, most of them downcast and silent.

I'm letting them down, he thought, picking up his helmet, inspecting the scratch he had made by heaving it into the locker.

I'm letting them down.

"We've been down before," Walker said, untying his cleats so he could tie them again. "It's no big deal."

"I know I'm going to break one," Barker said. "Just give me the ball over right tackle. Their whole right side is slow, man. I can get around 'em."

"I should have got rid of the ball," Jack said quietly to Walker. "I never should've let 'em get me in the end zone."

"It was my fault," Walker said. "I let that guy through. He just rolled over me like a tank. He must weigh a hundred and forty kilos. And he's only a sophomore."

Jack grabbed a paper cup of water and downed it. Then he took a towel and wiped the sweat off his face. From out in the stadium, he could hear the band going through its Homecoming routine. What was that song they were playing? "Zip-a-Dee-Doo-Dah"?

"I just lost my concentration," he said glumly, scratching his head. "I should've grounded the ball, just heaved it or something. Instead I stood there like a dork and ate it."

He reached into his locker and pulled out his black-and-silver Raiders cap.

I'm letting them all down, he thought. On Homecoming.

At least Lauren isn't here to watch me blow it.

Maybe that's the problem, he thought. Lauren isn't here to watch. At the party last weekend, he was only kidding about her being his good-luck charm. But it was obvious he performed better when he knew she was there, watching him, cheering him on.

Up at the front, across from the showers, Coach Hawkins slammed a locker with his fist, his usual way of getting their attention when they were losing at half-time. "You can beat these guys," he said, his high-pitched voice echoing off the low ceiling. "You just have to execute. It all comes down to who executes best."

"You wear that Raiders cap in the shower?" Walker asked, grabbing it off Jack's head and examining it.

Jack grabbed it back. "It's sort of a good-luck cap. Lauren gave it to me."

"Maybe that's your problem," Walker said, finishing with his cleats, leaning forward to grin right in Jack's face. "You're thinking about the dance."

"I'm not going to the dance," Jack said, his eyes on the coach, who was diagramming a complicated defensive formation on the small chalkboard.

"Huh? What?"

"You heard me," Jack said edgily. "Lauren is in Paris, remember?"

"I don't believe it!" Walker exclaimed, grabbing a plastic water bottle, tilting it over his head, and letting a stream of water run down his face. "The quarterback and the head cheerleader won't be at Homecoming?"

"You can go in my place," Jack said dryly. He tapped his hands nervously against the bench. He hated half-time. It was always his most nervous time of the game. "You got a date, Walker?"

"Yeah," Walker nodded, drying his face with a towel.

"With who?"

"I don't remember. I called so many girls. I don't remember which one said yes." He laughed.

Jack forced a laugh, but he was thinking about the game. And about Lauren.

My good-luck charm, he thought.

"Hey – did you hear me?" Coach Hawkins cried, glaring at Jack.

Jack looked up, startled. "Yeah, I heard you," he lied.

"Well, let's see you do it," Hawkins squeaked. "You guys can beat Lincoln in your sleep."

"We just can't beat 'em when we're awake!" Walker whispered.

"Let's get out there," Hawkins yelled, heading for the door.

"Go Tigers!" someone yelled.

"Go Tigers!" several voices repeated.

I've got to get up for this, Jack thought. I'm not going to be a loser on Homecoming. No way!

He jumped to his feet and stood up on the bench so the rest of the team could see him. "Let's kick their butts!" he shouted, gesturing with his helmet high over his head. "Let's kick their butts! Go Tigers!"

His cheers got them all shouting enthusiastically.

That's more like it, he thought.

Pulling on his helmet, he jogged out of the locker room, and led his team on to the field. His heart began to pound as he stepped under the bright, white lights, the cheers from the stands rising over the drums of the departing marching band.

He ran down the line of players, slapping everyone a high five, a tradition he had started. The quarterback has to be a leader, he told himself.

Now I'm going to show them I'm a leader.

Whoops of victory pierced the silence of the locker room as the Tigers swept in after the game, laughing, cheering, shoving each other, butting heads, a noisy, sweaty celebration that Coach Hawkins couldn't stop if he wanted to.

"We shut 'em out! We shut 'em out!" Walker was screaming, swatting his towel wildly at anyone who passed.

Well, we *did* shut them out in the second half, Jack thought, joining the celebration, chanting along with his team-mates. The final score was 14–9. But, secretly, Jack felt disappointed. The defence had been responsible for both Tiger touchdowns, scoring the last one on a fumble recovery in the final two minutes.

Of course, the stadium erupted into total bedlam. And Jack was thrilled that they were going to win. But happy as he was, Jack wished that he had had a little more to do with the Tigers' victory. He had played his worst game of the season.

I'm glad Lauren wasn't here to see this game, he thought, as he joined the raucous cheers, slapped hands, laughed and shouted with his team-mates, and pretended he was as happy as they were.

The only way Coach Hawkins was able to stop the locker-room victory party was by blowing his whistle until his round face grew as red as a balloon, and then reminding them that they all had to appear at the traditional Homecoming bonfire behind the stadium in less than ten minutes.

After a quick shower, Jack got into his jeans and T-shirt, pulled on his jacket and his Raiders cap, and started for the door, intending to hurry home and skip the bonfire.

"Hey – Singleton!"

It was Walker, pulling a green-and-white Glenview hoody over a T-shirt as he chased after Jack. "Wait. I'll walk to the bonfire with you."

"Is that what you're wearing to the dance?" Jack teased. "Couldn't you have at least found a *clean* hoody?"

"Hey, it's almost clean." Walker grinned. And then he added, "At least I'm *going* to the dance."

"You really are rubbish, man," Jack said, shaking his head. "You really know how to kick a guy when he's down."

"How can you be down?" Walker asked, pushing open the door. A rush of cold air greeted them, feeling even colder because they had just stepped out of a steamy shower. "We won the game, right? In spite of you." Walker laughed to show he was teasing.

"Hey, watch it," Jack said edgily.

"Friends have got to be honest with one another, right?" Walker asked.

"Wrong," Jack said.

"Oh. Then I take it back. You were awesome tonight," Walker said, grinning.

Jack punched him hard on the shoulder. Then the two of them began to jog around the car park to the back of the stadium.

"Hey, we're just in time," Walker said.

Mr Velasquez, the principal, was holding a long, flaming torch, about to light the bonfire. A crowd of two or three hundred Glenview students, parents, and people from the neighbourhood huddled in hoodies, jackets, and winter coats, looking exaggeratedly bright and colourful under the high stadium lights.

Jack followed Walker up to the front. Planks of wood, branches, logs, sticks, rags, old cushions, newspapers, and assorted flammable items had been piled into a mountain nearly two storeys tall.

Across the way, Jack saw three Glenview policemen eyeing the proceedings warily, shifting nervously, their eyes on Mr Velasquez's torch. The Homecoming bonfire wasn't the police department's favourite event, Jack knew. One year, Jack's freshman year, the celebration had got out of hand, and a house had been set on fire.

"Turn off the lights!" Velasquez yelled. A few seconds later, the high stadium lights obediently faded out, surrounding everyone in darkness except for the orange-yellow light of the wavering torch.

A strong gust of wind blew past, bending the torch flame, pushing it downwards. The crowd grew silent, drew closer. Jack pulled down his Raiders cap, then shoved his hands into his pockets.

Get on and light the fire, he thought. It's getting cold out here!

Velasquez, with his usual dramatic flare, raised the torch high over his head, then lowered the flame to the pile of wood. The flames took hold slowly at first. Sticks crackled. A small yellow flame began to spread.

Before long, the entire mountain burst into flame, the orange-yellow light licking up towards the black, starless sky. It's really awesome, Jack thought, looking around the circle of cheering faces. Everyone looks so orange and warm.

He took a deep breath. It smelled so good. A branch crackled and broke, making a group of kids jump back. The flames leaped higher and higher. The fire had become a pulsating, yellow mountain, warm and alive.

"Who brought the marshmallows?" someone shouted.

It got a pretty big laugh.

Jack stepped a little closer, allowing the darting, bright flames to warm him. Velasquez tossed the torch into the fire, then raised his hands over his head, trying to get everyone's attention.

"We had a victory here tonight!" Velasquez shouted in his booming, deep voice. "Let's let the team know we appreciate them. Let's really hear it for the Fighting Tigers!"

This was the excuse the crowd was waiting for to go wild. A deafening cheer rose up, kids slapped hands, and hats and gloves were tossed into the fire. A shoving match started between a group of guys very near the fire, and the three policemen moved quickly to break it up.

The crowd started to chant, "Tigers! Tigers! Tigers!" And when the team paraded in a single line in front of the fire, the wild cheers and celebrating started all over again. Jack got the biggest cheer of all. He grinned and waved at everyone, holding his hands over his head in a double victory sign.

What a night! Jack thought happily. He wished Lauren were there. It would've been so much more fun with her.

And then suddenly the crowd was calming down again, and Velasquez, his face bright red in the glowing firelight, was starting to talk. "We have another bonfire tradition," he shouted.

Jack searched the crowd for Walker, but couldn't find him. Faces looked strange and distorted in the orange light. A picture of rows and rows of jack-o'-lanterns popped into his mind.

What was Velasquez going on about?

". . . when we crown the Homecoming King and Queen," the principal's voice boomed over the crackling and spitting of the fire.

What? Jack wondered. What is he saying?

"And so I'd like to call our Homecoming King and Queen up here right now!" Velasquez shouted enthusiastically. "Jack and Lauren – get up here where everyone can see you!"

"Oh, no," Jack groaned out loud. "Didn't anyone tell him?" He could feel his heart sink down to his feet.

"Jack and Lauren! Let's give it up for them!" Velasquez shouted.

Didn't anyone tell him Lauren isn't here? Jack thought. What am I going to do? This is so embarrassing.

As the crowd cheered, he realized he had no choice.

Slowly, hands shoved in his pockets, keeping his eyes on the ground, he made his way towards Velasquez.

Oh, please, let me die right here, he thought. Before the jokes start. Before everyone has a good time laughing at me.

"Lauren? Where are you?" Velasquez called when the cheers died down.

"She stood him up!" some guy screamed.

The crowd roared with laughter.

Jack felt his face grow hot.

"She had another date!" another joker added.

Another roar of laughter. At Jack's expense.

"Where's Lauren?" Velasquez asked Jack.

"She's in the car park with Walker!" someone shouted.

The crowd thought this was hilarious.

Jack glared angrily into the fire. He had never been so embarrassed in his life, but he didn't want to let these clowns know they were getting to him.

"Lauren isn't here," he told Velasquez, leaning close so the principal could hear him over the crowd. "She's away with her family."

"Oh. Right," Velasquez said, slapping his forehead. "Someone told me that this afternoon." He turned away from Jack to address the crowd. "Lauren is away with her parents. What a shame! But at least we can crown the Homecoming King!"

206

Jack gritted his teeth and let himself be crowned with the stupid crown. He felt like a total dork.

Finally, after a few cheers by the cheerleaders, the bonfire ceremony was over. People started to wander off in groups, still laughing and cheering.

Jack tore off the crown and tossed it into the fire. Then, ignoring calls from a couple of friends, he put his head down and started to run at full speed towards the student car park. His face still felt hot from the fire. The rush of air was cold and refreshing.

"Singleton – you going to the dance?" someone called.

"Hey – where's Lauren?" someone else yelled.

He ignored them and kept running. A car squealed out of the car park, burning rubber as it roared off down Fairwood Street. "Good game, Jack!" a guy yelled from a car as Jack ran past. He acknowledged the compliment with a quick wave, but kept running.

His car, the old Ford his mum had bought second hand, came into view at the very end of the car park. Jack slowed to a walk and reached into his jacket pocket for the car keys.

He was struggling to unlock the front door when he saw something down low against the fence.

It was a girl.

What was she doing down there? Was she OK?

Jack stepped back from his car and walked over to her. As

he came closer, he saw that she was on her knees, leaning over a bicycle, which was lying on its side.

She was wearing a thin, pale green jacket. Her back was turned to him. In the white light suspended over the car park, he could see that she had long, red hair, which flowed down to her waist.

Hearing him approach, she turned her head and gave him a shy smile. "Hi." she said breathily.

Four

"Flat tyre?" Jack asked.

"Yeah." She made a face.

"That's really rubbish," he said, shaking his head.

She's very pretty, he thought. Her long, red hair falling loose behind her was really wild and sexy. And she had a high forehead, and big, brown eyes, and full, red lips.

He thought she looked very dramatic. Like an actress.

I've seen her around school, he thought. But he couldn't remember her name.

"It's a pretty cold night for a bike," he said.

"D'you want to buy me a car?" she cracked. Then she laughed to soften the remark. She had a light, breathy laugh, like her voice.

She got to her feet. He was surprised by how short she was. Her head didn't come up to his shoulders. She looked frail and light in the thin jacket, which flapped in the wind. "I think it's a puncture," she said, and kicked at the tyre. "I'll have to push it home."

"How about a lift?" Jack said, pointing to his car. "We can toss the bike in my boot."

She looked so light and fragile, as if a strong wind might blow her away.

"Thanks," she said, her big, brown eyes examining him. "I'm Shannon Smith."

Right, he thought. Shannon Smith. He remembered her now. She had only been at Glenview for a year or so. He'd seen her sitting in the canteen by herself. She didn't seem to have many friends. He remembered her wild red hair.

"I'm Jack Singleton," he said.

"I know." She looked down at her bike. "Everyone knows *you*," she added, her voice a whisper.

He ran his hand through his short hair. He suddenly felt awkward, nervous. "So? Want a lift?"

Another car squealed out of the car park, the kids inside yelling and singing, the radio blaring. He looked around. The car park was empty now, except for him and Shannon.

"Thanks," she said. "I'm pretty cold." She bent over to pick up the bike. He helped her carry it over to his boot. Then he opened the boot and shoved it in.

She lowered her dark eyes, smiled at him, a teasing smile, and slid into the passenger seat. He climbed in behind the wheel and started the engine.

"Aren't you going to the dance?" she asked, toying with a strand of her hair, tangling it and untangling it around her fingers.

"No," Jack said uncomfortably. He rubbed his cold hands together, waiting for the car to warm up.

"I don't have a date, either," she said softly, playing with her hair. She reached over and touched the back of his hand. "Thanks for rescuing me." Her hand was surprisingly warm. He could still feel the warmth of it after she pulled it away.

He backed up, then headed out of the narrow exit. Up at the school, he could see couples heading in to the dance. He looked for Walker, curious to see who his date was, but didn't see him.

I'm sure I'll hear all about it tomorrow, he thought.

He glanced over at Shannon as he pulled into the street. He liked the way she nibbled at her bottom lip. She glanced back at him, shyly.

"You were good tonight," she said softly.

"You mean at the game?" He shook his head. "I was rubbish. Totally rubbish."

"No, you weren't," she protested, letting go of her hair, dropping her hand to her lap. She scratched the knee of her jeans with slender fingers. "We won, didn't we?"

"No thanks to me," he said moodily, turning on to Park

211

Street.

"Are you always so modest?" she asked, touching the back of his hand again.

Her touch sent a shock of electricity up his arm. "Where do you live?" he asked.

"At Sharpes Corner," she said, looking out of the window. "You know, in the Old Village."

"Yeah, sure," he said. He didn't go to the Old Village much. None of his friends lived there. The houses were old and small and close together. He remembered hearing on TV about a big effort to restore the Old Village to its former glory, or something.

"Do you like football?" he asked, glancing away from the road to look at her. She was playing with her hair again, winding it around one hand. He realized he was very attracted to her.

"Not much," she replied and then laughed at her answer. "But I like going to the games. My brothers all like football. I guess that's why I don't like it."

"How many brothers do you have?" he asked, slowing for the light at Harbour Crossing.

"Three," she said, making a face. "Three big louts."

"Let me guess," he said. "You don't like your brothers?"

"We don't have much in common," she said, sliding down in the seat, raising her knees to the dashboard. "They're all older than me. They're all big. Really big. The oldest one, Joe, was a pro wrestler. A pro. Do you believe it?"

"Wow," Jack said. "Remind me to stay on your good side!"

He had meant it as a joke, but he saw her face turn serious. "I will," she said softly.

They drove in silence for a while. She's so pretty, Jack thought. Why doesn't she have a date tonight?

"D'you want to stop and get a hamburger or something?" he asked. The words popped out. He hadn't really thought about it. As he said it, it felt as if someone else were talking.

I haven't been out with another girl in . . . *how many years?* he asked himself.

Never, he realized.

He'd been with Lauren since sixth grade.

Well, I'm not really *out* with Shannon, he told himself. This isn't a date or anything. I'm just helping her get home. So what's wrong with stopping for a hamburger on the way?

"I'd love to," she said breathily, her voice so soft he could barely hear her.

"Great," he said. "I'm always starving after a game." He turned the car around and started to drive to Henry's, the hamburger restaurant near school where everyone hung out. He had gone half a mile when he decided that wasn't a good idea.

There'll probably be a lot of kids I know there, he thought. And they'll see me with Shannon. And they'll start making jokes. Or they'll start making up stories about me. Or word will get back to Lauren that I had a date with another girl.

Why look for trouble?

"Know any good places in the Old Village?" he asked.

She nibbled at her bottom lip, her expression thoughtful. "Well, there's a Burger Basket on Ridge just before the railroad tracks."

"Sounds perfect," he said. "Let's go there."

"OK," she said softly.

Did she sound a little disappointed, or was he just imagining it?

A few minutes later, he found the Burger Basket and pulled into the car park. There were only two other cars there, he noticed with relief.

This looks like a pretty rough neighbourhood, he thought, looking around at the low, dark buildings and empty car parks across from the hamburger restaurant.

As they walked in through the glass doors, Shannon took his hand. Her hand felt so warm, so light, so fragile. She smiled up at him, a playful smile. Her hair smelled sweet, like cinnamon and oranges.

He guided her to a booth at the back, away from the windows.

Hey, I'm not doing anything wrong, Jack thought.

So why do I feel so strange?

Five

He liked the way she kept touching his hand as she talked. She was always gesturing with her small hands, tugging at her hair, reaching across the table to touch his arm or his hand, as if she had known him for years.

And he liked the way her red hair fell, tangled and wild. Lauren was always fussing with her hair. It had to be perfect, not a hair out of place. But Shannon didn't seem to care. She tossed her hair back over her shoulder as she talked, or twirled a strand around her fingers, or tugged at it, smiling, as she leaned forward to listen to him.

She smiled at him with those dark, pouty lips. Her smile was knowing, almost smug, not at all an innocent little girl's smile.

The restaurant was empty except for a pair of silent old men hunched over cups of coffee, and four tough-looking teenagers Jack had never seen before sitting in a booth next to the window.

He felt comfortable knowing that no one from school would see him here. And he felt excited sitting here with Shannon, a kind of excitement he had never felt in his life. The excitement of doing something wrong.

Or of *thinking* about doing something wrong.

Of course, he kept reassuring himself, there's nothing wrong with having a hamburger with someone and driving her home. It's not like Lauren and I are *married*, he thought, scolding himself for feeling guilty.

"You're a senior, right?" Shannon asked, wiping hamburger juice off her chin with a paper napkin.

"Yeah. You too?"

She nodded. "What are you doing after graduation?"

"Oh, I'm going to Princeton," he said casually. "Where are you going?"

She looked down. "Probably look for a job, I guess."

He could feel his face redden. She must really think I'm a rich jerk, he thought. Why did I assume she was going to college?

"I'm . . . uh . . . hoping to get a scholarship," he added quickly. "My mum can't really afford it unless I get a scholarship."

"Where's your dad?" she asked.

Jack was a little startled by the question. He responded with a broad shrug, as if to say, "Who knows?"

For some reason, this struck Shannon as funny. Her laugh was high and fragile, like the tinkling of a glass wind chime.

They talked for an hour after their hamburgers were finished. Jack was usually exhausted after a football game, but being with her was keeping him wide awake.

They didn't have much in common. She hated school, hated Glenview, seemed generally unhappy with her life but didn't have any plan for changing it. Unlike Jack and Lauren and their friends, she didn't seem to have any ambition, any goals, any dream.

When he asked her what she'd really like to do with her life, she had to think about it. Finally, tugging at her hair, she said, "I don't know. Be a rock star maybe. Maybe be like Madonna."

As he drove her home, she slid low in the seat, her knees on the dashboard. She turned on the radio and cranked up the volume until the entire car throbbed and vibrated, and sang along in her whispery voice, ignoring Jack entirely except to point the directions to her house.

The house was a little box, so small Jack nearly drove right past it. It was entirely dark. He drove up the dirt driveway, his headlights rolling over a rusted pick-up truck, tyreless, up on blocks in the middle of the narrow front garden. The house was white clapboard but looked as if it hadn't been painted for a long time.

Jack clicked off the blaring radio.

"Home sweet home," Shannon said, sighing.

How do her three big wrestler brothers fit into that tiny house? Jack wondered.

He jumped out, ran around the car through the twin white headlight beams, and pulled open the car door. She reached up her hands, and he pulled her to her feet on the soft dirt drive.

To his surprise, she didn't let go of his hands. Squeezing them tightly in her warm hands, she leaned forward, raised herself on tiptoe, and pressed her mouth against his.

Her lips were wet and burning hot.

Her soft hair brushed against his face.

She leaned forward, pressing against him. He started to back away, but realized she didn't want the kiss to end. Giving in to it, he put his arms around her.

She kissed harder, harder.

Hungrily.

Finally she let go. Backed away. Smiled up at him. That sexy, knowing smile.

Wow, he thought.

"Thanks for the lift," she said, breathing hard.

"Uh . . . no problem." He couldn't think of anything else to say. "Hey – almost forgot your bike."

He could still feel the heat of her mouth on his, could still feel the brush of her hair against his face. Feeling crazy and exhausted and excited and confused all at once, he walked quickly to the boot, opened it, and pulled out the bike.

"You can just leave it here. One of my brothers will fix it for me in the morning," she said, pulling the light jacket around her.

He set it down beside the drive.

"Shannon – are you busy tomorrow night?"

"What?"

He walked back towards her. "Do you want to go to a film or something?"

She smiled. The half moon in the dark, starless sky above them sparkled in her eyes.

I don't believe I just asked her out, he thought.

What am I *doing*?

"Yes. OK. Cool," she said.

"I'll come by about seven."

What am I *doing*?

She turned and ran quickly to the dark house without looking back. He climbed into the car, closed the door, and looked for her. But she had disappeared. Probably already inside.

The car bumped over the dirt driveway as he backed out into the street.

One date is no big deal, Jack thought.

Lauren is off in Paris having the time of her life. Why shouldn't I have a little fun, too?

Besides, Lauren will never know . . .

Six

Saturday was grey but not as blustery. It felt to Jack more like a day in late September than November. He had slept in, then had a long, leisurely breakfast. When Walker came over to help rake leaves as they had arranged, Jack was still in his pyjamas.

"You ill or something?" Walker asked, walking in through the back door without knocking, as usual.

He startled Jack from his thoughts about Shannon.

"You look pretty serious this morning," Walker said, grabbing a piece of cold bacon off Jack's plate and stuffing it into his mouth.

"Oh. I was just thinking about . . . the game," Jack said, thinking quickly.

"Great game," Walker said, wandering around the kitchen on his long, lanky legs, looking for more food to scavenge.

"Yeah," Jack agreed, trying to clear the fog from his head. "I'll get dressed. Be right back, man."

"Sure. I'll just make myself a sandwich or something," Walker called after him.

He eats as much as a herd of elephants, Jack thought in his room, pulling on jeans and a hoody. But he's the skinniest, lightest tackle on the team.

A few minutes later, they were raking the front garden, attacking the large, dead leaves with enthusiasm. "Hey, you guys," Mrs Singleton called, poking her head out of an upstairs window. "What are you doing?" She had a pink bath towel wrapped around her head.

"What are we doing?" Jack shouted up to her. "What does it *look* like we're doing? We're raking the leaves!"

"Well, why are you raking in one direction and Walker raking in the other?" she demanded. "You're making two separate piles!"

Jack and Walker looked at each other. "That's just the way we rake," Jack replied.

"The earth is round, Mrs Singleton," Walker added. "Jack and I are bound to meet sometime!"

"Very funny!" she called sarcastically, and slammed the window shut.

"No sense of humour," Walker muttered, leaning on the rake, then pretending to fall off it. He toppled sideways to the ground. Walker loved falling down. He thought it was hilarious. And he was very good at it.

"How was the dance?" Jack asked, thinking about Shannon as he started to rake again.

I can't believe I asked her out, he thought. Am I really going to go through with it?

Of course.

He realized he hadn't heard Walker's reply.

"Hey, everyone was asking about you and Lauren," Walker said. He was raking with the wrong side of the rake. Anything for a laugh.

"Stop messing about. We'll never get finished," Jack said, laughing.

"So what did *you* do after the game?" Walker asked.

"Oh, I just went home and . . . watched a dvd," Jack told him, avoiding his glance.

"Yeah? What'd you see?"

"Uh . . . I don't remember, man. It was just some stupid film Charlie rented."

I'm such a bad liar, Jack thought. I can never think fast enough when I want to tell a lie, and I bet my face is bright red.

Walker, raking in long, slow sweeps, didn't seem to notice. "So what are you doing tonight? Want to come over and play pool or something?"

"I can't," Jack said quickly. Too quickly.

Walker looked over at him. "How come? Hot date?"

"Yeah, sure," Jack said sarcastically, still avoiding Walker's eyes.

Walker laughed at the idea. "Lauren would murder you," he said.

"I . . . uh . . . have to do some schoolwork tonight," Jack lied.

One lie after another, he thought, feeling guilty.

"You? Work?" Walker exclaimed, and fell backwards into the leaf pile he had made. "I thought you got your perfect grades without cracking a book." He sat up. Flat, brown leaves clung to his hair. "Besides, man, they've already accepted you at Princeton. Why knock yourself out?"

"I can't just veg out for the rest of the year," Jack replied. "Then people would think I was *you*!" He laughed at his own joke and tossed the rake to the ground. "This is boring," he said, helping Walker to his feet. "Let's go and check out Ernie."

"You still have that snake?" Walker asked, loping along behind Jack, around the side of the house to the back garden.

"Yeah. I built this cool cage for him," Jack said. "On the side of the garage. I put a heater in it and everything, and Ernie gets plenty of sun and fresh air. Mum wouldn't let me keep him in the house since he got so big. She's scared of him."

"Scared of snakes? How weird!" Walker exclaimed.

Jack gave him a playful shove. Walker pretended to go flying into the side of the garage.

They stopped in front of the large mesh-and-glass cage Jack had built. "Hey, you've practically got a whole tree in there," Walker said, peering in from the top.

"Well, Ernie's a tree snake," Jack explained. "I wanted him to feel at home."

The bright green snake was coiled up in the V formed by two branches, its head hidden from view.

"That's the most amazing colour," Walker said. "That green is almost neon. I'd like to have a shirt that colour."

"I thought *all* your shirts were that colour," Jack joked.

"Just the smart ones," Walker said. "So, how about it, Jacko – change your mind. Come over tonight. You can work next year."

"No, really, I can't," Jack insisted. "I've . . . just got shedloads of work to do."

Going out with Shannon has *got* to be wrong, he thought. And here I am, lying to my best buddy.

But so what?

So I'll be *bad* for just one night.

"Hey, Jack!" His mother yelled from the back door. "Jack – are you there?"

He stepped away from the cage. "Yeah, Mum!"

"The post just came," she shouted. "Come and look. You've got a postcard from Lauren!"

Jack pulled his Raiders cap low over his forehead as he and Shannon walked out of the cinema. "How'd you like it?" he asked, his hand on her back, guiding her towards the car.

He had taken her to the old Westside cinema in the next town, deliberately staying as far away as possible from the multiplex at the mall, or anywhere else he might be recognized.

"It was pretty cool," she said thoughtfully. "But I didn't get some of the humour, I don't think. It was very dry."

He had watched her during the film and hadn't been able to tell if she was enjoying it at all. For the most part, she sat through it, expressionless, nibbling on her lower lip. Near the end of the film, she had taken his hand between hers and held it tightly, staring straight ahead at the screen.

He couldn't help stealing glances at her. She was wearing a tight wool jumper and a very short leather skirt over sheer tights.

I can't believe I'm sitting here with her, he thought.

He was so nervous and excited, he could barely follow the film.

"I thought Will Ferrell was awesome," he said, trying to keep the conversation going. So far, it hadn't been as easy to talk to her as the night before.

225

"Will Ferrell. Is he the funny one?" she asked, lowering herself into the car.

Of *course* he's the funny one, Jack thought as he walked around the car and slid into the driver's seat. Who *else* would he be?

He was starting to think that asking Shannon out was a big mistake when, without warning, she leaned across the gearstick and kissed him.

She smelled so sweet, like oranges. Her hair brushed lightly against his face, tickling his cheeks, sending a chill down his neck.

She leaned back into her seat, smiling at him, licking her lips.

He took a deep breath. "Would you like to go up to Rainer Point?" he asked softly, suddenly feeling nervous. Everyone knew that Rainer Point was a big make-out spot. How would Shannon react to that idea?

Shannon laughed and shook her head no.

Jack felt embarrassed. Too fast, he thought. I moved too fast. That wasn't too cool of me. I'm such a dork! And now she thinks I'm a dork, too!

But then she touched the back of his hand and said, "Let's go to my house instead."

He looked over to see a very playful smile on her face. "What?"

"Let's go to my house," she whispered. "We'll be all alone. My brothers are away, and my parents are at an all-night party."

"Really?" he gulped, his voice cracking.

She nodded her head, her long hair covering her face. "Really," she said, pulling the tangles of red hair away.

He turned the car around and headed towards her house. The night was clear and cold. There were a lot of cars on the road, people out looking for fun on Saturday night. An accident at Penn Crossing had the traffic at a standstill.

They sat in awkward silence. She smiled at him. He tried to think of something to talk about. But they'd already gone over last night's football game again, and they'd already discussed the film, and school, and the weather.

He was grateful when Shannon reached over and turned on the radio. Again, she turned it up until the car felt about to explode, and sang along, so softly he could see her lips moving but couldn't hear her sing.

We don't have much in common, he realized. This will have to be our only date.

But she really is a babe!

When he reached her house on Sharpes Corner, he pulled up the dirt drive and turned off the headlights and the engine. The house was completely dark, as the night before.

As soon as they got inside, she slammed the front door.

Then, staring boldly, almost challengingly into his eyes, she pulled off his Raiders cap and tossed it across the dark room.

Then she started covering his face with kisses.

Wow! he thought. This is *awesome*!

"You're *my* baby now," she whispered, holding his head with both hands as she kissed him.

"You're *my* baby now."

Seven

Jack was woken up the next morning by the phone ringing. He stirred, shook his head as if trying to shake away his sleepiness, and pulled himself up to a sitting position.

Downstairs, he could hear the thunder of Charlie's trainers against the living room floor as he ran to answer the phone. "I'll get it!" he screamed.

Jack yawned and stretched. His head felt like a lead weight. When had he finally rolled back home? It must have been after one in the morning.

And what time was it now? He tried to focus on the digital clock beside his bed, but it was a blur.

"Jack – phone for you!" Charlie shouted from the foot of the stairs, loud enough to wake the dead. "It's a girl!"

"Huh?" Jack said aloud, scratching his head.

Could it be Lauren?

No. Her plane doesn't arrive until this evening.

He lumbered over to his desk, tossed a dirty T-shirt out of the way, and picked up the phone. "Hello?" His voice sounded low and husky.

The voice on the other end woke him up immediately.

"Good morning, baby," Shannon chirped.

"Huh? Shannon?" His throat felt dry. He realized his heart was pounding.

"I had such a good time last night," she said softly.

"What time is it?" Jack asked.

Why is she calling me? he wondered. What does she want?

"It's early, but I just wanted to talk to you," Shannon replied in a little girl's voice. "Did you dream about me?"

"Listen, Shannon . . ." he started. He could hear his mum padding down the corridor, coming towards his room.

"Are you coming over to see me today, baby?" Shannon asked in a tiny voice.

"No, listen. Shannon, I . . ."

Mrs Singleton poked her head into the room. Her platinum hair was piled high on her head, tied with a purple ribbon, but she was still in her dressing-gown. "Who is it, dear?" she asked, her expression disapproving.

"I'll have to call you later about that," Jack said quickly into the phone. "Talk to you later, OK?" He hung up the receiver. "Just a girl from school," he told his mother, trying to sound nonchalant. "She had a question about history homework."

"So early?" Mrs Singleton asked, turning her disapproving gaze on the clock.

Jack could read it now. It was 8:08. Sunday morning.

"I guess she was getting an early start on it," Jack said. "I probably should, too."

He hated lying. Whenever he did it, he had the feeling lights lit up on his face, blinking on and off, "Lie! Lie! Lie!"

"When did you get in last night, Jack?" she asked, tightening the belt on the loose fitting dressing-gown.

"Not too late." Another lie.

"Well, I'm just going down to start breakfast. D'you want pancakes this morning?"

"No. Something light," Jack said, making a face.

He stood leaning on the desk, listening to her slippers thud down the stairs. He heard her ask Charlie what he was doing up so early. Charlie already had the TV on in the living room. Jack could hear the loud boings and crashes of some kind of cartoon show.

I've got to tell Shannon not to call, he decided.

I've got to make it really clear to her that it's over between us. I mean, we just had the one date. It was just a one-time thing.

When he had said goodnight to her, standing in the dark,

narrow hallway of her tiny house, he tried to let her know that he wouldn't be seeing her again. "I'll call you sometime." That's what he had told her. "I'll call you sometime."

The meaning of that is pretty clear, he told himself.

Shannon had smiled back at him in the dark, but she must have understood what he was telling her.

It was over, over, over.

After all, Lauren would be home tonight. He realized he couldn't wait to see her. An entire week was a long time without seeing Lauren.

Much too long.

He showered and pulled on a pair of grey joggers and a hoody. Maybe Walker and I can go to the park and play a little roundball, he thought. Shoot some hoops. Or maybe go on a long bike ride. He felt like getting some exercise.

He was down in the kitchen, finishing his cereal, sitting at the breakfast counter with Charlie and his mother, when the phone rang again.

Jack started towards the wall-phone beside the fridge, but Charlie got there first. "Who is it?" he asked into the receiver. Charlie never bothered to say hello. He always picked up the phone and asked, "Who is it?"

He held the phone out to Jack. "It's for you," he said. Then he grinned. "The same girl!"

Jack caught the surprised expression on his mother's face

as he hurried over and took the phone from his little brother. "Hello?"

"Hi, baby," Shannon said in her whispery voice. "Whatcha doin'? You didn't call me back."

"Uh . . . listen . . . uh . . ." Jack looked back at his mother and Charlie. They were both staring at him. "I'm going to take this call upstairs, OK?" he said. "It's homework stuff." He handed the receiver to Charlie. "Hang up when I get upstairs, OK?"

Grinning, Charlie took the receiver and held it up to his ear. "I can hear her breathing," he said.

"Just hold it for a second," Jack snapped. He hurried out of the kitchen, through the front hall, and up the stairs to his room, thinking hard about how to get Shannon to stop calling him.

"What does she think she's doing?" he muttered to himself aloud.

As he picked up the phone in his room, he was breathing hard from taking the stairs three at a time. "Hi, Shannon. Listen . . ."

He heard giggling, realized Charlie was still on the kitchen phone.

"Charlie?"

"Yeah?"

"Get off the phone. Hang up – now."

Silence.

Jack waited for the click, the signal that Charlie had hung up.

"Charlie?"

"Yeah?"

"Get off the phone!"

Charlie giggled, made a rude noise with his lips, then finally hung up.

"Who was that?" Shannon asked.

"My stupid kid brother," Jack said. "He's really rubbish."

"He sounds really cute," she said. "I can't wait to meet him."

Meet him? thought Jack. Why would she ever meet Charlie?

"When are you coming over, baby?" she asked. "I'm kinda lonely."

"I can't come over, Shannon," he said. He decided to be really straight with her.

"What?"

"Listen, I'm, like, really busy. You know, with school and everything. And I've got stuff to do around here for my mum. And a lot of homework to do."

"Didn't you have a good time last night?" she asked, suddenly sounding hurt.

"Of course, I did," he told her. "I had a great time,

234

Shannon. Really. But . . . but you shouldn't call. I'm very busy now." He took a deep breath. "And I'm not going to be able to go out with you again."

She giggled. "Aw, you're teasing me. Right?"

"No, really. I'm not," he said. "I have to go now. Goodbye, OK? I'll see you at school next week."

He hung up before she could reply.

The receiver was all wet from his hand perspiring. He stood there for a moment, leaning on the desk, waiting for his heart to resume its normal pace, staring at the phone, half expecting it to ring again.

But it remained silent.

Feeling a little better, he headed downstairs to finish his breakfast. Charlie had returned to the cartoons on TV. His mother was unloading the dishwasher. "I thought I'd go over to Walker's. Maybe play some basketball or something," he told her.

She turned around and stared at him, surprised. "Have you forgotten?"

"Huh? Forgotten what?" He picked up a piece of cold toast and chewed it.

"About Charlie's school fair? Remember? You promised to help out?"

"What?" Jack cried. "I did? When did I promise? In my sleep?"

Her expression turned stern. "Come on, Jack. You did promise me. I'm on the PTA, remember. How will it look if you don't show up?"

"But, Mum . . ."

"It isn't anything difficult. Just cloakroom duty. Come on, Jack. You promised."

He hated it when his mother whined like that. But it was starting to come back to him. He had been feeling guilty because he'd promised to take Charlie out bike riding, but then Lauren had come over, and he'd gone off with her instead. And so he'd promised he'd go and help out at Charlie's school fair.

"OK," he said despondently.

What a boring way to spend a Sunday.

His mother smiled. "Good. It should help the time pass for you. When the fair is over, Lauren should be almost home. That's exciting, isn't it?"

"Yeah," he said quietly. He couldn't let on to his mother how pleased he really was that Lauren would be back.

"I'm going to play video games at the fair," Charlie said, coming into the room to get a carton of juice from the fridge.

"You have video games at home," Jack said.

"So?" Charlie hurried back to his cartoons.

A few hours later, Jack was in the noisy, crowded front

hall of Charlie's school, taking coats as parents and kids streamed in for the annual fair. Luckily, it was a clear, dry day, so the coats weren't wet or snow-covered. Across the hall, Mrs Singleton and two other women were selling tickets from large ticket rolls.

"Where's Lauren?" a voice asked.

Jack, weighed down with two long, heavy overcoats, turned to see Mrs Farberson, a friend of his mother's, smiling at him.

"She's in Paris," Jack said. "With her parents. But she's coming home tonight."

"I don't mean to embarrass you," the large, red-faced woman said, handing Jack her fur-collared coat, "but you and Lauren just make the most wonderful couple."

"Thanks," Jack said awkwardly.

"I *am* embarrassing you. I'm sorry," Mrs Farberson said, taking the cloakroom ticket from him. "But you're just so cute together."

Jack smiled, an uncomfortable smile. "Thanks," he said again.

Please go away, he thought.

He hated it when people said that he and Lauren were "cute". This wasn't the first time he had heard it. But he wished it were the last.

"I know your mother is so proud of you," she gushed. She

237

turned. "Oh – there's your mother over there. I must go and say hello. Bye, Jack. Say hi to Lauren for me."

He watched her make her way through the crowd, then went to hang up her coat.

The rest of the afternoon was uneventful. Only three other people asked him where Lauren was, two of them friends of the DeMarcos, commenting on what a wonderful couple they were.

Jack realized he should have been used to the compliments. He and Lauren had been together since sixth grade, after all. But even though he really was nuts about Lauren, it never failed to embarrass him when people made a fuss about what a terrific couple they were.

It's *our* business – not theirs, he thought.

That evening, he, Charlie, and his mother had just finished dinner, fried chicken and chips from a take-away place down the street. He was about to go upstairs to do some homework, when the phone rang.

"I bet that's Lauren," Mrs Singleton said.

Jack hurried over to the kitchen phone and eagerly grabbed the receiver. "Hello?"

"Hi, baby. Aren't you coming over tonight?" Shannon half talked, half whispered, more of a plea than a question.

Jack looked back at his mother, who was staring at him expectantly.

"I'm sorry," he said coldly into the receiver. "We don't need double glazing." He hung up the receiver.

His mother was still staring at him, a thoughtful expression on her face.

"I don't believe those sales people," Jack complained, shaking his head. "They're so rubbish! Can you imagine – calling at dinnertime on Sunday night!"

Why was his mother staring at him like that?

Did she suspect something? Or was he just being paranoid?

He was halfway back to the table when the phone rang again.

Eight

Jack hesitated, staring at the phone on the kitchen wall. It rang again.

"Aren't you going to answer it?" his mother asked impatiently.

"Yeah. I guess." He walked over to it, let it ring a third time, then, with a heavy feeling of dread, picked it up. "Hello?"

"Hi, it's me."

It was Lauren.

"Lauren? Where are you? At home?" he asked, feeling happy – and relieved.

"Yes. I'm home. Totally wrecked. The plane was delayed for over an hour."

"How was it?" Mrs Singleton called from across the room. "Did she have a good time?"

Jack repeated the question. "I had a *great* time!" Lauren exclaimed. "Paris is so beautiful. Like a film set. Not like a real

240

city at all. I just couldn't believe it, couldn't see enough. One day, yesterday I think, I'm too tired to think clearly, we were at Montmartre, looking down from way up high, and it started to snow. This gentle, light snow. It was the most beautiful thing I've ever seen. I don't think I'll ever forget that moment."

"Wow!" Jack said. "Sounds cool!"

"Get down," Lauren said.

"What?"

"Oh. Sorry. I was talking to Fluffernutter. *Get down, you dumb cat.* She won't get off my lap. Jack, I think Fluffernutter missed me more than you did!"

Jack forced a laugh. "That's impossible," he said.

"You missed me?" she asked.

"Of course I did," he said. "It was really rubbish without you around. It just felt so weird."

He couldn't help it. As he said those words, Shannon forced her way into his mind. He thought of Saturday night in Shannon's steamy, dark living room.

"I'm happy to be back, too. I thought about you all the time," Lauren said.

Jack felt so guilty, his words caught in his throat.

"Jack . . . ?"

"Uh . . . listen, Lauren, let's spend all of next weekend together, OK? Just having fun. Just the two of us." He heard the clatter of dishes behind him. His mother was clearing up, noisily loading the dishwasher.

"Jack, have you forgotten? The Junior Chamber of Commerce thing? You know, the Autumn Ball, or whatever they call it?"

"Let's skip it," he urged. He really felt like being with her and no one else. He had to make it up to her for what he had done, for sneaking out with another girl, a girl he had no real interest in.

"We can't skip it, Jack," Lauren said, sighing. "We're being crowned Teens of the Year, remember?"

"So?" he asked, realizing he was sounding just like Charlie.

"So? So they're giving us a cheque," she said.

"Oh. Right. Well," he said, changing his tone, "I'm really looking forward to that!"

She laughed. "Maybe we can sneak out early," she said playfully. "Maybe we'll take the money and run."

"I like the way your mind works," he said.

"Fluffernutter, get down!" she shouted. "Jack, I'd better get off the phone. I'm really tired."

"OK. See you tomorrow at school," he said, not wanting to hang up.

"Yeah. See you tomorrow," she said softly, and then added, "I missed you."

"Me, too," he said and hung up feeling very guilty.

"Did they have a good time?" Mrs Singleton asked, struggling to close the dishwasher. The handle always stuck.

Jack hurried over to help her. "Yeah. She said it was great. It snowed one day."

"In Paris? That must have been beautiful," she said dreamily. "I've always wanted to see Paris in the snow."

Jack's mother had never been abroad. With the two boys to bring up, there was never enough money.

"Well, I'm glad they made it back OK," she said, giving the worktop a final wipe.

Jack suddenly had the urge to get out of the house, to get into the car, to drive somewhere fast, to drive anywhere, to just get away. "I'm going out for a short while," he told his mother, avoiding her glance.

"Are you going to Lauren's?"

"No. She's too tired. I'm just going for a drive, maybe stop at Walker's," he said, heading to the cupboard for his jacket.

"On a Sunday night? Don't you have homework?"

"I'll be back soon," he said impatiently.

"Do what you want." She disappeared up the stairs.

Jack pulled on his jacket and searched the shelf for his Raiders cap. Rummaging through the scarves and gloves and woollen ski hats, he couldn't find it.

My cap. Where could it be?

And then he realized. He had left it at Shannon's.

243

Yes. She had tossed it across the room, and he had never retrieved it.

Maybe I should drive over there and get it, he thought, stepping out through the door into a blustery, cold night. It *is* my favourite cap, after all.

I'll just knock on the door. Stay on the front porch. Ask for my cap.

No way, he told himself.

No way I'm going back to Shannon's. I'm never going back there. Never.

It was a promise he was making to himself, a solemn promise, to him – and to Lauren.

Never.

She can keep the hat.

He climbed into the old Ford and drove aimlessly around town for nearly an hour. Houses and shops whirred by in the darkness as a light fog settled in. Jack paid no attention to where he was or where he was going. He felt like driving, just driving.

He didn't think about anything. The darkness, the cold air, the wisps of soft, grey fog all calmed him. By the time he returned home and pulled the car into the garage, he was feeling very relaxed.

The next morning, he arrived at school early, a little past seven-thirty, and found Shannon waiting for him at his locker.

Nine

J ack stopped short, several metres away. "Shannon?" His voice echoed in the empty corridor.

A warm smile spread across her face. She didn't wait for him to come closer. She ran up to him and jumped up to give him a playful kiss on the cheek.

"Surprised?"

"Yeah," he said, taking a step back. He pulled off his school bag and let it slide to the floor.

She was wearing a bright red jumper that clashed with her red hair, and tight black jeans. Stepping forward quickly, she tilted her head up for another kiss.

"Whoa. Stop," he said sharply.

"It's OK, baby," she replied softly. "It's nice and early. There's no one around."

"Shannon – what are you *doing* here?" Jack demanded.

"I wanted to see you," she said, tossing her long hair back

over one shoulder. "You're my baby now."

"No, I'm not," he said angrily. He picked up his bag and slammed it against the wall. "Stop saying that."

Her dark eyes narrowed. "You liked it on Saturday night," she said. She looked like she was about to cry.

She's a good actress, he thought.

It made him even angrier.

"Saturday night was great," he told her. "But it was just one date, OK? It was great. But that's it. We can't go out. OK? We can't."

"But, baby—"

"Shannon – please!" He looked behind him. A few kids were wandering into the building. Lockers were being opened. Voices echoed down the long corridor. "I'm going out with someone," he told her. "Someone I'm very serious about. She's very important to me and—"

"Hey, man – how's it going?"

A hand grabbed Jack's shoulder from behind.

Jack wheeled around to see Walker grinning down at him. "Where were you yesterday afternoon?" Walker asked. "I called round at your house and . . ."

Walker stopped because he noticed Shannon. "Oh," he said, seeing the desperate expression on Shannon's face and realizing that he had interrupted a conversation. "Sorry, man. I didn't know . . ."

Walker's face filled with embarrassment. Waving his big

246

hand at Jack, he started to back down the hallway.

"No, Walker – wait!" Jack said. "Wait!" He picked up his bag.

"I've got to go," Walker shouted, still looking embarrassed, and disappeared around the corner.

Shannon stepped in front of Jack, blocking his way. The hall was crowded now. Jack looked towards the doors, expecting to see Lauren come walking in.

"You're not being nice to me, baby," Shannon said, putting a hand gently on the front of Jack's jacket.

"Shannon, give me a break—"

"I was so nice to you," she said softly, ignoring his anger, not moving her hand from his chest. "But you're not being nice to me." A tear formed in the corner of each eye.

The bell rang.

She lifted her hand off the front of his jacket. The single tears were rolling down her pale cheeks. She turned quickly and ran.

He stared after her, watching her run through the crowded hall, her hair flowing wildly behind her. A few seconds later, she turned the corner and disappeared from view.

Maybe I finally got through to her, he thought. Maybe she finally gets the picture.

Feeling a lot better, he unlocked his locker and got ready to start the school day.

"Shouldn't I get my coat?" Lauren asked.

"No. It isn't that cold out. Really," Jack urged. "You'll see."

She followed him through the door and on to the lawn behind the school. They were both carrying their lunchboxes. It was Jack's idea to eat their lunch outside, not only for the fresh air but for the privacy.

"It feels like you've been gone a lot longer than a week," he said, sitting down under a large maple tree, bare and wintery-looking. He patted the leafy ground beside him. Lauren sat down.

"You're just saying that to be sweet," she said, affectionately pressing her forehead against his cheek.

"Yeah, you're right," he said, and laughed, casually putting an arm around her shoulders.

It was so easy being with Lauren, he realized. So comfortable. So *right*.

"What have you got?" Lauren asked, removing his arm so she could open her lunchbox.

"Ham and cheese, I think. Every day it's ham and cheese. So boring."

"Well, who makes your lunch?" she asked.

"I do!"

They both laughed.

"It's not too cold out here. You were right," she said, unwrapping her tuna fish sandwich. Half the tuna fish fell out on to her lap.

"Smooth move," Jack said.

"The food was a little better in Paris," Lauren said, picking up a clump of tuna with her hand and putting it into her mouth. "The bread. The bread was the most spectacular thing. I could just live on the bread. It was so good!"

"Better than Hovis?" Jack joked.

"Hey, Jack?" Lauren's tone suddenly changed.

"Yeah?" he asked, with a mouth full of sandwich.

"Who's that girl?"

"What?"

Lauren pointed.

Jack looked up to see Shannon standing on the path a few yards away. Her jacket was open, and she had her hands on her hips as she stared intently at Jack and Lauren.

"Why is she looking at us like that?" Lauren asked.

"I don't know," Jack told her. "I've never seen her before."

Ten

Jack walked home after school, thinking about Shannon. The sky had turned grey and threatening. Gusting winds tossed waves of dead, brown leaves at his feet, but he stepped through them without noticing.

Shannon, what am I going to do about you? he thought.

How can I get through to you?

It had been so embarrassing at lunch. Shannon had stood there like a statue, staring angrily at Jack and Lauren for the longest time. What did she think I would do? Jack asked himself. Go running over to her and invite her to join us?

Why can't she take a hint?

I've been straight with her. I've told her exactly how I feel. What more can I do?

He turned the corner on to his street and saw Shannon sitting on his front steps.

Oh, man.

Now what?

She hadn't seen him yet. She was sitting with her head down, her knees tucked between her hands. His first impulse was to turn and run in the other direction.

But that wouldn't do any good, he realized. She'd be sitting there when his mother got home with Charlie. And how would he ever explain Shannon to his mother?

No. He had to face her. He had to make her understand that she had to leave him alone.

He took a deep breath and, with long, determined strides, walked over the leaf-strewn lawn to the front porch. "Hi, Shannon," he said wearily, letting his expression show how unhappy he was to see her.

"You have to break up with her," Shannon said, raising her head slowly. Her eyes were red-rimmed, as if she'd been crying. Her hair was more tangled than usual, a twisted strand falling down over one eye.

"What? Are you crazy?"

She didn't react to him at all, didn't even look at him. "You have to break up with her," she repeated in a low, steady voice.

"Shannon, there's no way I'm breaking up with Lauren," Jack said, standing over her, shifting his weight uncomfortably. He pulled off his school bag and heaved it on to the path. "No way."

"But you're *my* baby now." She tugged at the strand of hair, but didn't push it away from her face.

"No. I'm not," Jack said firmly. "I'm not! D'you hear me? I'm *not*!" He held himself back. He could feel his anger taking over, feel it turn to rage. He felt himself getting out of control.

Why didn't she listen to him? Why was she doing this to him?

He wanted to hit something. He wanted to hit *her*.

He closed his fists, then opened them again.

Get control, get control, get control, he repeated to himself.

"I'm not good enough for you?" she asked, looking up at him, staring into his eyes with her big, brown, sad eyes. "Is that it?"

"No, that's not it," he said coldly. "We had one date. Now it's over. I've already told you." He looked down the street, afraid he might see the Ford heading home with Charlie and his mother.

"You're hurting my feelings," Shannon wailed, tears running down her puffy cheeks. "You're hurting my feelings, Jack. I'm getting very upset."

"Don't be upset," he said, feeling helpless, nervously watching the street. "It was just *one* date, Shannon. Be fair – OK?"

"My brothers won't like this," she said, wiping her wet cheeks with her hand.

"What?"

"My brothers," she said, sniffling. "They don't like it when people aren't nice to me."

She's threatening me, Jack thought angrily. I don't believe this. She's threatening me with her three monster brothers.

"I'm trying to be nice to you," he said. "I'm trying to be honest. OK? I think you should forget about me. I think . . ."

He stopped. He saw his mum's car turn the corner, Charlie beside her in the front seat.

"Listen, Shannon – you've got to go – *now*." He grabbed her arms and pulled her to her feet.

"Let go of me!" she cried, struggling away from him.

"My mum is almost here," he said frantically. "You've got to go."

"But I want to meet Mum," she insisted, following Jack's gaze to the street. "I think it's time I met Mum, don't you?"

"No!" The car was halfway down the street. "Listen, Shannon – go now and I'll call you tonight," he offered, tugging at the sleeve of her jacket.

"Huh? Really?" Her whole face brightened.

"Yeah. I'll call you. After dinner. We'll have a long talk," he said. "Just go. Now. Please!"

"OK, baby. Call me tonight," she said, smiling for the first time. She started towards the driveway, but he grabbed her and pulled her the other way, to the side of the house.

"Go that way. Call you tonight. Promise," he said.

She ran off, stopping once to look back at him uncertainly, then disappeared through the hedges to the street just as his mum's car pulled up the driveway.

"AAAAAAGH!" Jack screamed, letting out only a little of his anger and frustration.

What am I going to *do*?

Furiously, he picked up his bag and heaved it towards the front door. He hadn't meant to throw it as hard as he did. It crashed into the storm door, shattering the glass.

"No!" he screamed. "Oh, no!"

He could hear the car doors slam around the back, could hear Charlie's high-pitched voice repeating, "I'm hungry! I'm hungry!"

Jack started trudging up the driveway to join them when something caught his eye. A shadow. A large one. Moving quickly from the side of the house, along the hedges towards the street.

"Hey . . ." Jack called out.

He saw a man, a very large man, wearing a long raincoat, appear between the hedges, then quickly duck out of view.

"Hey . . ." Jack called again, at first not believing his eyes.

He stood frozen on the driveway, more surprised than frightened, staring at the hedges that were now still.

Someone was here, Jack thought.

Someone was watching Shannon and me.

And then he realized. It must have been one of Shannon's brothers. "My brothers are enormous," she had told him, and this guy, even seen from behind, seen in a split second, was certainly enormous, his coat billowing behind him as he ran.

"My brothers don't like it when people aren't nice to me," Shannon had said. It was definitely meant as a threat. And one of the three hulks had been standing there the whole time, standing in the shadows at the side of the house, watching, listening.

Maybe the whole family is crazy, Jack thought, chilled by the thought.

What am I going to do?

Trying to conceal his troubled feelings, he hurried around to the back where his mother was struggling with the back door, several shopping bags in her hands. "Jack," she called out, "are you just getting home?"

"Yeah," he lied. He was getting used to lying.

"I'm hungry," Charlie whined.

"I know, I know," Mrs Singleton groaned.

"The front door is broken," Jack said. "The glass on the storm door, it's shattered."

"What?" His mother's mouth dropped open. "How?"

Jack shrugged. "I don't know. I saw it as I came up the drive. Looks like somebody threw something at it."

"Well, maybe we'll just remove it or put the screen back up," she said, frowning. "I can't afford a new storm door." She brightened and held up the shopping bags. "Especially after the money I spent on this."

"What's that?" Jack asked.

"I'm hungry," Charlie shouted.

She pushed open the door, and they went inside. "It's the new dress I bought for Saturday. You know. For the Junior Chamber of Commerce."

"You bought a special dress for that?" Jack asked. He started to open the fridge, but Charlie got there first, darting between his legs to win the race.

"Of course," his mother said, smiling as she held up the silky dress to show him. "It's a special day, isn't it? I had to buy the perfect dress in honour of the perfect couple. I'm just so proud of you and Lauren. Everyone is."

"I'm not," Charlie said. "I'm hungry."

In his room after dinner, Jack tried to concentrate on his history textbook. But he couldn't read an entire paragraph without thinking about Shannon. And about her brother, spying on them.

Slamming the book shut in exasperation, he reached for the phone. I'm going to call Shannon, he decided, and tell her once and for all that I don't want to go out with her again, that I don't want her to ever call me again.

But then he pulled his hand back. No. I've already told her. A hundred times. I promised to call her tonight. But I'm not going to. And when she sees that I'm not calling, she'll realize that I'm serious.

And then her enormous brother will beat me to a pulp, he thought.

He stared at the phone. No. No way. I'm not going to call her.

He opened the textbook again and shuffled through to find his place. He still hadn't found it when the phone rang.

He felt his heart skip a beat. He jumped to his feet.

It rang a second time. A third.

He didn't want to pick it up, but no one downstairs seemed to be answering it. "Hello?" he said softly, timidly.

"Where were you, man?" a familiar voice asked without any greeting.

"Walker?"

"Yeah, it's me. Where were you?"

Jack was so relieved to hear Walker's voice, he could barely hear what his friend was saying. "What do you mean?"

"Where were you? Why weren't you at practice?" Walker asked impatiently.

"Oh, no!" Jack slapped his forehead. He had been so obsessed with Shannon that he'd forgot all about his after-school football practice.

"Coach Hawkins was really steamed," Walker said. "He gave Berman extra time. Had him passing all afternoon."

Berman was the second-string quarterback. He wasn't bad. Jack knew if he slipped up, Berman would take his place in an instant.

"Tell me Berman wasn't any good," Jack pleaded.

"He wasn't bad," Walker said. "He's really got an arm. He can heave the ball a mile. I think Hawkins was impressed."

"You're a real pal," Jack said sarcastically. "I *asked* you to tell me he wasn't any good!"

"So where were you?" Walker asked.

"I was . . . busy," Jack said, struggling unsuccessfully to think of a good excuse. "I had to do some things . . . for my mum."

There was a long silence at the other end. Jack knew that Walker wasn't buying his story.

"You've been acting kind of weird lately," Walker said finally. "Who was that girl you were talking to?"

"Girl?"

"Yeah. You know. Really small. With the wild, red hair."

"Oh. I don't know her name. She has a locker next to mine, that's all," Jack told him.

I'm lying to everyone now, he thought.

He had a sudden strong urge to tell Walker everything, but held back. Walker would just make a joke, Jack thought. Or he might tell someone else. I've got to handle this on my own.

He knew he couldn't take a chance. What if word somehow got back to Lauren?

"Are you sure everything's OK?" Walker asked.

"Yeah. Fine," Jack said. "See you tomorrow, man."

He hung up and reached for the textbook. "How am I ever going to read this?" he asked himself aloud.

The phone rang again.

Walker almost always called back with something he'd forgotten. Jack picked up the receiver. "Hello?"

"Baby, you didn't call." Shannon's whispery voice reverberated in his ear. He could feel his neck muscles tighten.

His entire body tensed. He couldn't hold back his anger any longer. "I didn't call you – and I'm *never* going to call you!" he screamed.

He could hear a sharp intake of breath followed by a low whimper on the other end. He didn't care if he hurt her now. He was too angry to care.

"I don't *want* to call you, Shannon!" he cried. "I don't

want to *see* you! We're not going out. Not ever. Hear? I don't want to go out with you."

He took a breath. His heart was pounding. His mouth was dry. There was no sound at all on the other end of the line.

"Leave me alone," he continued. "I mean it. Leave me alone, Shannon. Don't call me again." He slammed the receiver down without waiting for any kind of reply.

"There," he said aloud and reached for his textbook. "That's done."

Eleven

Jack felt good the next morning, having slept well, a peaceful, dreamless sleep. Lauren called while he was eating breakfast. He was happy to hear her voice.

"I've been thinking about your birthday," she said.

"Huh?" He swallowed a mouthful of Frosties. "My birthday is two weeks away."

"So? How shall we celebrate?" she asked. "Should we have a party or something?"

"A party? No. I . . ." He realized he wasn't awake enough to discuss this. "Can we talk about it later?"

Lauren always did this to him. She couldn't bear to be thinking about something alone. If she had something on her mind, she had to call no matter what time it was and make him think about it, too.

"D'you want to meet after school?" she asked.

"No. I've got football practice," he said. A heavy feeling of dread sank through his body. He knew he was going to get yelled at by Coach Hawkins this afternoon for missing practice. "How about lunch?"

"OK," she agreed. "The usual place. And think about your birthday, OK?"

"OK," he said, and hung up. He gulped down the last spoonful of the sweet cereal, tilted the bowl to his mouth to drink the milk, then started to look for Charlie. "Charlie – where are you? We're going to be late."

Charlie came limping into the room, one trainer on, one off. "I've got a knot in my shoelace," he whined, handing the shoe to Jack.

How does he do it? Jack wondered, shaking his head. How does he get a knot in his shoelace *every* morning?

Jack dropped Charlie off at the elementary school, then continued on to the high school a couple of streets away. When he turned the corner and started down the corridor to his locker, he was relieved to see that Shannon wasn't waiting for him there.

He smiled, feeling better, feeling the sense of dread begin to lift. He locked up his jacket, then, carrying the books he'd need that morning, talked with friends until the bell rang. Shannon was nowhere to be seen.

After the fourth lesson, he met Lauren at their usual

meeting place outside the canteen. "You've had your hair cut!" he exclaimed, immediately noticing her new, short hair.

"Do you like it?" she asked, patting it in exaggerated fashion like a primping film star. "I wanted to look nice for Saturday."

"Are we really going to show up for that thing on Saturday?" he asked, rolling his eyes.

"No. You're going to turn down the money," she replied dryly. "What do you need money for?"

"OK, OK. We're doing it," he said. "But it's going to be so rubbish."

"It's only a few hours of your life, Jack," Lauren said, pulling him into the canteen. "What could be so terrible?"

As they ate their sandwiches, Jack kept alert, looking for Shannon. But she never appeared.

He didn't see her all day. Driving home after football practice, he wondered if she'd be waiting for him on the front porch.

The afternoon was warm for November, but grey clouds were rolling in, bringing a chill to the air. The bare trees seemed to shiver along the sides of the street as he turned on to his street and then pulled up the drive.

He glanced at the front porch then moved his eyes around the front garden.

No Shannon. She wasn't there.

"All right!" he shouted happily inside the car.

He jumped out of the car and stretched. He suddenly felt very light, as if a heavy weight had been lifted from him.

Finally.

I finally made her understand.

Carrying his school bag by the straps, he walked towards the back door. But he stopped on the path, suddenly remembering Ernie, his snake, and lowered the bag to the ground.

I'd better check on Ernie, he thought. I forgot all about him yesterday.

Walking quickly, he headed to the side of the garage. Two fat, grey squirrels scampered along the fence at the back of the garden, kicking up the dead leaves as they ran.

When the cage came into view, Jack stopped.

And gaped.

The top of the screened cage was off, lying on the ground.

Had Ernie escaped?

Jack started to run. How had the top come off? It was too heavy to be blown off by the wind. Someone had to have *taken* it off.

But – wait. The snake hadn't escaped. It was still in the cage.

Yes. As Jack came up to it, he could see Ernie on the glass cage floor.

"Ernie, what's . . ." Jack started to say. But his mouth dropped open in horror, and he never finished his greeting.

The snake, he saw, had been cut in two.

Twelve

"You have to break up with her, baby."

Shannon called him right after dinner. He was upstairs, pacing back and forth in his room, unable to get the picture of his pet snake out of his mind. Ernie had been sliced cleanly across the middle, cut into two almost perfect halves.

Jack was standing right next to the phone when it rang. Startled, he uttered a short cry, then picked up the receiver before the first ring had ended. "Hello?"

"You have to break up with her, baby."

Shannon didn't even bother to say hello. Her voice was as whispery as ever, but there was a hard, determined tone to it, an edge Jack had never heard before.

"Shannon – did you kill my snake?" he asked angrily, balling his free hand into a tight fist.

"You have to break up with her. You *have* to."

"Did you? Did you kill my snake? Answer me!"

"You have to break up with her, Jack."

Jack made the fist tighter and tighter until his hand ached with pain. Slowly, he relaxed his hand. His voice trembled from anger as he spoke. "Stop repeating that and answer my question."

"You've hurt me, baby," she said, her little-girl voice returning. "Please don't make me hurt you again."

"Again? What do you mean by *again*, Shannon?" he screamed. "You're admitting it? You're admitting that you did it?"

"Come over tonight, and we'll talk about it," she whispered.

"What? Are you serious . . . ?"

"Come over," she repeated playfully. "There's no one here but me. I'm very lonely, baby."

"Shannon – I – I'm going to call the police," he said, surprising himself. He didn't know if he was serious or not. He hadn't really thought about it. The words just popped out.

"The police?" her voice grew even tinier. Then, to his surprise, she giggled. "My brothers wouldn't like that."

"I don't care about your brothers," he declared. "I've decided. I'm calling the police."

There was a pause. Then she said softly, "No, you're not. Because then Lauren would find out. Wouldn't she? And her parents. I'd have to tell everyone then, wouldn't I? Everyone would know about you and me, baby."

"Now, wait . . ." He didn't know what to say next. Shannon was right, of course. There was no way he could go to the police. If Lauren found out, she'd break up with him. He'd lose her. He'd lose . . . everything.

Besides, he had no way of proving that Shannon killed the snake. The police would laugh at him, wouldn't listen to him at all.

"Come over, baby," she urged. "Stop being so silly."

"I'm never coming over," he said slowly, speaking each word clearly and distinctly. "Hear me? I'm never coming over. And if you call me, or threaten me, or do something else to me – *anything* – I'll call the police, Shannon. I really will."

He hung up the phone and realized he was trembling all over.

A loud knock on the bedroom door made him jump.

The door swung open, and Charlie came skipping in, a big grin on his face. "What do you want?" Jack snapped, not meaning to sound so harsh, trying to calm down, not wanting Charlie to see how upset he was.

"Can I ask you a favour?" Charlie asked, fiddling with the homework papers on Jack's desk.

"Yeah. I guess."

"It's a pretty big favour," Charlie said.

"That's OK. Go ahead and ask."

"It's kind of a *really* big favour," Charlie said reluctantly.

"Charlie . . ." Jack snapped angrily.

"Could I borrow Ernie?" Charlie asked. "We're having a science show-and-tell, and I told everyone I was bringing a snake."

"No. Sorry," Jack said quickly. He pictured the snake, lying so still and straight, cut into two halves, its insides pouring out on to the glass cage floor.

"Why not?" Charlie asked angrily, shoving Jack's papers across the desk.

"Ernie escaped," Jack said, thinking quickly. "I . . . uh . . . didn't get a chance to tell you."

"He escaped?" Charlie stared up at him, his face filled with surprise.

"Yeah. The lid came off somehow. It was off when I came home, and Ernie was gone."

Actually, Jack had lifted the two snake halves into a plastic bag and buried the bag behind the garage.

"You mean, Ernie is out in the back garden somewhere?" Charlie asked, looking upset.

"I don't think so," Jack told him, putting a reassuring hand on his shoulder. "I searched all over for him. I think he probably went to the woods. Snakes like it in the woods."

Charlie wanted to talk about it more, but Jack had

homework to do and guided him out of the room. That night, Jack couldn't get to sleep. The picture of his pet, sliced so neatly, so coldly, so cruelly, wouldn't fade from his mind.

It was already dark when football practice ended the next afternoon. The sky was inky black with eerie grey streaks of clouds, ghostly images floating low overhead. The air was cold and damp.

"It could snow for the Madison game on Friday night," Jack said, zipping his jacket up to the top, ducking his head into the collar for protection against the damp wind.

Walker pulled his Hard Rock Café cap low on his forehead as he loped along beside Jack. His glasses reflected the light from a street lamp. "I guess snow would help us and hurt them," he said thoughtfully.

"How come?" Jack asked.

Walker shrugged. "No reason. Just trying to sound as if I know something." He laughed. Jack punched him on the shoulder.

They turned the corner on to Jack's street. The wind seemed to blow into their faces no matter which direction they walked. Despite the cold, Walker had his jacket unzipped.

"What are you and Lauren doing after the game?" Walker asked.

"I don't know," Jack replied. "D'you think Hawkins will get off my case before Friday?"

"You know Hawkins," Walker said. "He thinks it's good psychology to make you angry. Thinks it gets you fired up."

"It only gets me angry," Jack said. "I didn't play so badly today."

As they reached the corner, Walker pretended to walk right into the postbox. He hit the postbox hard with his whole body and fell back on to the pavement. Walker was always doing things like that, walking into trees, falling down. It usually cracked Jack up, but he didn't feel like laughing today.

Jack helped Walker up. "I hope you throw better blocks than that on Friday night," he said.

He looked up and saw Shannon standing on the pavement in front of them. The streetlight above cast her in an eerie green glow. She was wearing the same green jacket. Her jeans were tucked into knee-high black boots. In the pale light, she looked frail and tiny, old-fashioned-looking with her long hair flowing freely behind her shoulders, like a Victorian painting of an angel.

"Hi, Jack," she said softly, smiling with pleasure at the shock on his face.

"Shannon, I warned you . . ." Jack said, looking at Walker, who was staring wide-eyed at Shannon and nervously re-adjusting his cap.

"Why didn't you come to see me last night?" Shannon asked, still smiling, stepping closer.

Jack didn't reply. He could feel his muscles tense. He was too angry to be embarrassed, but he wished Walker weren't there.

"Hi," Walker said to Shannon. "I'm Jack's good-looking friend. David Walker. But you can call me Walker like everyone else."

Shannon didn't look at Walker, didn't acknowledge that he was there. "You hurt my feelings, baby," she said to Jack in her little-girl voice. "Why didn't you come over?"

Jack's face was frozen in anger. He refused to reply, hoping his silence would force her to retreat, to disappear.

"Hey . . . if you two want to be alone . . ." Walker said, casting a meaningful look at Jack.

"No," Jack replied quickly. "Let's go, man. I don't know this girl."

"She seems to know you – *baby*!" Walker cracked. He smiled at Shannon, who continued to ignore him.

"Why won't you be nice to me, Jack?" Shannon asked, her tiny voice barely carrying over the wind. "I was very nice to you. Remember?"

"Wow!" Walker exclaimed.

"Let's go, man," Jack said, avoiding Shannon's stare.

He started to walk past her, but she stepped into his path, blocking his way. "Don't go, Jack."

Still ignoring her, he pulled to the right, walking fast. "Let's go, Walker," he insisted.

But Shannon grabbed his arm with both hands, as if making a high shoulder tackle. "Wait, baby."

"Hey – let go!" Jack protested.

Shannon slid her hands down the sleeve of Jack's jacket and squeezed his hand between hers. Jack saw Walker behind them, staring in disbelief. He tried to pull his hand away from her, but her grip was surprisingly strong.

"Don't go, baby," she pleaded, tears running down her cheeks.

"Come on, Shannon – let go of me!" Jack cried.

"You two want to wrestle?" Walker suggested. "How about two out of three? I'm betting on *her*!"

"Let go. I don't want to hold hands!" Jack yelled, surprised by how strong this frail-looking little girl was.

"Don't go. Please – stay with me!" Tears were streaming down her face. "Don't make me hurt you, Jack. I don't want to hurt you."

As she said this, she grabbed two of his fingers with one hand, the other two fingers with her other hand.

"Hey . . . !" Jack cried, struggling to free himself.

But she was so strong, so surprisingly strong.

And then, her face distorted with fury, Shannon pulled down hard, yanking the fingers in two different directions.

At first, Jack didn't feel anything.

He heard the loud *crack*.

It was loud enough for all three of them to hear it.

He screamed as the pain coursed up his arm, then shot through his entire body. Everything went red, then white. He dropped to his knees. He had never felt such pain. His entire right side throbbed. Gasping for breath, he held his arm close to his body, as if trying to protect it, to squeeze away the pain.

When Jack focused again, he saw Walker, looking pale, his mouth open, gulping air, his eyes wide behind the black-framed glasses, gaping at Shannon with shock and disbelief.

Shannon had stepped back under the eerie green light of the street lamp. She seemed to be shocked by what she had done. Wet tears slid down her cheeks. She tugged at the sides of her hair with both hands.

"Shannon – my hand . . ." Jack managed to cry out in a terrified voice he didn't recognize. He held the injured hand up by the wrist with his left hand.

"I'm so sorry, baby," she cried, shaking her head. "I'm so, so sorry." Then she turned and ran, her jacket flapping behind her.

"My hand . . ." Jack called after her. He looked round at Walker. "It's – it's broken!"

Thirteen

Behind him in the stands, Glenview fans cheered and shouted. Jack leaned forward on the bench to get a better view. On the first play from scrimmage, Berman went back to pass. He looked left, then right.

Too long. You're taking too long, Jack thought. You're going to eat the ball.

He was right. Berman was swarmed by three gold-and-green-uniformed Madison players. He hit the ground hard, sacked, and they piled on top of him.

The crowd in the stands groaned and then grew quiet.

Jack turned downfield to see the cheerleaders. They were facing the crowd, clapping in rhythm, shouting a "Go, Tigers" cheer. Lauren stood in the centre, leaping high in her short, green-and-white-skirted cheerleader uniform. She looks great, Jack thought.

Shifting the heavy cast on his hand, he turned back to the

game in time to see a handoff to Barker, stopped at the line of scrimmage. Third down. The Madison players seemed really fired-up. A cheer went up from the Madison supporters on the other side of the field.

Jack groaned as the next play began, and Berman fumbled the snap from centre. Luckily a Glenview player fell on the ball. But now it was fourth down. The Tigers had to punt.

I should be in there, Jack thought, pounding his knee with the heavy, white cast over his hand. He looked down at the cast, feeling his anger starting to rise.

But he realized he was more angry with himself than with Shannon. I let everyone down, he thought. I let Coach Hawkins down. I let the team down.

He looked past the bench towards the cheerleaders. Lauren had turned around to watch the punt. Her short hair glowed golden under the bright white stadium lights. She turned and looked back at him, her smile momentarily fading. Their eyes met. He waved at her with the cast. She turned back to the field.

I let Lauren down, too, Jack thought dejectedly. And her parents. And everyone else who believes in me.

The punt was short. The Glenview supporters behind the team bench groaned. Madison would be starting out on the Glenview forty-five.

"*Dee-fence! Dee-fence!*" the cheerleaders were chanting.

After Shannon broke Jack's hand, Walker had taken him to casualty at Glenview General. On the way, Jack had to explain a little bit about Shannon, after first making Walker swear to total secrecy.

"She's been after me for weeks," he lied, feeling bad, feeling guilty about all the lying he'd had to do. But what choice did he have? "She calls me, and comes to my house, and follows me everywhere," he told Walker. "She wants me to go out with her, but of course I won't. She's crazy. Just plain crazy."

"You've got to call the police," Walker urged.

"No, I can't," Jack said, resting his head on the seat in Walker's car, grimacing as his hand throbbed with pain. "The police won't do anything."

"But she broke your hand, man!" Walker exclaimed, nearly driving through a red light. "That's assault, isn't it?"

"She'd just say it was an accident," Jack said softly, afraid to tell Walker the real reason he didn't want to call the police. Afraid to tell Walker any of the real story.

"Well, at least you can call her parents," Walker suggested, turning into the hospital driveway. "Let them know what their daughter is doing. Tell them she's got to be put on a leash or something."

"Yeah. That's a good idea," Jack had said thoughtfully.

Walker was right, he realized. He *could* call Shannon's parents and tell them that Shannon was driving him crazy. Or maybe even talk to one of her brothers.

The whole family couldn't be as weird as she is – could they?

He told everyone, including his mother, that he had slammed his hand in a car door. Lauren had been terribly sympathetic. She called him a clumsy idiot, but she said it in a nice way. Coach Hawkins hadn't been as nice.

That night, trying to get to sleep, Jack kept hearing the crack his fingers had made as Shannon pulled them in different directions. The pain had subsided, but his hand itched constantly, and of course, he couldn't scratch it.

The next morning, he tried calling her house at lunchtime, hoping to catch someone at home while Shannon was at school. He had carefully rehearsed what he was going to say, repeating it endlessly in his mind. He was going to tell them that he was a friend of Shannon's and that as a friend, he was calling to say that she needed help, that he was very worried about her. He was going to tell them that she had been calling him constantly, following him around, and threatening violence.

It was the truth, after all.

If they weren't sympathetic, he was going to threaten to call the police. He hoped he wouldn't have to do that. He wanted to stop Shannon. But he didn't want to get her so upset that she'd do something drastic, like call Lauren.

Despite his endless rehearsal of what he was going to say, his heart was pounding as he punched in her phone number. The phone rang and rang, but no one answered.

He tried again right after school. Again, there was no one at home.

That night, he dialled her house again, hoping that one of her parents or brothers would answer. But he immediately recognized Shannon's breathy "Hello?" and slammed down the phone.

Her "hello" had sounded so eager, so hopeful, that for a moment Jack had felt sorry for her. But then he glanced at his hand in the big, white cast and remembered that the football season was over for him, as were his chances of being named player of the year, and he felt only anger.

He tried calling three more times during the week. But Shannon had answered each time, and each time he had immediately hung up. Finally he gave up the idea, and his carefully rehearsed speech faded from his mind.

Now, here he was on Friday night, sitting on the team bench in his hoody and jeans, balancing his heavy cast on his lap, feeling terribly guilty and terribly sorry for himself at the same time, watching the Tigers lose to a team he knew he could have beaten.

The final score was 21–3.

As the team trudged to the locker room, Jack stayed on the bench, slumping low, feeling chilled by the night air, staring across the now-empty field as people made their way out of the stadium.

"Hey, man, we missed you," Walker said, standing over Jack, his helmet in his hand, his hair matted down on his head, sweat covering his forehead despite the cold night air.

"Yeah, well . . ." Jack stared across the field uncomfortably.

"Only one more game," Walker said, breathing hard. "That girl still bothering you?"

"No," Jack told him, still avoiding his glance. "I haven't seen her all week."

"Hey – that's great!" Walker said. "That's terrific."

"You haven't told anyone about her?" Jack asked nervously.

"No. No way," Walker replied, looking hurt that Jack would ask that question. "You meeting Lauren?"

"Yeah. She's getting changed. Then we're going to get something to eat. Want to come?"

"No. Thanks. I'm going to hang out with some of the guys on the team. Later, OK? I've got to get changed." He jogged off towards the locker room.

Jack stayed on the bench for a while, staring at the shiny green turf, thinking about Shannon and about Lauren. He was startled when the stadium lights went out, casting everything in darkness.

Standing up, he turned to see Lauren watching him from the track at the edge of the field. "Hi," she called, waving. She had changed into jeans. Her coat was open, revealing a white jumper. "What on earth are you doing?"

"Nothing much," he said, hurrying over to her. "Just waiting for you."

"You were sitting there feeling sorry for yourself," she said, taking his arm and giving him a quick kiss on the cheek. Her nose and lips felt hot against his cold face. "Admit it."

"Maybe a little," he confessed, smiling guiltily.

"Well, I have some news that should cheer you up," she said, holding tightly on to his arm as they walked to the car park.

"The Junior Chamber of Commerce has disbanded, and we don't have to go to that stupid thing tomorrow?" he joked.

She slapped his arm, accidentally hitting the top of the cast. "Oh. Sorry. No. My news is that Dad has decided to take on an intern for the summer at his firm, and you're it."

"Huh?"

"You heard me, Jack. You can work as an intern there this summer, and he'll even pay you. Not a lot, but it'll give you some spending money for when we're at Princeton in the autumn."

"Wow! That's great!" Jack exclaimed, brightening.

"Am I cheering you up?" she asked, clinging to him, pulling the coat together with her free hand.

"Yeah. You're doing a great job," Jack said sincerely.

"Well, here's more," she said, grinning at him. "Dad says you can come up to Cape Cod with us in August and stay for two whole weeks."

Jack stopped and turned to her. "Really?" He hadn't been looking forward to August. He knew Lauren would spend the whole month up at the Cape with her family, and he wouldn't get to see her. "That's awesome!" he declared.

"Stick with me, kid," she said playfully. "I'll show you a good time."

"August is a long way away," he complained. "It's only November."

"Hey – I'm trying to cheer you up," she said, laughing. "Give me a break."

"Please – don't say *break*," he groaned, holding up his cast.

She gave him a playful shove. He reached for her, but then stopped short as the car park came into view.

There, leaning casually against the bonnet of his Ford, was Shannon. She was wearing the same clothes as the last time he'd seen her – jeans tucked into high black boots, the green jacket, which she always seemed to wear no matter how cold it was.

Had she seen him?

No. Not yet. She was looking towards the other stadium exit.

Looking past her, trying to decide what to do, Jack's eyes bulged in surprise. Someone else was standing a few cars down, hiding in the shadows, keeping low behind a black Jeep.

It was the large man Jack had seen running along the hedges from his garden. Shannon's enormous brother!

A wave of fear shot through him. Why had Shannon brought her brother? Why was he hiding in the shadows a few cars away from Shannon?

She had already broken his hand. Wasn't that enough? Now what did she and her huge brother have planned for him?

"Uh . . . can we take your car?" Jack asked Lauren, trying to make his voice sound normal.

Lauren looked at him, confused. "Huh? Why?"

"Uh . . . mine doesn't have much petrol," he lied.

"Well, OK. I'm parked on the street," she said, still clinging to his arm. "Your muscles are all tight," she said, squeezing his bicep through his jacket. "How come you're so tense?"

"You just excite me," he cracked, leading her quickly in the other direction, away from the car park.

"Hey – what's the rush?" Lauren protested.

"I'm hungry," he lied. "Let's go and get a burger."

Did Shannon see me? he wondered. What is she doing there? Is she going to wait there all night?

He turned back to look.

"Oh!" He gaped in horror as he saw the flames shoot out from the front seat of his car.

Still standing a little in front of the car, Shannon stared at him, hands on her hips, just stood and stared, as still as a statue, bathed in the yellow glow of the fire.

Fourteen

"I have to tell you something, Shannon, and you have to listen to me," Jack said, softly, seriously.

She tugged at a strand of her hair, but didn't reply.

They were sitting on the sofa in her living room, its cushions worn and sagging. The only light came from a dim bulb in the back hallway.

She edged closer to him, her face covered in shadow. He could smell the sweet, flowery perfume she was wearing.

"Will you listen to me?" he asked softly. "I have the feeling that you do not listen to me, Shannon."

She leaned forward, bent her head, and brushed her hair against his cheek. It sent a shiver of excitement through him.

"Shannon . . . ?" He really wanted to talk to her, to communicate with her. He had to set things straight, once and for all.

She pressed her head against his shoulder, a tender gesture.

"Shannon . . . ?"

"You hurt me, Jack," she whispered.

He leaned away, tried to get some room between them. "That's what I want to talk to you about," he said.

The ceiling creaked. What was that sound? Footsteps? Was someone walking around upstairs?

"You hurt me," she repeated. She raised her head and stared at him, her dark eyes burning into his. "And when I get hurt, I hurt back," she told him, still whispering.

"That's what I wanted to talk to you about," he said, edging away, trying to back away from the warmth of her, the fragrance of her perfume. "You see, I can't see you. Ever again."

She stared at him, her face expressionless, beautiful in the dim light.

"I know we had something really special," Jack said. "But you have to understand that it's over. I really can't see you."

She remained silent. The only sounds now were the creaking of the ceiling, her soft, rhythmic breathing, the insistent pounding of his heart.

"Do you understand?" he asked, raising his voice for the first time.

"Let me see your hand," she said, reaching for him.

He pulled his arm away. "You broke my hand, Shannon. Why do you want to see it?"

"Let me see the other hand, baby. I want to tell your future."

"No," he insisted. "I'm *telling* you the future. I cannot see you again."

Her lips puckered into a childish pout.

"Do you understand? Do you finally understand?" Jack demanded.

"I'm very hurt," she said, still pouting. "You have hurt me a lot, Jack. And my brothers don't like it when I'm hurt."

As she said this, the floorboards creaked and groaned. The room filled with dark figures, moving quickly through the shadows, large figures, lumbering noisily.

A light went on overhead. Three enormous men stood in front of the sofa, glaring at Jack. Even though they were indoors, all three were wearing long trench coats with wide lapels. All three had round, red faces, topped with short-cropped white-blond hair.

"My brothers don't like people who hurt me, Jack," Shannon said in her whispery voice, speaking tonelessly, without any expression at all.

"Now, wait . . ." Jack started, suddenly terrified. He looked up at the three identical brothers looming menacingly over him, so big, so muscular, their faces locked on him, seething in silent anger.

"Get him," one of the brothers said, raising his arms as if to perform a stranglehold.

"Get him," the others grunted.

Jack uttered a low cry and shrank back on the sofa as the three enormous men circled it, then closed in on him.

Fifteen

The phone was ringing.

He stirred, pushed himself up, and squinting against the morning light, looked for Shannon's brothers.

The phone rang again.

"It was a dream," he said aloud, his throat still clogged with sleep.

Of *course* it was a dream. An ugly, frightening dream. But just a dream.

He picked up the phone and cleared his throat. "Hello?"

The dream lingered in his mind. He expected to hear Shannon at the other end.

"Hi, did I wake you?"

"Lauren?" He was relieved to hear her voice. He glanced at the clock. Ten-twenty.

"Who were you expecting?" she asked teasingly. "Your mystery girl?"

Her joke sent a shock wave down the back of his neck.

Did she know something? Did she mean something by that?

Of course not.

Don't go completely mental, Jack, he scolded himself.

"I guess I slept late," he said uncertainly. "What's going on?"

"That was so horrible with the car last night, I just wondered how you were," she said.

"I'm OK, I guess. Mum took it pretty well," he told her, remembering the night before with a shudder. It all came back to him in a series of ugly pictures flashing before his eyes: the flames licking up from the car, Shannon seeming to disappear into thin air along with her mysterious brother, Jack running to the car, the fire engines, the hoses, the crowd of onlookers.

"Did the firemen figure out what caused the fire?" Lauren asked.

"Yeah. They think it was a match," Jack told her. "They think someone came out from the game, lit up a cigarette, and tossed the match into my front seat. It was so rubbish of me to leave the window open."

Of course, Jack knew that wasn't how his car was set on fire. He knew that Shannon had done it. He could still see her standing there staring at him and Lauren as the flames grew higher and higher behind her.

I've got to talk to Shannon, he thought. I've got to make her see that this all has to stop.

He glanced down at his broken hand. It itched like crazy. He banged the cast against the wall, but it didn't help.

This all has to stop. It *has* to!

"Mum's making her famous waffles for breakfast," Lauren said.

"Is *that* what smells so good?" he joked, sniffing loudly into the receiver.

"Why don't you hurry up and get dressed and come over for breakfast?" Lauren suggested.

"Well, no I—"

"Don't say no," she interrupted. "Say yes."

"But I'm going to see you in a few hours at this stupid Junior Chamber of Commerce thing."

"Oh, I see," she replied sharply. "And seeing me twice in one day would be too much for you, huh?"

"OK. I'll be there in fifteen minutes," he quickly agreed. "Don't eat all the waffles before I get there."

"Me?!" she cried with exaggerated indignation. "You pig! I'm not the one who swallows the waffles whole! I wouldn't touch your stupid waffles!"

"Don't yell," he said softly.

"Why not?" she screamed.

"Because I have a broken hand."

She laughed. "You're weird, Singleton. Hurry over, OK? I want to show you the dress I'm wearing this afternoon. Wait till you see it. It's hilarious. It looks like something my grandmother would wear."

"Can't wait," he said sarcastically. He faked a loud yawn.

"Hey – be a good sport about this afternoon," she said.

"Huh?"

"Be a good boy at the Autumn Ball and maybe I'll buy you a balloon."

"See you," he said, and hung up.

When he came downstairs, his mother was on the phone with the insurance company about the car. "Be home in a few hours," he whispered. She looked up, concentrating on her conversation, and gave him a quick wave. "But I need a car right away. Can you get me a replacement?" she was saying.

Feeling guilty, Jack headed out the front door and began walking to Lauren's house, only four streets away. It was a clear, crisp day. The sky was bright blue and cloudless.

Much too nice a day to be cooped up with the Junior Chamber of Commerce, he thought unhappily.

The waffles cheered him up a little. Mrs DeMarco kept pouring more batter on the waffle iron, bringing replacements to the table so fast Jack could barely keep up. Finally, feeling stuffed, he begged her to stop. "I won't fit into my jacket this afternoon!" he told her.

"Speaking of that hideous jacket," said Lauren, getting up from the table, "come and see my dress." She grabbed his hand and dragged him to her room.

"Hey, what's wrong with my jacket?" he asked, pretending to be offended. They'd had this conversation before.

"It looks just like a horse blanket I saw at the riding stable last week," Lauren told him.

"Yeah, but what's *wrong* with it?" he joked.

They both laughed. She closed the door to her room, threw her arms around his neck, and kissed him. "You always make me happy," she said.

Normally he'd feel happy, too. But this morning, every nice thing Lauren said just made him feel guilty.

She pulled the dress out of the wardrobe. He agreed that it was weird-looking. It was a blue sheath dress made of some sort of shiny material. "I'm going to look like a grown-up," she said, holding it up in front of her. "And you're going to look like a horse!"

"Lay off my jacket," he grumbled, making a sour face.

She whinnied at him, doing a pretty good imitation of a horse.

"Give me a break, Lauren!" he cried.

She whinnied again, laughing. He started to chase her around the room. Laughing, they stumbled out on to the landing.

"It's still early," she said, taking his hand. "We don't have to be there till two. Come out into the garden for a while."

She led him downstairs and out through the sliding glass doors. They crossed the terrace, stopped to look at the covered swimming pool, then started walking slowly, arm in arm, down the wide, sloping lawn.

"Dad's really excited that you're going to intern at his place this summer," she said, taking a deep breath of the fresh, sweet-smelling air.

"Not as excited as I am," Jack told her.

"I think it's so cute how he's kind of adopted you," Lauren said chirpily. "I think he always wanted a son. Instead he got me."

"You're all right," Jack said, grinning.

"Thanks a bunch," she said sarcastically, giving him a playful shove.

She stopped suddenly. "What's that?"

Jack followed her stare. There was a small, dark object lying in the grass near the wooden fence.

"That's odd," Lauren said. "Let's see what it is."

As they stepped closer, walking quickly over the wet grass, the object came into view. It was a black cap, lying upside down.

"Hey – isn't that the Raiders cap you always wear?" Lauren asked.

Jack gasped.

"How did your cap get back here?" Lauren asked him, puzzled.

"I don't know," he said, overwhelmed by a sudden feeling of dread.

He held back while she ran to get the cap.

"Lauren? Wait!" he called.

But he was too late.

She bent over to pick up the cap, looked inside it, then, raising her hands to her face, started to scream.

Sixteen

"What is it?" Jack cried, running over to her, his heart pounding.

"It – it's Fluffernutter!" she wailed.

Jack put an arm around Lauren's heaving shoulders and stared into the cap. The white cat was dead, its blue eyes already sunken back in a gruesome, glassy stare. Its body had been bent and stuffed tightly into the baseball cap.

"Who did this?" Lauren wailed, tears pouring down her cheeks. "Who did this?"

Jack stood gaping at her. Lauren had always seemed to be in complete control. He had never seen her cry before.

"Fluffernutter!" she cried. She picked up the baseball cap and cradled it against her chest. "Poor Fluffernutter."

Shannon did this, Jack realized.

I left the cap at her house. She never returned it.

Until now.

She'll do *anything*, he thought. *Anything.* She doesn't care what she kills or who she hurts.

He stared at the cast on his hand. First Shannon took out her jealousy on me. And now she has taken it out on Lauren.

What am I going to do? What *can* I do?

I've go to stop Shannon. But how?

"Who did this?" Lauren demanded, staring at him now, still cradling the dead cat in her arms. "Who?"

"I don't know," Jack said softly, his arm around her tenderly. "I just can't imagine . . ."

How long can I keep lying to Lauren? he asked himself.

How many more horrors is Shannon going to commit before I'm forced to tell Lauren the truth?

"Who did this? Who did this?" Lauren repeated, holding the cat tightly, closing her eyes. Then she opened them and stared at Jack, her expression hardening. "How did Fluffernutter get in your cap? How did your cap get in my back garden?"

"I don't know," Jack lied. "I haven't seen the cap for days. I lost it over a week ago."

"You lost it?"

"Yeah. I've been looking and looking for it," he said. "I think maybe I must've left it at your house sometime."

"Poor Fluffernutter," Lauren said, wet tears covering her eyes again. "I just don't understand this." She stared hard at Jack, as if expecting him to have an answer.

He gently took the cap with its twisted corpse out of her hands and set it back down on the ground.

I've got to tell her the truth, he decided.

I've got to stop lying. I just can't take this any more.

I'll tell her about Shannon. Lauren will be hurt and upset, but she'll forgive me. And once she knows the truth, we can both go to the police. We can stop Shannon once and for all.

Jack took a deep breath. "Lauren – I have to tell you . . ."

But before he could say another word, a large, dark figure stepped up from behind and grabbed Jack by the shoulder.

Seventeen

Jack spun around in terror.

"Mr DeMarco!" he cried.

Lauren's father grinned at him, squeezing his shoulder. "Sorry if I startled you. How is my favourite couple today?" He was wearing a smartly tailored, black wool suit, already dressed for the afternoon affair.

"Dad – Fluffernutter is dead!" Lauren wailed, pointing down to the cap on the ground. "Somebody killed her!"

Mr DeMarco's broad smile shrank to an open-mouthed look of shock, and his normally ruddy face paled. He let go of Jack's shoulder as he saw the contents of the cap.

He didn't say anything. His mouth froze in an O of surprise and puzzlement. He leaned his head down to examine the cat, then looked up at Jack. "Isn't that your cap?"

Jack felt his face grow red. "Yes," he muttered. "It's been lost for days."

"How strange," Mr DeMarco said, tucking his tie back under his suit jacket with a trembling hand. "How strange."

It isn't strange at all, Jack thought guiltily.

I could explain it to you in less than a minute.

But the desire to explain, to tell the truth, had left him. He knew he couldn't face both Lauren and Mr DeMarco together. They would be so disappointed in him. So hurt by his betrayal.

Things would never be the same again, Jack realized.

Silently, he walked back to the house with them. The walk took only a few minutes, but it seemed like an eternity.

The Junior Chamber of Commerce Autumn Ball was held in the ballroom of the Sheraton hotel. The room was vast, with rows of crystal chandeliers suspended from the high ceilings over the dozens of round banquetting tables spread over the room. There were tall flower arrangements as a centrepiece on every table. A large parquet dance floor stood to the right of the tables. In the front of the room, beyond the table of honour, stood a low stage where the dinner-jacketed orchestra sat.

Jack immediately saw that he and Lauren were just about the only young people in the room. They arrived a little after two to find the place already crowded, the orchestra already playing some lilting lift music, waiters passing through the room with silver trays of hors d'oeuvres, a long line at the punch bowl.

Jack's mother had her platinum hair piled high on her head and moussed until it stood as stiff as a sculpture. She wore her new cocktail dress, the brightest dress in the room. But Jack didn't mind. He was used to his mother's flamboyant style. Actually, he realized, the clothes she wore and her platinum hair were the only flamboyant things about her.

Mr and Mrs DeMarco were somewhat sombrely dressed, especially in comparison with Mrs Singleton. Mr DeMarco wore his black wool suit with a dark, narrow tie. Mrs DeMarco had chosen a tailored grey suit, the colour just a shade darker than her greying hair, with a high-collared white shirt, offset by a dark blue silk scarf worn loosely as a tie around her neck.

Lauren actually looked sensational in the blue sheath dress she had made fun of that morning. It had seemed dowdy and old-fashioned when she held it up in her room. But on her, Jack thought, it became a very sexy party dress.

But of course, none of them were in a party mood this afternoon.

Mr DeMarco had buried Fluffernutter by the fence in the back garden. Jack's Raiders cap had been thrown into the rubbish bin.

They had all come to the hotel together in Mr DeMarco's BMW. Mr DeMarco had tried to cheer everyone up by telling funny stories he had heard at work. But, still thinking about the murdered cat in the back garden, they were a pretty grim crowd.

Now they entered the ballroom with forced smiles. The adults hurried to greet friends, shaking hands, kissing cheeks. Jack and Lauren got in line for some punch, both of them feeling tense and uncomfortable.

Jack had dreaded this afternoon for weeks. He knew it would be boring and difficult, keeping a smile plastered to his face for hours as people, mostly friends of the DeMarcos, congratulated Lauren and him, slapped him on the back, and told them what a good-looking couple they made and how proud everyone was of them.

But after what had happened, it was even harder than Jack had imagined to keep it together. He didn't feel like smiling at these people, like making small talk about the warm winter they'd had so far, about school, and about the Tigers and what a shame it was that Jack had broken his hand and couldn't finish the season.

Knowing how his hand had been broken, knowing how Lauren's poor cat had been killed – knowing that he himself was largely responsible for the terrible things that were happening – was driving Jack over the edge.

He felt like tearing off his stupid sports jacket and the tie that was choking him and tossing them in the bin. Then he'd run out the door and keep running.

Away from Lauren. Away from the DeMarcos, even though they'd been so nice, so giving. Away from his mother. Away from Glenview. Away from everyone he knew.

Away from . . . Shannon.

He'd run and run and never stop.

"What are you thinking about?" Lauren asked, filling a glass with dark purple punch and handing it to him, some of the liquid spilling over the sides.

"I'm thinking about how great you look in that dress," he lied. He spilled a little of the punch back into the gigantic crystal punch bowl.

She forced a smile. "And I'm thinking how that jacket *still* looks like a horse blanket!"

He laughed, pleased to see her smile again. They headed towards a corner, away from the dance floor crowded with people talking and laughing, where they could drink the awful, sweet punch in peace.

But there was no escape today.

"Kids! Kids!" cried an excited woman's voice, and Mrs Benedict, the president of the Junior Chamber of Commerce and organizer of this event, came hurrying over. She was a tall woman, as thin as a rake, dressed in a straight, black skirt that emphasized her slimness. She wore four or five huge, sparkling rings on her fingers and had at least six strands of gold and emerald beads around her neck, which clattered noisily as she came running up to them.

"Oh, we're all so excited!" she gushed, beaming at them both. "You two look wonderful."

Lauren thanked her. Jack nodded, nervously straightening his light brown hair with one hand.

"We're going to have lunch. Then I'm going to present your awards to you," Mrs Benedict said. "And the cheque, of course," she added, and laughed a high-pitched laugh.

"Thank you," Lauren said. Jack repeated her words, shifting his weight uncomfortably, staring down at his empty punch cup.

"We're all so proud of you," Mrs Benedict said. "You're both just so exceptional. And I understand you're both going to Princeton next autumn. How wonderful!" She stopped. And blinked. "I'm embarrassing you, aren't I," she said in a subdued voice.

"No, not at all," Lauren said quickly.

"Everyone's being so nice to us," Jack added.

"I didn't mean to make you uncomfortable," Mrs Benedict said. "I know this must be hard for you. My son Oliver – you know Oliver – well, he refused to come today.

He's at home playing video games. I'm sure you'd rather be doing that, too. It's just so refreshing to meet two truly *nice* young people these days."

"Thanks," Lauren and Jack said. They both shook hands with Mrs Benedict, and she walked away, her necklaces clinking.

"She's not so bad," Lauren said, watching her stop to greet some late arrivals.

"Her son's a total nerd," Jack said, sniggering.

"I don't think anyone wearing that sports jacket should call anyone else a total nerd," Lauren cracked. "And what about that tie? Is that a clip-on?"

Jack made an unhappy face, but he was secretly pleased that Lauren was making jokes again. "Save my place against the wall here, OK?" he asked, handing her his empty punch glass.

"Where are you going? Are you ducking out?" she asked suspiciously.

"No," he told her. "I'm going to the gents. We can't be together *every* second, you know."

She stuck her tongue out at him. He rolled his eyes and started off across the room.

"Hey – what happened to your hand?" a middle-aged man in a red blazer asked as Jack passed.

"Hunting accident," Jack replied. He didn't know why he

said that. The words just came to him. He decided he was starting to feel a little better, too.

He was making his way past the rows of tables when a guy he recognized as a cousin of the DeMarcos came hurrying up to him, a concerned look on his face. "Hey, Jack!" he called.

Jack tried to remember his name. "You're Paul, right?"

"Right," the guy said, not smiling. "I think you should go to the lobby."

"Huh?" Jack wasn't sure he heard him correctly.

"I think you're needed in the lobby," Paul repeated, his forehead wrinkled with concern. "There's someone out there. A girl."

Jack had a heavy, sinking feeling. "A girl? In the lobby? Why do they need me?"

"Well . . ." Paul reached a hand over his shoulder and rubbed the back of his neck. "Sorry. Stiff neck. I woke up with it."

"What about this girl?" Jack demanded.

"She doesn't have an invitation, so they're not letting her in. But she says she's your date." Paul looked meaningfully across the room at Lauren, who was still talking to her father.

"My date? That's complete rubbish," Jack said. "They should just send her away. I don't know who it could be." He lowered his voice confidentially to Paul. "Why would anyone want to crash *this* party?" He laughed.

305

Paul didn't seem to catch his humour. "Well, the lunch is going to be really something," he replied, studying Jack's face. "You'd better hurry up. The hotel people are waiting for you, Jack."

"OK," Jack said, realizing he had no choice. He could feel all of his muscles tense as he turned and walked to the ballroom doorway. He could hear his mother calling him from somewhere near the stage, but he just kept walking, taking long, steady strides.

What am I going to do? he thought, trying to fight down the panic he felt.

What am I going to say to Shannon? How can I get rid of her before anyone sees her?

A gong rang behind him in the ballroom. He heard chairs being scraped across the floor. Lunch was being served. He had felt hungry a few moments before, but now his stomach was tied in a knot.

He stepped out into the hallway. Two uniformed hotel workers, serious-looking young men with slicked-back black hair and hard expressions, were standing beside a wooden desk that had been set up to check off guests on the list as they arrived.

And there was Shannon. Standing between them, her arms crossed over her chest.

Jack stopped at the doorway and stared at her.

What did she think she was doing? How did she have the nerve to come here?

Her hair had been carefully brushed for once, he saw, and tied back with a red hair ribbon. She was wearing a bright red dress, very tight, cut low in the front, very short, ending only halfway down her thighs.

She unfolded her arms to gesture at the two hotel guards, and Jack saw that she was wearing short, red gloves that matched her dress.

Is that her idea of dressing up? Jack thought. He was no fashion expert, but he knew that Shannon didn't look right for *this* place!

She looked so . . . tacky. Why had he ever thought she was cute? What had he seen in her?

He cleared his throat nervously and started towards her.

She saw him while he was still halfway across the lobby and called to him. "Jack – here I am!"

"Shannon – what are you doing here?" he asked coldly, stepping up to the desk. One of the guards kept Shannon back, holding her by the arm.

"Tell them who I am, baby. They don't believe me," she said in her little-girl voice, making her eyes really big.

"She doesn't have an invitation, sir," the guard said, letting go of Shannon's arm. "Is she with you?"

"I'm your date, right, Jack?" Shannon asked before Jack could reply to the guard.

Jack stared at her. "Shannon, I can't believe you're doing this," he said, his heart pounding but his voice low and steady.

"Tell them, Jack," she said, smiling at him, ignoring his words. Her lips were covered with bright red lipstick. Some of it had smeared on to her front teeth.

"Why, Shannon?" Jack asked, more of a plea than a question. "Why are you here?" He glanced back to the ballroom entrance, hoping no one was coming to look for him.

"I'm your date, baby," she insisted in her tiniest voice. "Tell them." Her voice remained tiny, but her eyes narrowed and her expression grew hard.

She pulled away from the guards and latched her arm around his.

"Sir, is she with you or not?" the guard asked impatiently.

"Tell them, baby," she said, pulling him towards the ballroom doors, her face hard, determined. "I'm your date. I'm coming in. I want to meet everybody."

Eighteen

"No," Jack cried, trying to disentangle himself from her. "You can't!"

"I'm going in with you, Jack." She clung to his arm, holding him tightly, staring up at him, her dark-lipsticked mouth set in a stubborn pout.

My life will be ruined, he thought, feeling himself overcome with panic. If I walk into the ballroom with her, if Lauren sees me with her, if everyone sees her – my life will be ruined.

That's what Shannon wants. She wants to ruin my life.

"No!" he cried again, and pulled himself free of her grasp.

"Miss . . ." one of the hotel guards called, stepping around the desk, an alarmed look on his face.

"Stop, miss," the other one called, looking suspiciously at Jack.

"I'm your date. I'm going in there!" Shannon screamed. Her dark eyes flared angrily. Then she spun away from him and started to run across the lobby towards the ballroom, moving awkwardly in her red high-heeled shoes.

"Stop her!" Jack pleaded.

She's going to humiliate me, he thought. She's going to humiliate me in front of everyone I care about.

He hesitated only a second. Then, seeing that the two guards were frozen in indecision, he took off after her.

She turned her head back as she ran and saw him coming. "I'm going in!" she yelled.

"No!" He leaped after her, and, ignoring the cast on his hand, made a diving tackle.

"Let go!" she shrieked.

His arm circled her waist. The force of his dive sent them both sprawling to the lobby carpet.

"Aaaiii!" he screamed in pain as she landed on his cast.

Heads turned. A woman across the lobby gasped. The two guards were moving fast towards Jack.

"Let go! Let go! Let go!" Ignoring the pain shooting up his arm, he pulled himself up and forced her down on to her back. She swung her fists up at him. But he had her securely pinned on the floor.

Crying out, she reached up and pulled his tie hard, choking him. As he struggled to loosen the tie with one good hand, she pulled herself out from under him, shoved him hard, and rolled on top of him.

This can't be happening, Jack thought, looking up to see a horrified crowd around them. The two guards were bent over them, trying to pull Shannon off him.

"I'm going in!" she shouted, as the guard lifted her up by the arms. "I'm going in!" Her hair had come loose from the ribbon and was flying wildly about her face.

"What's going on here?" an important-looking man in a dark blue suit cried, breaking through the circle of onlookers.

"I'm going in," Shannon insisted, as the two guards struggled to pull her to the front exit.

Somewhat dazed, Jack climbed to his feet. He touched his cheek. It felt wet. Looking at his hand, he realized his face was bleeding. Shannon must have scratched him as they scuffled.

Trying to catch his breath, he glanced towards the ballroom. Luckily no one had come out to witness the embarrassing scene. He looked around the crowd in the lobby and didn't recognize anyone.

"Are you OK?" the man in the dark suit asked.

"Yeah. I think so," Jack said, holding his cheek. The hand under the cast throbbed with pain.

Shannon was being pulled, struggling and screaming, out of the lobby. People gasped and moved quickly out of the way as the two guards, one on each side, tried to remove her.

I've got to get back inside, Jack thought, feeling a little relieved. Lauren must be wondering where I am.

First, I've got to find a gents and wash off this blood.

Then he gasped as he saw Shannon kick one of the guards hard in the knee. The guard cried out in pain and dropped to the floor.

With a burst of speed, Shannon broke away from the other startled guard, and came running back towards Jack, heading for the ballroom.

"I'm your date, Jack!" she yelled, staring at him, her eyes wild and frantic as she passed him, running awkwardly in the heels. "I'm your date! You can't keep me out!"

"Shannon – stop!" he yelled. He grabbed her again with his one good hand, and held on tight.

"Young man, I – I cannot allow this," the man in the blue suit sputtered. "You and your girlfriend must leave at once."

"But I'm going in," Shannon insisted.

"Shannon – please," Jack begged, holding on desperately to her arm.

Suddenly, she stopped struggling. She looked up at him with her little-girl face and brushed his bleeding cheek tenderly with her gloved hand. "Tell them I'm your date, Jack."

"Young man, I must insist . . ." the important-looking man, obviously the hotel manager, said.

An idea flashed into Jack's mind, an idea born of panic, of desperation.

"Shannon – if I take you out next weekend, will you go home now?" he asked, not loosening his grip on her arm.

"You're hurting me," she cried, staring into his eyes.

Reluctantly he let go of her arm. "How about it, Shannon? Please? I'll take you out on Saturday night. I promise."

"Really?" she asked in her tiny voice. "Just you and me?"

"Yes. Just you and me," he said quickly, seeing that she was considering it. "You go home now, and I promise I'll take you out next weekend."

"You promise?"

"I promise."

"Hope to die?" she asked.

Something about the way she said that gave him a chill. "I promise," he repeated, still breathing heavily, his chest heaving, his heart pounding. "Please, Shannon. Go home, OK? And Saturday night will be our night."

She stared up at him for a long moment, pulling loose strands of hair away from her face, "OK," she said finally.

He breathed a loud sigh of relief, then bent down and picked up her red hair ribbon from the floor. "Good," he said softly, handing it to her.

He looked back towards the ballroom. No one had come

out. He could hear voices and the clink of dishes and glasses. They must be halfway through lunch, he thought.

"Walk me to the door?" Shannon asked, pulling the red ribbon back and forth through her hand.

"OK," Jack quickly agreed.

Anything to get her out of here!

What am I going to tell Lauren?

He felt his cheek. The bleeding seemed to have slowed. Some dark, dried blood flaked off on his fingers.

"I didn't mean to hurt you, baby," Shannon said softly.

"It's OK," he replied, leading her quickly to the door. People were staring at them from all over the huge lobby.

"You'll come to my house on Saturday night?"

He pushed open the glass door and guided her out of the building. "Promise," he said.

The sky was overcast with dark clouds hovering low. It looked as if it might snow. The sudden cold made the cut on his face sting.

She looked up at him one more time as if trying to read in his face whether or not he was telling the truth. Then, without saying another word, she turned and began running along the path that led past the hotel car park, her clunky red shoes clicking over the pavement.

What have I done? he thought. And then: What am I going to do?

314

He watched her as she passed the car park, running so awkwardly, not looking back. And then he saw the figure step out from behind a parked car in the main drive.

It was Shannon's brother. Jack recognized him immediately even though he had never clearly seen his face. He recognized him from his enormous size and from his long coat.

The man was moving quickly towards Jack, pointing at him, calling to him even though he was too far away for Jack to make out the words.

Does her brother follow her everywhere? Jack wondered. What does he want?

Jack had no intention of waiting to find out. He spun around, pulled open the door, and nearly knocking over an elderly couple who were trying to exit, bounded back into the hotel.

He won't follow me into the ballroom, Jack decided. Taking long, quick strides, he headed across the lobby and down the hall towards the ballroom at the back.

He was nearly there when he remembered that his face was cut. Looking down, he saw that his shirt had come untucked during his wrestling match with Shannon, the white flaps hanging down over his trousers. A button had been torn off his sports jacket. His tie hung loose and crooked.

What should he do now?

Behind him, he saw Shannon's brother lumber into the lobby, looking in all directions, obviously searching for Jack.

The ballroom offered safety. But Jack knew he couldn't go back in there looking the way he did. He had to get himself cleaned up a bit first.

Praying that the hulking figure hadn't spotted him, Jack ducked into the gents, pulling the door closed behind him. He looked for a door lock, but there was none.

Moving to the mirrors over the row of sinks, he examined himself. The cut wasn't as bad as he had feared. It was just a scratch, actually. He picked up some paper towels from beside the sink, wet them, and dabbed the dried blood away.

Unfortunately, he had bled on to his shirt collar. He tried dabbing at the stain with the wet paper towel, but it only smeared the blood, making a larger stain.

He combed his hair, surprised that his hands were still trembling. Then he tucked in his shirt and retied his tie.

I don't look too bad, he thought.

Maybe I can go back in and pretend nothing happened.

And then, in the mirror, he saw the door open and Shannon's brother step in.

Nineteen

Gaping into the mirror, Jack hesitated for only a second.

As the big man moved through the narrow corridor that led to the sinks, Jack darted to the cubicles. He leaped into the nearest one and pulled the cubicle door closed, latching it silently.

Did he see me?

Does he know I'm in here?

His heart pounding, Jack climbed up on to the toilet, hunched on the seat, keeping his feet off the floor so they couldn't be seen in the space beneath the cubicle door.

His chest felt tight. He had a strong urge to cough. His fright was making it hard to breathe.

Hunched on top of the toilet seat, he held his breath, forced himself not to cough . . . and listened.

The heavy footsteps against the marble floor grew louder. Closer.

Peering down beneath the cubicle door, Jack could see the man's shadow on the floor. He was standing right in front of the cubicle.

He knows I'm here, Jack thought, still holding his breath even though it felt as if his lungs were about to burst. He knows.

He's standing there, waiting for me.

He's not going to make a move until I come out.

The shadow on the white tile floor shifted. Jack could hear the man's shoes scrape as he moved.

Is he coming to get me? Jack wondered, frozen in fear.

Is he going to force open the door, grab me, and pull me out?

The shadow on the floor seemed to freeze in place. Then, as Jack stared down from his uncomfortable perch, it slid out of sight.

The shoes scraped heavily, moving away.

Jack still didn't breathe, listening to the shoes move against the tiles. When he heard the gents door squeak open and then close, he exhaled loudly, but still didn't move.

He listened carefully.

Silence.

Struggling to catch his breath, he climbed down off the toilet seat. He unlocked the door, pulled it open, and stepped out.

Shannon's brother was waiting for him at the first sink. "Tricked you," he said, smiling. He had short blond hair, a round, red face with small grey eyes over a pug nose.

He took a step towards Jack and pointed with two fingers. "I want to talk to you." He had a reedy, high-pitched voice, a voice much too small for a man his size.

"I've got to g-go," Jack managed to stammer. With a determined burst of speed, he ran towards Shannon's brother, then dodged away from him and raced through the narrow corridor to the exit.

"Wait . . ." the brother cried, lurching towards Jack.

But Jack already had the gents' door open. He ran through it and across the lobby, past the two uniformed guards at the desk outside the ballroom door and into the ballroom.

Dessert was being served from trolleys. Coffee was being poured from silver coffeepots. The room was quiet except for a few low murmurs.

Why isn't anyone talking? Jack wondered, his eyes surveying the room. He quickly understood why. Mrs Benedict was standing in the centre of the main table, about to speak.

Forcing a smile to his face, hoping he looked at least a little normal, Jack made his way through the tables to the front, being careful not to look at anyone. He didn't stop until he reached his table. Then he found his seat and slid in silently beside Lauren.

She turned immediately and stared at him questioningly. "Jack, where've you been?" she whispered. "You missed lunch."

"We're so proud of both of them," Mrs Benedict was saying into the microphone, standing just a few feet away, holding a stack of notecards in front of her. "Before I call them up to award them their prizes, let me tell you a little about these two young people and their accomplishments."

Lauren continued to stare at him, searching his face. Suddenly, her eyes widened in surprise. "Jack – you've been bleeding. What did you do to your face?" she whispered.

"I tripped," he whispered. "In the gents. I fell on to the sink."

Her expression remained one of bewilderment. He wasn't sure whether she believed him or not.

"As you can see, both of them are citizens of the community as well as students," Mrs Benedict was saying. She looked over at Jack and Lauren and blinked hard when she saw that they weren't paying attention to her speech.

"You're sweating like a pig," Lauren whispered loudly. "Jack, are you OK?"

I'll *never* be OK, Jack thought.

Never.

Not as long as Shannon is around.

She's never going to leave me alone. She's never going to quit.

All my plans, all my hopes – my whole life – it's all ruined.

"I'm going to to call Jack and Lauren up now, so let's give them a warm round of applause," Mrs Benedict said.

Twenty

Jack called Lauren on Wednesday night. He had carefully rehearsed what he was going to say, but he was very nervous, uncertain of how she would react.

The phone rang once, and he dropped the receiver. Doing everything with one hand was really difficult, he had discovered. The big cast had been removed on Tuesday, replaced by one that was smaller but just as clunky.

He fumbled around on the floor of his room for the receiver. When he managed to return it to his ear, Lauren was already on the other end. "Hello? Hello?"

"Hi, it's me," he said.

"Jack, have you been avoiding me?" she asked.

"Huh? What are you talking about?"

Did she suspect something about Shannon?

"I haven't seen you since Saturday afternoon," Lauren said.

"Yeah. I know," he said. "I've been working and stuff."

"You've been kind of weird lately," she said. "I mean, weirder than usual."

"Is that a compliment?" he joked.

"Is anything the matter?" she asked.

What a question!

"No," he said. "Not really." There was an awkward silence, and then he began his prepared speech. "Lauren, would it be OK if we don't go out on Saturday night?"

"What?" The question seemed to take her by surprise.

"You see, my cousin is sick up in Meritville, and I thought I'd drive up and see him on Saturday night."

"I thought you didn't have a car," she said suspiciously.

"Mum got a hire car from the insurance company. It's actually much better than our car," he said.

"But can you drive with one hand?" she asked.

She suspects something, he thought. That's why she's asking so many questions.

"Yeah. No problem," he said. "I know we usually go out on Saturdays, but Eddie has always been a real pal and—"

"Jack, I think you're confused," she said, suddenly sounding very cross.

"What?"

This wasn't going right, he realized. She was supposed to be sympathetic. She was supposed to tell him it was perfectly all right for him to go and visit his sick cousin.

"How could you forget your own birthday?" she cried.

"Huh?"

"You can't visit your cousin on Saturday night, Jack. That's the night we're celebrating your birthday, remember? I've made big plans. I'm picking you up at your house at nine and taking you somewhere very special." She paused and then added sharply, "Doesn't *any* of this ring a bell?"

"Oh. Yeah," he said.

How could he have forgotten his own birthday? Lauren had made such a fuss about how she was going to plan something really cool.

Oh, well, he thought, sighing. Lauren isn't picking me up till nine. That'll give me time to get over to Shannon's early. I'll talk to Shannon, tell her I can't ever see her again, get everything straight with her once and for all, and be back at my house by nine.

"I feel like a total dork," he told Lauren. "I – I just wasn't thinking clearly. Forget everything I said. I'll go and visit my cousin on Sunday."

"That's better," she said. But she still sounded very suspicious.

"Uh . . . Lauren?"

He had this sudden urge to tell her how sorry he was. He wanted to tell her that he hadn't meant to mess everything up. He wanted to tell her that Shannon didn't mean anything to him, that he didn't even like Shannon, that she was a mistake, a horrible mistake that he had regretted from the first night he had met her.

He felt like telling Lauren everything, just letting it all spill out. Not to cleanse himself. Not to make himself feel better. But just to let Lauren know that he didn't like having to lie to her, that he didn't like what Shannon had forced him to become.

"Yes?" Lauren asked, a little impatiently.

"I just want you to know I care about you," he said. His throat tightened. He couldn't say any more.

"Me, too," she said quickly.

"No matter what happens," he added.

"What?" she cried. "What do you mean? Jack?"

"I'll call you," he said and gently hung up the phone.

Twenty-One

Saturday was grey and cold. A sharp wind blew down from the north, toppling rubbish bins, sweeping the fallen dead leaves over the front garden like a crackling, brown river. The sun never appeared, and by late afternoon it was as dark as midnight.

Jack didn't notice the wind or the cold as he climbed into the white hire car a little after six o'clock to drive to Shannon's house. Thinking about her, about all she had done, about all she *could* do to ruin his life, he had felt edgy all day. But now, as he backed down the drive and headed towards the Old Village, his nervousness gave way to anger.

He had had only one date with Shannon. He had made no promises to her. He hadn't misled her in any way. What right did she have to keep pestering him, to follow him, to call him constantly, to try to invade his life?

She had no right. No right at all.

His mind whirled as he repeated over and over the things he planned to say to her. All of his attempts to get through to her, to make her stop, to get rid of her, had failed.

But not tonight, he told himself. Not tonight.

Tonight would be different. Tonight he would *make* her understand. Tonight he would make her *promise* to leave him alone.

And if she didn't agree?

He would talk to her parents. Or her brothers. He would tell them how unbalanced Shannon was. How dangerous.

Dangerous.

Well, Jack thought, I can be dangerous, too.

I can get tough if I have to.

Distracted by his angry thoughts, he sped through a stop sign. The squeal of another car's brakes alerted him to what he had done, but he didn't look back.

I'm going to make this short, he told himself, glancing down at the digital clock on the dashboard. Six-twenty.

He knew he had to be back home by nine, when Lauren planned to pick him up.

No problem, he thought.

As he drove into Shannon's neighbourhood, the houses passing by in the darkness were smaller and closer together. A burst of wind shook the car. He gripped the wheel tighter with his left hand, his other hand resting uselessly on his lap.

Halfway down the street, he squealed to a stop. He had driven right past Shannon's house. Cursing to himself, he threw the car into reverse and backed up along the curb. He parked at the bottom of her dirt driveway. Then he turned off the engine and climbed out, slamming the door behind him.

The house was dark except for a dim yellow light glowing behind the lowered blind in the front window. Jack jogged up the drive, ducking his head against the strong wind.

Why did I ever come here? he thought.

Why did I ever get involved with her?

He couldn't decide if he was more angry at Shannon or at himself. His temples throbbed as he climbed the two steps of her front porch. He felt strange, out of control, angry, and nervous – and a little frightened.

Taking a deep breath, he raised his hand to knock on the front door, and it was pulled open.

Shannon stood in the pale yellow light. She was dressed all in white, in a short, straight skirt and a white cotton jumper. Her red hair shone in the light, falling softly down in front of her shoulders.

She smiled at him, her dark eyes lighting up.

She looks like a little angel, Jack thought.

What a joke.

"Hi, baby. You're late," she said softly.

Stepping into the small front room, he didn't return her smile. "Hi," he said, keeping his expression hard.

"Let me hang up your coat," she said, reaching up to help pull off his jacket.

"No. I'm not staying long," he said sharply, looking around at the threadbare furniture, the peeling wallpaper, the bare floorboards. "Are your parents at home? Or your brothers?"

She gave him a devilish look. "No, baby. Don't worry. No one's at home. We're all alone." She took his jacket and hung it up.

She smelled sweet and flowery. He realized she was wearing a lot of perfume.

"Please don't call me baby," he said sharply.

When she turned around, she had a slightly mocking expression on her face. "Why not, baby?" she asked in her whispery voice.

"Because I'm *not* your baby!" he shouted.

She put her hand gently on his shoulder. "I made you a special dinner. Because this is such a special night."

He stared at her, surprised. "You cooked dinner?"

"Yes. Just for the two of us. Look." She pointed to a small table in the adjoining room. It had been set for two. A single candle glimmered in the centre. "Surprised?"

"Shannon, I'm sorry. I'm not going to stay," Jack said. He struggled to remember what he had planned to say, what he had rehearsed over and over in his mind all week. But he was drawing a blank.

"Come and sit down, Jack," she said, taking his hand.

He pulled his hand away. "Didn't you hear me?"

"How's your hand?" she asked, studying the cast. "It doesn't hurt any more, does it?"

"Shannon – don't ignore me," he said, feeling his anger rise.

"That was such a shame, such a nasty accident," she said, pushing her lipsticked mouth into a pout.

"It wasn't an accident," he said, glaring at her. "You did it deliberately."

"I wouldn't hurt you. You're my baby," she said softly. She reached up and grabbed the back of his head with both hands. Then she pulled his head down and pressed her lips against his.

She smelled so sweet. Her lips were so soft.

"*No!*" he screamed.

It was hard to pull away from her, especially with just one useful hand. She grasped the back of his head, holding him tightly. It was no longer a tender hold. It was violent, desperate.

Finally he managed to duck out of her grasp. He backed

away, holding his hand up as if it were a shield. "Stop it, Shannon."

"But what's the matter? Don't you *like* me any more?" Her voice sounded tiny and hurt.

"No," he said flatly.

She stared into his eyes. "You're not being nice to me, Jack."

"I came here to say leave me alone," he said, staring right back at her. "Leave me alone, Shannon. Don't call me. Don't follow me. Don't come to see me."

"I made such a nice dinner for us," she said.

"I want you to leave me alone. And I want you to leave my friends alone," he continued.

"I want this night to be special," she said softly.

"Aren't you listening to me?" he screamed. He could feel himself losing it, but he didn't care.

He had to make her hear him.

He *had* to!

"Listen to me, Shannon. I'm leaving now. Right now. And I'm never coming back. Do you hear me?"

"Don't leave," she said, her face expressionless now. Her smile had faded; her eyes lost their sparkle. "I don't think you should leave."

"What are you going to do? Break my *other* hand?" he cried.

"No," she said softly, "if you leave, I'll do something worse."

"Worse?" His chest was heaving. He had never felt such anger, such frustration.

"I'll tell Lauren," she said.

She waited for him to react, but he just glared at her.

"I'll tell Lauren everything," Shannon said, her face a pale, cold mask, revealing no emotion at all. "I'll go and see her. I'll tell her that you want to be with *me* now."

"No, you won't!" he screamed. "You won't!"

In a total rage, he grabbed her narrow shoulders and began to shake her.

The next few seconds became a noisy blur.

He suddenly felt as if he weren't here in this shabby, dimly-lit living room, as if he were somewhere above it, hovering over the room, watching the boy and girl struggle beneath him.

It wasn't him shaking Shannon so violently. It wasn't him roaring out his rage and frustration. It wasn't him making her head snap back like that, her long hair tossing wildly over her face, then behind her shoulders.

He wasn't doing it. He wasn't struggling with her, pushing her, choking her, slamming her small body against the dark wall.

"You've ruined my life! You've ruined my life!"

He wasn't crying out like that. He wasn't making her cry out.

He was above it, outside it, away from them, watching them.

And then suddenly the blur, the violent blur cleared.

And he saw everything so clearly.

Shannon was on the floor, crumpled in such a strange position, her head tilted at such a strange angle, her white skirt up over her pale thighs.

Her eyes were closed.

He could see everything so clearly.

Her eyes were closed, and she wasn't breathing.

So clear. So clear.

He had killed her.

Twenty-Two

I didn't kill Shannon, he thought, staring down at her, his eyes focusing and unfocusing.

I didn't kill her.

I'm the quarterback. I was player of the year last season.

I should've been player of the year again *this* season.

I'm too young.

I hardly knew her.

So how could I have killed her?

Lauren and I are the perfect couple. Everyone is so happy for us.

So happy.

I couldn't kill Shannon.

I've already been accepted at Princeton. Of course, I haven't heard from the scholarship people yet. But it's almost a sure thing.

Lauren and I will be there together.

It seems we've always been together.

We belong together. We're the perfect couple.

So I couldn't have killed Shannon.

"Get up, Shannon!" he yelled. He nudged her side with the toe of his trainer.

"Get up! Get up – please!"

He stood over her unmoving form. He couldn't bend down. He wanted to, but he couldn't move. He could only stand there.

Maybe I'm dead, too, he thought.

No. That's crazy. Crazy.

I'm the quarterback, Jack Singleton.

I'm the perfect couple.

There's a place waiting for me at Mr DeMarco's agency.

So I can't be dead. And neither can Shannon.

He could see everything so clearly, every detail in the room, every thread in Shannon's white cotton jumper, every hair on her head. Her hair was splayed out on the floor. Her legs were bent beneath her.

Lauren and I are the couple of the year, he thought.

He tried to remember his little brother's name. Why couldn't he think of it?

I'm not thinking clearly, he realized, staring down at her hair, so tangled and wild.

I can see very clearly. But I'm not thinking clearly.

He turned and walked over to the worn sofa. He dropped down on to it, closed his eyes, and rubbed his eyelids with the fingers of his good hand.

Charlie. That's his name.

OK. That's a little better.

He sat with his eyes closed for a long time, waiting for the panic to subside.

I'm just not thinking clearly. I've got to think clearly.

What do I do now?

She can't be dead. So what do I do now?

After all, I'm the quarterback.

Coach Hawkins is really going to yell at me about this.

I'm still not thinking clearly.

Charlie. His name is Charlie.

That's good. That's good for a start. But what do I *do* now?

He got up and walked back to her. "Aren't you going to move?" he asked softly. "Isn't dinner going to get cold?"

Aren't *you* going to get cold?

He had to do something to clear his head. He would never think clearly if he stood staring down at her, waiting for her to move.

He would never get his scholarship.

He would never pass Go and collect two hundred.

I've got to get out of here, he realized.

I've got to go somewhere and think. I'm not thinking clearly here. If I go away, I'll be able to figure everything out.

And then I'll go to Princeton. With Lauren.

I'll call Lauren right now. We can go to Princeton tonight.

No. He wasn't thinking clearly. Lauren wasn't at home.

She wasn't at home.

An idea flashed into his spinning head. Even in the confusion, he knew he could work out what to do if he got out of that house. He knew the cold air would help clear his head. Getting away from her body would help drive away his panic.

Her body?

Why did he think of her as a body now? She couldn't be dead.

He was too young.

And he was very smart. All the tests showed it.

He moved quickly to the front door, grabbed his jacket, and struggled into it, pulling it over his broken hand first, then easing his good hand through the other sleeve.

I'm not thinking clearly. I'm just not thinking clearly.

He searched the jacket pocket until he found the car keys. Then he pulled open the front door and started out.

A strong gust of wind blew him back.

I'm not thinking clearly. I've got to get away, go somewhere quiet, somewhere peaceful to think.

But I can't leave Shannon here.

She's not dead. But what if her parents come home? What if they find her lying on the floor, all twisted like that? They might *think* she's dead.

And I could get into trouble. Bad trouble.

Or what if her brothers come home? They could make a mistake, too. They could think she's dead. And then they'd come after me. Like that one huge brother of hers.

I'm not thinking clearly.

I'd better take her with me. Yes. I'll take her with me. And when I'm feeling a little better, a little calmer, a little quieter, I'll know what to do.

Picking Shannon up was hard, especially with only one good hand. Slinging her over his shoulder was even harder.

Luckily she was small and light.

Not as light as a feather, he thought. But light enough to carry out to the car.

She still felt warm as he draped her over his shoulder, holding her around the back of her legs with one arm. He made his way unsteadily to the front door, thought about getting her a coat, but decided he couldn't put her down again.

Out into the blustery wind. The front garden was dark. There was no porch light. The neighbours couldn't see him.

She started to get heavier as he carried her down the dirt drive. She was slipping off his shoulder.

Just a few more feet, he thought. The wind seemed to be blowing at him from all directions at once, making it hard to move forward, and hard to balance this heavy, sprawling weight.

He was breathing hard by the time he reached the car. Bending down, her arms dangling in front of him, he pulled open the back door. Then he bent lower until she was even with the seat, and he lurched forward, letting her go tumbling off his shoulders and on to the car seat.

She landed face down. He waited, expecting her to pick herself up. But she didn't move.

He pushed the rest of her on to the seat, straightened her skirt, and tucked her legs in. Slamming the door shut, he leaned against the car, gasping for air, struggling to catch his breath, his shoulders aching, his broken hand throbbing all the way up his arm.

Where shall I go?

Got to think. Got to think.

Lauren isn't at home. The words flashed into his mind again.

Lauren isn't at home. She's picking me up at my house.

So he'd take Shannon to Lauren's house. The back door was always unlocked. He'd hide her down in the cellar. Just for a short while. Just long enough for him to start thinking clearly again.

Having this plan made him feel a little better. He stepped away from the car and started to walk around it to the driver's side. He opened the car door, but dropped the keys on to the street.

He found them easily, then climbed behind the wheel.

"Are you still back there?" he called, struggling to slip the key into the ignition with his trembling hand.

No answer.

"Have you put your seatbelt on?" he asked.

Again no answer.

He glanced at her in the rearview mirror. She still lay face down, her hair splayed out at odd angles all around her head.

"I know you're breathing," he called back to her. "I'm just not thinking clearly."

But that would change as soon as he dropped her off at Lauren's. He'd leave her in the basement, in the cedar wardrobe in the rec room. Then he'd go somewhere quiet and think.

The drive to Lauren's was another blur. There didn't seem to be much traffic on the road. Or maybe he just didn't see the other cars.

It seemed like an instantaneous trip to him. A second later, he had pulled up the smooth, curving drive to the back of Lauren's house.

The house was dark except for the outside lights, front

and back. A spotlight above the middle door on the three-car garage shone in his eyes. He climbed out of the car to get away from it.

No one is home, he realized, peering into the back windows.

Breathing a sigh of relief, he opened the rear car door. Then he bent down and started to pull Shannon out of the car. It took a long time to get her back on to his shoulders. For some reason, she seemed much heavier now. By the time he reached the back door, he was breathing noisily, and bathed in sweat.

His entire body ached. He shifted her on his shoulders and reached for the doorknob. She was draped over his shoulders now, like a shawl, her arms dangling down to his right, her legs to his left.

He turned the knob. And breathed a sigh of relief as the door pushed open.

Yes. Unlocked as usual.

He stepped forward, but her arms and legs caught on the sides of the door. Backing up, he turned sideways and slipped into the dark kitchen.

It was warm inside, and smelled of baked apples.

For a long moment, he stood in the doorway, inhaling the sweet smell, waiting for his eyes to adjust to the dark, balancing Shannon on his shoulders.

I'm starting to feel better already, he thought.

Just being away from her house has helped.

Now I'll take her down to the basement and work out what to do.

He turned carefully to the wall and clicked on the kitchen light.

Then, balancing Shannon awkwardly, he turned around.

And as he turned, Lauren, Walker, the DeMarcos, his mother, and about twenty or thirty other friends jumped up from behind the kitchen units, all shouting in unison: "SURPRISE!"

Twenty-Three

"Happy birthday!" Lauren cried, and then her eyes bulged and her mouth dropped open in horror as she saw the girl's body around Jack's shoulders.

Jack reeled back and stared into the crowd of familiar faces. Their smiles seemed to fade in slow motion as their expressions changed to horror and confusion.

Shannon slid off his shoulders and hit the floor with a soft thud. She groaned as she hit the floor and her eyes opened. "Huh?" she cried groggily.

"I knew she wasn't dead," Jack said aloud.

The shock of seeing Lauren and everyone was helping to snap his mind back to normal.

"Jack – who is that? What's going on?" Mr DeMarco demanded. He hurried over and knelt down beside Shannon, who was groaning loudly, lying on her back behind Jack.

"It – it's hard to explain," Jack said, feeling dizzy and weak.

Everything that had happened was coming back to him all at once. He was finally thinking clearly.

"I thought I'd killed her," he said.

There were loud gasps. Everyone started to talk at once.

Walker came over and put a hand on Jack's shoulder. "I recognize her, man," he said quietly. "She's the one who did your hand."

"I really can't talk about it now," Jack said, turning to watch Mr DeMarco, who was still tending to Shannon.

"Jack – who is she?" Lauren demanded.

"I think I need to sit down," Jack said weakly.

Her features drawn with worry and confusion, Lauren took his arm and started to lead him out of the kitchen. The counter, Jack noticed as they passed, was piled high with colourfully-wrapped birthday presents.

"We didn't even have time to get the presents organized," Lauren muttered. "How did you know we were here?"

"I didn't," Jack said honestly. He decided he was going to be completely honest with her, completely honest from now on. He'd tell her everything, and pray that she'd forgive him.

She led him to the kitchen table and pulled out a chair for him. He dropped down on to it gratefully, his head spinning, the loud, excited voices echoing in his ears.

Across the room, Shannon was on her feet. Mr DeMarco

was holding her by the arm. She was tugging at her hair, pulling it behind her shoulders.

"Who is she?" Lauren demanded, standing beside Jack, staring across the room as Shannon talked to Mr DeMarco and several others.

"She's a girl from our school," Jack said quietly. "I met her at Homecoming, the night you were away. In Paris. I did a really rubbish thing. I – I took her out while you were gone."

"You what?" Lauren looked down at him in surprise.

"It's a long story," he said. "I feel really bad. I'm really sorry. But she – she's crazy, Lauren. She wouldn't leave me alone. She killed Ernie, and she broke my hand. She killed your cat, too, and . . ."

He stopped his explanation and jumped to his feet, his eyes growing wide with fear.

Across the kitchen, Shannon had stepped away from Mr DeMarco. As Jack watched, she darted over to the pile of birthday presents, her eyes wild, her expression hard and determined. Without saying a word, she tore the blue and green ribbons off a pair of ski poles propped against the counter.

She grabbed a ski pole by the handle, letting its companion drop to the floor. Her eyes moved slowly around the room until they found Jack.

"Whoa! Hold on!" Jack heard Walker yell from somewhere across the kitchen.

Jack stepped away from Lauren and called to Shannon. "What are you doing?"

She didn't answer him. She glared at him with pure hatred, and raised the pointed end of the ski pole towards him.

"You're not my baby any more!" she screamed, her voice loud and raspy, unlike any sound he had ever heard from her before.

"Shannon, wait . . ." he cried.

But she came rushing at him, holding the ski pole like a sword.

"No!" he cried, frozen to the spot, realizing she meant to kill him.

Screaming at the top of her lungs, she lunged towards him.

He dodged, and the pointed ski pole slid a few centimetres past his side and rammed the wall with a loud *crack*. The handle flew out of Shannon's hand. But she quickly picked it up and came after Jack again.

"No, Shannon – please!" He turned and ran across the kitchen. The back door was open. He heaved himself towards it, thinking only of escape.

And then he stopped short.

Shannon's enormous brother stood on the other side, his face twisted in menace.

Twenty-Four

J ack backed away from the door. "She's OK! I didn't kill her!" he screamed.

Behind him, Mr DeMarco and several others were wrestling the ski pole from Shannon's hands. She was screaming and struggling to keep it away from them.

"Your sister is OK," Jack repeated, his trembling voice revealing his fear as the big man pushed open the door and came towards him.

"Sister?" the man asked in his high-pitched voice. He stared at Jack questioningly and reached into his pocket.

He's got a gun! Jack thought, stumbling backwards.

"Look out – he's going to shoot!" Jack screamed.

But the man pulled a small leather card holder out of his pocket and flipped it open, revealing a police badge. "Lieutenant Jarmusch, juvenile division," he said, and quickly replaced the badge.

Then he bounded across the room, moving very fast for someone of his size, and grabbed Shannon by both shoulders.

She stopped screaming and struggling. She seemed to recognize him. "Uh-oh," she said quietly, rolling her eyes.

"Is everyone OK?" Jarmusch asked, holding Shannon firmly, looking around at the startled faces. "This one can be dangerous," he said.

"Uh-oh," Shannon repeated, shaking her head. "Busted again."

"You – you're not her brother?" Jack asked, his head still spinning.

"Brother?" The big police officer laughed, a high, wheezy laugh. "She doesn't have any brothers. No family at all, as far as I can tell." His expression changed. He looked accusingly at Jack. "I've been trying to talk to you, son."

"I – I thought you were her brother," Jack said, embarrassed.

"Uh-oh," Shannon said and laughed scornfully at Jack.

"This one was sent up for manslaughter," Jarmusch said, holding tightly to Shannon's shoulders. "But she only did juvenile time. You know. Like ten minutes." He sniggered, shaking his head.

"She's been seeing her parole officer regularly. Has her parole officer convinced that she's got her act together. But I had a hunch she was up to no good again. So I've been doing a little surveillance work on her in my spare time. Spare time? That's a joke."

"Uh-oh," Shannon muttered. "He made a joke."

"Just chill out," Jarmusch told Shannon. "It took me till yesterday to get a legal search warrant for her house. Just as I suspected, she's been lying to us about living with her mother. She's all alone in there. No family. Nobody. I've been trying to get enough hard evidence to show that she still needs help. I don't want her to do more time. I just want her to get the treatment she needs."

Shannon puckered her lips and, looking at Jack, made loud kissing noises.

Jack looked away.

Jarmusch did a little more explaining, told Jack he'd need a statement from him tomorrow, then led Shannon away. She didn't resist, looking back longingly at Jack before disappearing through the back door, followed by the bulky policeman.

"I think maybe we'd better postpone this birthday party," Mr DeMarco announced when they had gone. "I think we're all too confused to feel like celebrating."

Jack slumped at the kitchen table as everyone filed out, retrieving their coats from the cupboard. His mother stopped to put a hand on his shoulder. "Are you coming home now?"

"Soon," Jack said. "I want to talk to Lauren first."

When everyone had left, Lauren, sitting across the table from Jack, shook her head. "You sure know how to pick 'em," she said dryly.

He looked up at her guiltily. "Don't be angry with me, OK?"

She reached across the table and squeezed his hand. "Maybe we're just trying to do things too soon, you know." Her face grew serious. "We've been acting like an old, married couple since we were twelve. Maybe it's a mistake."

"I'm the only one who made a mistake," he said softly.

"We don't have to talk about it tonight," she said, still holding his hand. A smile slowly spread across her face. "I'm just angry that that girl spoiled my birthday present for you."

"Present? What present?" he asked.

"The ski poles, of course!"

They both laughed.

"What a birthday!" Jack exclaimed.

"Well," said Lauren thoughtfully, "I'll tell you one thing. This was one surprise party that was a *surprise* – for everyone!"

They were both still smiling as she walked him out to his car to say goodnight.

R. L. STINE

HORROR HIGH

DEADLY RUMOURS

One

The first time I saw Louis Morgan, he terrified me.

I probably should have known then – at that very first moment, staring into the sun at him from my bike – to stay away.

Danger here.

Danger and fear.

I think I knew at that moment that Louis meant trouble. But a person doesn't always listen to these signals. A person doesn't always listen to her sensible self. At least, I didn't.

And before I knew it, I found myself trapped by Louis.

Caught up in his sadness. Caught up in his mystery.

A mystery that began in murder.

It all started on such a beautiful day, warm and promising, fresh as only a day in late April can be.

I borrowed my brother Jake's bike and went riding. I wanted to explore Shocklin Falls, our new home.

Jake's bike was a clunky BMX, heavy and slow, and the seat was too high for me. (Do you *believe* I'm shorter than my little brother? It's so annoying.) But my 21-speed had been stolen just before we moved. So what choice did I have?

I'm seventeen and I have my driver's licence. But you can't really explore in a car.

Bike riding is my passion. I love the rush of wind against my face, the feel of the pedals under my trainers, the control, the way it makes my legs throb and my heart pound.

The total *freedom* of it.

You can't feel that in a car.

Dad promised I could buy a new bike as soon as the insurance company paid for the stolen one. I really didn't want to wait that long. But Dad wasn't in any mood for arguments.

He and Mum are still unpacking boxes. I think they'll be unpacking boxes until next Christmas! You just don't realize how much *stuff* a family of four owns until you move to a new town.

Anyway, I took off on Jake's bike. I'm such a shrimp. I should've lowered the seat. But I was too impatient to get away and explore.

I was wearing shorts and a bright blue sleeveless T-shirt. It was the first really warm spring day, and the afternoon sun felt hot on my back.

I had just washed my hair, which is long and blonde and very straight. I had tied it up. I knew the sun would dry it.

The air smelled so sweet! All down my street, the dogwood trees had blossomed. It was like riding under majestic white arches, so pretty and unreal.

Prettier than real life, I thought.

I get these kinds of thoughts when I'm out bike riding.

It didn't take too long to explore Shocklin Falls. It's a very small town, a suburb of Glenview. The college where Mum and Dad are going to start teaching next term is at one end. Then come quiet streets, shady under rows of old trees, lined with small, nice-looking houses.

The big, expensive houses are out by the falls on the other side of town. And in the middle is a small shopping district – two-storey buildings, mostly, a two-screen cinema, a bank, and a post office. Not much else. The nearest mall is in Glenview.

I rode slowly past the small shops. For a Saturday afternoon, the town wasn't very crowded. I think most people were at home doing spring-cleaning or gardening.

An old car rumbled past, filled with teenagers, its windows open, radio blaring. The noise drew frowns and headshakes from two elderly women about to cross Main Street arm in arm.

A bike shop on the corner caught my eye. I climbed off

Jake's bike and walked it up to the front window. I pressed my nose against the glass, peering inside. It looked like a pretty good selection. I'd definitely have to check it out later.

I climbed back on to Jake's bike and coasted unsteadily off the curb back on to the street. Is that all there is to town? I wondered.

Yep. I'd seen it all.

I circled round once again, then headed towards the falls.

I hadn't seen the famous falls yet. Mrs Pratte, the estate agent who sold us our house, couldn't stop raving about how beautiful and spectacular they are.

So I was saving the best part of my tour for last.

Mrs Pratte described the falls as rising up high on a sheer rock-cliff, then cascading straight down like a steamy, white curtain into the wide river below.

She was good at describing things, which I guess you need to be if you're going to sell property. Anyway, she said it was as pretty as Niagara Falls, except much smaller, of course, and you could see three towns from up at the top.

I followed Main Street past the shopping district and soon found myself in the fancy part of Shocklin Falls. Big houses. Some of them looked like *mansions* to me! A lot of them had teams of gardeners working, planting beds of flowers and weeding and clearing away the dead leaves.

I had a little scare when a snarling German shepherd

came bounding after me. Its owner was yelling for the dog to come back, but of course the dog paid no attention.

I began pedalling furiously, standing up to get better speed. Luckily, the dog gave up halfway down the street and contented itself to end the chase and bark out a warning for me to stay away.

"OK, OK. I can take a hint!" I called back to it, still pedalling standing up.

The big houses gave way to woods. The trees were still mostly bare, the spring leaves just beginning to open. A squirrel scampered up a tree, startled by my silent, gliding intrusion.

I found the cycle path Mrs Pratte had described. It curved through the woods, climbing higher as it went, becoming steeper and steeper as it made its way up through the thick trees.

After about a ten-minute ride, I found myself at the top. I was pleased to see that I wasn't at all out of breath. Being in good shape is really important to me. It's one reason I always prefer my bike to a car.

I kept pedalling. The woods were all to my right now. To my left – the steep cliff-edge, a sheer drop to black rocks below.

I slowed down. There was no fence or anything. At some

points, the cycle path came within a half a metre of the cliff-edge. And the path was really curvy.

I heard the falls before I saw them. A soft, steady roar that grew louder as I approached.

And then the path curved, and the falls were right in front of me.

How can I describe them? They were dazzling.

The white water fell straight down, sparkling like a million diamonds, splashing back up in a shimmery white mist.

Looking down, I could see the wide brown river flowing between green banks. And I could see far into the distance, over trees, over fields. I could see the town, tiny like it was miniature, and beyond it another town, and then, in the misty distance, a third town.

I slowed to a stop. The cycle path ended abruptly at a tall pile of grey granite rocks.

I shielded my eyes from the sun.

And then I saw him.

A teenage boy. Wearing jeans and a yellow T-shirt. He was standing over the falls. Right on the edge.

I gasped and gripped the handlebars. I hadn't expected anyone to be standing there.

He didn't see me. He was staring straight down, down to the jagged black rocks below the falling water.

Still staring straight down, he took a step forward.

My heart stopped.

I realized what he was about to do.

"Stop!" I screamed, trying to be heard over the roar of the falls. "Don't jump! Please – don't jump!"

Two

He cried out and stepped back.

My screams had startled him.

I jumped off the bike and hurried towards him. The bike clattered on to the rocks behind me.

"Hey!" he called. His expression changed from surprise to confusion. He jammed his hands into his jeans pockets and he moved away from the edge, towards me.

He was tall and very good-looking. He was really tanned. He had a cleft chin. He stared at me with striking green eyes.

I guess I was staring hard at him. That's how I managed to see his face so clearly.

"I thought you were someone else," he said, shouting over the sound of the falls. He smiled. A crooked smile, but very gorgeous.

I think I fell in love with him then. Or something like

that. I'm not sure. It's impossible to explain. I was so embarrassed about shouting like that.

"I thought you were going to. . ." I started, but I didn't want to finish my sentence.

He was still smiling, hands jammed into his pockets, his yellow T-shirt fluttering in the wind. "You what?"

"I'm sorry," I stammered. "I saw you at the edge, and. . ."

I get a slight stammer whenever I'm really nervous. And believe me, I was really stammering now!

He laughed. He had a great laugh. Sort of tossed his head back and crinkled those incredible green eyes.

"You thought I was going to jump?" The smile faded. His eyes burned into mine, studying me.

I nodded. I could feel my face turn red.

I tugged at my hair. It was still wet.

"I'm just waiting for someone," he said. "Looks like they're not coming."

"I – I've never been up here before," I stammered, lowering my eyes. I didn't like standing there. I don't normally have trouble with heights. But we were so high up, and the drop was so straight, so steep, and the rocks below looked so sharp and pointed.

"D'you go to Glenview High?" he asked.

I shook my head. "Starting on Monday. We've just moved here. From Ohio. I'm Abbie Kiernan," I said awkwardly. I always find it so hard to introduce myself like that. I don't know why.

"Louis Morgan," he said. He removed his hands from his jeans pockets and shook my hand. Very formal.

He grinned.

I loved the cleft in his chin. And I loved the way the wind blew through his hair but it stayed standing up, every hair in place.

I should have seen the sadness in those green eyes.

I should have seen the fear. The dread.

But of course I didn't.

I should have asked him why he was standing right on the cliff-edge like that, staring down so intently into the crashing waters.

But of course I didn't.

Instead, I said, "It's so awesome up here." Pretty lame, but at least I had stopped stammering.

"Yeah," he replied, scratching his chin.

"The town is so ordinary," I went on. "I mean, it's OK. But it's nothing special. You don't expect to find something like this." I motioned to the falls.

Louis's eyes were on the woods behind me. "I . . . uh . . . left my bike back there," he said. "Wait right here. I'll go and get it."

"D'you like to bike ride?" I asked as he headed past me.

"Yeah. A lot," he called back without stopping. He disappeared behind the wide pile of granite rocks.

I wrapped my arms round my chest and stared out at the town below. Even with the afternoon sun high above, it was a little chilly up here.

What a fabulous spot, I thought.

I knew I'd be riding my bike up here often.

I suddenly wondered if I'd be riding it beside Louis. I had this silly idea that we were fated to meet up here. Like an old black-and-white romantic film.

Maybe I'll ask him to go riding next weekend or something, I thought.

I saw him approaching, walking a sleek black racing bike.

No. He must have a girlfriend, I realized, a sinking feeling in my stomach.

He's too good-looking not to have a girlfriend.

He said he was meeting someone up here.

He leaned his bike against one of the big stones and made his way towards me, taking long, slow strides. "So you've just moved here?" he asked, pulling a long strand of grass from my hair.

"Yeah. My parents are going to teach at the college."

"Weird time to move," he said, staring over my shoulder at the falls.

"Tell me about it," I groaned. "Changing schools and everything. It's horrible!"

He gazed at me thoughtfully. "Are you a senior?"

"Junior," I replied.

"Have you met anybody? Kids, I mean."

"Just you," I said, laughing.

He laughed, too. A silent laugh that sounded more like coughing.

"Then I guess I should show you around or something," he said, suddenly shy.

He should be on TV, I thought. He's so great-looking!

"I could give you a bike tour of Shocklin Falls," he offered, motioning to his bike. "That'll take a minute or two," he joked.

"Well, I've sort of had the bike tour," I said.

And instantly regretted it.

Why did I say that? I scolded myself. He was offering to ride around with me, and I told him no.

What an idiot I am!

I could feel my face redden again.

Louis stared at me thoughtfully. "I'll introduce you to some Shocklin kids," he said.

"Great!" I gushed. "I mean . . ."

He turned his gaze towards the woods, as if he saw something. "I have this friend," he started. "He's my best buddy. I mean, he's a total dork, but he's my best buddy. Actually, he's a wild man. You'll like him."

"Great," I repeated, starting to stammer again. Was he planning to fix me up with this wild-man friend?

"His name is Jacob," Louis continued, still staring towards the woods. "Jacob Dorsey." He sniggered, as if remembering something funny about Jacob.

"Jacob's parents have to work every Friday night," Louis continued. "So we all get together at Jacob's and have like a party. You know. Every Friday. It's great. It gets pretty wild sometimes."

"Sounds great," I said.

Why couldn't I think of some other word? I scolded myself. How many times in one conversation can a person use the word *great*?

He must think I'm a real dork.

"So would you like to go with me on Friday night? To Jacob's, I mean?" His green eyes seemed to light up as he stared at me expectantly.

"You mean, like a date?" I asked.

Abbie – get it together! I ordered myself. *It's not like you've never been on a date before. You were pretty popular back in Middletown.*

"Yeah," Louis said, grinning. "Like a date."

"Sure," I said. "Great!"

Great?

Did I really say it again?

"Great," he repeated softly. He kicked at the grass with his trainer and glanced at the falls. "I've got to go."

"Me, too," I said.

The sun dipped behind a wide white cloud. The air grew chillier. Shadows slid along the ground.

We made our way across the grass to get our bikes.

I was feeling really good.

It was only my third day in Shocklin Falls. And the first boy I'd met, a really great-looking guy, had asked me out.

Not a bad start, I thought.

Not bad at all.

Louis picked up his bike by the handlebars and walked it over to me. Then we headed round to the other side of the big rocks where I had left mine.

To my surprise, the bike was standing up, tilted against a rock.

I remembered just letting it fall when I went running over to Louis, thinking he was going to jump.

Strange, I thought.

And then I gasped loudly. "Whoa!"

I hurried over to the bike and bent low to examine it.

"Hey – what's going on?" I cried, my heart pounding in my chest.

Both tyres had been slashed to ribbons.

Three

"I don't believe this," I muttered.

I ran one hand over the cut tyre. A chunk of rubber fell off in my hand.

"Who. . ." I started, but the words caught in my throat.

I was crouched down, staring in total disbelief at the slashed tyres on Jake's bike. Louis was standing right behind me, his shadow falling over me.

"I don't get it," he said quietly. "There's no one else up here."

I gazed up at him. His eyes were narrowed on the woods, as if searching for someone there. I followed his glance. The trees were mostly bare. It would be easy to see someone running away.

The woods were empty.

I shuddered. I suddenly felt cold all over.

"Jake's going to kill me," I whispered, climbing to my feet.

"Who's Jake?" Louis asked, still searching the woods.

"My little brother. It's his bike."

Louis scowled. "I'll help you walk it home," he said glumly, avoiding my eyes.

"That's OK," I said. "I can—"

"No." He grabbed the handlebars of Jake's bike. "Take my bike. I'll walk this one," he snapped. He suddenly sounded very angry.

I obediently took his bike. We began to walk side by side along the bike path.

"This is so stupid," I said. "Why would someone do this to me?"

Louis didn't answer.

"I mean, who would climb all the way up to the top of the falls just to wreck some stranger's bike?" I continued, my voice trembling.

Louis still didn't reply.

His angry expression startled me into silence.

Why was *he* so angry? It wasn't *his* bike!

His mood had changed so quickly, it frightened me.

We followed the path as it curved down through the woods. The sun remained behind the clouds. The woods were shadowy now, shadowy and cold. As if spring had left and winter had returned.

It seemed to take forever to get down to the street.

I felt so awkward. I wanted to talk, to say something. Anything. But Louis kept his eyes lowered to the ground, his jaw clenched. I could see the veins throbbing angrily at his temples.

So I remained silent, too.

I just didn't get it. He volunteered to walk me home, after all. I wasn't *forcing* him.

Was he angry with me?

I was totally confused. It didn't make any sense.

The ground levelled out when we reached Main Street. The sun reappeared, but it was nearly evening and the air remained cool.

"I live on Edgevale Street," I said softly.

"OK," Louis replied, his expression a blank.

Then we heard a sound behind us. A girl's voice calling.

We both stopped and turned round.

A girl rode up on a sleek red bike. "Louis!" she called, flashing him a warm smile.

She had curly red hair, which cascaded down her shoulders like a waterfall, and a face full of freckles. She wasn't exactly pretty. Her blue-grey eyes were kind of close together, and she had a short stub of a nose. I guess you'd call her "cute".

She was wearing an oversized green-and-white Glenview High T-shirt with a big G on the front.

"Courtney!" Louis cried. Even though she was smiling at him so warmly, he didn't exactly seem pleased to see her.

"Hi," she said breathlessly, lowering her feet to the road. She glanced at me, then quickly returned her smile to Louis. "What's happening?"

"Bike trouble," Louis replied curtly.

Courtney giggled for some reason.

"This is Abbie," Louis told her. "Abbie . . . uh. . ."

"Kiernan," I said. "Abbie Kiernan. And that's my bike." I pointed to the bike Louis was walking. "I mean, it's my brother's."

"I'm Courtney Bonds," she said and, tossing her red hair behind her shoulders, quickly turned her attention back to Louis. I wasn't sure she had even looked at me.

"Courtney, where are you coming from?" Louis asked. "Up at the falls?"

"Uh-uh." Her smile faded as she shook her head. She blushed. "No way. I've just been riding around. I've been cooped up all day helping my mum with spring-cleaning. So I wanted to get a little exercise."

"Have you seen Emily today?" Louis asked.

"No. I'm going over there tonight," Courtney told him. "Just to hang out."

"Abbie's just moved here," Louis said, suddenly remembering I was still there.

"Oh," Courtney replied, not terribly interested. But then she turned, narrowing her eyes to check me out. "What happened to your bike?" she asked.

"Somebody cut the tyres," I told her. "I really can't believe it."

Courtney glanced dryly at Louis. "I believe it," she muttered under her breath. She flashed Louis a look I couldn't interpret.

Something was going on between the two of them, but I couldn't figure out what.

Was Courtney the person Louis was waiting to meet up at the falls? If she was, wouldn't he ask her why she didn't show up?

I decided he had to be waiting for someone else.

I had the feeling that Louis didn't like Courtney. She kept smiling at him, but I couldn't tell how she felt about him.

"I've got to go," Courtney said suddenly. She fiddled with the gear control on her handlebars. Then she turned to me. "Watch out for Louis," she said through gritted teeth. "Really. He's dangerous. A really dangerous guy."

"Courtney. . . !" Louis started to protest.

But Courtney called out, "Later!" and sped off, standing on her pedals and quickly disappearing round the corner.

"She's weird," Louis said. "She was kidding about me. You know? Courtney and I are old mates."

I saw that Louis was staring at me intently, studying my reaction to what Courtney had said.

"Yeah. I could tell she was joking," I said.

But I wasn't so sure.

She hadn't *looked* as if she were joking. She had looked very serious.

Was she really warning me to stay away from Louis?

Did she mean that he *really* was dangerous?

What a crazy idea.

I glanced once again at Louis. He looked perfectly OK to me.

Better than OK!

With those wild green eyes and that dark, tanned skin, he reminded me suddenly of a tiger.

Tigers are dangerous, I warned myself.

I don't care, I thought.

A short while later, we were standing at the foot of my driveway. We swapped bikes. "Thanks," I said, "for walking me home."

"That's OK. Sorry about your bike."

"D'you want to come in or something?" I offered.

He shook his head. "I've got to get home. See you at school on Monday."

"Yeah. Great," I said. And then I added, "Nice meeting you." It sounded really stupid and phoney.

He ignored it. "And don't forget Friday night," he said, climbing on to his bike.

"I won't. I'm looking forward to it."

That's for sure!

I watched him ride away, those long legs pedalling quickly, easily.

I turned and started to drag Jake's bike up the driveway. But then I stopped.

Who was that at the corner?

Someone was waiting under the shadows of a tall hedge. Someone on a bike, keeping close to the hedge. Waiting for Louis.

I stepped back towards the street, squinting hard to see who it was.

Courtney!

She was waiting for him at the corner. She pedalled away from the hedge, out of the shadows, as he came near.

They talked for a moment, close together, side by side on their bikes. And then I watched them ride off together. What's going on here? I wondered. What exactly is going on?

Four

Jacob Dorsey was the kind of guy who thought it was hilarious to smash Coke cans against his forehead and burp really loudly.

He had long, stringy brown hair that looked as if it hadn't been washed for a month. I spotted a thin gold earring in one ear. His face seemed to be locked in a wide grin, his dark eyes crinkled in laughter. I couldn't imagine a serious expression on his face.

Jacob was tall and lanky and never seemed to stand still. He was very fidgety, very hyper. He bounced around his small, crowded living room, wearing a T-shirt that was too small for him and baggy, faded jeans with enormous holes at the knees, jiggling his shoulders, slapping high fives, shouting and laughing.

At first I couldn't imagine Jacob and Louis being best friends. But after a few hours, I realized that Jacob brought out a lighter side of Louis. Around Jacob, Louis loosened up and became funny, and wild, and loud. Almost as if he were competing with his friend.

I was pretty nervous, being the outsider, the new kid. So I spent a lot of time on the outskirts of the crowd, studying the others.

It was Friday night. Louis had picked me up in a brand-new, silver Volvo and had driven us to Jacob's small box of a house for the usual Friday night blow-out.

Louis seemed pretty relaxed, and I pretended to be. But my stomach was knotted, and my hands were as cold as ice. I mean, it was our first date, and here we were going to a party where he knew everyone and I didn't know a soul.

I had spent at least an hour up in my room puzzling over what to wear. I'd finally ended up in a silky white, long-sleeved top and a short, black skirt over black tights.

As we walked in through the kitchen door, I saw that most of the girls were in jeans, but I didn't care.

Even though it was a cool night out, the house was steamy hot. I spotted about twenty kids, maybe more, jammed into the small living room and spilling into a narrow front hallway.

The music was so loud, the windows rattled. Everyone had to shout to be heard over the noise.

Some couples were dancing near the living room door. A big group of kids hung out in the middle of the living room, laughing and talking. Two couples were pressed together on the narrow stairway leading upstairs, making out, one couple on the bottom step, the other nearly hidden in darkness halfway up the stairs.

Most kids were carrying around cans of Coke, but I saw several with cans of beer. Even though they were away at work, Jacob's parents must know about his Friday night parties, I thought. But I wondered if they knew about the beer.

Holding my hand loosely, Louis led me into the crowded living room. Over the voices and music, I distinctly heard someone ask, "Is that Louis's new girlfriend?" I turned, but I didn't see who said it.

Jacob came bouncing over, grinning. His grin didn't fade as he checked me out. Louis introduced us, giving Jacob a shove.

"Watch out for this jerk," Jacob warned me, shoving Louis back. "He doesn't look it, but he's an animal."

I laughed. But it flashed through my mind that Jacob was the second person to tell me to watch out for Louis.

"You're not animal. You're vegetable," Louis told Jacob.

"You're not even vegetable," Jacob replied. "You're sponge."

"If I'm a sponge, *you're* the stuff you have to wipe up with a sponge!" Louis exclaimed.

The two of them collapsed, laughing.

Shaking his head, Louis said something to me, but I couldn't hear him over the music.

Jacob moved close to me and wrapped a heavy arm round my shoulder. "Don't pay attention to Louis and me," he said, bringing his face close to mine. I smelled beer on his breath. "We're both idiots."

"And proud of it!" Louis declared, grinning. He ran a hand through his hair as his eyes searched the room. "Where's Emily?" he asked Jacob.

Jacob shrugged and slapped a short kid hard on the back, making him spill his Coke on the carpet. The kid didn't even turn round, just kept talking to two other guys.

"Here I am," a girl's voice called from behind me.

I turned to see a tall, dramatic-looking girl with piles of long, curly black hair, big, dark eyes, and dark, lipsticked lips. Despite her black hair and dark features, she had very pale, creamy-white skin. She wore a really short, flowery skirt over black tights. Very sexy.

"Jacob, can't you turn the music down?" she demanded, stepping past me.

"No way." He gave her a goofy grin.

"I can't hear myself think," she shouted.

"Who wants to think?" was Jacob's reply.

"Jacob hates new experiences," Louis commented dryly.

377

He turned to me. "Abbie, this is Emily Pedderson."

"Hi," Emily shouted over the music. "You're here with *him*?" She pointed to Louis and made a face.

I nodded.

"You must be new here," Emily teased. She tossed her hair back over her shoulder. She seemed to play with her hair a lot, tugging at it, tangling it around her hand, then pushing it off her face.

"Yeah," I said. "I've just moved here."

I turned to Louis, but he and Jacob had disappeared somewhere.

I felt abandoned.

As I looked for him, my eyes stopped on the couple making out at the bottom of the stairs. I couldn't see her face, but I recognized the girl's red hair.

"Courtney!" I declared.

"Have you met Courtney?" Emily asked, stepping close beside me and following my gaze.

"Yeah," I said, staring. "Who's the guy?"

"I don't recognize him," Emily replied. "I don't think he goes to Glenview." She sniggered. "Courtney probably doesn't know his name, either."

I laughed. I liked Emily's nasty sense of humour.

"Some people do aerobics. Courtney does guys," Emily said. And then she turned her eyes to me and her expression grew more intense. "She has a thing for Louis, too. Did you know that?"

"A thing?" I asked. I wasn't sure I'd heard right. It was so noisy.

I couldn't hear what Emily said next.

The two of us found ourselves wandering back towards the kitchen, away from the speakers and the crowd. The kitchen was empty. Someone had spilled a bag of crisps across the worktop.

There was a stack of dirty dishes in the sink. I stepped around a brown puddle of Coke on the floor.

Emily and I leaned against the worktop, chatting and absently picking up the spilled crisps and eating them as we talked. She was nearly 30 centimetres taller than me. She kept complaining that she was overweight, but in my opinion, she was just well-built. I looked like a short little beanpole next to her.

I told her about moving from Ohio, how hard it was to leave my friends behind, to start at a new school so late in the school year.

We both jumped when we heard a loud crash from the living room. "Typical," Emily said, rolling her eyes. "I can't believe Jacob's parents put up with this."

"Jacob's a riot," I said, reaching for another crisp. "He's so funny!"

"Funny-looking," Emily muttered. "Jacob and I have been going out together for about six months. Off and on."

I gazed at her in surprise. I couldn't imagine Jacob and Emily as a couple. "Off and on?" I asked.

"Sometimes I get sick of him," she admitted, glancing to the kitchen doorway. "I mean, he's just never serious. That can be a lot of fun for a while. But sometimes I just want to shake him and say, 'Knock it off. Stop the jokes. Be serious!' He can be a real pain. I mean, he's always getting into trouble at school. Always. . ." She stopped.

"Yeah?" I urged.

She shrugged. "He's OK, I guess. He makes me laugh. And once you really get to know him, he's a good guy." She sighed and tapped a crisp against the worktop until it crumbled. Then she raised her eyes to mine.

"There's something you should know about Louis," she said, lowering her voice, her expression turning solemn.

"Huh? About Louis?"

"Yeah. He's been through a bad time. He—"

She didn't get to finish her sentence. Jacob burst into the room and grabbed her arm. "Come on, Emily – we're all going now."

She pulled out of his grasp. "Going where?"

"To Sportsworld," he replied, tugging her again. He turned to me. "You, too. Come on."

"What's Sportsworld?" I asked.

"Batting cages," Emily answered, making a face. "You know. One of those places with basketball courts, and table tennis, and—"

"You can watch me outslug Louis," Jacob said, grinning. "We made a little bet." He put his hands together and bent his knees in a ridiculously exaggerated batting stance. Then he swung all the way around, toppling into the kitchen unit.

"Jacob, how are you going to outslug Louis? You can't outslug *me*!" Emily declared, shaking her head.

"Are you kidding?" He cried, acting as if his feelings were hurt. "You swing like a *girl*!"

"Cute," Emily muttered. "That's really cute." She gave him a hard, playful shove, then followed him to the living room.

I followed Emily, then stopped in the hall way. Across the room, I saw Courtney standing with Louis. She had a hand on his cheek. They were talking with their faces close together.

I think he saw me because he pulled Courtney's hand away from his face and stepped away from her. I made my way across the room, pushing past a circle of kids who were laughing uproariously about something.

"Hey, I lost you," he said as I approached, flashing me a smile. "You remember Courtney?"

I said hi to Courtney, and she nodded. "Did you get your

bike fixed?" she asked, shouting over the laughter across from us.

"It wasn't my bike," I told her. "It was my brother's."

She didn't react. I thought maybe she didn't hear me.

Jacob grabbed my shoulder. "Come on, guys. Let's go!"

Louis flashed me a guilty smile. "Is it OK with you? I sort of made a bet with Jacob."

"Sure," I said. "Sounds like fun."

A few seconds later, about ten of us had piled into two cars, and we were roaring past town towards Sportsworld. I sat beside Louis in the front of his car, with four kids I didn't know in the back.

Louis drove like a madman. He had the radio cranked up as loud as it would go, and he kept careering deliberately from side to side on the road, going at least sixty the whole way.

"Louis!" I shouted when he bumped over the curb into someone's front garden. "Stop it!"

His eyes were wild with excitement, and his grin just grew wider. "I can handle it," he shouted.

He turned the wheel wildly, and the car squealed back into the street.

"Do you always drive like this?" I asked.

He stared into the windscreen, a strange grin fixed on his face, looking almost as if he were hypnotized.

"Louis. . .?"

I was so relieved when we finally reached Sportsworld, a brightly-lit, massive indoor-outdoor sports arena. Louis turned into the car park, the tyres squealing, and came to an abrupt, bone-jarring stop. I pushed open my car door and practically leaped out, grateful to be in one piece.

To my surprise, Jacob and his group were already going inside. Jacob must be an even crazier driver than Louis, I realized.

I slammed the car door and jogged after Louis, who was already moving across the car park towards the entrance. "Whew! What a ride!" I cried breathlessly. "That was scary, Louis."

He stopped and turned to me. His smile faded. Those amazing green eyes seemed to burn into mine. "Sometimes I just feel wild," he said. "Like, out of control. You know."

He stood staring at me, hands at his waist, as if waiting for me to reply. But I didn't know what to say. His driving had really frightened me. He *did* seem out of control.

His expression softened. He smiled. "Just kidding," he said. His green eyes seemed to twinkle under the car park lights. He was so gorgeous! "Come on. Let's go and hit some baseballs."

We started jogging across the car park to catch up with the others.

I saw Emily up ahead of us, and I suddenly remembered what she had started to tell me in the kitchen: "*There's something you should know about Louis.*"

What had she started to tell me?

Did it have something to do with the way he drove, with his need to get "out of control"?

He seemed to have such drastic mood swings.

Was that what Emily wanted to warn me about?

The batting cages were outdoors, at the back of the building, under daylight-bright lights. I could see a row of eight or ten of them, long canvas-and-wire mesh cages with pitching machines near the far end.

The place was incredibly crowded. Jammed with teenagers and a lot of loud, young, working people. We had to wait for a batting cage. I kept close to Louis, peering through the mesh into the cages, watching helmeted batters take their swings against ninety mph pitches.

"Look at that guy. He's swinging an hour late on every pitch," Louis said, sniggering.

It was a chilly night. It felt more like winter than spring. I shivered. I wished I'd worn a jumper or something.

Louis was shouting encouragement to the guy in the batting cage. He seemed to be enjoying himself. I wondered if he liked me.

Suddenly, I heard a loud, rattling sound above our heads.

Startled, I looked up to see Jacob clinging to the side of the cage, about five metres above the ground. He was holding on to the mesh with one hand, making chimpanzee gestures with his other hand.

"Oh, man!" Louis cried, and then he totally cracked up.

"Get down!" a man cried from somewhere behind us.

"Hey – that's dangerous!" someone else screamed.

"Me Tarzan!" Jacob shouted, climbing to the top of the cage.

"Jacob's so messed up!" Louis exclaimed gleefully. "He's crazy! He'll do *anything*!"

My eye caught Emily, a couple of metres away. She didn't appear at all amused. In fact, her face was bright red, and she looked really embarrassed.

I saw two guys wearing dark blue trousers and white shirts come hurrying over. They must work here, I realized.

"Hey – get down!" one of them waved furiously at Jacob.

"What are you doing?" the other one shouted.

Jacob ignored the two men. "Hey, Louis – join me?" he called down. "You get a better view up here!"

"Do you *believe* him?" Louis asked me, still laughing.

"Come on, man," Jacob called down to Louis. "You chicken?"

Louis stared up at his friend.

"Come on up, wimp!" Jacob called down.

The smile faded from Louis's face.

I shuddered.

Louis had the strangest expression on his face. Fear mixed with anger. His entire body went rigid. He stared up at Jacob without moving.

What is wrong? I wondered.

What is Louis thinking about?

Why does he suddenly look so strange, so frightening.

"Hey – chicken face!" Jacob called down, waving his free hand, clinging to the wire mesh with the other. "Chicken face!"

Louis glanced nervously at me. Then he started to call up to Jacob. But Louis's words choked in his throat, and his eyes widened with horror.

As Jacob motioned enthusiastically for Louis to climb up, his hand slipped away from the mesh.

He started to fall.

I watched Jacob plummet all the way down without realizing that the hideous scream I heard the whole time was coming from me.

Five

I was surrounded by screams and cries of horror.

Louis grabbed my shoulder.

Jacob landed easily on his hands and knees. He rolled over once. Twice. Then climbed to his feet, a goofy, triumphant grin on his face.

"Ta-*daa*!" he sang.

There were groans and loud sighs of relief. Excited voices rang out through the entire area.

The two grim-faced workers came up on either side of Jacob and grabbed his arms.

"Hey, what's the problem?" Jacob demanded. "I mean, what's the problem?"

Louis was still holding tight to my shoulder. I turned to him. He seemed somewhat dazed by the whole thing. "Are you OK?" I asked.

He shook his head. Seemed to snap out of it. "Yeah. I – I was just thinking about something else." Avoiding my eyes, he let go of my shoulder.

Jacob was arguing with the two workers, who wanted to throw him out. Emily came up to me, toying nervously with a thick strand of black hair. "Read any good books lately?" she asked dryly.

"I – I really thought he was going to kill himself this time," Louis said.

"*This* time?" I asked.

"Yeah. He's done it before," Emily told me.

"He does stuff like that all the time," Louis said, shaking his head. "He always lands on his feet."

"Or his head," Emily said with surprising bitterness. "But it never knocks any sense into him."

The two men were leading Jacob out to the exit. I watched Emily run to catch up with them. She seemed really angry and upset. Again I thought what a strange couple Emily and Jacob were. They were so different from each other. And she didn't even seem to like him that much.

Louis had picked a bat up from the bat rack at the side of the cage. He swung it hard once, as if hitting an imaginary pitch. "Looks like our competition is over," he said quietly. "Sorry."

"That's OK," I replied. I was shivering. It was a really cold night.

"Let's go," he said. He tossed the bat to the ground and headed towards the exit.

People were still talking and laughing about Jacob climbing on top of the batting cage. As I followed Louis out, I pictured again the strange expression on his face when Jacob had called for him to climb up, too.

Was it fear?

Was it anger?

Was it jealousy?

His green eyes had filled with such sadness. What had he been thinking of?

I realized I was probably reading too much into it. Louis was probably just afraid for Jacob's safety.

I do that a lot.

"You think too much." That's what my mum always tells me.

I over-analyse everything. I find dark meanings in things that have no meaning at all.

But why was I feeling so troubled as Louis and I made our way to his car?

You're just nervous, Abbie, I told myself. It's your first date with Louis, and you're not sure if he likes you or not.

And why should he like me?

I'd been so quiet all night. I felt like such an outsider among all these kids who'd known each other for ever.

He'll never ask me out again, I thought as I slid into the front seat of the car and pulled the door shut. The leather seat was ice-cold.

Louis started up the car. Two other couples had piled into the back. "Can you turn on some heat?" I asked, folding my arms round myself, trying to get warm.

"No problem," he said, reaching for the dials.

He drove home carefully, keeping below the speed limit. Everyone joked about Jacob and his climb. A boy in the back seat told a story about Jacob breaking into an indoor swimming pool and being caught swimming naked with a bunch of kids. A girl told a story about how Jacob was arrested one night breaking into his own house!

"He's been arrested twenty times!" another boy declared.

Everyone laughed except for Louis. "Jacob's not a criminal," Louis said earnestly. "I mean, he's never been convicted of anything. He always pleads *insanity*!"

Everyone laughed again, including Louis this time.

Laughing and joking, we dropped the other kids off.

I was feeling really good and had finally got warm by the time Louis pulled into my driveway. He left the engine running.

The porch light was on, and the lights were on in my parents' bedroom upstairs. The clock on the dashboard read 11:24. Still pretty early.

I wondered if Louis was going to kiss me.

Gazing at him in the pale white light from the porch, I realized I wanted him to.

His eyes studied the green lights on the dashboard. I wondered what he was thinking.

Was he trying to decide whether or not to kiss me?

Was he nervous, too?

Was he thinking about me at all?

His expression was a total blank. I couldn't read it.

"Well, that's a typical night in Shocklin Falls," he said, turning towards me and smiling.

"I enjoyed it," I said, smiling back.

"Me, too," he said automatically.

Was he going to lean towards me and kiss me?

No.

"See you at school," he said.

"Yeah. OK."

I gave him a few more seconds. But he kept both hands on the wheel. So I pushed open the door and climbed out.

The headlights rolled over the front of the house as I found my keys and pushed open the front door.

I felt disappointed.

I felt like a total idiot.

The front hallway and living room were dark.

Without bothering to turn on the lights, I hung my jacket in the cupboard.

Then I started to make my way through the darkness to the stairs when someone leaped at me and two hands grabbed my shoulders from behind.

Six

Uttering a silent gasp, I stumbled forward into the banister.

I heard footsteps pad across the floor.

"Goggles!" I cried out in a choked whisper.

I clicked on the hall light. The stupid cat was standing at my feet, staring up at me.

"Goggles, how many times do I have to tell you not to scare me like that?" I asked, picking him up.

He purred excitedly.

I touched his nose to mine.

"Don't jump on me," I told him for the thousandth time. "I don't have nine lives like you do."

I hugged him close, rubbing my hand down his soft, white fur. "You don't understand a word I'm saying, do you, stupid?"

He purred contentedly as I stroked his back. Then he

swiped at me with his paw, his way of telling me he'd had enough affection.

I set him down and he padded away.

Goggles has some bad habits. Jumping on people in the dark is one of his worst. But I love him just the same. He is so cute with all that fluffy white fur and those big, serious blue eyes.

I had started up the stairs, thinking about Louis, when my mother's voice interrupted my thoughts. "Abbie, is that you?"

Who *else* would it be?

"Yes, it's me," I called.

She appeared on the landing, her hair down, wearing a long pink nightie. "How was your date?"

"Fine."

I always give the same reply to that question. What does she expect – *details*?

"What did you do?" my mother asked, yawning loudly.

"Went to a party," I told her, starting the climb up the stairs. "Just a lot of kids hanging around."

"That's nice," she replied sleepily. "See you in the morning." She disappeared into her room.

A few minutes later, I was changed, in bed, thinking about Louis.

Once again, I heard the girl at Jacob's house saying, "*That's Louis's new girlfriend.*" I wondered if I *was* Louis's new girlfriend.

I wondered if he'd ever ask me out again.

Before I realized it, I drifted into a sound sleep. If I dreamed about Louis, I didn't remember it in the morning.

I ran into Emily at school on Monday morning. We talked for a while between classes. It turned out we were in the same geography class.

I decided I really liked her. I hoped we could become good friends.

During lunch break, I spotted Emily at a table in the corner of the canteen and I carried my tray over to have lunch with her.

We talked about our geography coursework. Emily and the others in the class had a real head start on me. They'd already been researching for three weeks. I knew I'd be spending a lot of time in the library and in the computer room, typing up all my research, trying to catch up with the others in the class.

Eventually, the conversation came round to Louis.

"Where'd you meet him?" Emily asked, taking a forkful of her salad.

"Up at the falls," I replied.

She put down her fork. Her mouth dropped open in surprise. "Huh? Where?"

"At the falls," I repeated, startled by her reaction.

She tossed a thick strand of black hair back over her shoulder and stared at me, studying my face as if trying to determine if I were telling the truth.

"I was bike riding," I said. "You know. Exploring. I followed the bike path up to the falls and—"

"I really can't believe Louis would go up there," Emily interrupted, still staring at me intently. She picked up her fork and started tapping it nervously against the canteen tray.

"What's wrong, Emily?" I asked.

Her dark eyes narrowed. "Are we talking about the same falls?"

"Is there more than one?" I asked innocently.

"No." She shook her head. "I just can't believe Louis would ever go up there again. I mean, after what happened."

I set down my slice of pizza. A sliver of cheese stuck to my thumb. I chewed it off. "Did something bad happen up there?" I asked. "To Louis?"

Emily nodded. "Yeah. A few months ago. Last January."

She stopped, then started again. "I guess I might as well tell you about it. I mean, everyone knows. It's not like a secret or anything. That's for sure."

"What?" I cried impatiently. "What? What? Stop being so mysterious. You're driving me crazy!"

"I don't think you'll like it once you hear it," Emily replied softly.

"*What*'s driving you crazy?" demanded a voice behind us.

I turned to see Courtney standing right behind me, a loaded-up lunch tray in her hands. She put the tray down beside me, across from Emily, and sat down. "You both look so serious," she said, moving the plates around on her tray. "What are you talking about? Your hair?"

"Our geography coursework," Emily answered quickly, casting me a quick glance that told me not to contradict with the truth.

Courtney brushed her red hair back over the shoulder of her green T-shirt and concentrated on pushing the straw into her juice carton. "We don't have coursework in Curtis's class," she told them. "We have a killer exam instead."

"I think I'd rather have the exam," I said, taking a bite of the small square of pizza. "I'm getting such a late start."

"You wouldn't want *this* exam," Courtney insisted, picking up a hamburger, watching the grease drizzle from the bun. "It has really easy, specific questions, like, 'Compare and contrast every country on earth.'"

Emily and I laughed appreciatively. That was a pretty good exam question.

We chatted about teachers and classes. All the while I was dying to hear what Emily had started to tell me about Louis. But it was obvious Emily didn't want to talk about it while Courtney was around.

What could it be? I wondered, my mind spinning with wild ideas.

Why was Emily so surprised that Louis was up at the falls? What happened up there?

We were nearly finished with our lunches when I felt a tap on my shoulder. I looked up to find Louis smiling down at me. He was wearing a pale blue jumper over dark, straight-legged jeans. He looked really great.

"Hi!" I cried, unable to hide my surprise. I'd looked for him all day, but hadn't seen him.

"How's it going?" he asked, glancing quickly at Emily, then returning his attention to me. He pointed to my tray. "You like cardboard pizza?"

"It's my favourite," I replied. "It's going OK, I guess. I keep getting lost. This school is so much bigger than my old school."

"Have you seen Jacob?" Louis asked Emily.

She made a face. "He's doing lunchtime detention."

Louis laughed. "What for?"

Emily rolled her eyes. "He said a rude word to Mrs Kelman."

"Jacob only knows rude words," Louis said, sniggering. "Abbie, have you got your new bike yet?"

I nodded. "I got a used one. The new ones were too expensive. It's excellent, though. Twenty-one speed."

Louis leaned close. "Great. Want to go riding on Saturday afternoon?"

I had promised my dad I'd help him unpack some of the boxes in the garage, but I knew I could get out of it. "Yeah. Great," I said. "Come and pick me up, OK?"

"OK." Louis disappeared as quickly as he had appeared.

I felt really happy. Maybe Louis *didn't* think I was a total drip. Maybe he *did* like me.

My smile faded when I caught Courtney's expression. She was biting her lower lip, her features in a tight frown. She was suddenly pale white, sickly white.

"Courtney – are you feeling OK?" I blurted out.

"No, not really," she replied weakly. She let the rest of her hamburger drop to the tray and scooted her chair back. "I think this food has made me ill or something."

"Can I help you. . .?" I started. But she jumped to her feet and hurried out of the canteen without looking back.

"D'you think we should go with her?" I asked Emily.

Emily shook her head. "She'll be fine." She'd been toying with her salad the whole time, but had hardly eaten a bite.

"Aren't you starving?" I asked.

Emily nodded. "Yeah. But I've got to lose weight. I hate having a boyfriend who's skinnier than I am."

"I think you're just about perfect," I blurted out, and then was immediately embarrassed that I'd said it. But it was true.

I'd give anything to look like Emily instead of having this short, little-boyish figure.

Emily picked up her tray and got to her feet. "Ready?"

I nodded. "Yeah. But you've got to finish what you were telling me. About Louis."

Her expression turned serious. "OK, Abbie. I'll tell you," she said softly. "But it may change everything. Really."

"I don't understand," I said. "Change what?"

"The way you feel about Louis, for one thing," Emily replied. "You see, it's about the girl who died. Have you heard about it?"

Died?

The word stuck in my mind. It stayed there, echoing as if it would never fade away.

Died?

What girl?

We deposited our trays on the dirty-tray counter. The floor seemed to tilt beneath my feet. The fluorescent lights above us appeared to flash like bright explosions.

Maybe I *don't* want to hear this, I thought, shutting my eyes till the flashing stopped.

"No. I haven't heard about it," I told Emily, my voice shaky.

I followed her out of the canteen. She led us up the stairs and down the hall that led to the principal's office in the front of the building.

The hall was crowded and noisy, filled with kids who had finished their lunch and were messing around, waiting for the bell to ring.

I didn't pay any attention to them. I followed Emily, wondering where she was leading us, what she was going to tell me. And as we walked, my stomach tightened with dread. My hands turned cold. My heart began to race.

"*It may change everything*," Emily had said.

Everything.

What could she be talking about?

We turned a corner. We were near the front entrance. The principal's office stood diagonally across from the big double doorways. And in the wall beside the office stood a large glass display case, the kind usually used for showing off sports trophies.

Emily stopped in front of the display case. She pushed her thick black hair back behind her head with both hands and peered into my eyes. "This is the girl who died," she said, gesturing to the glass case. "She died up at the falls."

I swallowed hard and stared into the case.

It was empty except for a single photograph. A colour enlargement of a school photo.

It was a photo of a pretty girl. She had it all. Bright blonde hair. Flashing blue eyes. High cheekbones like a model. A beautiful smile revealing perfect white teeth.

The photo was draped with black crêpe.

Under the photo stood a small black tag. It read: 1992–2009.

I stared into the girl's eyes. They stared coldly back at me.

After a few seconds, I had to look away.

"She died?" I asked Emily in a tight, shrill voice. "Who is she? I mean, who was she?"

"That's Phoebe," Emily answered softly. "Louis's girlfriend."

Seven

I stared through the glass at the photo of Phoebe.

I stared at those round blue eyes, at that perfect smile, at the honey-blonde hair, brushed casually back, so soft against her perfect skin.

The black crêpe draped round the photo didn't belong.

She was so light, so pretty, so . . . happy.

I couldn't picture her wearing black.

She shouldn't be in this dark, heavy case, I thought. She shouldn't be here with her dates under her photo.

The display case was like a glass casket. I was staring into Phoebe's casket.

Staring at her smiling face, her pretty blue eyes.

I turned away with a violent shudder. I felt that I was somehow invading her privacy.

"She was Louis's girlfriend?" I asked Emily.

Emily nodded.

I wanted to ask more. A hundred questions flooded my mind. I wanted to know everything about her. I wanted to know what she was like. And I wanted to know how she died.

And why did Emily say it would change my idea of Louis?

But the bell rang right over our heads. The hall was filled with kids stampeding noisily to class.

Emily gave me a quick wave and hurried away, leaving me standing there.

Standing there with Phoebe.

My eyes locked on Phoebe's once again. And as I stared, the voices and laughter echoing down the hall faded away.

Phoebe and I were alone.

What is your story, Phoebe? I asked silently. What happened to you up at the falls?

She stared back at me through the glass.

1992–2009.

The dates seemed to shimmer and then blur.

Was that *sadness* I detected deep in those blue eyes? Sadness behind the posed smile?

I had to force myself to turn away.

To my surprise, the hall was nearly empty. The second bell was about to ring, and I hadn't even collected my books.

How long had I been standing there?

I knew I had to talk to Emily, had to find out the answers

404

to all my questions. Avoiding the display case, I jogged past it and headed to my locker.

I'll call Emily later, I decided.

I'll make her tell me everything.

The afternoon seemed to drag on for days. I was very distracted. I don't think I heard a word anyone said.

After school, I spent a couple of long, dreary hours in the computer room, typing up my geography research. Normally, I enjoy doing research. I like digging around in old books for facts and information. It's sort of like being an archaeologist.

But I had joined the class so late, and I was so far behind everyone else, I felt really pressured. Glenview High seemed a lot more intense than my old school. Also, I wasn't used to the kind of computers they had in the computer room, so I kept making mistakes.

That night, struggling to concentrate on my maths homework, I found myself still thinking about Phoebe, still eager to unravel the mystery about her. I kept calling Emily all evening. At first, there was no answer. And then the line was busy for hours.

So frustrating!

I didn't get to talk to Emily about Phoebe until lunch the next day. I forced Emily to gulp down her lunch. (She was only having a salad anyway.) And then I dragged her to the display case at the front of the building.

"You have to tell me the whole story," I insisted, staring at the photograph, finding myself searching once again for the sadness in Phoebe's eyes. "What happened to her?"

Emily hesitated. She leaned against the tile wall, toying thoughtfully with a thick strand of black hair, wrapping it and unwrapping it round her finger. "You sure you want to know?"

"Yeah. I'm sure," I replied impatiently. "Tell me what happened."

"No one really knows," Emily said, still fingering her hair. "I mean, no one knows for sure."

I groaned. "Start at the beginning," I urged.

Emily waited for a group of cheerleaders to pass. They were in their green-and-white uniforms, laughing and playfully shoving each other into the walls.

When they had turned the corner, Emily let go of her hair and took a step closer to me. "It happened last January. It was a really warm day for January. Phoebe and Louis went bike riding up to the falls. Somehow, Phoebe and her bike went over the falls. And she died."

I gasped and shut my eyes. "Over the falls?"

I tried not to picture it. It was so horrible.

The falls were so steep. The water crashed straight down. Down on to those jagged black rocks.

406

"Over the falls," Emily repeated softly.

"But, Louis. . ." I started. I didn't really know what I wanted to say.

"Louis told everyone he had left Phoebe for a minute or two," Emily continued, staring into the display case, her hands knotted into tight fists at her sides. "Louis said he saw someone. Back on the bike path. Or, he thought he saw someone. Anyway," Emily sighed, "he went to see who it was. And when he came back. . ."

She didn't finish her sentence.

I swallowed hard, staring into the display case. Phoebe's photo was just a blur of colour to me now, all greens and pinks, surrounded by black.

"When he came back, Phoebe was gone?" I managed to ask.

Emily nodded. "Louis looked for her. And then he saw her bike. Down below. All mangled. It had caught on the rocks."

"And Phoebe?" I asked, my voice choked with the horror of it all.

"They dragged her body out downriver," Emily said in a whisper. "Two days later. She was cut to pieces."

I gasped. "Someone had cut her?"

Emily shook her head grimly. "The police said she'd been cut up by all the rocks."

I tried to focus on the photo in the display case, but it

wouldn't come clear. I rested one hand against the wall to steady myself.

Such a horrible story.

And to think that I'd just been up at the falls. With Louis. I could picture it all so clearly. I could hear the roar of the falls in my ears. I could see the winding cycle path and the woods behind it.

I could see the cliff-edge over the falls.

I could see the black, pointed rocks in the river below.

I could see it all.

I turned to Emily, who had folded her arms over her chest. "Why did she kill herself?" I managed to ask.

"What makes you think she killed herself?" Emily asked with surprising emotion.

"Huh?" I gaped at her, trying to figure out what she was trying to tell me.

The principal, Mr Velasquez, passed by, dabbing a wet handkerchief over a dark stain on his yellow tie. He glanced up as he walked by us, nodded solemnly, and disappeared into his office, still working on the tie.

"I was Phoebe's best friend," Emily confided. "I thought she was perfectly happy." She sighed and lowered her eyes to the floor. Then she added, "I guess you never really know another person. Even a close friend. You never really know what's in their mind."

"But—"

"The police decided it was suicide," Emily interrupted, still staring at her white trainers. "In case you didn't already know it, Louis's parents are very rich. They got the police investigation to end very quickly."

Emily's words stunned me. I raised my hands to my forehead and rubbed my throbbing temples.

"But no one suspected Louis – *did* they?" I asked, my voice choked with emotion.

"No, not really," Emily replied reluctantly. She raised her eyes to mine. "But there were stories. You know. You know how rumours get started."

"What kind of rumours?" I demanded.

"Just rumours," Emily replied edgily. "Rumours that Louis and Phoebe had had a big fight. That Louis wanted to break up with her and start going out with someone else."

"Someone else?"

"Well . . . some kids saw his car parked in Courtney's driveway one night."

I stared hard at Emily, trying to understand what she was saying, trying to read her mind, to figure out what she really believed had happened.

"Emily, *you* don't think that Louis killed Phoebe – do you?" I asked.

"No. Of course not," she replied quickly.

Too quickly.

She grabbed my arm and moved her face close to mine. "But I'd be careful, Abbie," she whispered.

Careful?

What did she mean?

"I'd be really careful," she repeated in a low whisper, gripping my arm tightly.

"Emily. . . ?"

"I've got to run," she said, letting go. "Later, OK?"

Before I could reply, she started jogging down the hallway.

Be careful?

Her words remained in my mind.

What did she mean?

Did she mean to be careful of Louis?

Did she really think that Louis murdered Phoebe? Pushed her over the falls? Then got his parents to hush it up with the police?

No. No way.

She *said* she didn't think that Louis had killed Phoebe.

So why was Emily warning me to be careful?

I shoved my hands into my jeans pockets and tried to stop from trembling. I wanted to walk away, to go to my locker, to go to my next class, to think about something else.

Anything else.

But Phoebe wouldn't let me go.

Her black-draped photo beckoned to me, called me, pulled me in. I stood there staring through the glass at her.

Emily had told me the whole story.

But she hadn't really told me any of it.

There is a story behind the story, isn't there, Phoebe? I asked silently.

There are secrets you haven't revealed.

Secrets you may never reveal.

I stood there in the brightly-lit hallway, hands shoved into my pockets, and stared at the photo as if searching the pretty face for the answers it hid.

I don't know how long I stared at it.

And I don't know how long it took me to realize that someone else had joined me. Someone else was standing right beside me, so close that his shoulder pressed against mine.

I don't know how long it took me to realize he was staring intently at me as I stared at Phoebe.

"She didn't kill herself," he said.

Eight

"What did you say?" I cried, startled.

I took a step away from him and studied his face. He wore round glasses with thin gold frames. He was short, shorter than me, and thin like a pencil. He had a lean face, with intense brown eyes, exaggerated by the glasses. His brown hair was short and spiky.

Taking another step back, I saw that he was wearing a green-and-black-striped polo shirt over jeans.

He flashed me a nervous smile and blinked two or three times behind his glasses.

"Hi," he said shyly. "You were in the computer room after school yesterday, right?" He had a surprisingly deep voice. He kept blinking nervously and shifting his books as he talked.

"Yeah," I replied.

"I was there, too. Did you see me?"

I shook my head and smiled at him. "I was concentrating

so hard on typing up my research, I didn't see anybody," I confessed.

His narrow face fell in disappointment.

"My name's Ryan," he said shyly.

"Hi," I said. "Is that your first name or last?"

"I have two last names," he replied, a smile slowly spreading across his face. "I mean, both my names *could* be last names. Ryan is my first name. Ryan Baker."

I laughed. "Do you have a last name for a middle name?"

"No," he replied seriously. "I don't have a middle name. Just two first names."

"I'm Abbie Kiernan," I told him.

"I know," he blurted out, then blushed. "I mean, I heard someone say your name. You've just started here, right?"

"Right," I said. I glanced up at the clock outside the principal's office. The bell was going to ring any second.

He cleared his throat nervously and turned his gaze to Phoebe's picture. "She was a really good friend of mine," he confided, his face completely expressionless. "I mean, we were *really* good friends."

"Yeah?" I didn't know what to say.

"We didn't go out or anything," Ryan continued, staring hard into the display case. "We were just really good friends. In fact. . ." He hesitated. He changed his mind about what he was going to say.

413

"What a terrible thing," I muttered awkwardly.

Something about Ryan made me feel very awkward and uncomfortable. I guess it was his nervousness.

"You've heard the whole story?" he asked, staring at Phoebe.

"Yeah. Most of it," I replied.

"Well, she didn't kill herself!" he cried with surprising vehemence.

That's what I'd *thought* he'd said before.

She didn't kill herself.

"How do you know?" I blurted out, taking another step away from him.

"I know it," he snapped. He blushed again.

The bell rang, startling us both.

I hesitated. He didn't move. "I guess we should get to class," I said, eager to get away from him.

He nodded, still not moving. "Are you busy on Saturday, Abbie? Would you like to go to the cinema or something?"

His question caught me by surprise. My mouth dropped open. I gaped at him as if I didn't understand what he was asking. I must have looked like a total idiot.

Why did Ryan make me feel so awkward?

"I guess you're probably busy," he muttered unhappily. "Well, some other time, maybe."

I remembered that I *did* have a date with Louis on Saturday, for the afternoon, at least.

"Yeah. Some other time," I said, feeling foolish. "Nice meeting you, Ryan."

He mumbled something, avoiding my eyes, and hurried away. I watched him disappear round the corner.

"Strange guy," I said out loud.

Then, taking one last glance at Phoebe's photo, I turned away and hurried to my lesson.

The afternoon was pretty much of a disaster.

I had done the wrong pages in the maths workbook, and Mr Woolrich insisted on making fun of me in front of the entire class.

Really sensitive guy, Mr Woolrich.

And then I was trying to drink from the water fountain next to the gym, and the water went down the wrong way and, in front of a big crowd, some boy I'd never seen before started slapping my back to help me stop choking.

Of course it didn't help. And I was totally mortified.

I was pretty well wrecked by the time I got up to the computer room after school. I probably should have just gone home and vegged out with some TV for the rest of the afternoon. But I still had several pages of research to type up.

The computer room was empty except for a couple of girls typing furiously away in the back. I looked for Ryan and was relieved to see that he wasn't there.

Just thinking about him made me uncomfortable.

Maybe I'm prejudiced against guys who are shorter than I am, I thought.

No. That wasn't the reason he made me feel awkward. It was just that he was so nervous and awkward himself.

And he was saying such revealing, frightening things to me, a total stranger.

"Phoebe didn't kill herself."

Why did he say that to me? Was he deliberately trying to scare me or something?

I shook my head hard as if trying to shake Ryan out of my mind. Then I found my disk in the file and inserted it in the computer I had used before in the front row.

The computer whirred, and the screen went black.

"Hey, wait!" I cried out loud.

Where were all the notes I had typed in yesterday?

I must have done something wrong. They must be here. They've *got* to be here.

"I *hate* these stupid computers," I muttered under my breath.

I turned off the machine and started again.

The name of my file appeared at the top.

But the rest of the screen was blank.

Completely blank.

My throat tightened. I suddenly felt sick.

"Where are you hiding my stuff?" I asked the computer.

I stared at the blank screen in angry disbelief.

My notes – all of my work – was gone.

Erased.

A heavy, sinking feeling in my stomach, I hit the keys, moving the screen down, page after page.

All erased. All a total blank.

Page after page after page.

"No!" I uttered a cry of total exasperation.

This can't be happening.

Wait.

There was something at the end of the file.

Two lines of type.

I was so upset, it took a while to focus on the words.

As I read the lines, the sinking feeling spread over my entire body, and I felt cold all over.

At the bottom of the screen were two short sentences:

STAY AWAY FROM LOUIS.
IT COULD SAVE YOUR LIFE.

Nine

It wasn't an accident, I realized.

My notes weren't erased by accident.

The computer didn't do it. A person did it.

Someone erased my work, then typed the threatening message at the end.

"Who?" I cried, not realizing I was talking out loud.

I turned and saw the two girls in the back look up at me.

I clicked off the computer and, leaving my disk in the machine, shoved my books into my school bag and burst out of the room.

I was breathing hard. My temples throbbed.

I ran down the corridor, my trainers thudding loudly on the hard floor, then down the stairs.

Who did that to me? I wondered.

All my hard work. And I was already so far behind everyone else.

I felt like crying. But I forced myself not to.

Who did it?

I ran past the empty classrooms, past a caretaker carrying two large grey rubbish bins, past rows of silent lockers.

I came to an abrupt halt in front of Phoebe's display case.

Don't stop, I told myself.

But something kept me from running further.

Phoebe stared out at me.

Her smile had changed.

She was *warning* me. Warning me to stay away from Louis.

No!

"Don't get weird, Abbie," I scolded myself aloud.

I forced my eyes away from the photograph and hurried round the corner.

Laughter. Up ahead.

I saw Emily leaning against her locker, books and notebooks at her feet. And I saw Jacob standing close to her.

They were laughing giddily about something.

They stopped when they saw me approaching.

"Got to go," Jacob said, reaching down and picking up some of the books and handing them to Emily. "How's it going?" he called to me.

"Peachy," I replied sarcastically. "Just peachy."

But Jacob had taken off, waving to Emily without waiting for my answer.

"Hi, Abbie. What's your problem?" Emily asked, stooping to pick up the rest of her stuff.

"Somebody erased all my work," I blurted out breathlessly.

Emily straightened up, leaving her books on the floor. "Huh?"

I repeated what I'd said. Her mouth dropped open. She shook her head.

I told her about the warning at the end of the file, telling me to stay away from Louis.

Her expression turned thoughtful. She tugged at her hair. "Who would do such a mean thing?" she asked.

I shrugged. "I don't even *know* anyone," I wailed. "This is only my second day in this stupid school!"

"D'you want to go somewhere and talk about it?" Emily offered.

"I don't know," I replied miserably. "I think I'll just go home. I'm having a bad day, and. . ."

I stopped when I saw Louis turn the corner. He had his head down and was loping along quickly. A smile spread across his face when he spotted me.

"Hey – hi!" he shouted. He came hurrying up to us, his bag over one shoulder, a tennis racquet in a blue case in one hand. "What are you guys doing here so late?"

"Jacob had detention, and I had to get some notes from him," Emily explained.

"Wow. You're in major trouble if you need notes from Jacob!" Louis teased her.

"They were *my* notes. I had to get them back from him," Emily said. She stooped and began picking up her stuff from the floor.

Louis turned his attention to me. "What are *you* doing?"

I felt a sudden tremor of fear.

The warning on my computer screen flashed in my mind. And I suddenly saw Phoebe's face.

Did you kill her, Louis?

The question popped into my mind.

I stared at Louis. Was I really afraid of him?

No.

The feeling of fear quickly faded.

He smiled at me warmly, running his free hand back shyly through his thick hair. His green eyes seemed to smile, too.

Louis is no killer, I decided.

"I was up in the computer room," I told him. "But something's happened to my disk. All my work has been erased."

"I'm not surprised," Louis replied.

"Huh?" I stared at him, startled by his matter-of-fact words. Emily glanced up at him, too.

"Those old Macs are terrible," Louis explained, bouncing the tennis racquet against his shoulder. "Some of them are practically falling apart. My cousin goes to Franklin Heights, and he says they have loads of brand-new Macs in their computer room."

"Well, I don't know if it was the computer's fault or not, but all my work is lost," I said unhappily, deciding not to tell him about the warning someone had typed at the end of the file.

Emily shoved the books and stuff inside her locker, slammed the door, and locked it. "I've got to run." She turned to Louis. "What are you doing hanging around so late? Did you have detention, too?"

He raised his tennis racquet. "Tennis team practice," he told her. "We're going to be champions this year."

"In your dreams," Emily muttered sarcastically.

Louis's grin grew wider. "No. Really."

"I've got to go," Emily said, turning to me. "If I'm late for work, they yell at me a lot."

"See you," I said, thinking about my lost notes.

"D'you want to do something on Saturday afternoon?" she called back to me, halfway down the hall. "I have a class in the morning. But later we could drive to the mall or something?"

"I can't," I called back. "Louis and I are going to test out my new bike. Want to come along?"

"No thanks. I'm in a shopping mood. See you around." And she disappeared out the side door.

Louis and I were alone now, alone in the long, empty hallway. He spun the racquet handle in his hand.

I struggled to think of something to say.

I wondered if I should tell him that I knew about Phoebe.

Somehow this didn't seem like the time or the place.

Maybe I'll tell him on Saturday, I thought. Or maybe not.

I mean, what's the point of saying anything about it?

And what could I possibly say?

"D'you want to walk me home?" I asked, my nervous stammer suddenly returning. "Or would you like me to walk *you* home?"

He smiled, but shook his head. "Can't. I've got to get back to practice. I just came in to make a phone call."

"OK," I said, shifting my bag on my shoulders. "See you later. I'm really looking forward to Saturday."

"Me, too," he said, twirling the tennis racquet.

We walked together to the side door, our footsteps echoing in the empty corridor. He started to push open the door, then stopped.

He hesitated. Then, to my surprise, he leaned down and

kissed me, pushing his lips against mine, softly at first, then harder.

I was so stunned, I swallowed noisily.

Looking over his shoulder as we kissed, I suddenly saw something.

A flash of colour.

Someone watching us from the corner where the hallway turned.

I backed away from Louis to see better.

Whoever it was pulled back out of sight.

But not before I saw a flash of red hair.

Courtney!

"Come here, Goggles. Come and sit on my lap."

I'd been calling to the stubborn cat for ten minutes, but he refused to budge. He just sat in the doorway to the TV room, staring up at me in the armchair as if I were crazy.

"OK, stay there," I said crossly, giving up. "Be as unfriendly as you like, you fat furry mop."

As soon as I said that, the contrary animal hurried across the room and leaped into my lap.

I laughed. "I should've used reverse psychology on you before," I told him, stroking the soft, white fur on his back. Goggles put up with me for about a minute, then scampered away.

It was Friday night. I was alone in the house and feeling restless. My parents had gone to a party at the college, and Jake had a sleepover at one of his new friend's houses.

I tapped my fingers against the arm of the leather chair, trying to decide what to do. There was nothing on TV.

I knew I should do more research for my geography coursework. But I just wasn't in the mood. I mean, who does homework on a Friday night?

"Goggles, where are you?" I called.

Then I scolded myself for pestering the cat. Goggles wasn't very good company.

I stood up, thinking maybe I'd do something with my hair. Wash it, then try to style it like that model I saw in a picture in *Sugar*.

As I started for the doorway, the photo of Phoebe flashed into my mind. I saw her hair. It was as blonde as mine, but prettier and wavier. It fell so casually, so naturally. It looked as if she didn't have to fuss with it at all.

She *doesn't* have to fuss with it any more, I thought grimly.

She's dead.

I tried not to, but for the hundredth time I pictured poor Phoebe plunging over the falls with her bike, screaming all the way down. Until she hit the sharp rocks with a sickening *splat*.

No!

Why did I keep imagining that horrifying scene again and again?

Why couldn't I stop thinking about her, about her hideous death?

Think about something pleasant, I told myself.

Force Phoebe out of your thoughts. Think about something good that's happening in your life.

And then I thought of Louis.

I wondered what he was doing tonight. I wondered if he was sitting around the house, as bored as I was.

Go ahead. Call him, I urged myself.

I dropped back on to the big armchair and picked up the phone from the end table beside me.

I hesitated.

I suddenly felt nervous.

Go ahead, Abbie, I thought. Call him.

What's the big deal?

Holding the receiver, I realized I didn't have Louis's number. I found it in the phone book and I quickly punched it in before I lost my nerve.

It rang once. Twice.

I realized I was squeezing the receiver so tightly, my hand hurt. So I loosened my grip.

Three rings.

He isn't home, I thought, disappointed. No one's home.

Someone picked up in the middle of the fourth ring. "Hello?"

"Uh . . . Mrs M-Morgan?" I stammered.

"Is that you, Courtney?" Mrs Morgan asked, sounding surprised. "Hasn't Louis picked you up yet? He left for your house a long time ago."

I froze.

My blood seemed to stop flowing. My body turned to granite.

I was a statue. A cold statue.

"Courtney?" Louis's mother asked.

"Sorry. I have the wrong n-number," I managed to say. And I slammed down the receiver.

Louis is out with Courtney tonight?

I scolded myself for feeling so hurt.

He had a perfect right to go out with Courtney, after all. It wasn't like Louis and I. . .

We weren't. . .

He and I never said. . .

I took a deep breath and held it.

I tried to chill out, to stop the angry, upset thoughts from careering through my mind.

I looked down and saw Goggles staring at me from the doorway with those big blue cat eyes.

"Louis's out with Courtney tonight," I told the cat.

I jumped a mile as the phone rang. Goggles scampered away.

I picked it up before the second ring.

A harsh, raspy voice began talking before I even said hello.

"*Computers don't lie,*" someone whispered loudly. "*Stay away from Louis Morgan. One dead girlfriend is enough.*"

Ten

I couldn't get to sleep after that. The raspy, whispering voice kept repeating its crude warning in my mind.

I hadn't been frightened at first.

Sitting in the TV room, staring at the phone beside me, I'd been more angry than frightened.

Did someone really think they could scare me away from Louis by whispering stupid threats over the phone?

The more I thought about it, though, the more frightened I became.

The phone caller knew about the computer. He or she obviously was the one who erased my coursework.

And did the caller also slash Jake's bike tyres that afternoon when I met Louis?

Whoever it was knew how to reach me, knew where I lived.

I shuddered.

I suddenly remembered a film I'd seen on TV where a babysitter is alone in a house, and she starts getting frightening phone calls – and the caller is upstairs, *right in the house with her*!

I got up and scurried round the house, making sure the doors were locked.

As if that would do any good if someone really wanted to get me.

"It's just a practical joke," I told myself out loud. My trembling voice didn't sound very reassuring.

And again I thought of Phoebe.

She was *really* dead. No practical joke.

Later, I went to bed and couldn't get to sleep.

The shadows on my ceiling looked like dark, pointed rocks.

I stared up at them wide-eyed, feeling the fear choke my throat, hearing the whispered threat over the phone, the raspy voice like water rushing over the falls.

Somehow I eventually fell asleep.

The next morning, I called Emily right after breakfast. I *had* to talk to someone.

"I'm rushing out," she said, surprised to hear from me so early. "I have this stupid electrical engineering class on Saturday mornings."

"You have *what?*" I demanded, certain that I hadn't heard her correctly.

"You heard me," she replied, groaning. "It's a beginner's course in electrical wiring and stuff. It's two hours every Saturday morning. You see, Courtney thinks that girls should know how to do stuff like that. You know. Have skills. And she talked me into taking the class with her."

"How did she ever do that?" I asked.

"Well, the instructor's this really cute guy. . ." Emily started. She sighed. "I don't know. We've only been doing it for a couple of weeks. It's kind of interesting. Circuits and stuff."

"Weird," I said.

"What's up?" she asked.

"I got this call last night," I said. I told her about the frightening call. The threat.

"That's really gross!" Emily exclaimed. "Did you tell your parents?"

"Well . . . no," I replied.

"Maybe you should tell them," Emily urged. "Whoever this nut is, he might be serious. I think your parents should know."

'What makes you think it's a *he*?" I asked.

Emily was silent for a moment. I could practically hear her brain working over the phone line. "Why? Who do you think it is?" she asked finally.

"Courtney, maybe," I said.

I hadn't really thought about it before that second. I hadn't really suspected Courtney.

But, suddenly, the whispered, raspy voice sounded a lot like Courtney's to me.

"Courtney?" Emily sounded stunned. "Hey, Abbie, I don't think so."

"But, Emily—"

"Courtney's OK," Emily interrupted. "You shouldn't trust first impressions. She's really OK."

"Well, you know her better than I do," I said reluctantly. "But something about the whispered voice. . ."

"Come on. Why would Courtney try to scare you away from Louis?" Emily demanded.

"Well, for one thing, they went out together last night," I said.

"Huh?"

Emily sounded really shocked.

"Are you sure?" she asked breathlessly.

"Yeah, I'm sure." I told Emily about my phone call to Louis's house, and how Mrs Morgan mistook me for Courtney.

'Wow," Emily kept repeating. "Wow."

"How come you're so surprised?" I demanded.

It took her a while to answer. "It's sort of a long story," she said. "I'm just surprised, that's all. I'll have to ask Courtney all about their date at our class. I'll tell you about it later. I'm late."

"But, Emily. . ."

"Are you still going bike riding with Louis this afternoon?" she asked.

"Yeah. I guess."

"Well, be careful, OK?" And then Emily hung up.

Be careful?

I stared at the humming phone receiver. What did she mean? Be careful of *what*? Of Louis?

Louis arrived a little before two. I watched from the living room window as he sped up our driveway on his bike and leaped off while it was still going, letting the bike topple to the grass.

He didn't see me. I watched him from the window as he pulled down his pale blue hoody and pushed back his hair with both hands.

It was kind of fun spying on him.

He's so good-looking, I thought. He should be in Hollywood starring on TV shows.

I suddenly remembered something my mum had said a long time ago about not hanging around with boys who were better-looking than I was.

It's funny the things that pop into your mind for no reason at all.

The front doorbell rang. I hurried across the room and pulled open the door.

Louis seemed really glad to see me. We talked for a few minutes, just making small talk. I pulled a long green blade of grass from his hair. "How'd you get this?" I asked, twirling it in my fingers.

"Mowing the lawn this morning," he groaned. "My dad always has to be the first on his road. Only *I'm* the one who has to do the mowing." He scratched his head, frowning. "And, then, Dad says since we mowed so early in the season, we have to rake. Only *I'm* the one who does the raking. I'm totally wrecked!"

"So you don't want to go riding?" I asked, unable to conceal my disappointment.

He laughed. "No. I *need* to go riding. Just as long as we don't ride on *grass!*"

My mum came by, carrying one of the still-unpacked boxes from the back. I introduced Louis to her. She put down the box and shook his hand. I could tell by the look on her face that she was impressed with how good-looking he was.

A short while later, I pulled my new bike out of the garage and walked it over to Louis on the driveway.

It was a warm, sunny day with a few puffy clouds in the sky. The air was heavy and wet, almost like summer.

434

"Excellent bike!" Louis exclaimed, rubbing his hand along the shiny blue frame. "Really excellent!"

"You can't tell it's used, can you?" I asked. "It has one tiny scratch on the side here. That's all."

He admired the bike for a while longer.

"Excellent." He raised his eyes to mine. "Let's get going."

"Great," I said enthusiastically. I lifted my leg over the frame and straddled the bike, preparing to glide down the driveway. "Where shall we go?"

He narrowed his eyes in concentration. "Well. . ."

The sun disappeared behind one of the puffy clouds. A shadow rolled over us. The air immediately grew cooler.

I felt a sudden chill as Louis stared into my eyes and said, "Let's ride up to the falls."

Eleven

Why did I feel that cold shiver of fear when Louis suggested we ride up to the falls?

I was angry at myself for feeling it.

I had no reason to be afraid of Louis. He seemed to really like me.

A horrible thing had happened up at the falls. But that was no reason to be frightened of Louis.

I reasoned that Louis was trying to get over Phoebe, trying to get over her death.

By returning to the falls with me, he was forcing himself to get on with his life. He was putting Phoebe behind him, putting all of the horror behind him.

That was my reasoning. I wished I had the courage to ask Louis if I was right. But I didn't feel I knew him well enough yet to bring it up.

He had never mentioned Phoebe to me.

I didn't think it was right for me to be the first to bring her up.

We rode in the middle of the street. There was hardly any traffic. Lawns were being mowed. And raked. Flowers were being planted. Gardens were being tended. Weeds were being pulled.

A group of little kids were gleefully climbing through the open walls of a new house being built. "This is *my* room!" a little boy cried. "No – that's the kitchen!" another boy corrected him.

"How are you doing?" Louis called back to me. He had got about three car-lengths ahead.

"Fine. I like this bike," I shouted.

"That's Jacob's house, remember?" Louis said, pointing to a square, white clapboard house with a ragged low hedge running along the front.

And just as Louis pointed, Jacob appeared on the gravel driveway. "Hey!" he called, spotting us immediately. "Where are you going?"

Louis wheeled around and pedalled on to the drive, his tyres sliding over the gravel as he hit the brakes. His front tyre came to a stop about a centimetre from Jacob who, grinning, raised both hands over his head in surrender.

I pulled up beside Louis and lowered both feet to the gravel.

"Hot day, huh?" Jacob said, grinning at me, pushing his

437

scraggly hair back off his forehead. The gold earring in his ear sparkled in the sunlight.

"Why don't we talk about the weather for a while," Louis said sarcastically. He gazed up at Jacob's house. Someone was watching us from the front window. Jacob's mum, I guess. "Did you get your bike fixed?" Louis asked.

"Pretty much," Jacob replied, grinning.

"Want to come with us?" Louis offered.

Jacob nodded. "I haven't had any better offers." He wiped his hands off on the legs of his jeans. "I'll get my bike. The tyres are low, but that's OK."

He started towards the back of the house, kicking up the gravel as he walked. After a few steps, he turned back. "Where are we riding?"

"Up to the falls," I answered.

"Huh?" Jacob's mouth dropped open. "What did you say?" His eyes were on Louis.

"Up to the falls," I repeated softly, surprised by Jacob's reaction.

Jacob continued to stare at Louis. "You sure?"

"Yeah. We're sure," Louis snapped. "Are you coming before suppertime or not? My bike is rusting, waiting for you."

"Hey, you're in a good mood," Jacob muttered. "Sure you want me to come along?"

"Get your bike," Louis instructed him.

Jacob disappeared round the back of the house. "Someone should mow Jacob's lawn," I said, gazing at the tall, overgrown grass and flourishing weeds.

"His parents won't trust him with a lawnmower," Louis replied, grinning. "They know he'd probably cut his foot off."

After a short while, Jacob came sailing down on a rickety old BMX bike, the seat raised up as high as it would go, both tyres nearly flat. "To the falls!" he cried, rolling past us, out of the driveway and into the street without slowing to look for cars.

"He's really messed up," Louis muttered to me, shaking his head.

Jacob was twirling his bike in tight circles, waiting for us, singing at the top of his lungs.

"He's your best friend," I said dryly.

"Why?" Louis asked, making a bewildered face.

Laughing, we followed Jacob into the street. We pedalled single file to town, which was crowded and busy, with cars actually double-parked on Main Street. Most people were going into the garden centre and the hardware store. Spring DIY time.

Past town, the road started to climb through the woods. Louis and I rode side by side behind Jacob, who zigzagged wildly from one side of the road to the other, riding no-hands most of the time.

After a bit, the road levelled out, and I could see a large red lorry coming towards us in the near distance.

"Hey, get over!" Louis called to Jacob. Jacob was riding no-hands on the wrong side of the road.

Staying in the wrong lane, Jacob turned back to us, a devilish grin on his face, his dark eyes glowing. "Watch what I do to this guy," he called.

"No way! Get over!" Louis screamed.

The red lorry seemed to grow larger and larger as it approached.

"Watch!" Jacob cried.

"Get over!" Louis screamed.

Jacob stayed on the wrong side, pedalling steadily, calmly, as if he had every right to be there, as if there wasn't a huge lorry barrelling right at him.

"This is stupid!" Louis screamed. His eyes were bugging out with fright.

The lorry honked its horn, a long, earthshaking diesel honk.

"Get over, idiot!" I could barely hear Louis's shout over the roar of the lorry's horn.

A wild grin on his face, Jacob just kept pedalling.

The lorry wasn't slowing down. It rumbled closer. Closer.

"Jacob – please!"

I closed my eyes as the blaring horn became an angry, deafening scream.

Twelve

The ground seemed to shake.

I felt a powerful rush of hot air, which nearly blew me over.

When I opened my eyes, I saw Jacob seated on his bike, both feet on the ground on the other side of the road. He grinned at Louis and me and raised his fists triumphantly, cheering loudly for himself.

Louis tossed down his bike and angrily strode across the road to Jacob. I could hear the lorry rumbling away from us. It still felt to me as if the ground were shaking.

My heart was thudding in my chest. I felt dizzy. Straddling my bike, I stared across the road at Jacob as if he were a mirage.

"You could've been killed, man!" Louis screamed angrily at him.

"No way," Jacob insisted, his arms crossed over his chest,

his face bearing its usual goofy grin. "I've got timing."

"Timing? You're crazy!" Louis insisted.

"It's all timing," Jacob bragged, ignoring Louis's anger. Jacob turned his eyes to me. "Did you see the look on that lorry driver's face?"

"No, I didn't see anything," I admitted, "I closed my eyes." My legs were all trembly. My mouth was dry.

"I thought his face was going to explode!" Jacob laughed.

"That was really stupid," Louis said, scowling.

"I didn't get hit, did I?" Jacob demanded. "If I got hit, *that* would be stupid. If I'm lying here as flat as a pancake, then *that's* stupid. But I've got the timing down to an art. You know that, Louis."

Louis glared angrily at Jacob. He leaned close to his friend and lowered his voice. But I heard what he said anyway. He told Jacob, "You're just showing off for Abbie."

"Huh? Who – me?" Jacob glanced over Louis's shoulder at me. "No way, Louis."

Louis tossed up his hands, as if conceding defeat. "Are we going to ride or not?"

"Yeah. Sure. Let's go," Jacob replied, sounding hurt.

Louis walked quickly across the road, picked up his bike, and climbed on to it without looking at me. I could see that his mood had changed. Jacob's game of chicken with the lorry had really upset him.

442

"He could have bought it that time," Louis muttered, more to himself than to me.

We started to pedal, slowly picking up speed as the road curved through the woods, climbing towards the falls.

"Why does Jacob like to play such dangerous games?" I asked.

"Because I'm a dangerous guy!" Jacob exclaimed, overhearing me. He laughed gleefully. "I'm so *dangerous*!"

Louis just scowled.

A few minutes later, we turned off the road on to the bike path that led up to the top of the falls.

The falls were more beautiful than I'd remembered, the water sparkling like silver under the sun as it washed straight down from the cliff-edge.

"It smells so fresh and clean up here," I said, closing my eyes and taking a deep breath.

We left our bikes on the cycle path. I turned away from the falls to look at the woods. The leaves were all opening. The woods were so much brighter and greener than the week before.

I hoped that the beautiful scenery would help return Louis's good spirits. But when I turned back to the falls, I was startled to see that he had stepped right to the edge and was peering down, a grim expression on his face.

That's just where he'd stood when I first met him, I realized, feeling a sudden wave of dread sweep over my body.

That's just where he stood. On the very edge. Staring down so sadly.

I had thought then that Louis was going to jump.

I could feel my face grow hot, remembering that.

I suddenly became aware that Jacob had moved beside me. He was staring at Louis, too.

"I knew we shouldn't have come up here," Jacob said to me in a low voice, keeping his eyes on Louis. "I knew he wasn't ready to come up here yet."

"He was in a really good mood before," I said, feeling the cold spray off the falls on my face.

"Now he's not," Jacob said sharply, shaking his head. "We shouldn't be here."

He moved away from me and headed towards Louis, stopping a few feet from the edge. "Hey, Louis. . . ?"

Louis didn't turn round. He stood motionless, staring straight down into the streaming rush of white water.

"Louis, let's go," Jacob insisted, reaching out a hand as if intending to pull Louis away.

No reaction.

"Louis, let's go – OK?"

I took a few steps closer, suddenly very worried about Louis.

What was he thinking about?

What was he looking for?

Why wouldn't he answer Jacob?

Why wouldn't he step back from the cliff-edge?

I stepped up beside Jacob, who looked really worried. I think it was the first time I had seen Jacob with a serious expression on his face.

"Louis. . ." he called. "Earth calling Louis."

"Just a second," Louis said, not turning round.

"Come on, man," Jacob urged.

"Just a second," Louis repeated. "That's all it takes. A second. A split second. And then you're dead. Gone forever."

Jacob glanced at me, his features tight with worry. Then he grabbed Louis by the shoulder and pulled him back.

"Hey, what's the problem? Let go!" Louis protested.

"You're scaring us, man," Jacob told him, not letting go. He was pulling Louis back from the cliff-edge with both hands.

The spray drenched my face and hair. I suddenly felt cold, despite the bright sun overhead.

"I'm fine," Louis insisted.

"I don't like to hear you talking like that," Jacob said.

"Let's keep riding," I suggested, trying to sound cheerful.

"Yeah. Good idea," Jacob said.

I turned towards the cycle path and screamed. "Hey!"

Someone was back there, messing with my bike.

"Hey – get away!" I screamed.

Brushing the spray from my eyes, I began running to my bike.

The intruder had picked my bike up off the ground and was doing something to the handlebars.

I had only gone a few steps when I recognized who it was. Courtney!

Thirteen

"Hey – get away!"

My trainers pounded the ground, kicking up dust as I ran towards Courtney. I could hear Louis and Jacob running behind me.

"Huh?" Courtney stood holding my bike by the handlebars, staring at me open-mouthed, her red hair dishevelled, gleaming in the bright sunlight.

I pulled up in front of her, gasping for breath. "What are you doing to my bike?" I demanded angrily.

"I'm just *looking* at it," she snapped back. "It's a lot like my cousin's bike."

I glared at her angrily, trying to catch my breath.

"I wasn't going to steal it or anything," she said, turning her snub nose up.

"What's the problem?" Jacob asked, running up beside me.

"Abbie thought I was going to run away with her bike," Courtney told him, frowning. "I just wanted to look at it. Here." She pushed the bike towards me.

I grabbed the frame and the seat to keep it from toppling over. "Courtney, I'm sorry. . ." I started.

"I'm not a thief, you know," Courtney said nastily.

"Hey, Abbie didn't mean it," Jacob said, trying to be helpful.

"Remember? Someone slashed my tyres last week," I told Courtney. "That's why I thought—"

"Well, it wasn't me!" Courtney interrupted.

I felt really embarrassed. I'd come running after Courtney like a crazy person, screaming at her, accusing her. And she was just looking at the bike.

"I'm really sorry," I said sincerely. "Really. I didn't mean. . ."

"OK, OK," Courtney said impatiently. Her bike was lying on its side a few feet down the cycle path. She picked it up and walked it back towards the tall granite rocks.

I wheeled mine after her, and Jacob followed.

"Where's Emily?" Courtney asked, shielding her eyes from the sun with one hand as her eyes followed the curve of the sloping bike path.

"Is Emily with you?" Jacob asked, following Courtney's gaze.

448

"Here she comes," Courtney announced.

I saw Emily, standing up as she pedalled, moving slowly up the hill. A few seconds later, she hopped off her bike and walked it up to us. She was red-faced and out of breath. Her dark hair was wet, a large strand matted against her perspiring forehead.

"Wow. I'm a little out of shape," she exclaimed breathlessly. "I've *got* to lose some weight."

"You look fine," Jacob said gallantly. He laughed. "You just need a better bike. Yours is too heavy. You should get one like Abbie's."

"But don't touch Abbie's, whatever you do," Courtney warned sarcastically, flashing me a dirty look. "If you touch her bike, she freaks."

"Huh?" Emily gazed at me, puzzled.

I leaned back against the rocks. "I made a mistake," I muttered. "I didn't mean. . ."

"Did you get that bike new or used?" Courtney asked.

"Used," I told her.

"It looks brand new," she said.

"It was such a pretty day," Emily said, pushing the hair off her forehead. "I told Courtney we should ride up. I was hoping you'd still be here."

"It's cooler up here," Courtney said.

"We should keep riding," Jacob suggested. "Keep going to

Glenview, maybe."

"I want to cool off a bit first," Emily said, leaning her bike against the rocks.

"You know, we should start a bike club," Jacob said with great enthusiasm.

"Huh?" Emily narrowed her eyes at him.

"Yeah. A bike club," he repeated, undiscouraged. "We're just about the only ones in Shocklin Falls who like to ride around everywhere on our bikes, right?"

"Give me a break, Jacob," Emily said, rolling her eyes. "You ride that beat-up bike of yours because you can't afford a car, and your parents won't trust you with theirs."

"Smart parents," Courtney muttered, grinning.

"Hey, no way," Jacob protested. "I'm really into bikes, you know."

Emily made a sarcastic face.

"I'm just saying we could get together every weekend or something and maybe ride all over the place. You know, plan different routes. Bring food and stuff."

"I like the food part," I said, starting to feel hungry. I hadn't had much of a lunch.

"Forget it," Emily told Jacob. "I *hate* riding with you. You're too crazy. Always showing off. Trying to get yourself killed."

"Who? *Me?*" Jacob protested, grinning.

He had somehow conveniently forgotten about his little

game of chicken with the lorry a short while before.

"Hey, where's Louis?" Courtney asked suddenly. "Isn't he up here with you?"

Louis.

I was so worked up about Courtney and my bike, I had forgotten all about Louis!

"He was with you," I told Jacob.

"No," Jacob replied. "I don't think so."

We all turned towards the falls.

No one there.

The water roared down, a fine white spray rising from the cliff-edge.

"Louis!" I called. "Louis, where are you?"

No reply.

I turned towards the woods. No sign of him.

When I turned back, Jacob was running to the cliff-edge, a frightened expression on his face.

Emily and Courtney were staring at me. "Where *is* he?" Courtney demanded, as if I were hiding him.

A wave of dread swept over me. Heavy fear, weighing me down, making it hard to breathe.

I raised my eyes to Jacob, standing at the cliff-edge over the falls.

The exact spot where Louis had been standing.

Jacob peered straight down, his features twisted in fear.

"Did he jump?" he cried. "Did Louis jump?"

Behind me, Courtney uttered a high-pitched scream of horror.

Fourteen

"No! No!" I heard a frightened voice shriek.

It took me a while to realize it was *me*!

Jacob took a step back from the falls. "I don't see anything down there," he called, cupping his hands over his mouth to be heard over the roaring waterfall.

"Look!" Courtney cried.

We turned to the cycle path.

There was Louis. On his bike. Dust flew up on both sides of his bike as he pedalled furiously away.

The four of us stood frozen in silence, staring after him, watching him disappear into the trees.

He never looked back.

When he vanished from view, I let out a long sigh of relief and dropped to my knees on to the ground.

At least Louis hadn't jumped.

I raised my eyes to Courtney and Emily. Emily had tears

in her eyes. Her shoulders were trembling. "I – I was so scared!" she stammered.

Courtney put a hand on Emily's shoulder to calm her.

"I mean, first Phoebe. Then. . ." Emily's voice trailed off

Jacob made his way back to us, his hands shoved into his jeans pockets, his head lowered.

"Why did he do that?" I asked him, my heart still pounding. "Why did Louis run away like that?"

Jacob shrugged grimly. "Beats me."

"I really thought he'd jumped," Courtney said in a quivering voice.

"Do you think he's *angry* with us for some reason?" Emily wondered. She leaned back against the rocks and pushed her damp hair off her face. She looked very pale, very upset.

"I *knew* we shouldn't have come up here," Jacob said heatedly. "It was too soon for Louis."

"But he had already come up here," I told Jacob. "Last week. I. . ."

"Was it *your* idea?" Jacob demanded loudly, staring angrily at me.

I gasped.

In that instant, I realized that Jacob didn't like me.

His outburst cut through me. I felt a stab of pain in my chest.

He doesn't like me, I thought, staring up at him, studying his angry expression.

"No. It wasn't my idea," I replied coldly, turning away from him.

"Well, it was a bad idea," Jacob insisted. "Don't you have any idea what Louis's been through?"

"Give her a break, Jacob," Emily said, coming to my defence. "Abbie knows the whole story."

"Let's get out of here," Courtney suggested, pushing away from the rocks and reaching for her bike. "Let's ride somewhere else, OK? This place gives me the creeps. I keep picturing Phoebe standing there."

"Yeah. Let's keep riding," Emily quickly agreed.

"I – I think I'd better get home," I told them. "I'm so behind on my coursework. I threw away the notes I'd typed on to the disk. And then it was all erased. I'm practically starting all over again."

"You sure?" Emily asked, pulling up her bike. "It's too nice out to be stuck inside doing schoolwork."

"I know," I sighed. "But I'd better do it."

"Don't be upset about Louis," Emily said as I retrieved my bike. "He's moody." She chuckled. "I guess you've noticed."

I said goodbye to them and headed down the hill, pedalling hard.

I *am* upset about Louis, I thought unhappily.

I'm *very* upset.

I thought this was a date. Why did he ride away and leave me there without saying a word?

Why did he do it?

That night, I had a frightening nightmare.

The dream was in black and white. Somehow the darkness of it, the sombre grey shadows, made it all the more horrifying.

In the dream, I was standing at the falls.

The water rushed down silently.

The whole dream was silent. Not a sound. Not a voice.

I stared at the rushing water, watched it plunge to the dark rocks below without making a splash.

It was cold up there. A wet chill fell over me, over everything. The sky was a cold charcoal-grey, a dead grey.

Someone stood at the edge of the cliff. Someone dressed in black.

I stared at her and listened to the silence.

Mist rose up from the plunging waters, grey and cold.

Even with her back turned to me, I realized it was Phoebe.

I called to her, but no sound came out of my mouth.

She turned round slowly.

I stared at her face.

I uttered a silent scream.

Her skin was gone. Her beautiful, wavy hair rested on top of a grinning skeleton.

Empty eye sockets stared at me blindly.

Her jawbone lowered, revealing a mouth full of perfect white teeth.

She turned quickly away from me.

Once again, she resumed her stance at the edge of the falls.

The water continued to sweep down in total silence.

The sky darkened. Shadows rolled over the hard, grey ground.

I crept up silently behind Phoebe.

Closer. Closer still.

I knew what I was going to do.

I raised my hands.

I was going to shove her over the edge.

Hands ready, I took another step. Another.

Suddenly, my voice returned. I spoke.

"I'm Louis's new girlfriend," I said as I prepared to push Phoebe. "I'm Louis's girlfriend now."

I said the words in a flat monotone, without any emotion at all.

The water flowed down, down, down. Silently.

I reached forward. I started to push her.

But as my hands lowered to her back, we suddenly changed places.

To my horror, I realized that I was now dressed in black.

I was now standing at the very edge of the silent falls.

"I'm Louis's new girlfriend," I said. "I'm Louis's dead girlfriend."

Was Phoebe behind me now?

Was Louis?

I couldn't turn round. I could only look down.

I knew that I was about to go over the edge, into the silently plunging waters.

I knew that I was about to die.

Silently. So silently.

Into the grey churning shadows below.

The ringing of the phone by my bed woke me up.

I sat up, startled, wide awake.

The dream faded slowly. The grey shadows lingered.

I blinked. Once. Twice.

The phone continued to ring.

I reached for it, then hesitated.

The cold fear I felt – was it from the dream? Or from the ringing of the phone?

Should I answer it?

Reluctantly, I lifted the receiver to my ear.

"It's me," said a dry, whispered voice.

Fifteen

My breath caught in my throat.

I shut my eyes.

"Abbie?" the voice whispered. "Is that you?"

I swallowed hard.

"It's me. Louis," the voice whispered.

"Huh?" I cried. "Louis?"

"Who'd you *think* it was?" he asked, still whispering.

"What time is it?" I asked, squinting through the darkness at my clock radio. "Louis, it's nearly two."

"Oh. Sorry."

"Why are you whispering like that?" I demanded, my heart slowing to a normal pace.

"I don't want my parents to hear," he replied. "They'll take away my phone if they hear me calling so late."

"You scared me," I admitted. "I thought – I thought you were someone else."

"I just called to apologize," Louis said. "You know. For this afternoon."

"OK. Go ahead," I said. "Apologize."

"I apologize," he said earnestly.

I chuckled. "Apology accepted," I told him. "You could've called earlier, you know."

"I wanted to, but I had to go somewhere with my dad. Listen, Abbie, I shouldn't have run off like that. But . . . well . . . it's hard to explain."

"That's OK," I said, hearing how hard this was for him.

I was so relieved that he wasn't angry with me, that he didn't blame me for some reason.

"I shouldn't have suggested that we go up there," he continued. "I mean, it was just too soon. You probably don't know about Phoebe—"

"Yes. I heard," I interrupted.

He was silent for a long moment. "Yeah. I guess everyone talks about it," he said finally, with some bitterness.

"Emily told me . . . about Phoebe," I said softly.

As I said it, the dream washed over me. Again I saw the silent falls, the shifting grey shadows, the girl dressed in black, standing on the very edge, about to fall.

Was it Phoebe – or was it me?

"D'you want to get together tomorrow?" Louis asked, abruptly changing the subject. "We could go and see a film or something."

"I wish I could," I replied.

"I won't run away. Promise!" he quickly added.

"I've got to work on my research," I said. "I'll never get that coursework done at this rate."

"Oh. I see." He sounded very disappointed.

"Sorry," I said, and then I yawned loudly.

"Guess I'd better hang up," he whispered.

"I'm glad you called," I said honestly.

We said goodnight and hung up.

I lowered my head to the pillow and pulled up the duvet.

When I closed my eyes, images from my frightening dream returned, as if they'd been waiting for me.

No, I thought, opening my eyes wide, trying to drive the pictures away. No, I don't want to think about Phoebe now. I don't want to think about this.

"Louis didn't push Phoebe," I whispered to myself, staring up at the dark ceiling. "Louis didn't push her. I *know* he didn't!"

I had just got down to work the next afternoon, papers and books spread out all over the dining room table, when the doorbell rang. Since I was the only one at home, I ran to answer it.

"Emily!" I cried out in surprise.

She smiled at me. She was wearing a blue jumper over white tennis shorts. Her hair was tied loosely behind her head.

"I really have to work," I told her, holding open the screen door. "I don't have time to. . ."

"I know," she said, stepping past me into the front hallway. "I brought you a bunch of books." She lowered her shoulder so I could see the bulging bag on her back. "You know. For research."

"Hey, thanks," I cried, genuinely grateful. "That's really nice of you. The library is closed on Sundays, so. . ."

"I think it's all stuff you can use," she said, groaning as she pulled the bag off.

I led her into the dining room, and she emptied the contents of the bag on to the table. "I'll only stay for a minute," she said, pulling out a chair and sitting down. "Have you talked to Louis?"

I told her about his late-night apology.

"Weird," she said. And, then, fiddling with her hair, she added, "Poor guy." Her expression changed to anger. "I've just about *had* it with Jacob."

"Huh? What do you mean?" I asked, sifting through the books she had brought, glancing at the titles.

"He's just impossible," Emily complained, frowning. "He's

such a dork. He can never be serious. We went to the cinema last night, and he called out funny remarks through the whole film. The people around us were really angry. They didn't think he was funny at all. I thought they were going to punch his lights out."

I tsk-tsked, only half concentrating on what Emily was saying. I really did want to get back to work.

"Jacob's parents actually let him take the car last night," Emily continued, sighing unhappily. "They haven't let him drive it in weeks. So what did he do? He drove it into a ditch, and we had to be towed. *Aaaaagh!*" She uttered a cry of total frustration, pounding both fists on the table.

"What a drag," I said, trying to sound sympathetic. "Jacob really is a crazy guy."

"I'm going to make a change," Emily said, locking her eyes on mine. I had the feeling that she had made up her mind just that second. "I'm going to break up with him. I really am. I don't know why I've put up with him for so long."

She got to her feet and picked up her empty bag. She started to the doorway, then stopped. "Don't say anything, Abbie. To Jacob, I mean. Or to anyone."

"OK," I agreed.

"In case I chicken out or change my mind," Emily said.

I suppose I should have said something nice about Jacob. Maybe that's what Emily wanted. Maybe she was confiding in me so that I'd defend Jacob and make her change her mind about breaking up with him.

But I remembered Jacob's angry outburst, the way he shouted at me up at the falls. I remembered the intense look of dislike on his face as he glared at me.

And I guess I had decided that I didn't like Jacob, either.

So I didn't defend him.

Emily left, determined to break up with him. Before the screen door had slammed behind her, I had buried myself in my research books.

I worked for a couple of hours, but my mind kept wandering. The hideous dream wouldn't fade away. It kept invading my thoughts. And I found myself daydreaming about Louis, making up conversations with him in my mind.

My thoughts wandered to Phoebe. I wondered what she was like, what her voice sounded like, what her laugh was like.

I glanced up at the clock. It was a little past four, and I hadn't covered much ground at all with my research.

I stood up and stretched, feeling restless.

I couldn't sit there any more. I had to get out, get some exercise. I had to clear my mind.

I pulled a long-sleeved shirt over my T-shirt and hurried outside to get my bike out of the garage. It was a grey, overcast day. Heavy, dark clouds hovered menacingly low. I could hear the rumble of thunder in the distance.

But I didn't care. I had to ride for a while. Maybe a long while.

As I pedalled down the drive and into the street, the cool, damp air felt good against my hot cheeks. The wind brushed my hair back as I stood up and pedalled harder, picking up speed.

Faster. Faster.

I wanted to ride faster than my thoughts. I wanted to ride away from the frightening dream, from Phoebe's smiling face – from everything and everyone.

Houses and lawns rolled past in a grey-green blur. A little kid in a yellow raincoat waved to me from his driveway, and I waved back but didn't slow my pace.

Faster. Faster.

My heart was pounding. I could feel the blood pulsing at my temples.

There were cold drops of rain in the air. The sky grew even darker.

I rode past the college where my parents worked, then turned on to a path that led round the back. The path ended behind the car park, dark and empty.

The distant thunder had become a steady rumble, moving closer. I headed my bike towards the woods behind the college.

I hadn't had a chance to explore these woods. Someone had told me they stretched on forever.

The tall trees with their freshly unfurled leaves blocked out most of the remaining light. I felt a sudden flash of fear as I realized it was nearly as dark as night here.

But I couldn't stop riding. I wasn't ready to turn round. It felt so good to be speeding through the cold air, under the dark trees.

At first, the only sounds were the whisper of the trees, the low rumble of thunder, and the scud of my bike tyres along the curving path.

But then I heard another sound.

Behind me.

Close behind me.

I turned and saw someone on the path. Someone dressed in dark clothes.

Running.

Running after me.

My dream suddenly flashed into my mind. All black and white.

Black and white like the figure chasing me.

Panic gripped my legs.

I wanted to speed up, to get away from the dark dream.

He was closing the gap, running at full speed, his shoes slapping the ground noisily.

"Ohh!"

I cried out as my front tyre hit something in the path. A rock, probably.

I didn't have time to see it.

The bike flew out of control.

I saw the trees tilt. Then the ground came up to meet me.

I landed hard on my side with a jolt of pain that ran up and down my entire body.

The bike fell on top of me, the front tyre spinning rapidly.

He's got me, I thought.

Sixteen

My heart thudding in my chest, I tried frantically to push the bike off me.

I heard my pursuer's footsteps stop. He was standing over me.

I glanced up.

"Ryan!" I cried

Breathing hard, he bent down, grabbed the handlebars, and pulled the bike away.

He leaned it against a tree, then wiped the sweat off his forehead with the sleeve of his black hoody.

"Ryan – what are you *doing* here?" I demanded in a high-pitched, shrill voice I barely recognized.

He took my arm and helped me up. "Are you OK?" he asked, ignoring my question. "Are you hurt?"

"No, I don't think so," I replied shakily. I tried to brush the mud off the leg of my jeans.

It started to rain. First I heard the *tap-tap-tap* of raindrops on the leaves overhead. Then I felt large, cold drops on my hair.

"Why did you race off like that?" Ryan asked, staring at me, a bewildered expression on his slender face.

"I – I don't know," I admitted, embarrassed. "I thought you were. . ."

Someone from my dream?

What *did* I think?

Why *did* I panic like that?

"I thought I was alone," I explained. "When I saw someone chasing me. . ."

"Didn't you hear me calling you?" he asked. He pulled a leafy twig off the sleeve of my shirt.

The pattering of raindrops against the leaves grew louder. I could feel the rain on my shoulders now. "We're going to get soaked," I said. I picked up my bike and examined it. It seemed OK. It wasn't bent or anything. "I think I hit a rock."

"Yeah," Ryan agreed. He pointed to the path. A square-shaped stone jutted up right in the middle. "You were really moving!" Ryan exclaimed, still studying my face intently.

"Yeah," I said, starting to catch my breath. "So what were you doing here?"

I began walking my bike back towards the college. Ryan followed, walking close beside me.

"Phoebe and I used to walk here all the time," he told me, turning his eyes to the trees up ahead. "This was where we used to hang out."

I waited for him to continue, but he didn't. We walked on in silence for a while.

The rain was cold but gentle. The trees shook as if shivering. My hair was soaked, but it felt refreshing. Cleansing, somehow.

"Phoebe was such a good friend," Ryan said, breaking the silence. His expression was thoughtful. His narrow shoulders were hunched under his hoody as he trudged along beside me, hands shoved in his pockets. He avoided my eyes.

I think he expected me to reply, but I didn't know what to say.

"We used to talk about everything," he went on. "She told me things she'd *never* tell Louis." A strange smile formed on Ryan's face. He kept his eyes straight ahead.

I wondered if what he'd said was true.

Why was he telling me this now?

I barely knew him. I'd only talked to him once. Why was he confiding in me?

He seems terribly lonely, I realized.

"She was my best friend," he said softly. He stopped suddenly. He grabbed my shoulder, forcing me to stop. I nearly dropped my bike.

Ryan turned his eyes to mine in an intense stare. "I want *you* to be my friend, too," he said with emotion.

"W-well. . ." I stammered. He was squeezing my arm so hard, it hurt. "Ryan, I. . ."

"I want you to be my good friend, too."

Still squeezing my shoulder, he pressed his face against mine and tried to kiss me.

I was so startled!

My breath caught in my throat.

His lips felt hot and dry against mine. He pressed them against me too hard, too desperately.

He was really hurting me.

With a bit of a struggle, I shoved him away. "Ryan – stop!"

He looked surprised for a moment, then hurt.

I felt terribly confused. And frightened.

He was so violent. So needy.

I jumped on my bike and started to pedal, standing up. "Bye," I shouted, without turning back.

The rain flew into my face, coming down heavier now. Thunder roared nearby, seeming to shake the dark trees.

"You'll be sorry if you hang around with Louis!" I heard Ryan shout. "You'll be sorry!"

I turned back to make sure he wasn't chasing after me.

Thunder roared.

"Poor Phoebe!" Ryan shouted as it echoed through the trees. "She was sorry. I tried to warn her!"

He shouted something else, but it was drowned out by thunder.

I was too far away to hear him now. The back of the college came into view with a flash of bright white lightning.

I pedalled faster, soaked to the skin.

"Ryan's crazy," I said into the wind, his voice still lingering in my ears. "Ryan's really crazy."

After school on Monday, I was on my way to the computer room. It was going to be my hangout for the rest of the week. I was determined to get all my research notes typed in so that I could organize them and then start writing my paper.

If only we had a decent computer at home, I thought.

My birthday was only a week away. But with all the expense of moving into a new house, I knew my parents wouldn't buy me a computer.

As I hurried down the hallway, kids were pulling out their school bags, slamming their lockers shut, and heading out of the building.

I saw Courtney speeding off in the other direction, her red hair dishevelled, an intense, thoughtful expression on her face. "Hey, Courtney!" I called to her as she passed.

But she didn't seem to hear me. She kept right on going.

What's *her* problem? I wondered.

For a brief moment, I suspected that she had deliberately ignored me. But I decided that couldn't be true.

"Hey, Abbie, wait!" a familiar voice called. I saw Emily waving to me from behind a group of laughing kids who were blocking the hallway.

"Hi, Emily. How's it going?" I asked when she finally managed to get over to me. She had her hair up high on her head in a new style. She was wearing a white top tucked into a very short, green-and-white skirt.

"Listen, the cheerleaders are having a cake sale in the gym," she said breathlessly, staring at the stack of books in my arms. "Courtney and I are meeting down there. D'you want to join us?"

"I'd really like to," I said, sighing. "But I can't, Emily. I've really got to get these notes done. I'm going to be staying late every afternoon."

Emily made a face.

"No. Really!" I insisted. "I'm so far behind. Especially since my disk was erased."

Emily waved to someone down the corridor. Then she turned back to me. "Why don't you type really fast, then hurry down to the gym?"

"No. No way," I told her.

"OK. Call you later," she said, giving me a little wave, then turning and hurrying down the hallway.

I trudged into the computer room, lugging my armload of books.

Miss Elwood, the ICT teacher, was at her desk in the back of the room, studying a thick software catalogue. She glanced up as I entered, smiled, and returned to her book.

There were a couple of other kids I didn't recognize, typing away at keyboards, their faces illuminated in green from the glow of their monitor screens.

I put down the stack of books beside the computer I always used. It wasn't one of the new Macs, but I really liked the keyboard. No one else seemed to like this computer, so it was always free, ready for me to use.

I really enjoyed doing research. I found it strangely satisfying – digging up little bits of information, then putting them in some kind of order. It was sort of like a puzzle. And it was fun to see the pieces come together.

I turned on the power, and the computer hummed to life.

I got my disk from the disk file, and I lowered my fingers to the keyboard.

I felt the first painful jolt as my fingers pressed the keys.

Bright light – like lightning – shot over my hands, with a loud crackle.

I heard a buzz.

Felt another jolt of pain.

Electricity crackled over my hands. Shot through my body.

Gasping, I tried to pull my hands away.

But the crackling blue-white current held me prisoner.

"H-h-h-h—" I tried to call for help. But the current was forcing my entire body to tremble out of control. "H-h-h-h—"

Out of control. . .

The crackling grew louder. The blue-white light snapped around me.

It grew brighter. Brighter.

The pain was so intense!

Then everything went black.

Seventeen

A thin blue light trailed through the utter blackness. The light glowed brighter. Brighter.

Cold blue light, ribbon-thin.

It exploded into a wash of bright colours.

I opened my eyes.

Miss Elwood's worried face came into sharp focus.

Everything seemed so bright, so clear. As if all the lights had been turned up. As if the white electricity had given everyone a brighter-than-daylight glow.

"She's opening her eyes," Miss Elwood told someone else in the room.

I slowly realized that I was no longer sitting at the computer. Staring up at the ceiling lights above Miss Elwood's frowning face, I saw that I was flat on my back on the floor.

Everything seemed to be vibrating. Pulsing. Buzzing.

"Miss Elwood?"

My voice came out flat, nearly a whisper.

"She's talking," Miss Elwood told someone near the door.

I heard shuffling feet, murmurs, muffled voices.

Miss Elwood peered down at me, her face just a few inches above mine. "Abbie, can you hear me?" she asked anxiously.

"Yes." Again, my voice didn't sound like me.

"Can you see me?" Miss Elwood demanded, so close I could smell peppermint on her breath.

"Yes," I told her.

I tried to sit up. But I felt dizzy, so I dropped back down.

Why was everything vibrating like that?

I thought I heard the crackling sound. The crackling of electricity. But it was only in my mind.

I turned my head and saw several other kids and a few teachers huddled against the wall.

"What happened?" I asked.

"You got a bad shock," Miss Elwood said.

"Huh?" I stared up at her. She pulled her head back a little. I felt a little stronger. I sat up.

The lights were dimming to normal. The crackling stopped.

"You got a bad shock. From the computer." She pointed. The old computer had been unplugged, the wire draped over the monitor.

"Those machines aren't supposed to do that," Miss Elwood said.

Right, I thought bitterly. *That's pretty obvious, isn't it!*

"The electricity just shot out from the keyboard," Miss Elwood explained.

I got to my feet. I felt strange. Not weak or dizzy.

I felt *crazy.* Really *pumped.*

I felt like running for ten miles. Or putting my fist right through the wall.

It was from all that electricity, I guess.

"Did you touch the plug or something?" Miss Elwood demanded, biting her lower lip.

"Uh-uh," I said. "Only the keyboard."

"I can't understand it," she said, staring at me intently.

I can, I thought.

I can understand it.

The anger surged in my chest like a jolt of electricity.

I saw the white light again.

My anger raged through me like a powerful current.

Courtney!

Courtney had tampered with the computer.

I knew it in a burst of angry white light.

That's why Courtney was running down the hall with that wild look on her face.

That's why Courtney ran right past me without seeing

me, without stopping.

Courtney had wired the keyboard.

She took that electrical class on Saturdays. That's where she learned how.

And now she had tried to kill me with electricity.

She had tried to kill me to keep me away from Louis. To make her threats come true.

She had wired the keyboard. To kill me.

Kill me. Kill me. Kill me.

"Abbie – come back!" Miss Elwood shouted.

I didn't even realize that I was running until I reached the hallway.

"Come back!" I could hear her scream.

But I kept running. I couldn't stop myself.

I couldn't stop my rage.

It raced through my body like a powerful jolt of current.

I heard the hideous crackling sound again. I saw the eerie blue light. It filled my eyes, shimmering brighter and brighter as I ran – until it suddenly burst into the brightest, angriest red, so red, so angry; I shut my eyes.

Courtney did it, I told myself.

Her name repeated in my mind until it became an ugly word.

Where was I running?

I'm not sure I knew.

The anger was driving me forward. The red electric anger was moving me blindly through the halls, past rows of lockers, past doorways, all red, all blazing red.

When I burst into the crowded gym, I wasn't sure where I was. Faces came into focus, bright focus. I saw smiling faces. I saw cheerleaders in their uniforms. I saw kids milling about the tables of the cake sale.

I'm here, I told myself. My anger, my *fury*, had brought me here.

To do what?

And then I saw Emily and Courtney against the tile wall. And standing next to Courtney was Louis.

She had one hand on the shoulder of his jumper.

They were laughing.

Their laughter, the hand on his shoulder, her dishevelled red hair – it was all too much.

With an angry shriek that I didn't even realize had come from me, I lunged across the gym. Ignoring the startled cries around me, I threw myself on Courtney.

Her eyes bugged out in shock as I wrapped my hands around her throat.

I leaped at her with such force that we both toppled to the floor.

As the red light crackled and buzzed, I wrestled her down.

I heard screams. Loud cries. Alarmed voices.

Red. I saw only red.

Then I felt strong hands on my shoulders, pulling me up, pulling me away.

As the hands held me back, Courtney scrambled to her feet.

She was red-faced, as red as my anger, and her eyes were filled with tears.

I turned to see who had pulled me away. It was Emily.

"Just chill!" she was shouting in my ear. "Chill, Abbie! Just chill!"

Courtney stood hunched over in front of me, her hands pressed against her knees, panting loudly.

The gym buzzed and crackled with excited voices.

With a swift motion, I jerked myself free of Emily.

Courtney raised herself warily, glaring at me, her chest heaving.

"You tried to kill me!" I screamed at her.

Her face filled with surprise, but she didn't reply.

"But you're not going to scare me away! You're not!" I shrieked.

"Abbie, what's your problem?" Courtney snapped, rubbing her throat with one hand. "What is your *problem*?"

"You know what I'm talking about," I said through gritted teeth, lowering my voice as I saw two teachers approaching.

"No, I don't. I *don't*!" Courtney insisted. "You're messed up, Abbie. You really are!"

I opened my mouth to say something, but no sound came out. Angrily, helplessly, I turned to Louis. He stood staring at me, his hands balled up tensely at his sides.

"Well, say something!" I shouted at him. "Aren't you going to say *anything*?"

His face reddened. All expression seemed to disappear. He stared back at me, a stone face. "Abbie, I don't know what's going on," he said.

The teachers were making their way across the gym to see what the fuss was about.

"Louis. . ." I started. But I didn't know what to say, either.

My anger, I realized, had faded. The bright red current that had brought me storming into the gym had vanished, as if someone had pulled the plug.

Now, with everyone staring at me, with everyone talking about me, I felt embarrassed. Humiliated.

"You're messed up, Abbie," Courtney repeated. "I mean it. You're really messed up."

With a groan of defeat, I turned and ran.

I pushed my way through a group of gawking kids and kept running.

My chest heaving, my head throbbing, I shoved open the gym doors and raced through them.

I heard Emily calling me from the gym. But I never looked back.

I ran up the stairs, panting loudly, stumbling, as I climbed. Then I started down the front hall, my trainers thundering over the hard floor.

I turned into the corridor where my locker was. Some of the lights had been turned out. The hall looked like a dark, empty tunnel.

My loud gasps echoing against the tile walls, I stopped short when a figure stepped out of the darkness.

She moved silently towards me. And when her face came into the light, I uttered a silent gasp of horror.

It was Phoebe.

Eighteen

I stood in the centre of the hall and stared at her, my eyes practically popping out of my head, my mouth wide open.

She stopped, too. Her blonde hair caught the light. She was very pale, paler than her photograph.

Pale as a ghost.

She wore a dark green jumper over brown shorts. She had a blue bag slung over one shoulder.

Phoebe, what are you doing here? I thought. *You're dead.*

I suddenly realized I'd forgotten to breathe. I exhaled with a loud whoosh.

"Are you OK?" she asked. Her pale forehead wrinkled in concern.

"I – I don't know," I stammered. I couldn't stop staring at her. I'd never seen a ghost before.

I took a step back, suddenly frightened.

"It's so dark in this hall with most of the lights out," she said. "Don't they usually leave them on?" She had a smooth, soft voice.

I didn't answer her. I just stared in disbelief. The photograph, the sad, sad photograph had come to life.

Phoebe had come back.

But how?

"I'm Natasha Powell," she said, shifting the bag to her other shoulder. "You're new here, right?"

"Huh?"

I was speechless. I couldn't seem to focus on anything. "What did you say your name was?" I managed to ask.

"Natasha," she repeated.

And then she gasped, and all the life seemed to drain from her face. "I'm not Phoebe," she said softly, so softly I could barely hear her. She took a few steps towards me, her pale blue eyes suddenly moist. "Is that what you thought? Did you think I was my sister?"

"They never told me she had a sister," I mumbled, still shaken.

"What?" She hadn't heard me. She gazed at me with concern. "Listen, are you feeling OK?"

"I'm sorry, Natasha," I said, shaking my head as if trying to clear it. "I'm having a really bad day."

"Tell me about it," she replied, rolling her eyes. "I just had to stay late to re-take a physics exam."

"I'm Abbie Kiernan," I said, starting to recover my wits. "I've just moved to Shocklin Falls, and. . ."

"You're Louis's new girlfriend," she said with an odd smile.

"I don't know," I told her. "I haven't really seen him that much. I. . ."

"D'you want to get a Coke or something?" she asked, starting towards the door. "Physics exams make me really thirsty. And this dark hall is giving me the creeps. It's like a tomb." She blushed, probably thinking about Phoebe.

"Yeah. Great," I said, following after her. "I'll be glad to get out of here, too."

Courtney flashed into my mind. Courtney, glaring angrily at me.

Had I made a fool of myself back in the gym? Or had Courtney really tried to electrocute me?

I tried not to think of it as I followed Natasha out of the building, into the sunlight of a warm spring afternoon. We walked to a small coffee shop a couple of streets towards town and slid into a booth near the back.

"I really want to apologize," I said, after we'd ordered Cokes and chips. "I mean, for the way I stared at you. You must've thought I was *nuts!*"

"Yeah, I did," Natasha said, smiling. Her eyes crinkled when she smiled, and a dimple appeared on her right cheek.

I wondered if Phoebe had the same dimple.

"I guess I freak a lot of kids out," she said softly, lowering her eyes to the tabletop. "Since I look so much like Phoebe. I'm a year and a half older than she was. But people were always mistaking us. I suppose you know what happened to Phoebe."

"Yeah. Some of it," I said awkwardly. "I mean Emily told me the story. I'm so sorry. Really."

"I feel so bad for Louis, and Courtney, too," Natasha said. The Cokes arrived, and she took a long sip from the straw.

"Courtney?" I asked, startled.

"Yeah. You know. The three of them went biking that day, the day Phoebe . . . died." She took another long sip, nearly emptying the glass.

"I didn't know Courtney went, too," I said, unable to conceal how stunned I was. "Emily never told me. . ."

"She was probably protecting Courtney," Natasha said. "You know Emily and Courtney have been friends since they were tiny."

"I'm sorry to be so nosy," I said, spinning my glass between my hands. "You don't have to answer if you don't want to. But –" I took a deep breath – "do you think that Louis or Courtney. . . ?"

I couldn't finish my question.

It was too horrible.

"Do I think they had anything to do with my sister's death?" she finished it for me. She closed her eyes, then shook her head. "No. Maybe. No."

"Natasha, you really don't have to answer," I said, putting my hand on her slender wrist.

"I don't know *what* to think!" she declared emotionally. "I've spent so many nights unable to go to sleep, just thinking and thinking about it."

She slurped up the rest of the Coke. The waitress brought the chips. Natasha asked for another Coke.

"Louis and Phoebe were always fighting," she confided to me. "Always. They were always breaking up, then making up. It was a really stormy relationship. But I really don't think Louis would *kill* her because of any stupid fight."

"And Courtney?" I asked.

"I think Courtney was jealous of Phoebe. I don't know. I don't know Courtney very well. I think Courtney probably liked Louis. A lot. But, come on, Abbie. People don't kill people over things like that."

"Someone tried to kill *me*," I blurted out.

"Huh?" She dropped the ketchup bottle. It clattered on to the tabletop, but didn't break.

I told her what had happened to me in the computer room.

Natasha frowned, wrinkling her pale forehead thoughtfully. "Those old computers," she muttered. "It probably shorted out. You have no proof that someone rigged it up."

I reluctantly agreed. I was instantly sorry that I'd told her about it. I mean, she had enough problems, enough sadness of her own. She didn't need to hear about my problems.

After that, we chatted for a short while, being careful not to talk about anything important. I liked her. She seemed like a really sweet, thoughtful girl. Even though she was so pale and slight, she seemed to have real strength, the strength to deal with all of the sadness she'd experienced.

We lived in different directions, so we said goodbye outside the coffee shop.

The sun was lowering itself in the late afternoon sky, a red ball sinking below the green trees. The air carried the chill of evening.

I gave Natasha a little wave, then stood watching her walk away. She was so light, she seemed to float away, like a pale ghost, disappearing into the cold, blue afternoon.

The ringing phone woke me up late that night.

Still half asleep, I lifted the receiver.

Again, a frightening, raspy voice whispered angrily in my ear:

"Louis will kill you, too, if you don't stay away. Louis will kill you too."

Whoever it was hung up.

I was wide awake now.

I replaced the receiver.

As soon as I hung it up, the phone rang again.

My hand hovered over the receiver, trembling.

Should I pick it up?

Nineteen

As my hand hesitated over the phone, something hit me hard in the stomach.

I uttered a silent gasp and leaped to my feet.

To my relief, it was only Goggles. I guess the phone had woken him.

The phone rang again. Goggles mewed and lowered himself on to my pillow.

I picked up the phone receiver. "Hello?"

"Hi, Abbie. It's me."

"Emily?" I read the time on my clock radio. It was nearly one.

"Did I wake you?"

"It's so late," I said, sitting down on the edge of the bed. I reached out a hand to pet Goggles, but he jumped off the bed.

"I'm sorry," Emily said, "but I've just been so upset. I've

been thinking about you and Courtney all night, Abbie. You know. What happened in the gym."

I shivered. The bedroom window was open. The breeze blowing in was really cold.

"Yeah. What about it?" I muttered, the whole angry scene flashing through my mind.

"Courtney was terribly hurt," Emily continued. "I've never seen her so hurt. And upset."

"Too bad," I said sarcastically.

"You really should apologize to her," Emily said.

My mouth dropped open. I was speechless at the suggestion.

"Abbie? Are you still there?"

"Apologize to Courtney?" I cried. "Emily, are you out of your mind? She tried to *kill* me!"

"Abbie, listen—"

"She wired the computer keyboard to *electrocute* me!" I screamed, forgetting that I might wake up the rest of the family.

"She couldn't have," Emily replied softly.

"Huh? What do you mean?"

"Courtney couldn't rig up anything like that."

"What about that electrical class you two are taking?" I demanded.

"We've only had two classes," Emily told me. "We don't

know anything. There's no way Courtney could wire up a computer. She can barely change a lightbulb."

"Then *who* did it?" I asked shrilly. I could feel myself going out of control. My throat tightened in anger. And in fear.

"How should I know?" Emily replied. "It was probably an accident, Abbie. But you shouldn't have blamed Courtney. She called me tonight. She couldn't stop crying."

"Boo-hoo," I said nastily. But I was beginning to feel guilty.

This afternoon, I had been so frightened and so angry, I didn't know *what* I was doing. When I ran into the gym, all I could see was bright red. I could've strangled Courtney then. I really wanted to harm her.

But maybe Emily was telling the truth. Maybe I blamed the wrong person.

"Why are you sticking up for Courtney?" I demanded, pulling the duvet over my bare legs.

"She's my friend," Emily said. "And she's really not a bad person, Abbie. I know you got off to a bad start with her. But Courtney is really OK."

"Well, how come you didn't tell me that Courtney was up at the falls when Phoebe died?"

That question caught Emily off-guard.

There was a long silence.

Finally, she answered, speaking slowly, carefully. "It was old news, Abbie. I didn't think you needed to know it. I didn't want to turn you against Courtney. I thought all three of us could be good friends."

She sighed. There was another long silence.

"I guess I should tell you the whole story," she said quietly. "Courtney had a thing about Louis for a while. I don't think Louis was ever seriously interested in her. He just saw her as a friend. But sometimes when he and Phoebe were fighting, he'd go out with Courtney. And that's all. After Phoebe died, it was all over between them."

"Oh, really?" I said, not intending it to come out so nastily. "Then how come Courtney and Louis went out together last weekend?"

"It wasn't a real date," Emily said. "Really. Courtney told me all about it. At the class on Saturday. It wasn't a date at all."

"Listen, Emily," I said impatiently, watching the curtains flutter in front of my open window. "Someone is trying really hard to frighten me away from Louis. And I think it's Courtney."

"I don't," Emily replied quickly. "I don't think it's Courtney. No way. For all I know, it could be Louis himself."

"Huh?" It was my turn to be caught off-guard.

"What are you *saying*, Emily?" I demanded, squeezing the phone cord tightly in my free hand. "Louis?"

"You don't know him very well," Emily replied. "Sometimes I think he's really crazy. Maybe even dangerous."

"Louis? Dangerous?"

"Maybe."

"Well, I don't know, Emily. He's really moody, but. . ." I didn't know what to say. "I *will* apologize to Courtney," I told Emily, changing the subject. "I guess I really owe her an apology. I'll invite her for Saturday night. To my birthday party. It's not really a party. Just sort of an open house. You and Jacob are coming, right?"

"Yeah," she replied. "I mean, I am. I don't know about Jacob. I might break up with him before Saturday. He's just too big a dork." She yawned. "But we've been through that before. I think I have to go to sleep now," she said, yawning again.

I said goodnight and we both hung up.

"Goggles? Are you here?" I called softly.

I had an urgent need to hug something.

But the bad cat had run from the room.

Everyone seemed to be having a good time at my birthday open house on Saturday night. Our living room isn't exactly enormous, but no one seemed to mind being jammed in like sardines.

The music was really loud, and the laughter was even louder.

I boiled up a huge pot of spaghetti. And everyone stood or sat around with their bowls of spaghetti, slurping it up as best they could. It was actually a very funny sight.

Emily showed up with Jacob. They seemed to be as together as always. I guessed Emily had changed her mind about breaking up with him during the week.

Courtney showed up, too. She even brought me a present. I could tell when I took it from her that it was a book.

I had called Courtney the morning after my conversation with Emily and apologized for twenty minutes, begging her forgiveness. I only did it because of Emily. I was still very suspicious of Courtney, in spite of Emily saying what a good person she was.

Louis seemed very relaxed. I could see he was having a good time, joking with some of his friends, laughing more than I'd ever seen him.

As I passed by him outside the kitchen, he grabbed both my hands and, smiling, started to pull me towards the corner of the living room where some kids were dancing. "Come on," he urged. "I really like this song. Come on. Let's dance."

I started to go with him, but I heard someone knocking on the back door. Louis got a pouty look on his face as I pulled away from him and headed through the kitchen to see who was at the back.

496

"Ryan!" I cried in surprise, pulling open the kitchen door and flicking on the back porchlight.

He looked terribly embarrassed. He fiddled with his glasses, avoiding my eyes. "I – I didn't know you were having a party," he stammered. "I just stopped by to . . . uh . . . say hi. See if you were busy, but. . ."

"Come in," I told him. "It's just an open house. For my birthday. Why don't you stay a while, have some spaghetti?" I pointed to the big, steaming pot on the stove.

I didn't really want Ryan at my party. Actually, he gave me the creeps.

But what could I do? There he was.

He came in, looking very reluctant. I hurried back to Louis in the living room.

"The song's over," Louis said, still pouting.

"I'll play it again," I said, moving to the CD player.

He grabbed my arm gently. "That's OK. Hey, want to go biking with me tomorrow afternoon? If it's a nice day?"

"Yeah. Sure. I guess," I replied.

Then he surprised me by wrapping his arms round my waist and lowering his face to mine in a really intense kiss.

I closed my eyes at first and returned the kiss.

When I opened them, I saw Courtney staring at us from across the room, an unhappy frown frozen on her face.

What's her problem? I asked myself silently.

Ignoring her, I kissed Louis again.

"What a mess!" my mother cried, her eyes surveying the kitchen.

"It's not as bad as it looks," I said. "It's *worse!*"

Mum and I both laughed.

"Maybe spaghetti wasn't such a great idea," she said, staring at a wide puddle of tomato sauce in the middle of the kitchen floor.

"It seemed like a good idea at the time," I sighed.

"I'll change my shoes. Then we'll get to work," Mum said, pushing a strand of blonde hair off her forehead.

"No. Really. You don't have to help," I told her. "You and Dad were so good tonight, hiding up in your room the whole night."

"We *were* good, weren't we?" Mum said, smiling. "But I'll come and help you clean up anyway, Abbie. Otherwise you'll be here all night."

She started towards the doorway, then stopped abruptly.

"Hey, you left the spaghetti water on," she said.

"No, I didn't," I insisted. "I turned it off. I remember."

"Well, it's boiling over," Mum said, irritated.

We both made a mad dash to the stove and turned off the burner. The lid was bouncing around on top of the pot, steaming liquid frothing up, running down the sides, on to the stove.

I lifted the lid. "Yuck. What's this white stuff?" I asked.

Bobbing on the top of the boiling water was a large white hunk of cotton.

"How did this get in here?" I asked, making a face. "What on earth is it?"

I poked it with a long wooden spoon.

As I rolled it over, two blank, blue eyes came into view.

When I finally realized what it was, I started to scream.

It wasn't a hunk of cotton bubbling at the top of the pot.

It was Goggles.

Twenty

Louis showed up at my house the next afternoon. He came walking into the kitchen, wearing a black-and-red sleeveless T-shirt and black shorts.

I looked up from my seat at the kitchen table, surprised to see him. "I told you on the phone I don't feel like riding," I said glumly.

"I know," he replied. "I wasn't going to come. But then I thought it might be good for you to get out of the house. You know. Get some sunshine. Take your mind off . . . what happened."

He put a hand on my shoulder and kept it there. His hand felt hot through the sleeve of my top.

When he had called at ten to see what time I wanted to go biking, I'd told him about Goggles. "Who would do that?" I had asked, still too upset to even think about it clearly. "Who would be so cruel?"

"It had to be someone at the party," Louis had replied thoughtfully.

Someone at the party.

"I can't go biking today," I'd told him, my voice trembling.

Every time I closed my eyes, I saw Goggles, a bubbling furball, boiled to death in that big pot.

"OK. I understand," Louis replied quietly. "Take it easy, OK?"

But now, three hours later, here he was, standing beside me in the kitchen. I turned and stared up into his startling green eyes. He had a grim, faraway look on his face.

I wondered what he was thinking about.

"It's almost like summer," he said. "It's really great. Come on out. For a short ride. It'll make you feel better. Really."

I turned my gaze to the golden sunlight pouring in through the kitchen window.

"It'll take your mind off Goggles," Louis urged. "Come on. You can't just sit and mope in this kitchen all day. It's too depressing."

"OK," I reluctantly agreed. I scooted the chair back and stood up. Then I called to my mum to tell her I was going out, and followed Louis out the back door.

It was a bright, beautiful day. Everything seemed to shimmer and glow from the sunshine. The grass and trees were that amazing fresh green you only see in springtime.

Two robins were fighting over a long earthworm beside the garage. Our neighbours on both sides were noisily mowing their lawns. I held my ears to block out the roar of the power mowers.

We rode side by side along our usual route. When we got past town, we picked up speed. At first, my legs felt as if they weighed a ton. But as we continued along the road, I started to gain my usual strength.

It took me a while to realize we were headed for the falls.

We left our bikes on the cycle path and walked towards the cliff-edge. The water sparkled pure white as it fell. Above us, the sky was solid blue, not a wisp of a cloud in sight.

Louis walked right up to the edge and peered down. It always made me so nervous when he did that. I stayed several metres back.

After a few seconds, he turned and came over to me. We both sat down on the ground, the falls roaring beneath us.

I decided to tell Louis about how someone was trying to scare me away from him. I'd been thinking about it all night and all morning.

Finally, I'd decided I had to tell him.

He listened to the whole story without moving, a vacant expression on his face. He kept his eyes towards the cliff-edge and didn't react to a thing I said.

"I think the same person killed Goggles," I said, finishing the story, my voice breaking. "But who could it be, Louis? Who?"

He didn't reply.

Turning towards me, he locked his eyes on mine. But he still didn't say anything.

His silence was driving me crazy.

"You *have* to say something!" I demanded. "You can't just stare at me like that after all I've told you."

"I don't know what to say," he said finally, lowering his eyes.

"You know, you can't just be silent all the time," I continued heatedly, "and never tell people what's on your mind. I can tell you're keeping something from me."

He shrugged.

"You've never once mentioned Phoebe," I blurted out.

I think it was the first time I'd mentioned her name in front of him.

"You've never talked about Phoebe once," I continued. "Not once."

He shut his eyes as if trying to shut out my voice.

"I know it's hard for you," I said, softening my tone, seeing the pain on his face. "I know it's hard, but I've got to know, Louis. You've got to tell me the truth."

He opened his eyes. "The truth?"

"You've got to tell me what really happened up here that day."

"Now, wait a minute, Abbie," he started.

I put a hand on his arm. "No. You have to tell me," I insisted. "You have to tell me the whole story about Phoebe. I know you cared about her so much—"

"*Cared* about her?"

His mouth dropped open. He jumped to his feet.

"*Cared* about her?" He stared down at me, his face twisted in excitement. "Are you *crazy*, Abbie? *Cared* about her?" Louis screamed.

"I *hated* Phoebe!" he bellowed. "I hated her so much, I *killed her*!"

Twenty-One

The roar of the falls grew louder, louder – until I felt as if it were roaring inside my head!

And then I suddenly felt as if my head were about to explode.

"*I hated her so much, I killed her!*"

The words repeated themselves in my mind, over the deafening roar of the sparkling white water beneath us.

Louis stared down at me, his expression wild, his features twisted angrily. His hands were balled into tight fists at his sides as he stood over me. Menacingly.

"*I hated her so much, I killed her!*"

A wave of dread swept over me as I scrambled to my feet.

He had just confessed.

He had just admitted to me that he had killed Phoebe.

And now I was here with him. Alone with him.

The only one to share his terrifying secret.

And he was staring at me with that crazed, dangerous look on his face, staring so intensely into my eyes, as if trying to decide what to do next.

As if trying to decide what to do about me.

As if trying to decide whether or not to push me, too.

"*I hated her so much, I killed her!*"

Why? I wondered.

Why did he do it?

"Louis," I said, taking a step back from the cliff-edge, away from him. "Louis, you . . . pushed Phoebe? Over the falls?" My voice sounded tiny and choked.

I wasn't sure he'd heard me over the relentless roar of the rushing water.

But his expression changed. His forehead wrinkled in consternation. His eyes narrowed. "No," he said. "I didn't push her."

I waited for him to offer more, but he lapsed back into silence.

My entire body shivered. I felt ice-cold despite the bright sunshine. I wrapped my arms round me for warmth, for protection.

But I felt totally alone. Totally vulnerable.

"You said you killed her," I repeated.

He shook his head sadly. "Yes. By bringing her up here. If

I hadn't brought Phoebe here, she wouldn't have died." He let out a groan of pain, of anguish.

"But you didn't push her?" I *had* to know the truth.

He trained his eyes on mine and moved closer to me. "Someone else pushed her," he said. "Someone else."

I stared back at him, searching his eyes, searching his face, trying to tell if what he was telling me was true.

"Someone else," he repeated.

"You mean . . . Courtney?" I asked. "Did Courtney push Phoebe?"

Louis nodded. "Yes."

Twenty-Two

A flock of birds, tiny dark Vs high in the sky, flew silently overhead, casting no shadow.

Louis took another step towards me.

He was breathing hard. His eyes were narrowed, his jaw clenched tightly.

"Courtney pushed her?" I repeated, not wanting to believe it.

"Yes," he said. "I brought Phoebe up here. But Courtney pushed her."

"*Liar!*"

The voice from the rocks startled us both.

"*Liar! You filthy liar!*"

We both turned to see Courtney running out from behind the tall pile of granite rocks. Her red hair flew wildly about her face, which was twisted in a frightening expression of pure rage.

"Courtney, are you still following me?" Louis cried angrily. "I told you—"

"Shut up!" she shrieked and shoved him hard in the chest, causing him to stumble back a few steps towards the cliff-edge. "Shut up! Shut up! Shut up!"

She tried to push Louis again, but he bumped her away with his shoulder.

Glaring at Louis, Courtney uttered an angry cry.

"I've been covering up for Courtney all this time," Louis said, turning to me.

"Shut up!" Courtney screamed. She turned to me, too. "Don't listen to him. He's a filthy liar!"

"I'm through with lying," Louis said heatedly. "I'm through with covering up for you, Courtney. I can't do it any more."

"Shut up – I'm warning you!" Courtney threatened.

"In January, I wanted to break up with Phoebe," Louis explained, eyeing Courtney warily. "Phoebe and I never got along. We were always fighting. I brought her up here to tell her. Courtney and I brought her here. We were both going to tell Phoebe. Courtney and I had been secretly dating. But, then—"

"Stop it," warned Courtney. "Louis, just shut up. Why are you telling her all this?"

"I started to explain to Phoebe," Louis continued,

ignoring Courtney, staring intently at me, "I started to tell her about Courtney and me. But then Jacob showed up on his bike. I went over there, behind the rocks, to talk to him." He pointed to the rocks.

"And, then," Louis's voice broke as he continued. "And then, while I was talking to Jacob, Courtney pushed Phoebe and her bike over the falls."

Courtney grabbed my arm and swung me around hard. "Don't listen to him, Abbie. It's lies. All lies."

"Courtney – let go of me!" I pleaded, twisting out of her grasp.

"Lies!" Courtney repeated, turning accusingly to Louis. "You've been lying since January. Lying to everyone. Even to yourself."

But Louis continued to ignore her, talking only to me. "After Courtney killed Phoebe, I was ill. I couldn't stand the sight of Courtney. She kept trying to get me to go out with her. But I felt so guilty. So horribly guilty. I didn't want to even *talk* to Courtney again. But she kept following me. She would never leave me alone."

"Liar!"

"Even today!" Louis accused. "Even today you're still following me! Leave me alone, Courtney! Leave me alone!"

Courtney uttered another roar of rage. "Liar!" she cried, giving Louis another shove towards the cliff-edge. "*You* killed

Phoebe! *You* pushed Phoebe! I didn't! *You* were the one! Admit it!"

Courtney turned to me. "Louis, Phoebe and I were up here. We had just started to talk. Then Jacob showed up. Louis went back towards the woods to talk to him. Phoebe and I were standing by the falls. Then I heard someone calling my name. I thought it was Louis. So I left Phoebe and hurried to the woods to find him. When I came back, Louis was standing on the cliff-edge, staring down. And Phoebe was gone. Phoebe was dead."

"Not true!" Louis declared. "I didn't push her – *you* did!"

I cried out as their anger exploded. Louis grabbed Courtney furiously round the waist and wrestled her to the ground.

Shrieking at the top of her lungs, she pounded him with her fists, hitting his face, his chest, his shoulders.

"Stop it! Stop it!" I screamed.

But they didn't hear me.

Locked in a bitter struggle, they wrestled, screaming.

"Stop it – *please!*" I cried.

They were rolling on the ground, rolling towards the cliff-edge.

Courtney was pulling Louis's hair, pummelling his face, batting his chest with her head.

I ran towards them, screaming, begging them to stop.

They were only a metre or so from the cliff-edge now.

"Stop it! Stop it, please!" My voice sounded tiny and far away over the roar of the falls.

Courtney scratched her nails down the side of Louis's face. The side of his face turned scarlet, and a line of bright red blood appeared.

He cried out in pain.

"Stop it! *Stop* it!" I didn't recognize my shrill, desperate voice.

Louis grabbed Courtney's head, twisted it round, and pushed her face into the ground.

Her hands thrashed the air wildly as she tried to break out of his hold.

They were only centimetres from the cliff-edge now.

"Stop! Please! Look out!"

They couldn't hear me.

They were out of control, I realized. I was watching the explosion of months of guilt, months of suspicion, months of rage.

Louis and Courtney hated each other because of the secret they shared.

And their hatred was about to kill them both.

"No!" I cried as Courtney rolled away from Louis and, crouched on her knees, pushed him with both hands towards the falls.

I made a lunge for them, reaching to grab Louis's arm and keep him from toppling over the side.

But as I hit the ground, Louis rolled on to his back, reached up, and grabbed Courtney around the knees.

She screamed in protest and broke free.

Then with a breathless snarl of rage, she lunged at him.

He rolled underneath her.

And she plunged over the cliff.

Twenty-Three

Courtney screamed all the way down.

I didn't hear a splash.

I didn't hear the crack of her body as it slammed on to the jagged black rocks below.

The relentless roar of the falls drowned it out.

The water continued to sparkle and flow. As if it hadn't claimed another victim.

Panting like a wounded animal, Louis raised himself to his knees.

Bright red blood rolled down his cheek.

His eyes were wild, confused.

Still on the ground, I stared at the cliff-edge in disbelief.

Louis was there alone now.

Courtney was gone.

I stared at the spot until my eyes watered over.

I had the urge to run to the edge. To peer down. To see what had happened to poor Courtney.

But I couldn't move. I couldn't breathe.

I had the sudden, crazy thought that if I just stared at the cliff-edge, if I just concentrated hard enough, Courtney would reappear.

I closed my eyes to stop them from watering.

When I opened them, Courtney had not returned.

Only Louis remained, gasping, sucking in deep breaths, his chest heaving under his torn, dirt-stained T-shirt.

It took me a long while to realize that the terrified whimpering sounds I heard were coming from me. My entire body shuddered.

Louis climbed slowly to his feet, still struggling to catch his breath.

I was on my knees, my arms wrapped round my chest.

The roar of the falls grew louder.

Louis stared down at me.

Such an odd expression on his face. Such an odd, hateful expression.

As if he hated me, too.

He took a heavy step towards me, his eyes wild, his jaw clenched tightly.

The blood oozed down the side of his face.

He's a murderer, I realized.

I'm alone now. With a murderer.

He murdered Phoebe. He just murdered Courtney.

And now he's coming to murder me.

Get up, Abbie, I told myself, feeling cold panic tighten my throat.

Get up! Get up!

Louis slowly moved towards me.

But I couldn't stand up.

Twenty-Four

"Louis? W-what?" I stammered.

My entire body was trembling.

The falls roared angrily in my ears.

He was a murderer.

He wanted to murder me.

I had to get away.

Uttering a terrified cry, I leaped to my feet. I turned and started to run.

I ran right into Emily.

"Oh!" I cried.

Emily! She was hurrying towards me, running from the cycle path.

"Emily – thank God you're here!" I cried.

I let out a loud sob of relief and threw my arms round her.

"It's OK now," she said softly. "Really, Abbie. It's OK now."

I let her guide me back towards Louis, back towards the cliff-edge.

"But Courtney. . . !" I sobbed. "Courtney fell over the edge! Did you see?"

"I saw it all," Emily said softly, soothingly.

Louis stood at the cliff-edge, hands at his waist. He stared at Emily suspiciously. "What are *you* doing here?" he asked Emily nastily.

"I saw it all," Emily told him. "I was back at the rocks, and I saw everything that happened."

"You mean. . ." Louis started.

"I saw Abbie push Courtney over the cliff," Emily said.

"Huh?" I cried out in confusion. *What* had Emily just said?

I pulled away from her, but she blocked my path. She took a step forward, her eyes narrowing.

I had no choice. I took a step back, towards the falls.

"I saw Abbie push Courtney over the cliff," Emily told Louis.

"No!" I shrieked.

"Then," Emily continued calmly, ignoring me, speaking only to Louis, "Abbie tried to push *you* over the side. But Abbie slipped, and she accidentally fell herself."

An odd smile formed on Emily's face. "Isn't that a shame?" she asked Louis sarcastically. "Poor Abbie."

Twenty-Five

Listening to Emily and her deliberate lies made something inside me snap.

My terror disappeared, replaced by anger.

I felt the red current of anger I had felt that afternoon in the gym.

"Why are you *doing* this?" I demanded of her. "Why are you saying all this? You *know* it isn't true!"

Emily laughed. "But it *is* true. Isn't it, Louis?" She turned back to me, tossing her dishevelled black hair behind her shoulder. "At least, that's what Louis and I will tell everyone after you're gone, Abbie."

Louis rubbed his cheek where the blood had turned dark and was starting to cake. "I don't get it, Emily," he said quietly.

Emily uttered a moan of frustration. "No, Louis. I guess you *don't!*" she exclaimed bitterly. "Well, let me explain it to you. Why do you think I've put up with that idiot Jacob all these months?"

Louis didn't answer. He stared back at her, rubbing his wounded face.

"I couldn't stand Jacob," Emily said angrily, practically spitting the words. "But I stayed with him just to be close to you." She took a deep breath. "After I killed Phoebe, I thought that you and I. . ."

Louis and I both let out loud cries of surprise.

"*You* killed Phoebe?" Louis asked, his face bright red, his eyes revealing deep pain along with his surprise.

Emily laughed bitterly. "All these months, you and Courtney suspected each other. What a riot. I enjoyed that. I really did."

"But, Emily—" Louis started.

Emily cut him off. "I thought it would be you and me after that, Louis. But you didn't know I was alive. Even after I killed for you. First, Courtney wouldn't let you alone. Then. . ." Emily raised her eyes to me, her features twisted in hatred.

"Then, Abbie came along. With her perfect blonde hair and her perfect little figure. I tried to scare Abbie away. I really tried. But. . ."

It had been Emily all along, I realized. Emily, who slashed my bike tyres, who rigged the computer, who made those threatening calls, who murdered Goggles.

Crazy Emily.

My friend.

My friend, who was crazy enough about Louis to kill for him.

And kill again.

"Enough talk," she said in a low whisper. "Louis, say goodbye to Abbie."

I stiffened my muscles, readied myself, prepared to duck away from her and run.

But she was faster than I'd imagined.

Before I could react, she lunged forward.

She ran into me, lowering her shoulder like a football lineman, backing me to the edge.

And before I could even cry out in horror, I went sailing over the falls.

Twenty-Six

I mean, in that blind second of heart-stopping panic, I imagined myself toppling over the falls.

I cried out and sank to my knees on the edge as I realized that Emily had failed. As I realized that I was safe.

The water rushed loudly below me.

My heart pounded even louder.

I was safe. Safe on the ground. Safe on hard, solid ground.

I raised my eyes to see Louis with his arms round Emily's legs. He had tackled her from behind.

And now he was holding her face down on the ground, pinning her there with both hands as she thrashed and squirmed and tried to free herself.

A blue light started flashing in the sky.

Was I going crazy?

No.

I pulled myself to my feet, blinking against the flashing blue light.

The flashing blue light of a police car.

Two uniformed policemen were hurrying towards us.

"Throw me over!" Emily screamed to Louis, struggling desperately to get out from under him. "Throw me over, too! I know you want to! I know you hate me enough!"

But Louis kept her pinned to the ground until one of the policemen pulled him away and grabbed Emily's arms.

"H-how did you get here?" I stammered to his partner. "I mean, how did you know we were here?"

"Your friend," he answered flatly, his face completely expressionless.

"Friend?" I stared at him in total bewilderment.

He pointed down over the falls.

I took a step towards the edge and looked down. An ambulance stood on the near bank of the river.

"She was lucky," the policeman said in the same monotone.

"Courtney?" I cried, staring wide-eyed as two paramedics helped someone into the back of the ambulance.

"Yeah. She's got a broken arm. Some broken ribs. But she walked out. She told us you were up here. Good thing, huh?"

I uttered a sigh of relief. Courtney was going to be OK.

When I turned back, both policemen were leading Emily to their car. She was still struggling. Still screaming hysterically, "Throw me over! Throw me over, too!"

Louis made his way to me and put his arm round my shoulder.

"Do you two need a ride home?" one of the policemen called, holding the driver's door open.

"No. We can ride our bikes," Louis answered.

"Get cleaned up. Then come to the station. We'll need statements from you both," the policeman instructed. He slid behind the wheel and slammed the door hard.

His partner was in the back seat with Emily, who was still screaming and crying.

A few seconds later, the police car squealed away.

Louis took my hand and led me back to our bikes. He sighed wearily. "Who says nothing ever happens in small towns?"

I shook my head. "I think it's going to get a lot more boring from now on," I replied.

"Hope so," he said quietly.

Then he let his bike fall to the ground as he put his arms round me, pulled me close, and kissed me.

He was sweaty and smelly. He was covered in dirt, and his face was caked with dried blood.

I kissed him back.

I hardly even noticed.